Three Sleeps

to Double Happiness

In the tradition of Herman Hesse's spiritual journey of self-discovery in *Siddharta* and Santiago's "Personal Legend" in Paolo Coelho's *The Alchemist,* Coerte V.W. Felske's *Three Sleeps to Double Happiness* sets the imagination afire in an exhilarating allegorical tale of love, loss, vindication, and triumph. Written in hauntingly spare prose TSDH is the story of an unlikely hero, Gonzalo, an alternatively-abled albeit functional Spanish boy who travels to India to seek out a legendary tiger in order to achieve what he has uniquely interpreted to be "Double Happiness" from his childhood teachings. The tale is told primarily in flashback as "the young teen of indeterminate age" perches in a Dhok tree in India's Sariska jungle and awaits the appearance of the Great One at the territorial beast's waterhole for "three sleeps," his term for days. As the boy waits and unwittingly fends off aggressive lemurs and the menacing leopard, his pinwheeling, Kaleidoscope mind conjures disjointed reminiscences of a devastating childhood in Spain. Abused mercilessly for perceived disabilities, the boy and his sister, the beautiful and exceptional Aravella, live north of Barcelona in the coastal town Llavaneres with their mercenary foster father. Not only has the greedy Tuko adopted the two for government subsidies, he sells hashish and procures women for the notorious drug lord Don Pepe whose sprawling *finca* overlooks the town. Still, the siblings form an unbreakable bond and the sacrificial Aravella, Gonzalo's Sister the Angel, teaches him Spanish, biology, religion, folklore, even the Chinese love fable Double Happiness. Gonzalo's best friend is the Old Man, Santoro, a local spice farmer who offers the boy paternal guidance and recounts fantastic adventures traveling the world. Gonzalo marvels at Santoro's trip to India when he came face to face with Zephyrles a thirteen-foot Bengal tiger. The Old Man, stricken with cancer, laments he hadn't offered himself to the tiger to die an honorable death rather than to rot ignominiously in a field shack. After the Old Man passes, misfortune and tragedy beset the boy and he is left to fend for himself. In his sweetly configured, contemplative mind he decides on a plan to go to India to confront the Great One and discover the meaning of Double Happiness. Back in the jungle the boy entertains a rush of memories; he gets a job on a pleasure yacht and cruises the Spanish coast, then is offered work on a hashish farm in Morocco before taking the overland train to India. He recalls the physical abuse of classmates and his foster father, and all the dark memories of his past. But the boy who only sees the good in people finds his mind to be repairing itself. He gains the capacity to process the teachings taken in these years, allowing him to understand the world and identify and evaluate all the love and cruelty he has encountered. With this raised level of awareness and fresh clarity of thought, Gonzalo is not dissuaded but rather emboldened to carry out his mission. After his third sleep, Zephyrles the Great One emerges and the boy must decide on his own ultimate fate. The tale is a scalding treatise recounted in a simplistic, meditative, almost poetic style, the prose so beautiful, it sings. Unintentionally the ultimate "green" novel and at once mystical and magical while no less brutal and unforgiving, TSDH excites the imagination long after the boy's final "Celebration" attended by a very special guest concludes.

— *Kenneth Nichols*
Professor of Playwrighting
State University of New York, Oswego

Reviews

"**Tom Wolfe rewrites American Gigolo**. Felske, a veteran of the New York fashion scene, makes a fiction debut marked by sheer chutzpah and this satire commands attention. Behind every tottering runway diva, every pouting cover girl, every buffed swimsuit babe, the author would have us believe, there's one guy who sleeps with them all. Here it's narrator Nick, who loves the breed of woman he calls "Thing," that rare Amazon who renders civilian females hopelessly schlubby by comparison. Astride his Harley, a copy of *The Letters of Vincent Van Gogh* jammed in a pocket, the chest of some Scandinavian demigoddess pressed against his leather-jacketed back, Nick knows he has a leg up on the average male. Mercifully, Felske makes almost no effort to redeem this fool for sex. Cruising Gotham's fashionable haunts in search of fresh material, Nick is more an artist of physical pleasure than the misogynist he at first appears to be; nevertheless, he receives his overdue comeuppance in spades by book's end. Though Nick jets to Miami's South Beach on a brief detour of debauchery, his story is fundamentally one of New York days: the flashy parties he promotes, the circuit of trendy enclaves where people pose fabulously and smoke a lot, the whole scene populated by a pumped-up tribe of neo-Cheeverians endlessly in search of love. By minimizing Nick's obsession with his mother's untimely death, Felske avoids the Jay McInerney first-timer's error of laying too much blame for the indiscretions of an American rude boy on the altar of family and Nick's unrepentant offensiveness carries things on. Fun stuff."

— Kirkus Reviews

"**Boys In Babeland**. No scruples or psychological doses of saltpeter daunts the narrator of Coerte V.W. Felske's *The Shallow Man*. This novel's hero, Nick Laws, is a club-hopping hedonist who exclusively targets models as bedmates and makes no apologies. Rather than waste time with names, he refers to each of his model-dates as Thing. After greasily chomping on nubiles and discarding them like spareribs, the narrator flirts with the prospect of maturing and settling down, a momentary lurch which takes the form of an affair with a non-model. The frustrating interlude leads him to decide, The hell with it—real women are nothing but hard work. The novel is crass, entertaining, slangy, egotistical, and reeking of sun bronze and the fresh turnover of fleshy delights makes the narrator's decision to become an aging roué instead of a responsible adult seem like an honest, if not admirable, choice. He's willing to go with the flow even if it leaves him stranded. Where *Zoe* belongs to the sadder-but-wiser category, *The Shallow Man* ends up neither sad nor wise, which seems right. The novel is prefaced by a remark from Oscar Wilde—'Only the shallow know themselves.' Felske writes like a gigolo and treats seduction as a dirty sport. Ambitious-minded literary types fasten on models as subjects and objects because their smooth blankness and mute mystique (the silencing effect of a beautiful woman entering a room) allow so much space for inscription and speculation. The bodily landscape becomes a sacred scroll. The model, reduced to abstraction, becomes Other: exotic animal, extraterrestrial, goddess, cyborg, or billboard archetype. Unlike Felske's Shallow Man, Jay McInerney knows what he wants to be when he grows up: F. Scott Fitzgerald, bugler of lost promise. But McInerney is a case of arrested development. His new novel *Model Behavior*, an urban safari of superficial people saying superficial things in a superficial culture, seems like an attempt to squeeze the last bit of wattage out of *Bright Lights, Big City*. Bret Easton Ellis's *Glamorama* with its supermodels, terrorists, and globetrotting story line, is an absurd escapade that's smirkingly aware of its own glossy anachronisms. The 'angry feeling' Ellis nurses about models reflects a deeper aversion to women, who are pretty much chopped liver in his fictional universe. Perhaps the biggest letdown of model fiction is that, aside from *The Shallow Man*, its boyish irresponsibility doesn't explode into sexy fun. The writers seem to have hangovers before they've even gotten looped. Who knew going to all these fictional parties would be such work?"

*— James Wolcott, **Vanity Fair***

"**Model Citizen**: the story of a man who never met a stunningly beautiful woman he didn't like. Love, H.L. Mencken said, is the delusion that one woman differs from another. Nick Laws, a marginally more enlightened fellow, claims that one in every 50,000 is quite different from the other 49,999: she's drop-dead gorgeous, and he's determined to sleep with her. Nick, who narrates Coerte V.W. Felske's amusing first novel, "The Shallow Man" is 30 years old, lives in Soho and works by day as a hand model, by night as a party promoter for clubs with names like Café D&A. He knows how to ask "Would you like to take a bubble bath with me?" in 10 languages, and he has committed to memory the Victoria's Secret 24-hour toll-free number. With the exception of his Harley, all he cares about is what he calls collectively, "Thing": "Fashion models, beautiful women and general hotness." He happily acknowledges his obsession right from the start. When Nick contemplates "the sweetest joining of limbs known to man," his company is agreeable. But during the couple of weeks he tangles with his brother, his confidante, and of course, models' boyfriends, all of whom demand he re-evaluate his life. By his own account, he is neither very bright nor very witty, and a dullard's earnest ruminations can only be dull—or, as Nick would put it, as exciting as York Avenue. Before long, though, he is back to his old, unreflective self, proving that the unexamined life is well worth living. To Nick, everything resembles conjugating the verb, and if your mind works in similar fashion, you'll probably understand his ruling passion. One feminist writer has used the term "penised humans" to refer to men. Mentally, at least, Nick Laws is as penised as a human can get. When he awards Audrey Hepburn the crown for "pinnacle hotness," it is only because Mr. Felske has nodded. Nick detests the beach but this novel is perfect for it. "The Shallow Man" is also perfect for shallow men. On the other hand, women may think the title is redundant."

— David Kelley, *The New York Times Book Review*

"In his first novel, *The Shallow Man*, Coerte V.W. Felske spins a clever tale of the narcissistic world of fashion modeling. In this comic send-up, Nick Laws is the shallow man whose every thought and word reflect his sole interest in life: boffing models. From the late-night clubs of Manhattan to the art deco bars of Miami, Nick searches for beautiful women to take to bed. He's so perfect, he's hilarious. Is there a man with a soul so noble that he has not entertained this fantasy? In real life, no one could stand around all day in his motorcycle jacket and sunglasses, purring platitudes to curvaceous dimwits. But Nick's relentless, self-conscious pursuit is very funny. Nick reminds us, "Never judge a book by its contents." Certainly not this book. *The Shallow Man* is fun, flash, and filigree–a sexy, witty spoof of the Nineties."

— Digby Diehl, *Playboy*

"**Shallow Waters Run Deep**. This stunning, but unreflective man knows a lot more than you think. Behind those big blank eyes and that deep tan is … well, something that women find hopelessly tempting: a healthy disdain for thinking too much. Since he can't be bothered connecting the dots, he maps out the politics of the jejune and Gitanes with an easy straight line. Reading the quick-witted prose, one begins to think less about things and more about Thing, the Shallow Man's tag for the women he dates: gorgeous, seemingly unattainable models. Nick Laws is like Hamlet without the mental baggage, tumbling Ophelia by Act II. So what if behind all that cigarette smoke and charm lies a lean mentality. Felske's *The Shallow Man* makes a case for the unexamined life."

— *Esquire*

"I may not have been the king of Generation Face," proclaims hipster Nick Laws, invoking his superficial peers in screenwriter Felske's first novel, "but I was definitely one of its princes." Nick can't get enough of "Thing" his catchphrase for models and other impossibly stunning women; his every waking moment is devoted to bedding them and their friends—as long as they're not Civilians (regular-looking women). It would be easy, but inaccurate, to dismiss Nick as a misogynist. For one thing, his acidic classification system extends to men too. "Guys can be Dialtones," he concedes. Spiked with original Nickspeak and hilarious dialogue, Felske's depiction of the physically elite is so clever in its anthropological detail that we can forgive his protagonist for just about anything. Besides, *The Shallow Man* harbors a few glimmers of Nick's humanity. You just have to dig to find them."

— *People*

"Coerte V.W. Felske's novel *The Shallow Man* turned the fashion world on its head—and introduced the term 'modelizer' into the collective consciousness. One of Nick Laws's dictums is "don't judge a book by its contents" ostensibly delivered in support of his 'beauty = truth' theorem. The novel is presented as a comment on our society's obsession with models, and therefore its cultural relevance outweighs any criticism of its craftsmanship. It's a notion that had its day during the genre of the hip urban novel of the 80's, a genre characterized by its most prominent literary agent Amanda Urban as, *'and then they fucked.'* *The Shallow Man* fits in perfectly with this body of work. It's an entertaining book, a pleasant diversion. Like its protagonist, *The Shallow Man* doesn't take itself too seriously, and it urges you to do the same. It's a fantasy, a lark, a good time. The Shallow Man has his moments of doubt and pain, wherein he questions the basis of his existence, but they are brief, and far from mending his ways he vows to indulge in as many in as many places for as long as he can, in retaliation for all the 'politically correct bullshit' he's been assaulted with. And, in a way, after several years of that 'politically correct bullshit' *The Shallow Man* is refreshingly moral-free."

— *Detour*

"Deep thoughts from a hand model, *The Shallow Man,* by Coerte V.W. Felske, humorously portrays Nick Laws, a model and club promoter who's happy to let "Thing" (the allure of beautiful women) dictate the conversation if not his life—to the point where he's mastered how to say "Would you join me for a bubble bath?" in every language spoken by supermodels. Aware that his lifestyle annoys "dromes" (average-looking people who resent the beautiful), Nick argues that it's not his fault that "4-B girls" (beauty, breeding, brains, and bank account) were created, or that men are compelled to pursue them. He frequently hauls out his tattered copy of Van Gogh's letters to prove that history's purest artist was also a model muncher. Set up by a "catsuit feminist" (one with beauty and brains), wary of "donuts" (male models who are stuck on themselves), a too-frequent partaker "the Dracula nap" (sleep all day, come out at night), Nick is a lot of laughs even as his promiscuity takes on the aspect of an addiction passed from father to son. Fans of Jay McInerney and P.J. O'Rourke should be amused."

— *Glamour*

"Cruising Manhattan's young and beautiful scene on a Harley Davidson, Nick Laws is on a desperate search for supermodels or, as he puts it, "Thing." Whether throwing parties or that one in 50,000 who is "hot, Thing hot," fending off "Civilians," (everyday girls with everyday looks) or convincing Thing to dump "Guy" (everyday boy, everyday looks), Nick is driven by Thing—how to get it and how to enjoy it. Though the world Felske paints is self-consciously hipper-than-thou, he holds his portrait of it in check with a ribald sense of humor and an understanding of the limitations of Nick's ways. Tight prose and smooth dialogue impel the story along, while the names of so many trendy New York night spots dot the text that hipster wannabes can use it as a guidebook. This first novel captures the gloss of its characters with a smart shine of its own."

— *Publisher's Weekly*

"Make no mistake, Coerte V.W. Felske's literary Lothario Nick Laws, the Shallow Man, is no ordinary ladies' man. He is an uberstud for the '90s, otherwise known as a model hound, modelizer, beauty junkie, or, as fashion insiders prefer, model fucker. Is this an accurate depiction of modelettes and the men who pursue them? While the book may be fictional, the modelizer phenomenon most definitely is not."

— *Details*

"**Move Over, Jay McInerney**: Coerte Felske, the author of *The Shallow Man*, wants you to know : he is not his title character. The narrator of his forthcoming novel, he says, is a composite of a number of men whose antics he witnessed on the model circuit. 'I used to live with a fashion photographer,' he explains, 'and these characters would show up at all the fashion shows. They'd fly around the world. They could be lawyers, restaurant owners, party promoters.' Felske says he himself doesn't even date models. 'OK,' he admits, 'I have gone out with a few, but only very briefly. All my girlfriends, though, have been Catsuit Feminists.' This is Felske's term for women who are both intelligent and gorgeous. He introduces a number of such swell terms for young women in his book, which he says he wrote in five weeks. For example, Civilian Girls (anyone not fortunate enough to be a model) and Dialtones (women so stupid they might as well emit one each time they open their mouths). 'One of the challenges of the book was keeping the shallow man from being too smart,' says the Ivy League-educated Felske, who until recently lived in Hollywood writing screenplays, including one for Mickey Rourke he'd rather not discuss. "The shallow man doesn't care to be deep. He's introspective but tries to avoid it. *The Shallow Man*, Felske insists, is a book for the nineties. 'It's different from the eighties,' he says, 'when money and power were the big things. Now glamour is eclipsing substance even intelligence in a lot of ways, rightly or wrongly.' In any case, Felske asks, 'what's wrong caring about beauty? The shallow man thinks it's life-enhancing.' As Forrest Gump might have put it, shallow is as shallow does. The *Bright Lights, Big City* of the 90s."

— *Buzz Magazine*

"**Shallow Waters**: This is where **Coerte V.W. Felske's** protagonist wants to be—sandwiched between the most beautiful women in the world. Surrounded by the most life-enhancing supermodels there are. Amid *hotness*, as his anti-hero Nick Laws would say. Felske is a native New Yorker and author of *The Shallow Man*—a book that details one man's pursuit of sleeping with that one woman who is agonizingly, physically superior to every other. I would hereby like to make Felske's book required reading this rainy summer, and, at the same time, inform the author that, in writing the book that I always intended to write, he basically devastated me. I am not applying for a job with the Kirkus Reviews, but I do think the book is important enough to describe and appropriately gush over certain parts. The Shallow Man is narrated through Nick Laws, the hand model/club promoter who refers to all models as *Thing*, friends who get you closer to *Thing* as *Conduits*, guys who are bitter over never being able to land *Thing* as *Dromes* and women who possess both brains and beauty as *Catsuit Feminists*. Some people are calling *The Shallow Man* the new *Bright Lights, Big City*. Others say as soon as Felske's agents find a film home for his tome, it will be the 'Shampoo' of the 1990s. In fact, as we speak, **Johnny Depp**, **Brad Pitt**, and **Keanu Reeves** are being pegged. 'The whole this is mind-blowing,' Felske told me. 'I always liked books where you can climb into a character's obsessed head and see what drives him. In this case, what drives him is his quest for these beauties.' Sadly, I hear area party promoters are laying claim to the book's title character being modeled after them, but Felske shoots that down. 'That's absurd. It's no more based on me than it's based on those guys,' he said. 'I was born in Manhattan. The 70s, the 80s. I was at Club Area and Nell's and M.K. I moved to L.A. in 1991, but still way before these tourist promoters started working the scene.' Still, it's all pretty heady stuff for the author. Just last week at a book signing party at L.A.'s Monkey Bar, Felske was floored when **Jack Nicholson**, **Harvey Keitel**, and **Kiefer Sutherland** all asked for his John Hancock. But the better story comes from a book bash in the Hamptons last weekend when a woman waltzed past doormen without an invite. 'I don't need one,' she said. 'I slept with the Shallow Man when I was 16.' Felske confided, 'She was right.' To his credit, Felske is not a kiss-and-tell guy, so there was no chance he and I were going to compare notes on, perhaps, at one time chasing the same *Hotness*. He also didn't care to battle feminists who might get frosted at his character learning the phrase, 'Do you want to take a bubble bath with me?' in eight different languages. Some will call that shallow. I call it being prepared. Meanwhile, Elite supermodel **Frederique** is not surprised at Felske's success. The supermodel told me she was his designated first-draft reader—and the woman he based his Catsuit Feminist on—and knew the book would blow everyone away. 'I am honest and direct,' Freddy said. 'There were so many recognizable moments that I saw from the personal end of modeling. And, for the most part, he's right, and women should not be upset with it. There are women who are *Dialtones* (a less than eloquent lady) and there are women where you get an answer. But ours is one of the few businesses where you can get work if you're just a *Dialtone*. This book says more about the way men think and feel than *Bright Lights*. And Coerte is not the Shallow Man himself. He's a voyeur ...' "

— A. J Benza, *"Downtown," The New York Daily News*

"**Useful New Word** (from the novel *The Shallow Man* by Coerte V. W. Felske): 'Dialtone'—a girl or guy who is so stupid, the sound of a dial tone hums in their brain and comes out their mouth."

— *Vogue*

"**Generation X's answer to *Less Than Zero*.** The (anti) hero is shallow. Nick is a New York party promoter and part-time hand model, simply so he can shag as many models as possible. Only one in 50,000 girls reaches his standards of 'pinnacle hotness' and the rest are 'Civilians' and 'Dromes.' He never recalls names, so models are 'Thing,' as in, 'I thought about the imminent arrival of Spring thing fresh from Europe. Then a new sea of Baby Thing would come along in the summer.' Nick never got over Robert Palmer's 'Simply Irresistible' video and this book would bring Naomi Wolf out in a nasty rash. If Jay McInerney had written the expose Model, it would read a lot like *Shallow*. Our hero also fantasies about a time when the world will be one big stretch of black tarmac—suitable for his Harley—and zoned for a 7-Eleven every 10 miles. It is not so much politically incorrect as politically indecent and I loathe Nick—but I love the book, which is worth it for the jargon alone. It is probably Generation X's answer to *Less Than Zero*, although Nick, of course, doesn't believe in Gen X. There is only Generation Face. And Thing."

— *Sydney Morning Herald (Australia)*

"In Deep With The Shallow Man. Linda and co. might not get out of bed for less than $10,000, but the vainglorious, model-toting Nick Laws of *The Shallow Man* won't climb *into* bed with anything other than the one woman in 50,000 who is hot. Nick, a hand model and party promoter, is drawn to hotness like a heat-seeking missile. In his shallow life, models are 'Thing's and are 'Thing hot.' If he is having a *very* good day, he'll meet a '4B' model—with beauty, brains, breeding, and bank account. 'I never met a model I didn't like,' he proclaims. With the rest of us, he's not so generous. There are Dromes (men who have Hotness Deficiency Syndrome and an inability to land 'Thing'); Civilians (women with real looks and real personalities—read average face and ordinary figures); Donuts (male models, because … well …); and Dialtones (the mentally challenged). With *The Shallow Man*, Felske skims along the glossy surface of club glamour, exposing the ugly facts of an industry where beauty is truth. A first novel for Felske, who was a scriptwriter on Mickey Rourke's 'Homeboy,' it's funny, brutally clever and, when the shallow man gets deep, can also be surprisingly insightful. And not a politically correct sentiment on the page."

— *Elle (Australia)*

"The book world's preoccupation with megamodels and glamazons continues with this New York-based tale of nipples and nightclubs. The man drooling on the end of the catwalk is Nick—also known as Dick—Laws, the kind of guy who checks out the trim of his lovers' privates before allowing sexual progress. He's a real character, which is why you might enjoy seeing what happens to him at the end of the story."

— *Cleo (Australia)*

" 'I never met a model I didn't like.' That still makes Nick Laws choosy, because he can only go for one woman in 50,000. Not a 'civilian,' but a girl who is on a model agency's books and who has that *je ne sais quoi* that Nick, with more economy than elegance, calls 'thing.' Nick is a model himself and a philosopher in his spare time, sharing with us his thoughts on life, love, the letters of Vincent Van Gogh and the significance of being asked to hold a girl's lipstick. Slick, self-consciously funny, occasionally sentimental, *The Shallow Man* by Coerte V.W. Felske is a modern morality tale."

— *Marie Claire (Australia)*

"*Vogue, The New Yorker, The New York Times, W* and *USA Today* don't usually turn out for parties to mark the publications of first novels by unknown authors. But they made an exception for a recent bash in Southampton, N.Y., for Coerte V.W. Felske's 'The Shallow Man.' A sendup of society's obsession with superficial beauty and glamour, the novel chronicles the life and times of Nick Laws, hand model, club promoter and lover of Thing; his name for all exceptionally beautiful fashion models. Just published by Crown, it is knee deep in good reviews: *Playboy* lauds it as 'fun, flash and filigree,' *The New York Times Book Review* calls it a perfect beach read,. and *Buzz* concludes that it 'very well may be the 'Bright Lights, Big City' of the '90s.' But rave notices weren't the only attention-getters at the party hosted by department-store heir Ted Field. As anyone who's flipped through a fashion magazine or turned on MTV's 'House of Style' knows, the media are as drawn to Thing as Nick is, and on hand were Sports Illustrated swimsuit models Ingrid Seynhaeve and Daniela Pestova, and fashion stars Yasmeen Ghauri and Gail Elliott. 'The model phenomenon is absurd. These girls could be running for office at this point,' says Felske, 34, referring in his candid, politically incorrect style to models as 'girls.' On the telephone from his home in New York's Upper East Side, Felske denies . that he's anything like his fictional hero. 'Every interview, certainly the question comes up, 'Are you the Shallow Man?' I only have one thing to say about that—absolutely,' he says, laughing. 'Not really. The whole idea came from thinking of a new Marvel Comics hero, the Shallow Man, who just appears on the scene like Batman. I just thought it was funny.' Amusing. and appalling, Nick Laws makes his appearance in the novel with the lines: *'I never met a model I didn't like. The revelation came to me early one morning when I was in that dreamy state, beyond the point of sleep but too comfortable in the Ocean of Love to get up. ... Since I don't have a great attention span, I thought about this for a short while, then went on to other thoughts.'* The novel follows Nick from SoHo nightspots to a Miami modeling agency, through the small world of hipsters, photographers, bookers, designers and stylists that revolves around models. What plot there is involves Nick's relationships with his best friend, a woman who is both beautiful and smart, whom he refers to as the Catsuit Feminist, and some unresolved issues from his childhood. It's a milieu Felske knows well. A former denizen of the club scene he documents, he counts as friends photographers Peter Beard and Richard Bailey and model Frederique Van der Wal, all of whom are noted in the novel's acknowledgments. He says he got his first exposure to the world of the fashion model when he was growing up in Quogue, N.Y., and a neighbor was Eileen Ford, the head of Ford Models Inc., the pioneering modeling agency that represented Christie Brinkley, Cheryl Tiegs, Lauren Hutton, Jean Shrimpton and just about every other big name in the 1960s and '70s. After studying romance languages at Dartmouth College, he attended Columbia University's Graduate School of the Arts in the film division. For several years after college, he labored in the other big glamour industry—the movies—as a screenwriter. But after a frustrating experience writing four drafts of a script called 'Homeboy' for Mickey Rourke, he turned to the novel. 'The Shallow Man,' written in six weeks in May and June two years ago, was his first. It comes on the heels of 'Model: The Ugly Business of Beautiful Women,' an expose of the modeling industry by former New York Times reporter Michael Gross that hit the best-seller lists this spring. Felske says his focus is less on supermodels and the fashion and beauty industries than on their effects on the rest of the population—especially men. 'The new trophy has been advertised and she's the fashion model. It's like the new Corvette or the new beautiful home in the Hamptons,' he says. Felske sees the rise of the model as linked to the boom in cable and its nearly insatiable appetite for programming. 'So the media thrusts these girls' faces in your living room and you end up wondering, who are they? People have been asking that question for a while and it just fed onto itself,' he says. 'I also feel that while you have the pressures of society out there, people seek out whatever flecks of beauty that are left—whether it's a van Gogh, a beautiful piece of literature, Proust, or a beautiful face. It takes you away from the dehumanization that's part of contemporary life.' "

— *Orange County Register*

" 'I never met a model I didn't like,' goes the opening line of 'The Shallow Man,' the first novel by **Coerte Felske**, the 33-year-old screenwriter who has met a few himself. The book is about a man obsessed with covergirls. His best friend, the Catsuit Feminist, is said to be loosely based on **Frederique**, the Dutch beauty who decorates those Victoria's Secret catalogues. As for the title character? 'He's a composite of all the shallow men I know.' The book won't hurt their feelings. 'Most of them will never read it,' Felske said, 'because they are too shallow.' "

— *"Page Six," The New York Post*

"**Chandler for the 90s:** ***** There are two reasons to write a Hollywood novel, and they're both the same: everyone will shell out for a peek backstage. Some Hollywood novels—Jackie Collins's oeuvre, for example—exist to perpetuate the fiction that stars' lives are as glamorous off-screen as on. Others are written, with equal commercial savvy, to expose the shocking vice and greed of the industry. Ultra-glam or ultra-scum; we love to read about either, and the very best back lot potboilers dish out both at once. Coerte Felske is an ex-screenwriter and he seems to have dug enough dirt during his time in the industry to fill several bookshelves. His hero in *Word* is Heyward Hoon: a failed screenwriter whose hobby is Hollywood anthropology, observing the local Wannabeasts, 8x10s, Noguls, Starmen, and Muffin Heads, and so on. Girls, though, are Hoon's real area of expertise—all 2,000 of them that he happens to know. When lonely studio magnate Sidney Swinburn sees him stagger out of a bathroom with four lovely Bullets on his arms, Hoon sees the perfect opportunity to sell his years of research for a slice of success. It's an old story, and in a way this is an old book. The flicks and chicks may represent 90s excess, but the style of *Word* is pure 40s cool, all choppy sentences and dry wit. It's a pastiche, but no more than anything else these days; people are getting used to judging authors on what they borrow rather than what they create. And if you like the original—in this case, the work of Raymond Chandler—the throwback can be terrific fun to read. Felske knows this and has gotten his chosen style down perfectly. Whole paragraphs swing with voiceover rhythms that put Harrison Ford's famous Blade Runner monologues to shame. 'He told me work was totally uncommercial. Sure, I'd heard it before ... But I was damn good at producing work that didn't sell. So why ruin a good thing? He told me I should look for new representation. I told him he should look at my tallest finger.' It's all good, punchy stuff and Felske never falters. Beautiful babes, New York wasps and sleazy zillionaires all flit through *Word*, larger than life and twice as interesting. The only bit of Chandler that Felske has chosen not to pilfer is the labyrinthine plot, which is a pity in a way: a long, zippy book like this could use a few more twists and turns. In the end, though, *Word* is lovable for the addictive dry wit of Felske/Hoon: 'As I massaged number 4 into her back, my mind drifted from its search of all that is original, and plopped splat on the cliché.' Can you blame him?"

— Carrie O'Grady, *The Guardian (England)*

"**Magnificent Obsessions:** *Word* is the book Bret Easton Ellis didn't write. It's a satire of Star Camp, USA, Felske's term for the movie colony. His narrator, Heyward Hoon, is a winning and wicked Ivy League prepster trying to conquer Hollywood. He's a screenwriter, and things are going miserably except for his not-so-little black book of gorgeous L.A. women. Felske does a great job with female characters, and his playful language introduces Strugs (struggling actors), WAMs (waitress-actress-models), and Noguls (wannabe movie moguls). Felske also has one eye on the screen, still, sometimes a book is meant to be just a good read, and we're grateful for it."

— Christopher Napolitano, *Playboy*

"**The return of *The Shallow Man*!** His first novel turned the fashion world on its head—and introduced the term 'modelizer' into the collective conscious. Now, with his tough-talking *Word*, Coerte V.W. Felske is back, red-eyeing it over Tinseltown's turf, but navigating much of the same Faustian topography. Catch a ride on this tale of a street-savvy screenwriter who sells his soul—but meets a lot of 'Wams,' 'Fundies,' and 'Mom-I-Got-the-Part girls'—on his trek toward the fabled Hollywood sign."

— *Detour*

"*Word: The Talk of L.A.*: By page 3 of this sharply funny send-up of all things Hollywood, you will agree that author Coerte V.W. Felske shares his lead character's talent for language. While threading his way through the Tinseltown jungle, Felske's wannabe screenwriter Heyward Hoon desperately tries to maintain his sanity. You will be patting yourself on the back for having discovered Hoon's story before *Variety* announces its inevitable arrival at a theater near you."

— *Marie Claire*

"If We Gave Out Book Awards: Great Read Gift Guide; Edgiest Girl, *Bridget Jones's Diary*, Edgiest Boy, *Word* by Coerte V.W. Felske. Felske's hero, an out-of-work screenwriter who calls himself a 'Blip' on movieland's radar, hilariously manages to find some beating hearts inside the hippest Hollywood hyphenates."

— *Glamour*

'*Word* is Coerte V.W. Felske's second novel. Like Peter Farelly's *The Comedy Writer*, Michael Tolkin's *The Player,* Peter Lefcourt's *The Deal, Word* belongs to the growing genre of Hollywood novels in which idealistic would-be screenwriters and filmmakers experience disillusionment as they come up against the madly illogical Hollywood system, in which liars, con artists and charlatans occupy almost all of the positions of power. In *Word*, the hapless seeker of the Hollywood jackpot is Heyward Hoon, scion of a privileged WASP family of declining fortunes. Many tales of American success involve a person of Jewish descent changing their name and trying to pass themselves off as WASP. In Hoon's case, however, he determines that he may best get ahead by blending in and not provoking envy of his upper-class WASP background. So he dies his blonde hair black and changes his name to Hoonstein. When we first meet Heyward, he has written 13 unproduced screenplays. What he does have command of, though, is his perspective on L.A. and its inhabitants, whom he has minutely categorized and labeled with hundreds of buzzwords. Hollywood, for instance, is "Star Camp." "Strugs" and "8x10's" are struggling actors, "Wams" are waiters/actress/models, while "Starman" and "Stargal" refer to those who have crossed over into success. (A specific star can be reassured to by a quality that made their reputation, such as "Starman Steroids.") "Thickies" are the omnipresent bodyguards that escort Starman and Stargals. "Noguls" are overly self-important producers who lack the one thing that would make them genuinely important—the power to greenlight a film. All agents are called "Agent Orange." A "Storage Guy" is a man so uninteresting that you feel safe leaving a beautiful woman with him at a party when you go to get drinks. A "Stowaway is a woman you can call up in the middle of the night for steady no-strings-attached sex. In addition to his general categorizing of the L.A. scene, Heyward has made what he calls a science project out of the study of individual women in L.A. In his attempt to fathom the mysteries of the female sex, he has catalogued and made a computer file of hundreds of L.A. women. A part of the key to his success at unraveling their secrets is that he has willfully chosen to remain "inactive," or celibate, thus making it easier for him to gain women's trust as they surmise that, unlike most men, he is not after sex. Wall his mastery of the L.A. scene, we are taken by surprise to discover, fifty pages into the novel, that Heyward's primary income comes from his day job as a temporary filing clerk. However his fortunes soon begin to change when, after crashing a party at the Bel-Air mansion of genuine mogul, Sydney Swinburn, the head of Novastar Studios, Heyward is taken under Swinburn's wings. Swinburn is impressed by Heyward's social ease with beautiful women, and he makes a pact with him. In exchange for lessons on how to successfully score with women, he will allow Heyward stay in a bungalow on his estate and encourage him as a screenwriter. The only rule: He must keep his hands off Teal, the beautiful woman who also lives on his estate and who, of course, is the only woman Heyward really wants. The more Swinburn learns from Heyward, though, the less he begins to feel he needs him, and Heyward soon finds he may have unwittingly entered into a pact with the devil. The more he becomes aware of Swinburn's deceitfulness, the more his struggle becomes whether he can voluntarily choose to end an association through which he feels he might gain so much potential Hollywood status."

— *USA Today*

"Language is what this novel downloads—a torrent of L.A. buzzwords and insider cynicism unmatched since Odets and Lehman's 'Sweet Smell of Success' took on Manhattan's nightlife. As with Tony Curtis's Sidney Falco, Felske pumps Heyward Hoon with so much film babble he's ready to burst. Insecure but WASPish Heyward, who's written scripts on spec, with not one green-lighted, tars everyone around him; leading men dismissed as 'Starmen,' struggling actors as 'Strugs,' and pretty faces with few goals, '8x10s.' When Heyward, accompanied by his beautiful but alcoholic arm piece, Baby Garbo, meets mega-mogul Sydney Swinburn, he sees a way of perhaps getting his masterpiece, the script of his 'Age of Astonishment,' sold at last. A wonderfully literate script, Sydney says, but, sadly, uncommercial, and he is in the business to make money. Still, he sees in Heyward a bookish ladies' man who can bring into this boorish super-producer's life just what he needs to fill a void: intimacy with the type of woman he has always challenged himself to attain. They strike a Faustian bargain to help each other as Sydney attends Heyward's charm school. Heyward, however, must not pursue Sydney's sought-after and mysterious Teal. When Heyward and Teal find each other irresistible, Sydney, the fearsome dark lord, assures Heyward's destruction in Hollywood. Cynics may snap their fangs at that big-bucks ending, but for film lovers the Hell-A hypechat will flick all of your fuses."

— Kirkus Reviews

"Heyward Hoon is yet another brilliant, but uncommercial and unproduced screenwriter careening around L.A. looking for a life amidst the clichés. His tale? Hollywood newcomer strikes a Faustian bargain in exchange for entrée into inner circle. It's winningly told, with often ferocious humor, including a fresh, funny argot (e.g., 'Wams' are waitress-actress-models). Recommended for fiction collections."

— Library Journal

"Flashy and dark, this energetic Nathanael West retake offers a rich Hollywood menu of pandering, ambition, power, and retribution. Narrator Heyward Hoon—30-year-old Ivy League New Yorker, creditless screenwriter, friend to a thousand Wams (waitress-actress-models), self-described 'wannabeast, a fame-seeking hound' and compulsive social taxonomist—hates L.A. but examines it closely. In company with some of the women he calls 'the Bullets' (the best of the L.A. party girls), he crashes a party where he meets Sydney Swinburn, mega-mogul studio head. Divorced after a long marriage, Swinburn seems humble and naïve, looking for female company. He and Hoon make a deal: Hoon will introduce him to attractive, available women, and Swinburn will improve Hoon's non-career by setting him up with a powerful agent. This turns out to be a Faustian bargain—with none of the upside for this Hollywood patois-spouting Faust, who gets into hot water after he moves into Swinburn's luxurious guest house and meets beautiful, mysterious Teal poolside. Sexually ante-diluvian and with the sharp wit of recent tinsel tales like Bruce Wagner's *I'm Losing You*, Felske's second (after *The Shallow Man*) is bright, bitchy fun and it's up to date with name-dropping local atmosphere and cutting edge jargon. *Author tour.*"

— Publishers Weekly

"In a vicious story of the Hollywood lifestyle, Coerte V.W. Felske transports the reader into the movie-driven anathema of depth that is L.A. Struggling screenwriter Heyward Hoon narrates our journey through 'industry' parties, dinners at the hippest eateries, and sexy encounters. A gaggle of questionable characters inhabits this story including 'Wannabeasts' (fame-seeking hounds), '8x10's (all look, no content), and various other movie types that exist in this insular, elitist community. This story about aching for success and the price of achieving it in Hollywood is good, fluffy fun that will remind you why you live in Northern, not Southern, California."

— *San Francisco Metropolitan*

"His latest tale, *Word,* is a jazzy, ironic appreciation of writing, filmmaking, and chasing skirt. In two of those arts, at least, downtown novelist Coerte.V. W. Felske seems more than passingly adept. It's an unexpectedly hot, sticky night in late November, and though the police are trying to persuade the hundreds of revelers gathered around the iron gates of Joe's Pub to move along, inside the three-week-old Lafayette Street club a wild party is in full swing. Pink and red spotlights swirl over the sunken dance floor as models in backless dresses dance to Abba with the men who love them—arch-rivals Donald Trump and Roffredo Gaetani, photographer Sante D'Orazio; tank-topped club impresarios Jeffrey Jah, Mark Baker, and Nur Khan; and a couple of well-known gossip columnists. An open-shirted Kevin Costner takes a breather in a banquette with Chuck Pfeifer, Bob Shaye, and Peter Brant; from their table nearby, Emma S., Kara Young, and a few more models edging over 30 wriggle their fingers seductively in greeting. A movie premiere? A supermodel's birthday? No, it's a book party. But one befitting Coerte V.W. Felske, the author of 1995's *The Shallow Man* and the upcoming *Word,* both of which are taut, clever character studies centered on this posse of older roués and slightly over-the-hill models—all of whom the author considers close friends, the kind who come over for late-night glasses of port in the SoHo apartment he shares with gallery director Michiel van der Wal, brother to Frederique, and whichever South African or Dutch or Italian models are passing through town. That is, when he's not in Quogue playing tennis with Taki, or in St. Tropez with his new Czech-Croatian girlfriend who lives in Switzerland, or hanging out in L.A. at Monkey Bar with his old friend Jack Nicholson, who helped arrange for the filming of *The Shallow Man* (for protagonists, Felske's thinking 'Pitt, Penn, Downey, DiCaprio, or Cage'). With his surfer's patois, a mellow constitution that he chalks up to being a Libra, and a practiced way of speaking similar to Mister Rogers's, Felske is beloved by all: a guy's guy and a model's guy, whose novels neatly refract their own lives through a highly ironic prism. He does take his shots at pony tailed, Vespa-riding, mannequin-addicted, SoHo-loft-living thirtysomethings who are hand models by day and party promoters by night. But Felske sympathizes with the dudes at the end, attributing their flaws to societal shortcomings and a general millennial ill will. In Felske's world, models are called 'Thing' (young ones are 'Baby Thing,' stupid ones are 'Dialtones'); the rest of womankind is 'Civilians.' His girlfriends are 'Catsuit Feminist's, and we, 'Generation Face,' all live in the notoriety-obsessed 'Age of A' (for Astonishment). His characters often think in these terms; what's more, their feelings are italicized: '*No one wants to be sentenced to life at someone else's table … I want the reservation in my own name. I want my own table and I want to fill it with whomever I fancy.'* Less self-consciously writerly than other colleagues who are concerned with this tribe, like Bret Easton Ellis or Jay McInerney, Felske confides that he writes his books in only a few weeks. 'It's all about the voice,' he says, often, as if it were a mantra. Just tonight, Felske comes up with a theory he calls the Ten-Year Window. 'Women only have the years from 20 to 30 to really make it happen,' he says, taking a seat at the bar next to Joaquin Phoenix. 'For some, maybe 24 to 34.' How to take this comment, delivered, to all appearances, by a guy who's apparently spent a little too much time with Things and not enough with Civilians? Auditing women's-studies classes while a grad student at Columbia's film school, he tells me, qualifies him as a feminist—yet he suggests that women are different from men because they're "ruled by the moon." As a samba band tunes up onstage at Joe's, a sunglasses-wearing Ralph Lauren model named Zofia jumps up on a table near the D.J. booth. 'God, do I adore Coerte, he is so wise,' she announces, narrowly avoiding the approaching gang of Felske's high-school buddies, who smother him with bear hugs and painful-looking noogies. 'This dude,' gurgles the beefiest one, grabbing him by an Armani lapel, 'was so popular with chicks in high school that cheerleaders from the other team were asking for his number.' Sipping an Amstel Light with three or four undone shirt buttons revealing dark tufts of chest hair, Felske runs a hand through his white-blond, shoulder-length locks before jumping onto a conga line between Mark Bavaro and Daniela Pestova, his five-foot-eleven stature greatly diminished by their hulking figures. He leans in close and confides, in utter mock seriousness, 'I'm the Mad Hatter.' Over the din at Da Silvano's a few nights earlier, Felske takes gulps of San Pellegrino and looks over the crowd—David Duchovny, Helmut Lang, and, to his delight, Robert De Niro eating penne with his family at a corner table: the perfect setting for what he wants to discuss. 'See, the most important businessmen, bankers, film producers, and studio heads often don't know anything when it comes to women,' says Felske, winking indiscreetly in De Niro's direction. That's what Word is about: the Faustian bargain struck between a film writer struggling for credits and a 50-year-old studio head trolling for dates. It's a relationship not unlike Felske's with Ted Field, the fiftyish head of Interscope Records, who is rarely seen without a woman hovering around legal age ('Ted has no problem getting dates,' Felske retorts, denying buzz that the character is based on Field). Not to mention Felske's friendship with Mickey Rourke, with whom he lived for five months while rewriting Rourke's boxing movie, *Homeboy*. 'I only got respect once he realized that I knew pretty girls,' says Felske. After dinner, Felske suggests a trip to Lot 61—'I hear it's the hot joint'—but I beg off. He asks if I have a boyfriend, and walks me home. Running his fingers through his mane he has one last thing to say before stepping off into the night: 'So, what's going on with my hair?' "

— *New York Magazine*

"**The word on *Word* is all good**. No sophomore slump for **Coerte Felske**. The young author has followed his well-received first novel 'The Shallow Man,' with 'Word,' which is due next month from Warner Books and already is getting good reviews. Plus, Felske just sold his third book, 'The Millennium Girl,' to St. Martin's Press. Pretty good for an Eastern-raised screenwriter who was banging his head on West Coast studio walls a few years ago unable to get much of anything going. The protagonist in 'Word' happens to be a good-looking young screenwriter himself, who happens to make friends with a powerful studio executive who in some ways resembles **Ted Field**, the Interscope mogul who was close with Felske for a couple years. Kirkus Reviews found 'an insider cynicism not matched since [Clifford] Odets' and [Ernest] Lehman's 'Sweet Smell of Success' took on Manhattan's nightlife.' Publishers Weekly calls it 'flashy and dark,' and said 'This energetic Nathaniel West retake offers a rich Hollywood menu of pandering, ambition, power, and retribution …bright, bitchy fun and up-to-date name-dropping, local atmosphere and cutting-edge jargon.' Detour was so taken by Felske's lingo, the glossy is publishing a glossary to go along with its excerpt of the book. Among the terms are modelitis: 'a fashion model's personal self-corrosion and character contamination as a result of her beauty. Affects her mind and behavior.' And model repulsion: 'a severe distaste and dislike for fashion models due to galactic maintenance behavior and prima donna needs.' "

— *"Page Six," The New York Post*

"**How to Catch a Man at the Century's End:** This happens to be written by a man, the novelist-journalist-screenwriter Coerte V.W. Felske. It's a face-to-face encounter with 'diggers,' women who troll resort towns in search of the perfect millionaire. *The Millennium Girl* is based upon Felske's own research. We all know women like this exist, but until now we didn't have all the gory details. Our heroine is a nubile 28-year-old named Bodicea, who dies her hair incessantly and has a wicked habit of giving her fellow diggers nicknames like 'Operation: I Do,' and 'Ellen B. Generous.' We go on tour with the charming Bo as she uses men and vice versa, and along the way she dispenses various nuggets of self-analysis like 'if women weren't so jealous of one-another, we'd be the rulers of the planet.' The book is hilarious and sympathetic and even stops to examine a gay man's search for the perfect mate in the midst of all its heterosexual sex scenes. Bo gains her humanity and has a real soul which is perhaps the surest indicator that this is fiction."

— Melanie Rehak, *The New York Times Book Review*

"*People Are Talking About: Books*; Novelist-cum-boulevardier Coerte V.W. Felske explains how to marry a billionaire. The outtakes from the life of Coerte V.W. Felske teem with glamour: the portrait of the novelist as a young man by good friend Peter Beard; a snapshot with model Frederique Van der Wal; another with his book party hosts director Peter Berg and Janice Dickinson. To Felske, whose previous book launches were held at Joe's Pub and Lot 61, the velvet rope simply does not exist. For tonight's out-on-the-town interview, Felske suggests we start with drinks uptown at Fifty Seven Fifty Seven ($110). From there, perhaps we'll move on to dinner at Harry Cipriani ($500) before finishing up with nightcaps at Au Bar ($175). An evening with Felske is enough to make a girl's Prada habit seem positively economical. By 7: 30 P.M., Felske is stretched out at a table in the cavernous bar, ready to talk about his new novel and what inspired it. He runs a hand through his shaggy Caesar cut, cocks his head forward, and tries desperately to be heard above the din. 'It's a good night, Wednesdays,' he says, surveying a room of Armani-clad tycoons, endless martini glasses, and the high-pitched laughter of well-dressed women. 'The men have finished their business day; maybe there's a meeting tomorrow, but now they have a night or two before they have to go home to their wives. And you get everyone here—Europeans, South Americans, everyone. It's prime Digger territory.' A 'Digger,' mind you, is Felske's term for a woman who targets wealthy men like a heat-seeking missile. And Diggers are at the center of *The Millennium Girl* (St. Martin's Press), Felske's much-buzzed-about new novel, a fictionalized account of his gimlet-eyed social observations. *The Millennium Girl* takes the reader through the marriage market of the nineties. His heroine, Bodicea, is determined to land herself not just a husband but a husband who meets a strict set of financial and social criteria. According to Felske, it's women's lib for the nineties: Bodicea's point of view takes a quick tussle with the fifties (for that perennially chic retro feel), spins through the eighties (for a dose of glamour), and lands firmly in the next century—the goal is still the same (landing the guy), but the white picket fence has morphed into a classic six, several vacation homes, and a Gulfstream V for the commute. The difference is that these women, like Bodicea, approach finding a husband with the steely-eyed acumen of a CEO: Wine and dine at Le Cirque 2000, shop at Gucci and Manolo, summer in the Hamptons, and winter in Aspen. Beyond having the money that allows them to traffic in global finery, these women are looking for men who can spend it with style. But *The Millennium Girl* is not just another collection of insider's jargon and 'Page Six' gossip. Felske is the real thing: He knows his territory, and he writes about it with wit and style. *Girl* may have taken him only a few weeks to write, but he's been steeped in its culture since childhood. He grew up in New York City and on the Eastern Shore of Long Island, navigated his way around Manhattan from a very early age, spent his undergraduate years at Dartmouth, and then did graduate work at Columbia University's film school—after which he co-wrote *Homeboy* for actor Mickey Rourke. Then came two novels that, like *Girl*, glitter with a diamond-sharp deconstruction of modern life in the fast lane. Both got solid reviews, including *The New York Times*'s: both are being produced for the big screen by New Line Cinema. 'It's all about the voice,' Felske says, describing what makes his novels different. 'I believe the book is honest. It's not an indictment, rather, it's in praise of women, in a reverse angle way, women who are trying to better themselves, empower themselves any way they can. To not be dependents, but independents. Occasionally, you write a certain piece of music and people respond to it, and I think *TMG* strikes those universal chords.' "

— Dana Wagner, *Vogue*

"His debut novel, *The Shallow Man*, introduced us to Manhattan 'Modelizers.' His second novel, *Word*, brought us Tinseltown's 'Blips,' 'Bullets,' and 'Strugs.' Now, in *The Millennium Girl*, pulse-of-the-Zeitgeist author Coerte V.W. Felske sets his sights on 'Diggers,' a.k.a. the globe-trotting hotties on the hunt for 'Walletmen,' the ultra-rich men of their dreams."

— *Detour*

"**Let's Hear It for the Girls:** They're baaaack, and in the latest reads, they rule the world. So much for that un-p.c. term 'girl' becoming as obsolete as 8-track tapes. It's back with a passion. Who are these lit It Girls? The Millennium Girl, by Coerte V.W. Felske ... 'I'm not a hooker ... but I do live off men,' says the title character. 'Why shouldn't I take what I can while I can?' Bodicea is a 28-year-old knockout with lips she's tattooed an even deeper red. Her work alias is 'Digger'—she globe-hops in search of filthy-rich 'Walletmen,' some to be kept by in high style, and one to marry before she turns 30. I wanted to hate her, but I couldn't: She was too shameless and too hilariously over-the-top."

— *Mademoiselle*

"**Prolific Pen: COERTE Felske** is alive and well on a 49-foot ketch in Barcelona. The author of 'The Shallow Man' and 'Word'—quite the man about town in the 90s—vanished when he fell in love and had a daughter with a gorgeous Swiss woman. Without the distractions of Gotham, Felske, now repped by CAA, has finished two more novels: 'Scandalocity,' the speed it takes for a disgrace to turn you into a star, and 'The Dolce Vita Diaries and the Final Phantasmagoric Flight of the Ivory Stretch Limousine into Freedom and Destiny.' Meanwhile, **Heather Graham** is planning to produce and star in 'The Millennium Girl,' and **Morgan Freeman** is slated for 'Wild Blood.' "

— *"Page Six," The New York Post*

"Another from the resourceful and amusing Felske, whose satire of the fashion industry, *The Shallow Man*, and knifing of Los Angeles, *Word*, are both in the pipeline at New Line Cinema. His latest topic is international gold diggers, the sweet lovelies more shark-like than Anita Loos's or Truman Capote's who speak of Walletmen (fat cats of Fortune 500 and Forbes 400 fame), of Chanel, Bulgari, and Armani, and of the seasons of Gstaad, Cannes, Nice, and Ibiza. Felske's narrator, Bo (Bodicea), has jade-green eyes, has had her lips tattooed deep red for a strong lip line, changes hair color every six weeks, and has just gone off-Tour and arrived in Manhattan to see an English sugar daddy whom a fellow Digger (Travels With Men) has asked her to entertain. Bo, part Native American Zuni, builds the ego of her Walletmen with wise words lifted from astrology columns, and, since seeing *Dances With Wolves*, she nicks all her fellow Diggers with names like Earns Every Penny and Every Little Bit Helps. She has a Ten Year Window, from 20 to 30, to hit the Mother Lode, a Walletman she can mine for lasting, lifetime security. For the time being, she lives in a cute two-bedroom on the 34th floor of Trump Tower (rent: $4,800 a month) that she shares with her best friend, the snowman (that is, gay) budding psychologist Napoleon Dieudonné, to whom, as his only patient, tells her steamy life story: her pursuit of the Rich Rebel, Bradley Lorne-August; her tie with late sister Vicky's daughter, Maximilia; and her own rise to true self-empowerment. Felske laces every page with a masterful cynicism that Bo sees as he own Millennial Smarts while still charming all. A novel with legs."

— *Kirkus Reviews*

"Meet Bodicea Lashley, 'the millennium girl,' living by her wits, and various other attributes, as a 'digger'—a species of jet-set hooker who gets paid for her tricks in clothes and rent instead of cash. She travels an annual circuit from Gstaad to Ibiza and points in between, following the money in hopes of catching some crumbs from some generous older gentleman. Bo fills us in on the tricks of the trade as she relates the story of her twenty-eighth year. The digger jargon is kicky, as is the device of giving fellow diggers pseudo-Native American monikers a la 'Dances With Wolves': Travels With Men, Earning Every Penny, Smiles to Your Face. *The Millennium Girl* is based on a magazine article Felske wrote in 1997 about young women hustling in Aspen. As a novel, it is snappy fun, a box of candy wrapped up with a black latex bow."

— Booklist

"Bodicea Lashley has definite goals. She is a 'Digger,' a woman who makes her living sponging off of supremely wealthy 'Walletmen' and an active participant on the 'Digger Tour.' The tour takes her all over the world, from Gstaad to St. Tropez, Palm Beach, and Aspen, to trade her feminine wiles for wearables from Prada and Gucci and for cold, hard cash. The goal of the Digger Tourists? To marry a Walletman, and Bo is trying her hardest to land the big one. A likeable character despite her excesses, Bo speaks in catchy phrases and, for her compatriots on the Digger Tour, finds hilarious nicknames like the Three Minute Princess and At these Prices. This is a strong follow-up to Felske's previous novel, Word, which delved hilariously into the Hollywood screenwriting scene. Here he uses his trademark insight and detail to peer into the lives of sassy but sad women. Learning how Bo got started in her line of work and observing encounters with the richest of the rich is a complete hoot. Sexy, hard to put down, and 100 percent fun, this is recommended for all fiction collections."

— Library Journal

"Of the slew of new single-girl manhunt novels, Felske's (*The Shallow Man, Word*) third novel scales new heights, aiming to describe the art of gold-digging women and the folly of their prey: wealthy, high-living "walletmen." Bodicea Lashley, hailing from a small factory town in Ohio, relocates to New York to pursue a career as a Digger, a woman who lives off well-heeled lovers, hoping to lure one into marriage. Her perfect body, satirically described, provides the bait. After dumping two-timing multimillionaire Giles, Bo decides to marry Napoleon, a gay friend who can access his family's considerable fortune if he weds. But while visiting Napoleon's family in Palm Beach, Bo takes up with Bradley Lorne-August. Bradley's attentions wane and Bo resumes with former lover Warren Samuels, America's 11th-richest man whose tastes run to sex in airplanes, religious role-playing and sadism. During the Aspen leg of her Digger Tour, Bo falls for a young journalist and keeps tabs on her ailing sister and niece, both living in poverty back in Ohio. Bo realizes that all that glitters is not gold and decides to become independent. Clever Bo invents cute nicknames for her fellow Diggers: "Travels With Men" and "Operation: I Do." Bo's discovery that wealth isn't love is unrelieved; sex scenes mix with lessons for Digger survival—'Don't depend. Independ.' The acidic jibes at upper-class hypocrisy are good for chuckles and the novel's stabs at satiric revelations of vision and subject."

— Publishers Weekly

"**Fast Lane:** *Coerte Felske's new book shows that life is no stranger than fast track fiction.* **Latest Felske Fiction:** *Millennium Gold Digger.* 'It's not a Gary Cooper-Jimmy Stewart world out there. I don't write fairy tales,' says Quogue native Coerte V. W. Felske, author of The Shallow Man, Word, and, out this month, *The Millennium Girl.* Mr. Felske will be reading excerpts from his new book this Saturday, October 9, at Book Hampton (20 Main Street in East Hampton) before departing on a book-signing tour of major U.S. cities. His new book—his third in a loosely constructed trilogy devoted to exposing the grit-behind-the-glitter lifestyles and moral ambiguities of those who would make their way among the rich and famous—marks a departure in tone and voice from his two previous works. Last week, Mr. Felske took a few moments before heading out to Los Angeles for film meetings on his first novel to sit down over lunch at the Blue Parrot in East Hampton to discuss this shift in tone, along with his past, present, and future. *The Millennium Girl* is the story of Bodicea, a nice girl from Fort Lowell, Ohio, who happens to be a quarter Native-American, quarter English, quarter Brazilian, and a quarter Eskimo. Bodicea's primary attributes, 'nice full breasts and an ass that's high, tight, firm, and about the size of a grapefruit,' have allowed her to slide smoothly from a broken home and onto the Digger Tour, the fast-paced world of globe-trotting gold diggers chasing the fat cat men of their dreams from party to party against a backdrop of fashionable vacation destinations. But Bodicea is not all evil or cold calculation. Her heart's in the right place, if her values aren't quite there yet, and she's on the path to enlightenment. As written in the first person by Mr. Felske, Bodicea is possessed of a wry sense of humor and an eye for detail that sustains the narrative. She's a sympathetic character (with a love for Chanel) who Mr. Felske insists is emblematic of the sort of 'conflicted modern people who interest me.' Throughout *The Millennium Girl,* Bodicea picks apart her own insecurities and those of the other girls on the tour. And, in the end, Bodicea manages to raise herself above the fate of her cohorts—amusingly referred to as Travels With Men, Earning Every Penny, Never Flies Coach, and For Your Wallet Only. 'This is an odyssey about female empowerment,' Mr. Felske explains, adding that he finds women inherently more interesting than their male counterparts. 'It's about getting to a position of strength and the opportunities available to women today. *The Millennium Girl* title is a loaded one, particularly ironic, but about how women should be addressing themselves to empowerment, given the societal restraints of their peak years and today's societal pressures.' But above all, it is the 'double-sided nature of human beings' that has drawn Mr. Felske to map the morally dubious interiors of characters who live on razor's edge of scruples. In *The Shallow Man*, Mr. Felske examined the life of Nick Laws, a celebrity-obsessed, supermodel-pursuing rake. *Word* presented Heyward Hoon, a writer of substantial but commercially non-viable screenplays, who procures women for a producer. And, Bodicea, Mr. Felske's millennium girl, follows in their tradition: decent people trying to make the best of the outrageous situations in which they've found themselves. Although Mr. Felske insists his work is not a case of art imitating life—'I wish I had had as good a time as I wrote about," he says—he is no stranger to the worlds he documents. From 1990 to 1994, he was a resident of Los Angeles, living the life of a struggling spec writer, churning out script after script, all highly praised but never made into movies. Now however, the likes of Jack Nicholson have proclaimed him 'the voice of the late 20s to early 40s group of people.' After the success of *The Shallow Man*, published in 1995, Mr. Felske moved back east, where he finished *Word*. But it was when he was sent by *Esquire* magazine to write a feature story on the above ground gold digging happening on the hills of Aspen that Mr. Felske discovered the material at the heart of his latest oeuvre. Granted two weeks of access to the parties that cap the social year in the famed Colorado mountain resort, Mr. Felske says that he found it difficult to get any women to open up until after New Year's. Then, 'they gushed. A purge took place when they were disillusioned, when they hadn't gotten their man.' Eventually published in *Manhattan File*, Mr. Felske's piece revealed the secrets of real women on the real-life husband-hunting circuit—mind boggling proof that fact is far stranger, and dirtier, than fiction. Mr. Felske, 39, writes in a style that mixes Brett Easton Ellis's precise obsession with designer labels with Dominick Dunne and Louis Auchincloss's insider looks at the over-the-top, rarified lifestyles of the super rich. 'It is what it is,' says Mr. Felske who sees himself as something of a documentarian and, at the same time, a writer who 'likes to play with, and invent, language.' Mr. Felske uses his 'literary anthropology' in hopes of 'allowing a reader to come into one of my stories and get a sense of the world, even if they are not familiar with it.' Mr. Felske's blond, unpretentious good looks, his laid-back approach to life (he carries his wallet, business cards, pen and paper in a fanny-pack) and gregarious, California sun-drenched personality seem to have served him well in the shark-infested waters of the movie business. He has just put the finishing touches on the script for *The Shallow Man* to be produced by New Line Cinema and directed by Gary Fleder ('Things To Do In Denver When You're Dead,' 'Kiss the Girls') and casting for the movie begins soon. He's also been teamed with the writer of 'Things To Do In Denver When You're Dead' and 'Armageddon' to develop a script based on *Word*. Film offers for *The Millennium Girl* have already started to come in. But Mr. Felske is a cautious optimist who'd rather wait to see the reviews of his book before committing to any deals, and he does not consider himself on top of the world. He feels simply that, 'I've been fortunate in a lot of ways. I'm having fun. I'm doing what I love. I make my own hours.' Appreciative of the 'less-touched' ocean vistas at the end of Long Island, Mr. Felske plans to divide his time between a house in Montauk and his apartment in SoHo. His next book, tentatively entitled, *The Bossa Nova Diaries*, is about the Hamptons in the 1970s. He will also publish next year, under a pseudonym, a 'traditional, classical' literary work set further back in time. 'The most significant aspect of my writing is the voice,' Mr. Felske says, explaining his productivity. 'Once I can get that, everything else falls into place.' For *The Millennium Girl*, finding Bodicea's voice was 'my biggest challenge. But when I had it, I had it.' After one draft, he submitted it to his agency, William Morris. After a 'mild, two-day modification,' the book was sent out to publishers and quickly sold. In the literary world, where authors are known to labor for days on sentences and years on books, this kind of productivity marks Mr. Felske as a rare bird indeed. With five more novels already planned out and plans of purchasing a house in the South of France or Tuscany, Mr. Felske seems poised to document a good deal more of pre- and post-millennial, American high life. Although he speculates about someday settling down and having children, right now he says, 'my books have been my children. I've given them all my attention. I travel extensively and write as I go. It's a pretty nice life.' "

— Nick Snyder, *The Southampton Press*

"**The Millennium Girl:** Coerte V. W. Felske. Despite its portentous title, this novel about a gold digger's calculated search for love is more than a racy rehash of *Pretty Woman* or any number of similarly old-fashioned hooker-with-a-heart-of-platinum tales. That's not to say it isn't great trashy fun too. Felske who covered the 'digger' scene in an investigative article for *Esquire*, clearly knows the turf (New York, Aspen, Hong Kong). Female empowerment, a having-it-all ending, a pampered husband hunter, and a flaming gay sidekick perpetuate these pages."

— *Entertainment Weekly*

"**Sugardaddy Sinderellas**: *Author* **Coerte V.W. Felske** *mines America's goldigger circuit in his new novel* The Millennium Girl. **Bill Powers** *learns why honey makes the world go round.* At a high-profile fete in Manhattan, Coerte V.W. Felske was once introduced to **Christy Turlington** as 'the man who never met a model he didn't like.' Just recalling the incident is enough to give him chills. 'It's stuff like that that really makes me cringe,' says the scribe, taking three steps back as if to punctuate via pantomime, 'but I guess it sort of comes with the territory.' When your first novel is *The Shallow Man* and follows the antics of an urban model hunter leading a barely examined life, there's some inherent baggage an author must learn to accept. Nevertheless, his 1995 debut put Coerte's name on all the right lips, including those attached to **Jack Nicholson**, New Line Cinema, and *Esquire* magazine. That winter, the men's glossy assigned Coerte an investigative feature on Aspen's yearly Christmas break influx of goldiggers. The $18,000 expose was ultimately killed due to changes in *Esquire*'s editorial leadership but

Coerte's encounters with these 21st century courtesans on the slopes of Colorado's toniest ski town left a lasting impression. Eventually they would serve as foundation for his latest tale of woe and dough entitled *The Millennium Girl*. Coerte recalls his Rocky Mountain excursion over a round of St. Pauli Girls at the Time Hotel in New York: 'I interviewed about 25 or 30 girls. At first no one wanted to talk and, really, what woman in her right mind would want to draw this kind of attention?' he asks with the annunciation of a TV anchorman. 'Then after New Year's Eve it was interesting, the women who hadn't managed to land their guy sort of felt this need to purge. I promised I wouldn't use their names and they gave me the full rundown. That's when I heard about girls studying the names on the *Fortune* and *Forbes* lists. Some girls were going to Brunei the next week. They just disappear for a while—tell their family that they're going to model in Europe or something—and wind up making $25,000 a week. It's a totally viable financial undertaking for a woman. I mean, there's no question what they're doing is prostitution, but they get paid incredibly well.' The assembled anecdotes have been fictionalized into the life of *The Millennium Girl*—a twenty-eight year old Digger named Bodicea—who lives in Trump Tower with her gay best friend Napoleon. Bo is looking to get off Tour permanently, meaning no more St. Moritz in March, June in the Hamptons, July in St. Tropez. She's tired of constantly chumming the bigwig waters hoping to get hooked on the purse strings of unreliable, though often generous, Walletmen. But, she's also wary of settling down. To paraphrase a rhetorical pondering of Bo's: Why have one guy who treats you like shit when you can have 20 who treat you a Goddess? 'Many of the girls I spoke with think a woman should get what she can,' says Coerte. 'Let's face it, survival is where it's always been at and some women are more hard-nosed than others. There's a very low success ratio [when it comes to goldigging] and if they play *the game* too long, these women often end up making compromises they never would have in their youth. In this modern age, as things get more stressful and Darwinian, people start doing things they never would have found acceptable back when life was a little more homespun. My whole thing was to show the warmer side of these women so you that you know where that money gravitation comes from. Ultimately Bo prevails and gets what she wants on her terms, but it's definitely a low-percentage racket.' "

— *Bikini Magazine*

"*The Millennium Girl*: Coerte V.W. Felske's novel is a *Breakfast at Tiffany's* for the year 2000. Bodicea Lashley, a former poor girl from Ohio, is a gorgeous twenty-something fortune hunter who does the circuit—Gstaad at Christmas, Aspen at New Year's, February in Palm Beach—hunting for what she calls "walletmen." But as the 20th century draws to a close, Bodicea begins to take stock not just of her finances but her way of life. A totally titillating read."

— *Woman's Own*

"**BEAUTY THRILLS**: Main Street in East Hampton was invaded by particularly beautiful people the other day for **Coerte Felske**'s book-signing, sponsored by Hamptons.com, of his thriller 'Scandalocity.' Felske—recently seen on 'Real Housewives of New York City' kissing **Countess LuAnn de Lesseps**—was flanked by models **Irina Shayk**, **Jessica White**, and **Eugenia Kuzmina**. Shayk graces the cover in a photo taken by **Peter Beard**. 'Scandalocity'— defined as 'the speed at which scandal, measured in velocity, can turn you into a star'—features a hero named Harry Starslinger, an online gossip columnist who becomes embroiled in the police investigation of his girlfriend's murder."

— *"Page Six," The New York Post*

" 'People Are Talking About: Books,' Favorite Novel: *The Shallow Man* by Coerte Felske which begins with the line 'I never met a model I didn't like.' "

— Candace Bushnell, *Vogue*

"PLAYBOY CENTERFOLD DATA SHEET, 'Favorite Book: *The Shallow Man* by Coerte V.W. Felske. It's about a very shallow man and his involvements with models.' "

— Priscilla Lee Taylor, Miss March, 1996, *Playboy*

"COERTE: generous son—James Joyce and Ernest Hemingway never got plugged the way **Coerte Felske** just got plugged. Readers who plowed through the biographical data provided by Playboy's Miss March, **Priscilla Lee Taylor**, on the flip side of the centerfold learned that her favorite book is **Coerte Felske**'s *The Shallow Man*. But Felske, who's in Miami finishing up his second novel, doesn't seem too eager to meet the buxom blonde. 'I'd like to introduce her to my dad,' the shy writer tells us. 'He's had a dry winter.' "

— *"Page Six," The New York Post*

"A Model Wordsmith."

— *New York Magazine*

"A STRETCHED TITLE. Coerte Felske, who wrote *The Shallow Man* and *The Millennium Girl*, went for a longer title on his latest novel: *The Dolce Vita Diaries and the Final Phantasmagoric Flight of the Ivory Stretch Limousine into Freedom and Destiny*, which the author describes as 'an abduction story which takes place in the southwest.' The manuscript is generating buzz as it makes its way through publishers and talent agents who think it could be a vehicle for **Tom Cruise** or **Brad Pitt**. The novel is being compared to Ken Kesey's *Sometimes a Great Notion*, Jack Kerouac's *On the Road*, and **Robert Parsing**'s *Zen and the Art of Motorcycle Maintenance*."

— *"Page Six," The New York Post*

"That classic opening line from *The Shallow Man*, 'I never met a model I didn't like,' defined an era. Coerte V.W. Felske has given us a run of texts which skillfully chronicle the skin-deep and shameless age with laser-like precision. There are pretenders to the throne of the genre, but this resourceful and amusing novelist has it down. Like the late Stanley Elkin, Felske masters the pedantry of various trades and milieus, then creates a joyous poetry of jargon to float his novels on, setting sail on an ocean of buzzwords which continue to creep steadily into the daily vernacular. At the same time, he's not merely an inventor of neologisms, rather, a sorcerer of language and the written word, lacing each page with a masterful cynicism. I suspect we'll be talking about this author as the one who captured certainly the Nineties best. He one-upped fashionista literature with *The Shallow Man*, bested Nathaniel West with *Word*, and took Capote a step beyond with *The Millennium Girl*."

— *The Guardian (England)*

Three Sleeps

to Double Happiness

Also by

Coerte VW Felske

for

The Dolce Vita Press

The Shallow Man: 20th Anniversary Edition
Word: 15th Anniversary Edition
The Millennium Girl: 15th Anniversary Edition
Scandalocity
The Ivory Stretch

Completed Future Works

Chemical / Animal
A Touch of Noir

Coerte V.W. Felske titles for The Dolce Vita Press are available
at the author's Web site coertefelske.com, thedolcevitapress.com,
Amazon.com, BN.com, e-book distributors, and
independent book stores worldwide

Three Sleeps

to Double Happiness

by

Coerte VW Felske

The Dolce Vita Press, Inc.
New York

Front cover calligraphy by Peter Beard by permission of the artist.

Cover graphics, art, layout by Christian Toms for Red & Jacket or chris@redandjacket.com, cover design by CVWF for The Dolce Vita Press

The Dolce Vita Press series cover concept and logo by Jackie Merri Meyer for MeyerNewYork@aol.com and CVWF for The Dolce Vita Press

THE DOLCE VITA PRESS is a trademark of The Dolce Vita Press, Inc.

Manufactured in the United States of America

Library of Congress Cataloging-in-Publication Data

Felske, Coerte V. W.

The Ivory Stretch / by Coerte V. W. Felske—lst ed.

1. Title.

PS3556.E47259S53 2016

813'.54—dc20 94-47947

ISBN 978-0-9840786-7-7

10 9 8 7 6 5 4 3 2 1

First Edition: July, 2018

For Dad

Acknowledgments

I would like to thank the following individuals for their inspiration, friendship, and guidance now and through the years.

Gisella Aquije, Peter and Nejma Beard, Bill and Sally Beatty, Alison Blume, Clint and Mary Blume, Anneke Felske, Norman Felske, David Greeff, Douglas Greeff, Grace Holland, Richard and Sessa Johnson, Roger Moley, Kenneth Nichols, Ray Nicholson, Gonzalo Otoya, Tom Rees, Jr., Nora Sabrier, Waldo Sanchez, Cameron Winklevoss, Tyler Winklevoss, Diamond Felske, and Bodicea Felske.

I give special thanks to Peter Beard for his creative cover magic, to Christian Toms for his graphic artistry, and Jackie Meyer for the original design concept.

To cherished friends and fallen soldiers, great souls and spirits taken too soon, you will always be remembered and I'm honored for the time we shared: Alan Beeber, Noel Behn, Joe Cole, Doug Cummins, Frank Daniel, Robert Hattersley, John Kennedy Jr., John Rassias, Dr. Thomas and Nan Rees, and Billy Way.

Lastly, I feel the deepest gratitude toward my father Richard Norman Felske who always fought the good fight, never gave up, and who taught me about honesty, generosity, and family integrity, qualities I am honored to pass on to our own. We lost him this year and he will be greatly missed. I also thank my mother Anneke Felske who has always been there for me with an inspired idea, recommendation, maternal guidance, the perfect gift, or just pure love, and has been a constant source of joy in my life.

There are no facts. Only interpretations.

— *Friedrich Nietzsche*
1844-1900

… Me, we …

— Muhammad Ali
Harvard University Commencement Address
1975

Three Sleeps

to Double Happiness

India

1

The boy whom they said was not quite right was waiting near the Water Hole beneath a line of towering Dhok trees. It was nighttime in the Jungle and he was enveloped by the cacophony of restless nocturnal critters. He had been awaiting Two Sleeps now and this was his second night as he had his own way of marking the passage of time. He counted each day as a Sleep and he did not know how many Sleeps it would be before he saw the Great One but he hoped it would be soon.

The Dung Flies were no longer bothering him and he had developed an appetite during the long hot day and he decided then to tear off another wedge from the dried Mango spear in his pocket to give him Energy. He appreciated the dried Mangos for their tart and sweet flavor and the chewy gum drop texture and he chewed them like candy.

Waiting was not difficult for the boy and he felt he was getting good at it. Besides, the Old Man said he would have to wait perhaps a long while. The Great One had vast amounts of territory to cover every day. And standing by was part of the Jungle way of life.

'Everyone waits,' the Old Man said. 'The Rhesus. The Striped Hyena. The Golden Jackal. The Four-Horned Antelope. The Caracal. The Wild Boar. And silly men who want to make themselves a part of it too. You must have Paciencia. And let it be your Guide.'

The boy they called Gonzalo did not remember much but he remembered this as it was a Big Thing. He did not write the word down either as he could not read or write but the Old Man spelled it out for him and the boy studied the word and the shapes and curvatures of letters. From then on he repeated it to himself before bed and at first light, like a mantra. *Paciencia.* I must have *Paciencia.'* He copied the letters too, but as one would a drawing and not the transcription of words. He scratched it on the Docks in Cadaques, he drew it on the Beach in Llavaneres, on the red clay earth too in Alicante, on the giant Dunes in Tarifa, and in the sand by the Bus stop in New Delhi; and then he drew it again One Sleep before by the Watering Hole. And he realized it may be few or many Sleeps before he saw the Great One, but that *Paciencia* and thoughts of his Sister the Angel and his life growing up in Spain would help pass the time.

Though the boy did not know the Sariska Jungle he was getting used to it just as he had learned would happen with most things. The tall Trees, underlying foliage, and thick and thorny Brush reminded him of the thorn scrub Forest on the hillsides above the Old Man's Spice Farm in Mataró high above the Mediterranean; so this type of unruly and prickly verdant growth was not unfamiliar. Yet the tropical broadleaf forest that surrounded the Water Hole made for its own unique aesthetic. From the indigenous Flame of the Forest trees with their fiery orange-red flowers, the bright yellow blossoms of the lofty Kadaya and Gol, and the Ziziphus Ber bearing white petals and tight-skinned orange fruit; to the spiny white flowers of the Khair, the wide canopies of the Bengal Fig trees, the florescent green Bamboo stalks, the yellow petals of the towering Arjuns, and the pink and red blooms of the stout Gugal—the lush Ravine was ablaze and exploding with color.

The boy was not scared about being alone deep in the Jungle either; nor was he unhappy in his solitude. He had come to know solitude and it had become his friend though he could not conceive of it that way. He enjoyed listening to the Jungle's music, especially the night noises. The Secadas began in late afternoon and were buzzing endlessly around him like swarms of bees and they made him feel like he wasn't by himself even though he was not uncomfortable being alone. He did enjoy seeing people though whenever they came around to visit or to talk with their bright eyes and smiles and soothing voices. In the end he could be Happy with or without people around him. Because when people were not around he could just ponder, watch, and listen to his own random Kaleidoscope renderings of thoughts and memories, wondering and wishing too in no particular order.

'I wish the Old Man was here to see me,' the boy thought. 'I think he would be Happy I arrived without difficulty. And with some Pasetas in my pocket.'

The boy had learned if he had Money in his pocket he was Smart and after a long Journey if he had some Money left it meant he was even Smarter. He still wasn't sure the nice dark-skinned Man with the Giant Legs at the Bus Stop with the watery Eyes had given him the right amount of Change. The Man handed him so many more pieces of paper of the New Money in return for what he had given him. (The boy did not understand Money; he thought everyone should be able to have some.) But he knew too Money was precious and that you had to work hard at Jobs to get it. And he recognized he needed the New Money if he wanted to buy a bigger Knife or more Rice and dried Mangos or a Stamp for the Letter he promised to send Zosimus the Fisherman. But the watery-eyed man was such a Generous Man he was hoping he had not miscalculated and given him back too much (when in fact the handicapped swindler had cheated the boy as it took stacks of New Money to equal his Pesetas). The New Money had a new name too: Rupees.

The boy did not understand why the man's Legs were so enormous. They looked swollen and not well (like when the boy's eye grew large and black and purple the first time the School Boys 'disciplined' him on the Municipal School playground. His Father had taught him that hitting was discipline and necessary for him.) And if the man's Legs were not well it could mean the man was not well either. He prayed to the Man with the Brown Beard then for the Man with the Dark Skin and flooded eyes, just as he had prayed for Basilio and Tomaso and Guido and all the other School Boys after every Boom to his head and every Game of Wrestle or Underwear Wedgie in the schoolyard.

The boy had Faith the Man with the Brown Beard was helping him find his Happiness; the one he had first seen at the Pulpit in the Church in Llavaneres and then in many places and pictures, even on Padre Miguel's Cross and his own Sister the Angel's Paintings. He was taught that the Man was always listening (to whomever wanted to talk to Him) and ready to hear Prayers though he had never seen Him. He couldn't process this Concept entirely because of his Mental Problems, he thought, though he did recognize that saying Kind Words for someone was important. It meant that he was thinking a Good Thought and Good Thoughts, like Faith, helped the World.

He had learned both words. They were Big Things too.

Good Thoughts also helped his Sister the Angel, he was reminded. Wherever she was the boy hoped she was well and painting beautiful and imaginative (not 'Crazy') Paintings and dancing her Ballet beneath the Juniper trees and that he would see her very soon.

Wisps of clouds passed slowly over the shiny white metallic moon perched high above the Ragasthan's Aravalli Mountains giving the moonface a temporary mustache. Eventually the thin mustache moved on and the moonface was clean-shaven again. The moon was so bright it resembled silver sunshine. As the clouds continued to clear the stars popped out and made a holiday blanket of the deep purple sky.

The temperature had dropped dramatically since dusk; Sariska was much cooler at night. The September evening chill surrounded the boy and his arms were invaded by the little bumps. The boy opened the Satchel, now blood-stained, and drew out the torn blanket, unrolling it, and draping it over his thighs. As he spread the covering he thought of the Golden Jackal then, the trickster, and the tug of war they had had over the Satchel just before the previous night's Sleep. He remembered his sharp muzzle, fulvous-reddish fur, and light tread though he could never describe it this way. A faint smile made it on his face as he thought of how strong the Creature was even though the Jackal nipped him a little. His arms were still very sore from the struggle similar to the discomfort he'd endured after fighting a fish with Zosimus the Fisherman. He Prayed then for the Animal too, that he would find food somewhere else.

Reflecting on the contest with the Jackal One Sleep before it came to mind he needed to cover himself again. And he needed to rub the Dung on thoroughly this time; so that he would not be interrupted again late at night. The Old Man had told him about the Dung; that it kept the Animals he did not want to communicate with away. The boy liked the Animals, all of them, he loved them in fact. He wished more than anything that they could talk. He just couldn't play with them now, not now. He needed to conserve his Energy and Strength. It was what Aziz had taught him on the Hashish Farm. He did not always know about these things but he did now. He had learned through his Sister's method of teaching, devised specially for him.

Gonzalo drew from his Satchel the rolled cloth, the one Sofía had given him that Summer morning in Tarifa, and unfurled it. From the pile of Dung he broke off a chunk of the deep brown almost black dried droppings and spit on them and began to smear it on his hands, arms, legs, and face. He did this twice a day but waited after nightfall and before first light when the Dung Flies were asleep. The air was moist and the Dung could absorb the dusk and dawn dew in addition to his saliva and the moisture allowed it to spread better, like brown butter, and bring out the smell of the urine. He did not know this was why, it was what the Old Man told him, a traveled man whose life had been full of Adventures—that it needed to be done at these times. It was a Big Thing and he remembered it and as soon as he saw the village Women in Alwar dressed in the bright fuchsia, Yellow, Purple, and Orange Saris selling it he bought an entire sack full with many sheets of the New Money. He could not read their Sign but he saw the picture of the Great One and he recognized what it was.

Like the Man with the Giant Legs, Gonzalo wondered if he had given the village Woman with the colorful clothes enough money; he let her choose it from his hand as he always did because he could not count and others could. The Money was left over from the overland train ride from Paris, the same Pesetas the Dutch Girl had given him. He had given away a lot of it on the train to the passengers who spoke Spanish. To the Serbian man. And the Greek one too, though he did not know their nationalities. And the Pakistani Girl. They seemed Happy to take his Money and he thought it could help them. He knew Money was a Big Thing and that everyone should have some. He did not understand why it was not given to everyone. Or why these folk did not get enough from their Jobs because everyone worked and had a Job. He had had three Jobs and he seemed to always have some Money.

He remembered just then Zosimus had told him not to give away any Money and that it was a Big Thing. He usually remembered all Big Things and he could not understand how it happened. It seemed the passengers really needed the Money badly with faces that did not show Happiness. At the same time he recognized he had followed his Journey and arrived according to his Plan and that was Good and that the Old Man and his Sister the Angel would be Happy.

Once the boy had covered himself thoroughly from head to toe with the Dung, Gonzalo decided then it was time to build the Fire to keep Warm.

The Matchbook he had from the big Boat with the 7 Puertas restaurant written on it had gotten wet, but now it was dry and he had a few Matches left. He did not know what he would do when he would run out of Matches. He did not know how to build a Fire. He had been taught how but he always needed help and he could never do it by himself. It was because of his Mental Problems he was sure.

'Perhaps the Great One will see my Fire tonight,' the boy said hopefully and out loud. 'I will make it rise up very High so if he is far away he can look at the tall Flames and know that I am here and waiting for him.'

He spoke out loud from time to time to practice his voice. He did not want it to go out on him. Not now. He had things to say to the Great One still though he did not know what the words were yet. He was so looking forward to the Celebration and the Joy perhaps Doubled (to Double Happiness) that would come with it. But he didn't want to think about it. Somehow he felt if he thought about it he would be Taking Without Asking from it. And he knew Taking Without Asking was a Big Thing and not a Nice Thing or a Happy Thing.

Gonzalo never told the Old Man about his Secret. He did not want to make the Old Man lose his Happiness. He did not want him to be Worried for him either as his Father had taught him that Worry for a Child was not Good for a Parent. Though the Old Man was not his Parent or part of his family he was the boy's Best Friend. And he told his Friend something that was true but not the whole truth, as in the entire rendition—that he was going to a town further south on the Spanish coast, Alicante, to find a Second Job. But that was not a completely accurate rendition because he was traveling further on and the boy knew about renditions that were not true from his Father. And now he was not Happy about having not told the Old Man about his Secret and the Celebration and the Happiness and he thought about it a dozen times a day from dawn to dusk.

The Old Man's name was Santoro and he did not know why his Father did not talk to him. It was easy to talk to Santoro. Much easier than it had been to talk to his Father. The fact is, and the boy could not know this, Santoro did not care to speak to his Father either. He did not approve of him. His Father Tuko was from Moorish heritage and from the south of Spain near Marbella. He was known to be impolite and mercenary and money hungry, yes, but it was more corrupt than that. This unscrupulous greedy man did not care well for his children—Aravella or Gonzalo—in the Old Man's opinion. But it was worse than that too. Santoro knew people who owned and worked in the restaurants, those who bought his spices. And they knew Tuko. And those people told the Old Man the true renditions.

At home Tuko had few words for the boy and was short and dismissive with him while he spat frequently with his Sister the Angel. In addition to being a marvelous beauty, Aravella was intelligent, a good student, and a strong young modern woman though she was only Sixteen when she left. It could be stated Aravella did not care much for Tuko and was repulsed by his raw southern Spanish tongue, dominating manner, and his overtly male chauvinistic points of view. She did not appreciate the way he treated Gonzalo or Sama, Tuko's live-in maid, cook, housekeeper and instrument of servitude ('fiancé' as the naïve Sama termed it).

Aravella did not like the people Tuko associated himself with either, especially the men. She avoided him, their Father, as much as possible, and stayed away from the house nestled beside the busy Train Tracks with Trains passing noisily through the night. She preferred spending time with her School Girlfriends and having sleepovers or paying visits to Zosimus the Fisherman's Wife the Seamstress with whom she learned how to make her own stylish Clothes as Aravella was supremely talented in many areas.

The boy thought warmly of his Father though as he did of all Living Beings and he felt Happiness to greet the smiling Guests who would come to the house. They were usually youthful girls of all colors and sizes (though some youthful boys came too who helped prepare meals and acted like girls), some very pretty and slender, some plump and overweight perhaps, and it was always told to the boy and his Sister that the Guests were friends of Sama; and that they were staying with them until they could find Jobs as housekeepers, Nannies, and caretakers of young children for working or occupied parents.

As for the boy who had difficulty having conversations with his Father (though it was the Father who did not freely offer verbal exchanges), he could talk to Santoro about anything. The Tides. The Harvest. His Sister the Angel. And his Mother whom he had never met. And the great Nadal. And all Women because he contended they were different than Men. He even discussed cooking and taught the boy to make his specialty, a Frittata, a special Spanish omelet made with Potatoes and Eggs and tiny crushed Spices from the Farm. Of course it was the Old Man who did the talking as the boy had few words; mostly two in his early years—yes and no—and if he spoke it was with one word only though his thoughts often contained several. (Tuko taught him how to speak this way, to reduce his verbiage to a single word and that became his norm for many years until Padre Miguel taught him to extend his sentences and expand his meager vocabulary). And of course it was Santoro who told the boy about the Great One.

The boy missed the Old Man's Farm. It was sweetly tucked up in the wooded hills overlooking the sea and he had enjoyed working in the fields there. He liked picking the stems and washing the leaves with their varied sharp, bitter, floral, spicy, and sweet smells. Whenever he looked up he could see the Alive Big Blue that was the Mediterranean and how it lived majestically spread before him, like a changing

Painting that was beating and thrashing and living and breathing and was never the same Colors each day. That was what he liked about the Sea though he could not put it into words.

The Old Man had given him the Job, the first of his Three Jobs. He had a feeling about his Jobs that gave him Happiness. A Job was a Big Thing. If he had been able to continue at the School he would have learned that it was orgulla, a certain pride he felt about his Jobs. But he knew they were important in any case and they got you the necessary Pesetas and even New Money—like the Dirhams he got in his Third Job in Morocco—if work was found in some other place and Jobs made him feel good. And he thought nothing of giving the Money he made on the Spice Farm to his Father who patted him on the head each time he did.

The boy's favorite Job of all though was on the Spice Farm probably because he could talk to the Old Man. He couldn't remember the names of the Spices he picked other than Tarragon, but the meals Santoro made for him with the crushed leaves were always delicious. The Farm grew Basil, Parsley, Oregano, Dill, Garlic, and numerous types of Peppers. The Old Man even harvested Curry as a result of his days living in India as a young Adventurer. When Santoro prepared a meal he made the best food the boy had ever eaten, even better than Sama's cuisine. And customers came from all around to buy his Spices. Even proprietors who served foreign foods in restaurants as far away as Barcelona (36 kilometers south) were patrons.

Now the boy was missing his Father since it all happened, but not as much as his Sister. He had been told about flying Fairies with big white Wings called Angels who were Good and Generous and Thoughtful and sang beautiful songs before a Sleep and looked out over you in the night and when you were confused or unsure. He didn't comprehend a lot about Angels, the whys or hows of course, but he was certain they existed and his Sister was one of them.

Gonzalo could not remember who spoke to him about Angels. He had trouble remembering things. Little Things. And Big Things too. But remembering the actual person who had told him something he considered a Little Thing. He knew that if he didn't have Mental Problems he could probably remember all Big Things and Little Things and those who classified them. He was grateful to his Father for always reminding him about his Mental Problems because he did not want to Hurt or cause Pain or disturb his Sister or his Father or the Old Man or Father Miguel or the School Boys or anyone else with them.

The boy heard the sudden calls then and the violent flapping of wings that took him out of his dreamy reflections. He angled up and saw hundreds of black-bellied Sand grouses silhouetted against the purple sky though he did not know the species of bird. He did not know the names of any birds but marveled at their capacities to fly and soar. He'd often seen the *gaviotas*, the white and gray birds with the orange beaks perched on the jetties at the Port in Cadaques and as they followed the boat from Alicante to Tarifa, but he could not remember their proper name. Others knew them as seagulls.

Gonzalo stoked the fire with the blunt stick that he had forgotten to sharpen like the Man in the Olive Uniform with Stripes had advised him to do on his First Sleep the previous day. The boy watched the glowing orange sparks shoot up and dance in the air and become nothing. He rose to his feet then and felt the prickling sensation in his legs from having been seated so long in a pretzel position and he liked it. He walked unsteadily on an explosion of tingles attacking his knees beneath a row of lofty Kadaya trees and to the clearing with which he had become familiar. Though it was a dark Jungle the Ravine was glowing from the bright Moon and he could see all the Birds, hundreds of them, now feeding at the Water Hole. They were swarming the clearing, having obviously synchronized their arrival with the location calls the boy was hearing and converged from many distant points as was their habit.

The nearby deserts and semi-arid locales had experienced a long dry season and the Ravine had been an essential water source for all the Animals, including the fiercest of creatures. The Sand grouses usually avoided Water Holes with tree canopies and dense cover to avoid ambushes from predators, preferring the safety of open areas; but the arid climate had made water sources few in number and difficult to find.

The boy bent low to a squat so as not to frighten the birds. He watched them scour the earth for Seeds with their pigeon-like heads and sturdy compact bodies. Some sand grouses were mudders while others explored looser dry earth with their beaks flicking the soil sideways to separate. The thirsty ones were sucking water and raising beaks to let the water flow down into their crops.

'Paciencia,' he whispered to himself once more.

The Man in the Uniform with Stripes had inquired about the Leopard the Sleep before and the boy had never thought about Leopards. He hadn't known they shared the Jungle with the Great One, but he did not even make that connection. The boy did not wonder why the Man asked about the Leopard and not the Great One, either. Nor did he intuit the Leopard was the reason the Man in the Olive Uniform with Stripes advised him to sharpen his stick with the knife. If there was a Leopard, he thought simply, he was looking forward to seeing it.

'Maybe the Leopardo will come tonight,' he said hopefully and out loud.

The boy was thirsty himself and needed to take a drink but he did not want to disturb the Sand grouses that seemed Happy. So he waited his turn respectfully for quite a while.

I am getting good at waiting, he thought. *It is easier to wait in the Jungle than it was in the Port towns of Spain or busy El Hoceima where I had other Jobs. It is much quieter too.*

It was only when he had an itch did he move his forearm so sharply that it caught the eye of one bird and the bird shot up like a rocket making all the others fly up as well and the Ravine reverberated with the thwapping sound of hundreds of Birds in flight.

'I am sorry, mi Hermanitos,' or Little Brothers as he called them. 'I know you have come here to get Energy and become Strong for your next Journey. I did not mean to scare you.'

He was sorry and he did not know the term forgiveness, *perdón*, nor to ask for it but it represented a sentiment with which he was familiar and he felt it then.

As the birds had flown up and away, he converged on the Water Hole and squatted on the muddy bank, careful not to kneel and get wet. He did not want the Dung to wash off. He bent low and cupped his hands and took mouthfuls until he was satisfied. Then he wiped his hands on his drawstring pants and rubbed more Dung on his palms and fingers.

'I must sharpen my stick,' he told himself again speaking out loud.

Gonzalo came to a stand and sauntered off from the Ravine and returned back to the Fire that now needed more Wood. He quickly gathered another pile of the driest kindling branches he could find and held them over the Fire to dry them. His Sister the Angel had taught him this procedure one evening they had gone to the beach in Llavaneres when they needed Fire Wood but the driftwood pickings were damp with sea spray and evening dew. It was a Big Thing related to keeping a proper Fire alive.

2

His Sister Aravella whom the boy thought might be an Angel, had just turned Sixteen years old when he last saw her. She was not like any other girls he had ever met or known in School or seen. She had an elegant symmetry to her face, a refined nose, and thick and long raven hair though he could not express it that way. Her skin was olive and tanned the year round and so smooth he loved to rub his cheek against it. She sunbathed without a top on the secret hillside clearing and bathed and changed often in front of Gonzalo and performed her spreads of sweet-smelling lotions without worry. And she behaved like this not to be exhibitionist or perverse, but because the two were so close and she did not consider him a normal brother or even a normal boy, meaning someone to fear.

The boy marveled at Aravella's uncommon beauty in his own particular way as well; her smooth, curvaceous body, different from his own (as she explained to him in her Biology lessons) though he was not at all lustful nor could he see her as an object of desire, those feelings never registering on him nor did he understand them. Gonzalo saw his Sister more as a beautiful moving and lifelike version of the Statues Without Clothes he'd seen frozen in marble in the fountains of Cadaques and the gardens of the Fincas. He thought he even asked his Sister one time if the Statue makers had known her before they made their works of sculpture, the way she sometimes painted from Photographs. He remembered her saying at some point, 'Do I look a hundred years old?' but he was not sure that had to do with his thought about the statues but the two ideas were floating in his mind and he thought they belonged together. He did not understand the humor intended by her comment, regardless, or the reason for it.

The boy's only way to describe her was 'Ava'. That came about after his Sister left Llavaneres for good and the boy was on his Second Job with the affluent Carrion family on the yacht called Summerwind. The boy was a deck hand and servant whose duties included everything from washing dishes to serving food to cleaning the bathrooms on the 75-foot luxury yacht. He met the Carrions when they docked the big Boat briefly at the Port at Llavaneres and the boy was looking for a ride south. The Old Man had advised the boy to take only Boats for transportation because there were too many thieves from South America and other economically depressed nations combing the trains for vulnerable passengers traveling alone. The boy of course didn't really entertain the concept of a Thief or stealing though Santoro claimed it was a Big Thing. He could not wrap his mind around it, but he knew the word when it was spoken. He knew to give unconditionally to someone if asked.

The Carrions were refined, pleasant, and trusting of newcomers and they offered the boy a ride, but instead of going south they were headed north to Cadaques. The boy with the consent and recommendation of the Greek Fisherman Zosimus thought to go anyway. He remembered what Fisherman Zosimus had said to Sr. Carrion.

'He is a good boy. And loyal. He does not talk well. And he is a little off. But he is harmless and effective at simple work. He has a great passion for each task no matter how menial.'

Fisherman Zosimus then advised the boy to take the ride with the family because it would be easier to find a boat going south from Cadaques which was a comely and active Port town, touristy and international too as it was situated close to the French border. Zosimus was not entirely certain of his proclamation and the fisherman felt bad for the boy and to have advised him of something that was not a sure thing. But the Harbor Master and the Capitán of the Port had both informed Zosimus they did not want to be responsible for the handicapped youth loitering around the docks. It was okay when the Old Man was alive but now that he had passed the boy was only perceived as a liability or getting in the way or even a potential 'threat' (though this was not the case), making some boat owners 'nervous.'

Zosimus had never cared for the persnickety and elitist boat proprietors and considered their condescending attitudes to be wholly insensitive. The boy had lost his Sister, along with his Father who had disappeared, and his best friend the Old Man and he was living alone in the abandoned house by the train tracks with feral cats as he had been for months, ever since Sama had returned to her family in La Ronda. Zosimus promised Santoro (before he died of the 'Stomach Devil' which is how the Old Man described his illness to the boy) that he would look after Gonzalo and make sure he was safe and for this reason the man felt sad in his heart for the boy; he also felt waves of guilt to Santoro as he could no longer ensure the boy's security and safety as he had promised his old friend on his death bed.

The considerate netter had experienced a conundrum over his promise however as his ninety-year old parents who lived with him were getting more fragile, senile, and demanding and he could not have the boy reside with them in that atmosphere. For these reasons he counseled Gonzalo to take the ride. He was sure to give the boy extra Pesetas before he left and he had his Wife the Seamstress sew a special Pocket into his draw string pants to hide the Money and his Passport. Zosimus was confident, however, at least in the short term, that the boy would eat well and be better cared for with the Carrions than he had been living with potentially diseased cats in the deserted house, the place he had found shelter once Santoro died—and that was comforting to the man who made his living by the sea.

The final message Zosimus imparted to Gonzalo was philosophical in nature and he realized the boy would not understand. But the man whose family hailed from the island of Crete thought he must try to offer some wisdom as had Aravella and the Old Man. And perhaps one day Gonzalo might remember.

'In life there are no lucky or unlucky events,' Zosimus proffered. 'There is only Kairos and that is the right moment. Every event in one's life has meaning and proposes a challenge we must meet. Your journey now is a result of everything that has happened to you, which was not lucky or unlucky, and you are right to go. You make your own luck, Gonzalo. This is your opportunity. This is your moment. This is the right moment. This is Kairos, my son. And you must embrace it.'

Gonzalo's voyage to Cadaques turned out to be pleasant and positive (which indicated the boy who had seized his opportunity to make his own luck had gotten off to a good start). He was awarded his Second Job for which he was paid normally as in fairly. Sr. Carrion and his wife Maria José were educated and cosmopolitan Spanish folk and they treated the boy protectively and well. They had a shy, striking daughter

Signorita Sofía who was nineteen and well-mannered and she had abundant wavy hair the color of yellow and honey and there was so much of it she could get paid handsomely to display it for shampoo advertisements in magazines if she cared to or needed the money. Sofía wasn't a great student or traditional thinker and her full perfect breasts, accentuated posterior, and tall slender body seemingly made for contrast in mental and physical gifts, but she was thoughtful, dreamy, sweet and most agreeable in disposition. The fact is she had more aptitude than was perceived, but that understated quality was also part of her unique charm.

Sofía had a boyfriend, an Italian from Milan named Massimo, who was an incorrigible narcissist with a wandering eye and spent most of his time on his mobile phone making plans that did not include the reserved Sofía. The couple had bonded over his offer to introduce her to the people of influence in Italy's fashion industry. He brought her to Milan with Sr. Carrion's consent (though against Maria José's wishes) and their physical relationship soon commenced which was his priority. Massimo (known to his close friends affectionately as 'Lupo', the Wolf) did not treat her well and was playing at sentiments; nor was he polite or respectful to Gonzalo, teasing him often and without mercy. And yet when Massimo slapped him hard across the face the boy felt it was because he had hurt Massimo with his Mental Problems though this was not the case. Massimo slapped him three times in all. He often called Gonzalo 'retardado' too though the boy did not recognize the word from his Municipal School Special Class days when several classmates called him that. It was a sin to use the word around the boy and children like him and most civil folks responded appropriately to that sensitivity.

'Stop it, Massimo,' Sofía would say.

'Ma! He's dumb. He doesn't know what I am saying.'

'Of course he does.'

'Che dici, he's a pet. Like a dog. Here Gonzi. Fetch me the swine bone.'

'Yes,' the boy would say and he would sift through the dinner's trash to find Massimo a Bone, a word he knew well. One time when the boy was bringing Sofía the Pink White Wine that was her favorite (and easier for the boy to remember than the French rosé) he found the couple listening to loud music in her cabin and when he opened the door she was kneeling on the floor and had Massimo's Waste Pipe One in her mouth. That was the third time that Massimo slapped him and the wine bottle broke on the floor and sent shards of glass everywhere. But the boy never assimilated this indecent sighting as a Big Thing, it was a Little Thing, and he forgot about it forever. He did remember the three Slaps though as he processed violence waged upon him always as a result of something he had done wrong because he was not right in his mind. In that case his mistake was mishandling the Bottle and allowing it to fall and explode into many pieces and that was his fault even though it was a result of the cruel violent assault waged against him. The boy could not compute causal relationships, even though his Sister the Angel in her Goodness and generosity of spirit had constantly reminded him things were not his fault, never his fault, and that he should never blame himself for anything. But the boy could never comprehend this.

Massimo the drageur (a colloquial French Mediterranean coining for seasoned playboys likening them to fishermen with big nets), however, traveled with the family for only one trip to Ibiza and then he disappeared suddenly. Sr. Carrion did not like him though Gonzalo was unaware of this. The boy never saw the tears on the face of Sofía either after Massimo left though she did cry morning and night and once briefly in public, but her back had been turned to him. The fact is the Drageur was her first and only love and Sofía was not nearly his, nor would she be his last that week alone once he hit the beach fiestas and nightclubs of Ibiza.

The boy remained comfortably employed with the Carrions after the initial trip to Cadaques and for many voyages; to the Balearic Islands including Mallorca, Menora, Ibiza, Formentera, and nearby Sitia on the mainland; and then of course, the inspiring home and playground of Dalí, Miró, Picasso and the great architect Gaudí—Barcelona. Eventually Gonzalo was rewarded for his Paciencia and hard work with his southern passage—the very reason he initially joined the family—as the Summerwind traveled down the coast to Valencia, Alicante, Marbella, Puerto Banus, and the unforgettable (for the boy) high Dunes of Tarifa.

Before the boat ventured south, however, on one of several pleasure trips the Carrions made to Barcelona, the family brought him to a legendary restaurant, the favorite of bullfighters and movie stars, called 7 Puertas, the Seven Doors, the name advertised on the boy's final box of Matches. Along the walls of the eatery hung inscribed and signed photographs of famous people who had dined there—Welles, Hemingway, King Juan Carlos, Elizabeth Taylor, Cary Grant, Ava Gardner, futbol's the Great Messi, and Spain's finest Matadors including Joselito, Arruza, Pérez, and of course the greatest torero of all, the amigo of the famed Hemingway, Juan Belmonte.

The boy did not eat with the family of course but a plate of roasted lamb and sautéed spinach with pine nuts was served to him outside where he dutifully guarded their small white-haired Dog named Muci. When Muci began to bark uncontrollably the boy looked inside to see if the boisterous canine communication had reached Sr. Carrion (as the boy did consider the utterings of Animals to be speech) And yet, while looking through the restaurant window he glimpsed a stunning photograph in black and white affixed to the plaster and the boy was surprised as much as he could feel the sensation. He was sure the handsomely framed image was that of his Sister the Angel (though he had never seen her wear such lipstick except for once—the night of her Sixteenth Birthday). Later when he was in Sofía's cabin delivering a bottle of chilled White Wine he asked her if he could pay with Pesetas to take the photograph of his sister Aravella with him because he had none. That was when she told him who the woman captured in the photo really was, Ava.

'The names are very similar, though,' Sofía said with a smile and patted the boy on the head like his Father was known to after he handed him his earnings and she kissed him on the cheek too, twice, and he did not know why. That was the same night when the 'Bad Things' happened, as she referred to them later he recalled.

Gonzalo's sudden random delivery of that uncommon night with memories he could never forget was short-lived, however. He spotted a pair of glowing eyes bouncing up and down in the distance then gliding closer to a prowl past his line of sight, bright silvery yellow lamps alit floating past in the murky beyond and, then again, nothing.

It was then the boy was reminded what the Man in the Olive Uniform had said—that he should sharpen his stick. He could use it for protection in case the Leopard or any other creature attacked him. He would not want to get hurt or injured and ruin his chances for his meeting with El Gran. With that he drew from his specially sewn Pocket the small gutting Knife Zosimus the Fisherman had given him at the Port in Cadaques before the boy took off on the big boat. He began to quickly shave bark from the end of the blunt stick, the one he had used for balance on his journey to the Ravine on the uneven terrain and for alerting Snakes of his passing. He wasn't as strong as others his size, but he was fast and had unsighted determination. (No one was ever sure how old the boy was as no record of his birth had ever been found; it was safe to say he was beyond puberty and younger than eighteen.) He would toil at a task until it was completely finished perfectly to his abilities. The challenge at present was the Knife was no longer sharp that made carving difficult. Fortunately Zosimus had taught him to use a Rock to help sharpen the Blade so the boy scanned the earth until he found a flattened stone. He then scraped the blade against the flat stone for a while then resumed carving. After an hour of labor he developed bubbles on his fingers like it happened when he had attempted to row the skiff from the beach with his Sister.

When the Stick was nearly completed he decided then to scale his chosen Dhok, the one he had marked its bark, the one that he had borrowed overnight for his First Sleep already. High up the tree a convergence was formed, the union of four thick limbs ascending further and it made for a bowl configuration that was not uncomfortable for someone of medium height to lie upon. Though the convergence was not flat the rising limbs were strong and sturdy and with proper positioning of his body the boy felt secure enough to fall asleep without worry of falling.

Once Gonzalo was situated aloft from the clearing he resumed shaving and shaping his Stick into a fine sharp point just as the experienced Man in the Olive Uniform with Stripes had advised him to do in his broken Spanish one Sleep before (the day he arrived); the one who held the Clipboard and asked him if he had seen the Leopard. He recalled the conversation now, a memory suggested coincidentally or perhaps conjured by the Stick.

'Ladka!' the boy had heard called out suddenly. He did not understand what had been said and he looked to the base of the Dhok where the voice had come from and there was a Man standing there wearing an Olive Uniform with Stripes and holding up his Satchel.

(The Satchel had been the giveaway to the boy's whereabouts though the boy did not think of this. He was mixed up in his mind and he did not follow cause and effect. His basic understandings were fractured and wavering and in the area of logic his brain had the capacities of a small child.) 'Kya kare ho tum?' the Man asked in Hindi.

The man kept speaking and the boy did not understand. He noticed the man had a mustache too. His Uniform was Olive he recognized because his Sister the Angel had taught him all the Colors. He could not write them but he could identify them. The boy saw the Man was holding a Clipboard too and he had a Walkie-Talkie attached to his hip. There was a Gun in the man's holster too.

'Laraká bólaté haim!'

Though the Man was asking Gonzalo to speak up the boy could not know this.

'Ápa báta kara sakaté haim? Apa kahám sé á'é haim? Pákistána? Bángládésa? Angréjí? Francais?' the man kept on. 'Hello? Bon jour? Ola—?'

'Ola,' the boy picked up.

'Aah, Spénísa,' the Man realized. The boy could not recognize it but he was in luck as the man spoke some broken Spanish. 'Habla Español?'

'Sí.'

'You come down. Now,' he continued in fragmented Spanish. 'We speak.'

The boy immediately scaled down the tree and stood opposite the Man in the Olive Uniform With Stripes.

'What you do in jungla?'

'The boy took some time to respond which was his way. 'Zephyrles.'

'You see Zephyrles?'

'Sí.'

'No, no,' the Man countered. 'Zephyrles muerto. Long time.'

The news of the death of the Great One was not Joy to the boy; it was as different from Happiness as his undeveloped emotional cortex could register.

The Man could not decipher the boy's expression, whether he was encouraged or showing disappointment.

'Son of son. Son of son Zephyrles live here,' he qualified.

It was as the Old Man had said, the boy thought; that Zephyrles was probably dead but his family may still be here—the grandson of Zephyrles the Man was attempting to communicate.

'You see leopardo?'

The boy shook.

The Man pointed demonstratively at his watch. '6 o'clock closed. Cerrado. You go. Comprendes?'

The boy nodded but he was confused.

'Be careful. Atención!'

Just then the Man with saw the boy's walking Stick propped against the Dhok. He walked over and raised it.

'U have knife?'

The boy nodded.

'Jungla Khataranáka. Peligroso. Comprendes?'

The boy had another near blank expression like he often did whether he understood or not.

'Make stick—' And the Man pointed to the tip of the Stick. 'Cut.' Then he touched the end as if it was sharp and mimed 'Owww!' The boy recognized the Man was telling him to make a sharp point at the end of the Stick because the Jungle was dangerous.

The Man then smiled slightly and continued on his way. As he neared the edge of the clearing he spun back around.

'Síx o'clock! Vamos!'

The boy nodded again but he didn't understand completely. The Man in the Olive Uniform with Stripes wanted him to go somewhere—but he did not tell him where.

The boy was Happy The Man in the Olive Uniform with Stripes did not make him leave the Jungle. He could not know why he had changed his mind because, as the Man said, the area was closed at Six o'clock. The boy did not know why the Man wore the Uniform either or how he even spoke broken Spanish which enabled him to communicate in the first place. That had been a stroke of good fortune for the boy. But there was more to it.

The Man with whom the boy had conversed held a responsible position as a jungle operative working for Project Tiger, the state-sanctioned organization concerned with Bengal conservation. The Bengal population worldwide had been decimated and the situation was even more dire in India. At this juncture, each and every Bengal sighting in the jungle was important, so much so sightings were documented in a logbook. More crucial were the sightings of tiger cubs, an even more rare occurrence. A cub sighting would indicate a growing population and that conservation efforts were succeeding. But the boy could not know any of this.

As it was, there had been other Bengal sightings in the twenty-four territories of Sariska. But the Great One, grandson to Zephyrles, who presided over the Pánichéda, the Water Hole territory, had not been seen in years. Villagers in Alwar feared it was gone, that it had been stolen or killed for its valuable parts on the black market. The Project, however, would not confirm this or any disappearance of the prized Bengal.

Spain

3

As Gonzalo carved away at the tip of the Stick his mind spiraled back spontaneously and without reason to memories of his Sister the Angel on Llavaneres Beach and the Story she told him after they dried out the dampened driftwood and fed the pieces to the beach Fire Pit. He could not forget either how he had cut his fingers on the barnacles attached to the Wood releasing much of his hand's Red Waters, his term for blood.

He remembered the evening unlike any he had experienced with Aravella. While gazing upon the calm glassy evening sea they sat pleasantly in silence together for a long while and then spoke of Little Things. But there was one Big Thing his Sister said that was more memorable than most Big Things.

'You know Tuko is not our father.'

'Yes.'

'No. He is not. Not our real father.'

Aravella knew Gonzalo could not rectify properly the Concept of biological paternity in its entirety and he responded 'yes' to almost everything back then, but the tirelessly hopeful one thought she should try to teach him— as she did with all challenging Concepts—in case any part of his brain at any moment in time in the future would suddenly come alive, wake up, change, or be cured enough to make sense of her teachings, any teachings. Of course, she was informed by professionals that a turnabout of the sort would likely never happen. But that did not deter her. She would give him every opportunity possible to understand the world and better himself and be prepared so that he could survive on his own if possible and live the best life he possibly could.

'He adopted us.'

'Yes.'

'For money.'

'Yes.'

'Like a Job.' She hesitated and watched a firefly dance before them and fly away though the magical sighting didn't divert her into a consuming fantasy much less elevate her downcast meditation.

'Everything he does is for money.'

Her mouth separated to launch into the unnerving issue further but she decided to hold back. She initiated another conversational path.

'I don't like the people he brings around, his friends. Or those au pairs he invites for dinners. And sleepovers. Or the men he does business with. I speak of Don Pepe especially.'

The boy knew of Don Pepe, the one with the sparkling eyes. In reality they were the opportunist eyes of a predatory animal with the half shaved dark beard riding up his face. Oddly the eyes were the brightest swimming pool blue and could be considered quite attractive, but they were wild eyes and there were those who described them as 'demonic' as they exuded knowledge if not a mastery of the dark arts. He possessed a forewarning grin of consumption and conquest and the sheer joys of both were reflected in it that stirringly complemented the unforgettable eyes, the beacons to his unsettling expressions. There was much in the way of societal whispers of the infamous man and his character and unofficial reports concerned wild bacchanals, a passion for immature, underage girls, and a penchant for libertine and deviant desires. But Gonzalo could not know of the finer points to the man's profile as he could not be privy to or comprehend them.

For Aravella, however, interaction with this man of ill repute was altogether a different matter. Though a virgin and physically an innocent, she was savvy and wise beyond her years in her attitudes as well as her judgments of folk. She had laser-like perceptions, intuitions, even interior visions to deep character and she found Don Pepe to be on the darker side of evil. She remembered Tuko first introducing him to her and though the man was wearing large dark eye shields she could feel his eyes carving into her in a wholly invasive and devouring way. She was twelve at the time.

Beyond that she could never forget the time perhaps a year later when she spotted Don Pepe in town while returning from her friend's house and he seemed to follow her. She ducked inside a lavanderia only to watch him pass in trotting pursuit. Her heart pounded through her rib cage. It was her good fortune she knew the secret side alley from town the Old Man had showed both her and her Brother that allowed for safe and uninterrupted passage back to the path to their casa by the railroad tracks.

Aravella's decided aversion to Don Pepe included another phenomenon she never confessed to anyone. She had nightmares from time to time about this dreaded individual. She horrifically saw his arresting glowing eyes and despicably depraved grin in her sleep, a smile that reminded her of the Cheshire Cat. More than once she had awoken with a jump, covered in a cold sweat, with her heart leaping like a bullfrog after confronting the haunting and unwanted nocturnal visitations her mind conjured. She considered the visions an appropriate warning.

Seated on the beach there that night Aravella had grown upset though her cherished brother was unaware. She possessed a roiling intestinal tempest and it was disturbing her immensely to hold in the domestic bile. She waged delivering it to Gonzalo to free herself of the upset that had built up over time inside her; it boiled within her like toxic lava and she needed to release it. And she knew to be careful too, but she recognized also she would not face repercussions by telling the boy. He was safe like home base for a game of tag. Aravella wiped her eye then and hesitated and then decided to pause on the subject for good.

It was then the exceptional Aravella decided it was finally time to attempt to explain to the boy biology and the act of sexual intercourse; so that maybe some day he would process it properly and understand. She suspected everything in his head was jumbled, mixed up, and not classified, and held in one giant pile of information received in a spiral and it spun around his cranium like a pinwheel. So that anything could be delivered to him from memory at any time like a raffle ticket announcement while whatever the ticket said would merely represent the same undifferentiated life to him. Except for Big Things. And she explained this to him.

'Your beautiful mind, my brother, is like a Box that stores things; every day what you see or do or hear or say or learn—is stored in the Box. Studying can put things in the Box. Memory will take things out. Sometimes you can't find things in the Box—that's forgetting. Rather, that's trying to remember. Because you know it's there. Somewhere. So you have to think hard and search for the things you can't find. But it's all in there, all in the Box—everything you did as a baby, a little boy, and now as a young teen.'

The fact is Aravella did not speak down to the boy, ever. She preserved and maintained a level of intelligent interaction with him. Each day she would supply him with new Words. She felt he was worthy of it; that he deserved it. Her approach was similar to a grieving daughter who speaks to her dying mother lying prostrate with hours to live, yet believing in her unconsciousness, that she can still hear the spoken words and process them. Aravella hoped somewhere deep inside his cortex Gonzalo was receiving her consistent inputs. She prayed for it to the Man in the Brown Beard, her name for Jesus Christ with the boy. That was how she perceived Gonzalo's challenged mental faculties and how they functioned and how she attempted to counteract the disability.

As a credit to her Aravella was not far wrong. She was exceedingly bright this way. She had a way of understanding things without being taught or told; like the knowledge was within her always and she just needed to ask of it and the answers came to her. She was a finely tuned instinctual creature who also had the dedication and presence of mind to study subject matter that could be learned from outside sources like books she borrowed and the computer she used at the Library. (Tuko would never buy a computer for her or the household or even himself).

But the boy did not comprehend his Sister the Angel's presentation of Biology and Animal Reproduction at present other than she was speaking of several Body parts he knew by name and could identify; Eyes, Ears, Arms, Hands, Face, Fingers, Waste Pipe One for which on that night she added the name Male Organ, and Blood which he referred to as Red Waters. She concluded the impromptu lesson by saying 'this is how life happens ...'

Aravella reached over and clasped her brother's hand. She had the softest hands, even softer than her arms and legs. And they smelled exquisite, her hands. She had long slender, elegant fingers like those in Sienese Renaissance portraiture and nails always freshly painted with the most vivid colors, often the primary colors utilized by Miró, her favorite artist.

'But I am your sister,' she added to let him know their bond was special regardless of any lack of direct biological connection.

'Sister … Angel,' he said in a rare two-word offering.

'Yes. And I will always love you. And take care of you. No matter what happens. And you know what?'

'Yes.'

'You're my Angel too.'

She hugged the boy then and the evening continued to be very pleasant for him. There was Happiness on the Beach with her.

'We were meant to find each other on this Earth. And be together. Forever.'

'Yes.'

She thought to herself then, as she had many times, about how she would have long since departed Llavaneres from the household she considered in her heart of hearts corrupt, perhaps even wicked—if it were not for the boy.

'I love you, Gonzalo.'

'Birthday,' the boy said then.

'Yes!' she shrilled in instantaneous rapture and excitement as she always did when he spoke up, initiated conversation, or exhibited a form of undeniable comprehension. Those were the favorite moments of her young life, when her brother responded absolutely. It kept her hopes alive. She also felt gratified as she worked extremely hard to better the boy and enhance his learning and cognitive capacities. It made her feel she was in fact making a difference or at least some progress even if in the smallest increments.

'It is coming! My sixteenth! We will have a celebration and music and dancing and picante prawn paella!'

'Paella.'

'Yes! And I will buy a new Dress.'

'Yes.'

'What Color? Help me choose—'

'Cloud …'

'Yes, a White one! Or Red like Fire! Or Turquoise for the Sea! With frills and lace. I am so excited! Aren't you?'

'Sleeps?'

'Let me see—' she said and paused to calculate. '19 Sleeps, okay?'

And then his Sister the Angel laughed fully suddenly (which gave the boy much Happiness to witness) and thoughts of her coming Birthday removed her from usual selfless meditations and brought to mind her own private excitements. She began to spontaneously recount the Names of the Boys she had had crushes on since Kindergarten and how she met each and every one of them. There were six. And then she told Gonzalo her Secret; that she had Kissed Pablo Ruiz—on the Lips! And she broke up so uproariously with pure Joy emanating from her, but less because she thought she had gotten away with a taboo and more that it was so lovely to have experienced a taste of what she instinctually felt was the greatest offering available to living beings on earth: love.

'I did it more than once too! Because it was Good the first time!'

He was smiling and then laughing and he didn't know why but he felt such Happiness.

'And one day I hope you will experience love too my brother!' she said. 'Maybe I'm not so much an Angel,' she said as an afterthought falling to her side in the sand still howling.

'But don't tell anyone. Especially not Tuko. Or Padre Miguel. Okay?'

'Yes.'

'Say 'nobody.' '

He repeated it. And then he knew it was a Big Thing. Aravella had initiated the practice of Big Things and Little Things several years before, in an attempt to organize his mind.

'All the Big Things you learn add up to Knowledge,' she explained to him knowing he did not and would not likely ever understand. 'And with Knowledge you can achieve what we were put on this Planet for—to offer Love on our path to a higher understanding of the Universe which is Enlightenment—'

Aravella wrote down Big Things for him in his Journal and capitalized the words even though he could not read. She worked exhaustively in this vein and she was brilliant at it, honing her methods instinctually as she had no formal training. She was computer savvy and spent hours doing research on the human brain, getting medical advancement reports and modern psychology approaches to the boy's condition. She combed the latest children's disability and medical paper Web site sources globally in order to be on the cutting edge of the subject. From time to time she would visit with Dr. Alvarez in Barcelona, a top neurosurgeon to learn as much as she could and even did a research paper on the healing powers of the brain in school.

When Aravella was gone the Old Man continued her teaching practices for the boy's benefit (as he was well apprised of Aravella's techniques and though he did not have formal academic training his education had come from traveling the world; he was clever, sage, and streetwise and approved overwhelmingly of her methods). Her most successful mechanism was the introduction of the 'Big Thing' (in addition to 'Sleeps' which allowed him to differentiate between days). As it was, whenever his Sister the Angel made him repeat something the boy recognized it was a Big Thing. He would never forget what she had told him that night about the kiss. And he would never tell anyone.

But Aravella had not told her Brother the Biggest Thing yet. As she looked up at the blanket of shining stars she began to tell him the Story finally, her personally cherished story, so that he could absorb it and store it, in the hopes that his unconscious mind might gain the capacity to decipher it one day so that when the pinwheel delivered it forward into a random reflection he could consciously make sense of it, perhaps, or at least in part.

'I want you to listen carefully, Gonzalo. I am going to tell you a fable—it's an old story. I want you to repeat it. Not now. But someday. I want you to listen now and don't worry about repeating. Not today. Okay?'

'Yes.'

'It's a Good Thought, ok? And Good Thoughts help the what?'

'World.'

'And what else helps the World?'

'… Faith …'

'And what else?'

'… Love …'

'Yes, amor,' she said pridefully. 'In ancient China, there was an Emperor who needed a good worker—like you Brother—to help him at the Royal Court. So the Emperor held a Contest for young students and the winner of the Contest would receive the Job as Minister. The contest had two parts. First there was a written Examination to be followed by an Interview with the Emperor himself. One young student full of hopes and dreams of winning the Contest but lived far away was on his Journey to the City to take the Examination, but he got sick while passing through a mountain village. An herbal doctor and his pretty daughter came upon the sick young man and took him in and cared for him. When the young student recovered finally he found it hard to say good-bye to the doctor's daughter, and so did she. They had fallen in love. As a departing gift the girl wrote a Line of Poetry for the student to Match with a Line of his own words some day to form a Couplet if he would ever return. She wrote:

Green trees against the sky in the spring rain while the sky set off the spring trees in the darkness.

The boy watched his Sister the Angel as she spoke. It made him feel good to be there next to her even though he didn't know what she was saying. The way she sounded though and the way her face lit up in her delivery under the sharp moonlight, he could tell it was a Big Thing. He remembered too she was saying a Good Thought. And he knew what Good Thoughts did.

The young man who felt the same love for the girl promised he would return to her and match her Line of poetry.

The student was very talented, enough to score first place in the Examination and the Emperor congratulated him. For the second part of the Contest the Emperor interviewed the top scorers and tested them in a final exercise by having them match in writing a Line of poetry he had composed. He asked the students to form a Couplet by finishing his very own single verse that read:

Red flowers dot the land in the breeze's chase while the land colored up in red after the kiss.

After reading the Emperor's verse the young man had an idea. He had put to memory the mountain girl's verse as he could never forget it. He thought it could be a perfect fit to the Emperor's. So to complete the exercise he delivered it. When the Emperor heard the student's choice of verse he was delighted and the young student won the contest and was awarded the position of Minister at the Court. Before the student started his new Job he traveled back to the mountain village to see the girl as he had promised. There he offered back to her as promised a verse to match hers, giving her the Line the Emperor had written. Like His Royal Highness she was thrilled with the Match and she knew the student must be her true love. So they married. And for their wedding, the couple combined the two verses of matching poetry that had united them together to form their own Couplet and showed it to all their guests. Then they doubled a drawing of the Chinese character Happy on Red paper and displayed it to show the Happiness for the two events, the winning of the Contest and the Marriage.

'And this, Gonzalo,' Aravella said, 'is Double Happiness.'

As his Sister the Angel was a talented artist she drew the Chinese Double Happiness sign in the sand under the stars above the shoreline.

'It's a reminder,' she conveyed, 'of a couple who share a Connection, a Bond of the Mind, and a Bond of the Body too, and they come together like lines of poetry, as one. That is Double Happiness. I hope to find Double Happiness one day in this life,' she said almost sadly. 'I hope you do too.'

Back at home later, Aravella was sure to remind the boy of the Biology and Reproduction lessons while incorporating the Bonds of Mind and Body terms from the Double Happiness tale. She invoked the already familiar Concept of the Man on the Cross with the Brown Beard in explaining the Mind while adding the word Spiritual. She then wrote down, of course, all the new Words in Gonzalo's Journal.

The boy knew from then on Double Happiness was the only Big Thing for his Sister the Angel which made it an even Bigger Thing—the Biggest Thing he would ever know.

After concluding the Story for Gonzalo on the beach, however, it was at that moment that Aravella removed all her clothes suddenly. She helped Gonzalo do the same as he stood by patiently. She then took him by the hand and led him to the water's edge. That was the night he swam Without Clothes for the first time. He had never experienced unclothed swimming before and it gave him Happiness to do it. The sensation was strange and marvelous; he felt tingles on his submerged bottom half, his joints and sensitive anatomy liberated from constraints of the everyday two articles, short sleeve shirt and drawstring pants. He had swum often in the Sea but usually to wash his clothes once a week as his Father commanded, even in wintertime. But he never took off his clothes; he swam with them on and dried them while wearing them the rest of the day.

(Years before it was customary for Gonzalo to wear undergarments but when he would leave the Special Class classroom for children with disabilities, the School Boys consistently followed him into the Schoolyard and grabbed him by his Underwear and hoisted him high in the air pressuring his crotch until the Underwear ripped from the weight. The boy who saw no evil in anyone or any living thing would smile when they performed their cruelties as he witnessed all the boys and girls laughing and his positive reaction to their Happiness naturally followed. It was Aravella who decided it was better her Brother avoid wearing the undergarments because the Boys were ignorant and would never change their ways. She did slap Mario and Basilio hard across their faces in succession one time, but it did not curb their aggressive, sometimes violent, and mocking behavior toward Gonzalo; they performed the same stunts when they ran into him in town or at the beach.

Eventually Aravella had to take her Brother out of the Special Class for safety reasons and she home-schooled him instead upon returning from her day of classes. This was another supreme sacrifice for her. Due to her special dedication to her brother, Aravella was then unable to participate in school activities or be part of the school sports teams. She was a natural and gifted athlete and excelled in nearly every discipline she undertook: swimming, horseback riding, tennis, futbol, jazz dancing, and ballet. She even was a clever chess player. With her slender and sinewy perfect body and physical talents whether involving hand-eye coordination or balance she was akin to a thoroughbred racehorse. It must be stated that she did not consider her dedication to her Brother to be any 'sacrifice' either, which was a testament to her selfless, loving, giving, and exceptional character.)

In any case, after that evening on the Beach by the Fire with the tale of Double Happiness, whenever the boy contemplated his Sister the Angel in his spiraling merry-go-round mind, he envisioned a portrait of her from that night—alit by the silvery moon and surrounded by stars and the reflection of the glorious lights from the purple sky upon the Sea; from his pixilated and disjointed memory she was forever presented naturally and free of clothes, laughing and splashing the water at him, slapping it and giggling. The boy never saw her smile more and she never seemed more filled with Happiness than that night—19 Sleeps before her Sixteenth Birthday.

4

When his days in the Special Class came to an end the boy stayed in his small room the size of a wash closet in the House by the Railroad Tracks and waited for his Sister to return from school. From time to time he conjured the images of Pino the sclerotic boy and Ana-Luisa the deaf-mute girl because he did have the capacity to miss people and long for them and wonder where they were. But they shot to mind only when his grab-bag mental faculties would allow for it without any consistency or reason. He would sit in the chair by the window for hours and hear Train after Train pass and blow their Whistles.

Sama would prepare meals for the boy but it was no mystery she was not enthusiastic about his presence in the house. (Tuko commanded her to use scraps and lesser foods for the boy like one would choose for a dog, but when the selfish man was not around she would feed him like everyone else.) She was of Andalusian and Moorish heritage and as was often the custom in such lineage she entertained thoughts of superstition, witchcraft, and a general inclination toward paranoia. She felt that having a boy who was not right in his mind in proximity might affect her in her own hopes of having children free of any birth defects, retardation, or disabilities. After all she had high hopes of marrying Tuko, as he'd promised, and having his children. To this effect her mother often telephoned from La Ronda insisting that she keep the boy outside and at a distance. In the end, the boy's presence spooked her.

At the same time, Tuko wanted to have as little to do with the boy as possible and would not consider taking him along with him. The opposing points of view came to a clash once and the two had a great row. Gonzalo overheard their raised voices from the backyard chair he was sitting on that had been moved from his tiny room.

'I never understand you,' she piped angrily.

'Qué understand?'

'You have a choice and you choose the retardado!' she yelled.

'Adopting a child is not simple,' he droned not wanting to further the discussion.

'The shiny fruit in the basket! Not the rotten limón!'

' … mucho paperwork …'

'Like Aravella!'

'That was different.'

'Imbécil!'

Tuko charged the woman then and hit her repeatedly with his shoe. 'Mind your tongue, puta!' calling her a whore. She crumpled to the kitchen floor sobbing.

'Sí, it's different—for me! I know … That boy is three times the work! …'

That was when Tuko made his mistake.

'Because estúpida—you get more Pesetas for the handicapped one!'

There was silence for a while until Sama tossed out a few curse words in Arabic that involved a prostitute, a donkey, and a human posterior.

'It is a sin to talk that way,' he said.

'Money, money, money!' she fumed. 'It's always about money with you!'

'Who do you think pays your salary? Eh? That boy in the back yard—that lemon! that retard!—he gives you your wages, three times what you got in your slum life in Ronda!'

Sama let it go. She could end up further away from her domestic planning if she pursued the discussion.

The fact is, not only did Tuko adopt the children for money, he paid off the office clerk at the adoption agency to destroy the birth documents of Gonzalo, so that he could keep him under 14 years of age on the annual application. Foster parents for children of that age were entitled to more government money. For this reason the age of the boy was undetermined and strategically so.

Sama was fully aware Tuko was a mercenary; that he received money from the government for his adoptions as well as commissions in his other businesses. Yet it had never been presented to her so dramatically and emotionally. The fact is, Sama's parents had been pressuring her about her future with this sketchy man. At the same time Tuko never wanted to discuss marriage after the initial promises years before and the combination was amplifying her stress and upset in addition to eating away at her like a worm in her heart.

After the quarrel Sama threatened to return to her family over the issue, tossed her washrag in the kitchen sink, and said nothing more.

This placed Tuko in a quandary. Though he knew he would never marry Sama he needed someone to run the household and cook for him. Sama was also polite, positive, and a buffering feminine presence when the youthful girls in search of employment would come to the house. She helped them relax and be at ease with their new surroundings and Sama would make them feel at home and comfortable.

Though she was no great beauty and rather heavy-set, Sama was also at Tuko's disposal in the late hours to provide pleasure (that required no physical exertion from him) and other submissions for him whenever he wished.

In the end, Tuko relented. He decided to take the boy with him in his passenger van while he made his daily rounds around town. Always the savvy opportunist, Tuko found immediate use for the boy: he would remain in the van whenever Tuko parked illegally in town or Barcelona so that the vehicle was not ticketed or towed. The corrupt man also strategically introduced Gonzalo to new Guests—women or girls—or when in mixed company to enhance his profile and exaggerate seeming humanistic contributions; it made for a positive impression as folk would think better of the man, that he must be thoughtful, sensitive, and perhaps compassionate to care for a handicapped child as it appeared he was.

Gonzalo of course felt Happiness while driving around with Tuko as he preferred company more than sitting in the Chair or being alone. And no matter what Aravella had said to the contrary, an assertion the boy could not fathom, Tuko was his Father and he knew that was a Big Thing.

Of all the trips Tuko and the boy made spanning a year or so, it was the initial day they drove the boy's memory would serve up most, the first day the two went to the Port. Tuko had a medium-sized passenger van and Gonzalo sat up front with him, the driver chain-smoking as he drove.

The van passed through the Port Balis security gate and circled the roundabout and pulled into the parking lot of the marina. Tuko wedged the van into the only available space opposite a fire hydrant. He got out and strolled into one of the local Port cantinas and ordered a cortado. As he waited he sniffed his fingers as he often did for grotesque pleasures. After downing the cup, he walked down the docks aligned on either side by large boats in their slips. The boy remained in the unlawfully parked van of course to forestall any ticketing or tow truck removal of the vehicle.

The boy watched his Father as he boarded a Boat and met the boat's skipper and they shook hands enthusiastically. Tuko withdrew from his Wallet a wad of Pesetas and handed it to the man who placed it immediately in his Shirt. Then the skipper disappeared inside the boat's cabin. From within three youthful Girls with Chocolate Brown Skin emerged beneath the veranda and the skipper introduced them to Tuko.

After some brief conversation they all bid farewell to the boat's skipper and Tuko guided the girls down the dock and to the van and the three got in the back. Tuko introduced Gonzalo to them and to extend the conversation he told the boy that two of the young ladies were from Senegal, the one with lighter skin from Morocco where his friend Aziz lived.

The group drove to Barcelona in silence for a half hour with little traffic. Eventually, the van entered the City and passed the Pier turning north up La Rambla and then left into the ghetto section of the City where the impoverished internationals—Africans, Indians, Argentinians and Columbians lived. The van pulled up before a dilapidated apartment building and Tuko slotted it by the curb.

A wiry African-looking man with teeth capped in copper and a white tank top came out of the building to meet Tuko on the street. The man handed Tuko a thick white envelope. Then he kissed all three girls on the cheek and they followed the wiry man inside. Tuko ambled up to a fruit cart and bought a banana. He returned the van and handed the boy the banana stump and peel and told him he could finish it. Then he turned over the engine and the van motored onward.

On the outskirts of Barcelona the van pulled up on the opposite side of the street from a high school playground. It was lunchtime now and several youthful students, girls, approached the van and spoke to Tuko. They knew each other already. The young teens piled inside the vehicle as Tuko lit up a marijuana cigarette and let them smoke it though Gonzalo did not know what they were smoking, just that He had watched Tuko do it before and it always made him cough.

'Who's your friend?' Alejandra posed politely, clearly the one who knew Tuko best and the most assured of the three.

'This is Gonzalo,' he said. 'My adopted son.'

The girls all greeted him and he smiled.

'Yes,' the boy said.

They could tell the way Tuko looked at them that something was off with the boy.

'Gonzalo just graduated from the Special Class at The Llavaneres Municipal School,' he added to confirm their suspicions.

With that they understood and poured forth effusively with exuberant salutations, the way folks often treat a 'different' child. When the marijuana cigarette was finished the pretty blonde Blanca indicated she had to get to class and the black-haired Zara concurred. Tuko hung weighted and hungry eyeballs on Alejandra—with intent.

'I'll be a minute,' Alejandra said to her friends and the two took off saying good-bye to the boy. The girls got out of the van and returned to school, laughing and giggling as they went.

'I hear *estabas la bomba.*'

The young teen paused somewhat bashfully. 'I was very drunk.'

'I'm jealous.'

'You are not.'

He laughed, an insincerity exposed. 'He wants to see you again.'

She hesitated then. 'I had fun.'

'He pays well, no?'

'Él es un psycho …'

'And the pay?'

She paused again a moment then smiled sheepishly. *'Sí …'*

Alejandra's smile curved onward slyly but was nevertheless receptive, an invitation extended. Tuko reached forth to her in the back seat and unzipped her cut-off jean shorts. She leaned back accommodatingly and looked briefly but unconcerned at the boy who was now looking straight ahead at the street life with occasional glances at them. Tuko slipped his hand inside her powder blue cotton panties and down, his fingers slipping beneath her. His tallest one explored her, finding the break and the moistness and he sent it deeply within her and her eyes rolled in reverse slightly back in her head. He slipped his other hand inside her T-shirt beneath her bra. Her head cocked back and she let him swim around within her and caress her nipple at the same time for a while.

As if snapping out of a spell she then she drew his hand from her pants and collected herself.

'I must go,' she said, straightening her clothing. She finger combed her mussed up hair.

'Again?'

She sighed to reflect and perhaps posture a response too. 'I know it's not right.'

'Again? '

'Maybe,' she said. 'Text me.'

'Your friends?'

'Blanca can't know. She's a virgin.'

'So …' Tuko's grin was demonic.

'No,' the high school girl said emphatically. 'My friend Zara. She may be interested,' she added and hesitated again. 'If she's with me …'

His smile broke wide. 'Good news.'

She shoved him playfully. 'I knew you would like that.'

'There'll be a bonus for you. *Bueno?*'

'How do you know?'

'There always is—'

She smiled again and pecked him on the lips. Then she pulled away as he winked collusively. She grabbed her book bag, patted the boy on the shoulder, and exited the van.

'Text me …' she repeated.

As a result of the extended meeting with Alejandra in addition to suffering the thwarting effects of the THC in the cannabis he smoked, Tuko was late by eight minutes for the train at Barcelona Sants train station in the Old City. He parked illegally by the entrance to the station. As the boy looked on, Tuko withdrew two black and white photocopied sheets of two different girls who seemed blondish though it was difficult to tell from the poor quality of the images.

Tuko gave the images a last look then dashed out of the van. He hurried to the tracks and searched the ramps and emptied platforms. Off to the side beside a coffee stand he saw two blonde teenage girls sitting on their duffle bags as if waiting. He raised a hand as if to wave and they responded with spare smiles and rose up. When they did come to a stand Tuko could see they both possessed ample breasts and the figures of hourglasses. His smile widened and his own brand of primitive charm that always lay dormant and ready to spring into action given proper inspiration or erotic impetus.

Tuko met them guiding them out of the station and to the van where he placed their bags in back and they got in. The girls spoke English but not Spanish and Tuko spoke with them cheerily in broken English. He first introduced them to Gonzalo and that would become a habit for father and son with new passengers though the boy never processed this ritual.

'This is Ludmilla and Svetlana,' he said to the boy in Spanish. 'They are from Moldova.'

Then Tuko switched to his fractured English and introduced Gonzalo to them as his son and lightly tapped his brow for them to indicate the boy was not quite right in the head. Tuko fired up the engine and they motored off.

They got back on the highway and it required a good half hour to get back to St. Andreu de Llavaneres. Along the way the girls asked him if he had found jobs for them and he explained as best he could with abundant enthusiasm but minimal word choice or linguistic artillery that there was nothing available yet for a housekeeper or nanny; but he had a wealthy friend, 'rico' as he put it, who lived in a grand villa, or Finca, and though the friend had no children to care for he may have miscellaneous or odd jobs for them. Tuko wanted to introduce them to his friend immediately but extended the offer for the following day too though in all seriousness it was a hollow accommodation compromised by strategy. The Moldovan girls looked to each other and nodded with approval.

'Well—?' he posed.

'We go now,' Ludmilla said in her unintentionally harsh delivery and brusque English.

Tuko made a phone call to his friend who was offering the possible employment to announce their imminent arrival and in Spanish it sounded as if the guests were already expected. He drove the van high up the hillside and turned onto the prestigious Carrer Eucaliptus, the winding road that serpentined across the exclusive hilltop community. This constituted the wealthy section of the resort town where the Barcelona elite had their impressive *fincas* and estates with superb views of the Mediterranean. He pulled up before what seemed an enormous estate bound by high white stucco walls and with the number 33 inlaid in a run of bright turquoise Spanish tiles. Gonzalo's eyes were drawn to the numbers like magnets as number configurations with the curves held an immediate attraction for him.

Beside the wide retractable gate was a guard shack and the plump guard was seated inside. When he identified Tuko he waved and the motorized gate slowly slid open for his vehicle.

The van turned up the stone driveway and it took some time ascending all the way to the palatial villa. The van spun around the huge fountain and slotted to the side of it. The two Moldovan girls looked to each other and both offered nervous half smiles of approval.

The giant front door opened and the man in flowing white linen emerged. He was not shaven as usual and he was holding aloft a thick and long unlit cigar and his sea blue eyes glowed and shimmered like Caribbean waters infested with rum pirates. He looked the two girls up and down with a consuming glare that could be described as infected by disease and said:

'Fuego, Tuko—'

Tuko nodded dutifully as he introduced the girls to him and hurriedly snapped a light for Don Pepe. The man rotated his cigar in the lighter flame. Tuko then told him the girls only spoke English.

'What are your talents?' he asked in a perfect English-schooled delivery.

When each of them took turns in speaking of their capabilities to a point where Don Pepe's eyes became glossy and glazed with disinterest, the man stepped sideways and back and invited them inside his villa to have an informal interview and discuss things further. They looked to Tuko who nodded consent then inquired about their belongings in the car to which Don Pepe replied:

'Your bags? I asked you to talk. Not to stay,' he said with a smile but hinted omnipotence and the young women became girls and chuckled skittishly.

'Don't worry,' Tuko confided. 'Your bags will be safe.'

'But actually all our documents are in there,' Svetlana said the more cautious of the two.

'You don't need them,' he assured them. 'Not now.'

'Ladies. We are going to talk,' Don Pepe followed. 'I have a big place yes, but I'm not yet certain I have work for you. In which case we won't need your documents to sign anything, like a contract. If we agree on something then we'll get your documents and exchange signed copies. Ok?'

The girls hesitated respectfully at the professional quality of his reply.

'What do you think we're going to do?' the man in flowing white and the disarming grin pursued. 'Steal your passports?'

And the two men laughed a laugh that was not of the civilized world; it was more primitive, intimidating too and yet so confident even alluring and magnetic and it had the overall effect of making the girls feel foolish of their fears. They had a potential opportunity after all, something that did not come easily in their country, a chance for which their girlfriends at home would be desperate.

They paused to smile and followed Don Pepe inside. Tuko stayed back preferring not to go with them, nor did Don Pepe ever give him a second look or even know he was still there.

Once the heavy high door had closed Tuko waited for a minute, giving special attention to the fingers of his right hand, sniffing them with recent memories intact, in particular the long thick one. When he was released from the reverie of his finger's exploits, he got back in the car and turned over the ignition.

'Wait,' the boy said suddenly and it caught Tuko by surprise. It seemed like such a normal and timely reaction—an indicative reaction—and Tuko had never heard this from the boy. In essence, the boy may have understood what was happening to the slightest degree and responded with his Father-taught one-word phrasing.

Tuko looked at Gonzalo briefly and gave this development little consideration. The fact is he was not concerned enough with the boy's affairs to be passionate about any perceived cognitive progress. Nor did he ever repeat the stunning exchange to anyone.

'We're late for dinner,' Tuko said to him and he sped the van back down the stone driveway and out the retracted gate and motored down the winding road broaching the outskirts of town.

A week later in the late afternoon of a breathtaking watercolor sunset Tuko and the boy returned to Don Pepe's finca for the first time since the Moldovan girls Ludmilla and Svetlana had entered the house. The baggage for the girls was still in the back of the van.

Tuko got out of the vehicle and both he and the boy could hear the electronic dance music blasting inside. He phoned from outside and moments later Don Pepe's man servant Juno opened the front door for him. Gonzalo remained in his seat in the vehicle for the next three hours as music thumped away. It was not rare for the boy to wait in the car for long periods of time. Tuko often left him there, at times long past the dinner hour.

On this occasion, however, the unexpected took place. The Old Man (whom the boy saw occasionally in town after school with his Sister the Angel, or at the house of Zosimus the Fisherman) often recounted exciting tales of his Adventures, sometimes by the fountain with Statues resembling the boy's Sister Without Clothes in the village square. The Spice Farmer was often prodded to indulge his young audience with his experiences by the enlivened curiosities of Aravella. The exceptional one had a terrific capacity to dream and an unquenchable desire to travel to distant lands and shores—but never had the opportunity due to her life circumstances. It had nothing to do with her household's economically spared existence (artificially imposed as Tuko did have money but withheld it) as she was capable enough to make her own money and survive on her own; rather it was because of the boy. She could not leave him. She would have left this part of Spain long before if it were not for her beloved Gonzalo.

As it was, Aravella had accumulated travel books and magazines, consistently scanned the Web, and took extensive notes in a Journal for potential exotic and breathtaking future destinations—islands and beaches, mountains and rain forests—all the while envisioning awe-inspiring escapades and adventures of her own. Thereby when the Old Man shared details of his voyages she became entranced, hanging on his every word.

The Old Man spoke of squashing grapes in vineyards of Provence, laboring on a fruit Farm in North Africa, he spoke of the spicy foods of Marrakesh, and hiking up Mt. Kilimanjaro further south on the continent and delivering inoculations to African tribes on the Serengeti where he saw the most beautiful Animals and creatures on the planet; he told of the long boat rides across many Oceans, he traveled to the Canary Islands even and climbed the steaming, active volcanoes. And he spoke of his favorite place in the world—India—its Cities and Jungles, the palaces and the poverty, the disease and the hunger, Hinduism and the caste system, and the pitiable, impoverished but noble Untouchables. And he spoke most of all of the Great One, known to the Jungles of India, the beloved and feared one, the Lord's most sacred creation, the gorgeous Bengal.

The Old Man once described the Bengal as having 'golden-yellow eyes that took its fire from the boiling core of the Earth and the wand of God.' Gonzalo did not comprehend this description nor could he know the words would stick with him in his Kaleidoscope mind, but when the large black house cat with glowing eyes crossed before him on the stone driveway as he waited in the car at the luxurious finca of Don Pepe, he was transfixed by the sighting and drawn to the little animal—a miniature version of the great cat—as if possessed. As the cat prowled silently onward, as if his soul had been seized the boy was called into action and opened the door to the car to follow him.

The cat rounded the side of the house and slipped through a side door to a large garage that housed a row of bright colored sports cars from England, Italy, and Germany. The boy was in pursuit and he walked beside the line up of low, wide, sleek cars. He lost sight of the cat but noticed a crack of light to a door ajar at the far end of the garage. The pounding music was very loud to his ears now.

The boy slipped out the door and was effectively on the side lawn of the finca. He spotted the cat prancing down the side of the house beyond the back patio and down near the pool surrounded by tents and lounge beds. The boy kept his eyes upon the cat as it entertained a quick pee.

The boy then looked up and on one of the many lounge beds he saw a tussle going on belonging to an accumulation of Unclothed Bodies and bare Skin. He did not know what he was looking at but he did recognize the faces of Ludmilla, Svetlana, Don Pepe, and another Dark Skinned African girl he may have seen before. Their fully naked bodies were pretzeled and intertwined and an afternoon of hedonistic 'pleasure' (likely more derived for the men) was in full swing.

Svetlana was poised on all four limbs facing the boy whom she seemed to notice and register, but she was perspiring and feverish and her eyes were swimming in her sweaty head like goldfish in a glass bowl as Don Pepe advanced into her harshly again and again from behind her while clutching a twist of her stringy hair in his fist and pulling her back to him in rhythm to his thrusts. Occasionally she would yelp from the follicles being pulled and torn at her scalp but she was too far relieved of her mind to do anything about primitive maneuvers being waged upon her, borrowed from the Paleolithic era.

The boy could not process the scene before him any more than if it were a pack of animals cheerfully at play in the fields hopping at butterflies and exercising themselves. But if the truth were to be known this was a normal almost mundane occurrence at the house of Don Pepe. He paid Tuko for his capacity to bring women of all ages and nationalities to his *finca* under the guise of getting them work. And with little money, clothes, few if any personal contacts in a foreign country, and no travel documents; and, at the same time being supplied noon and night with large doses of narcotics and alcohol, they would easily succumb to Don Pepe's desires and depravities and usually in a rather short time.

The way the business operated was Tuko received commission money for professional types like the dark-skinned girl, but the procurer was awarded with double the denomination for girls who were conventional civilians and unsuspecting and had never given their bodies away for pay (of course young innocents who had never experienced intercourse were supremely coveted and Don Pepe paid more handsomely for that introduction. Tuko was also known to falsely advertise chosen offerings as such but that ceased for the most part at the finca of Don Pepe when he nearly slashed Tuko's throat once after a deception had been discovered).

Unknowing or virginal types Don Pepe appreciated and desired most as they provided him with the appropriate dosage of lewd and licentious excitement he was seeking. It must be stated there were times when the girls were unwilling to comply with the rules of the house in which cases the situations could turn nasty or violent until the unwilling ones let down their defenses, and, completely. The narcotics, whether euphoric mood enhancers or powerful horse tranquilizers that distorted reality, melted resolves faster. But Don Pepe was more it could be said psychopathic, when it came to the degradation process. He preferred the process of capitulation pure (which enhanced ego satisfactions and added the elements of domination and omnipotence) without the use of drugs that could be considered more of a cheat. And time was always on his side. He actually sought resistant types (or *resistentes* as he referred to them) as his pleasure index soared, likening conquests of the sort to the breaking of wild stallions and becoming their master.

No girl had ever escaped Don Pepe once she entered his villa walls—unless he did not desire her or need her as an hors d'ouevres for his colleagues in business or politics or law enforcement, or his close amigos. When he tired of a 'guest' he would let her go and give her a modest stipend. He did not worry about the law as the Policía Local was invited as well to his celebrations from time to time when off-duty to enjoy themselves with the party favors. He also made sure he had supportive documentation—the estate's videotape surveillance system boasted full spectrum coverage as a precaution to prove any compromising activities were consensual and not forced. The tapings would capture 'guests' willingly engaging in acts of prostitution as well as ingesting illicit narcotics. This evidentiary documentation would of course neutralize any credibility the participants may have in the eyes of the authorities or courts of law if action were action. That, along with Don Pepe's collection of influential lawmaker friends and law enforcement participants nearly ensured his immunity from prosecution.

The boy looked left and saw Tuko on a separate Bed covered by a tent-like apparatus. He was sitting down on the edge of the bed smoking a Cigarette while another Dark-Skinned Girl was knelt before him, her head bobbing up and down from his lap with his Waste Pipe One in her mouth. When Tuko spotted the boy he yelled something unintelligible and the boy took it as a sign to return to the car. And yet the boy didn't know which way to go or how to get out so he spun around awkwardly.

Tuko shouted again and pointed aggressively with gritted teeth to the far hedge indicating a break in it. The boy moved quickly and passed through the separation in the shrubbery and there he saw the great outer fence of the finca. He did not know what to do until he heard Tuko yell at the top of his lungs to make him heard beyond the noise of the music.

'Dig!' he yelled. 'Dig!!!'

The boy then dug deep into the earth for over an hour until his fingers were bleeding, but he was able to squirm a passage beneath the fence and deposit himself on the other side beyond the finca grounds. He then waited on the road a long while until Tuko passed out of the gate hours later in the van. Tuko picked up the boy seated patiently on the street curb, his fingers raw and covered with dried Red Waters. The digging had been very painful.

Tuko's direction for the boy to dig himself out of the compound did not seem on the surface to be a very prudent decision. But Tuko was out of his mind, relieved of his faculties due to the effects of having indulged in terrific quantities of cocaine powders and island rum. His paranoia was spiked just enough to fear the wrath of Don Pepe's need for secrecy, and, of what he might do to the boy if he had been seen watching or suspected of witnessing the orgy. And Tuko, always the mercenary, did not want to lose out on that income stream of government funding and no quantity of substance ingested could let him lose sight of that fact.

As it was, this occurrence if not interruption in Tuko's mind, brought the man's impatience with the boy to a limit. Tuko was a lone wolf as they say and independent and he had grown tired of having the boy in the car with him on a daily basis. Though the boy was nearly a non-person in his eyes who witnessed but did not register, and understood less, it was grating to have him in his proximity daily. He resented having to feed him too. For these reasons, the following day, Tuko drove the boy to the Church, the Iglesia de la Inmaculada Concepcíon to meet the revered local priest Padre Miguel.

Though certain small town gossip had reached Padre Miguel and perhaps he did not approve of him, Tuko intuited the man of the cloth could not turn him away with an impassioned plea. He apologized for his family's lack of contributions to the Church and not attending mass citing his Muslim upbringing as a source of confusion. He begged the Father for his forgiveness as well as that of the Almighty's, of course, and offered a handful of Pesetas. Tuko's request duly articulated was granted. He then asked the priest if his handicapped son could be introduced to God and taught the word of the Lord; and that perhaps the boy could help in the Church as an altar boy, the passing of the collection plate, or anything at all, even dusting the intricately carved ivory reredos, the impressive altarpiece for which the Church was known.

Father Miguel could not turn away a suffering boy with condition nor the passionate appeal of a widely acknowledged albeit alleged sinner—but seemingly a concerned father too, this being proof—so he invited Tuko to drop off Gonzalo whenever he wished. Tuko didn't inform Sama of the arrangement as he didn't want to make it an issue of it. The arrangement was finalized and from then on when Tuko finished with his business meetings and errands (or his brand of pleasure pursuits which would never cease), he would pick up the boy from the Church or Padre Miguel's rectory where the pious man resided.

Thus began the boy's sojourn under the tutelage of Padre Miguel in the house of God. In the first month he instructed the boy to expand upon his simple yes-no, one-word communication patterns and extend sentences by stringing together successive words. That accomplished to a functional degree, he had the boy sit in on catechism classes and Bible study with local kids. The boy found Happiness no longer isolated and enjoyed being around his own age group again. As these were the offspring of Church-minded, God-fearing parents the boy did not experience bullying and ridicule as he had at the Municipal School. The Church kids were sympathetic, even supportive of their new classmate.

Gonzalo learned to speak in phrases at first, and that grew to full sentences then series of sentences. Aravella was elated and proud when she first heard the lengthier sentence structures as would a parent when their child takes a first step. Not a knock against her efforts it seemed the boy's brain had not been ready for linguistic and cognitive advancement when working with him alone in the afternoons. But the daily combination of both Padre Miguel and Aravella teaching the boy words and grammar simultaneously brought terrific results.

5

The life and death scene played itself out before him in the middle of the night as he lay asleep on his back high up in the Dhok tree. He heard the screeching first then the high-pitched squeals of terror. The sounds of hooves pounding the earth followed and Gonzalo could feel the rumble. It would seem a clan of Wild Boar had been making their way to the Ravine, but had been ambushed by a pack of Striped Hyenas.

The melee was eventually reduced to a terrified Young Boar separated despicably by the Hyena tribe and the horrific shrills of the beast could be heard from far away. The cries grew louder in closer proximity to the boy until the chaos reached the Water Hole. The bright light of the full moon cast a silvery blanket over the clearing and the boy now sitting upright could see the desperate struggle unfold.

The famished pack had been chasing the Young Boar across the open plain, across the service roads, and back into the forest and onward to the Ravine. This was the end of the line as the young Boar did not know his way, only to the Water Hole and the violence erupted beneath. The young Boar plunged into the shallow water but the treacherous Hyenas were not stymied. It was the final standoff. They surrounded the little beast and it squealed at the top of its lungs. The Boar was not defenseless; its fangs were developed and the young beast slashed them back and forth while charging each attacker that came close.

The pack took its time. Time was always on its side. They could run and fight forever. And wait until their prey tired.

That was always the fiendish plan. Several Hyenas would attack at once, but cautiously, as any blood wound could likely result in their own demise, at the hands of their own brothers and sisters even. They would get close and nip the doomed creature's rough hide then retreat back as others resumed the onslaught from another flank. Then others followed suit. There were a dozen in all hissing and whining, snarling and moaning their battle cries and taking turns attacking and their teamwork as usual was rewarded. And soon. Red Water streamed from the back of the winded young Boar and the loss of blood served to weaken its strength and steely resolve.

The beast fought off the pack as best it could—until it could no more. And then the hyenas initiated their most diabolical stratagem yet. As the boar stood trembling there, exhausted from the exertion, unable to move another step, the assassins targeted its most vulnerable region; that which was soft. The testicles in a male; the vagina in a female. That was their death-blow technique. Once one bold assassin got hold of the young male's gonads in its powerful jaws the fight was over. The others dug snouts beneath the prey's underbelly and ravaged the soft belly tissue, upending the beast and forcing a collapse. The exposed Boar squealed from the torture, releasing the blood-curdling cries of impending death, of being eaten alive; until it lay in the mud getting ripped into pieces aggressively seized, stolen, and fought over.

The boy watched the bloody feast until the last chunks of stripped carcass disappeared into the brush with two Golden Jackals. All that remained of the fallen creature was the ribcage and as Gonzalo spotted it laying in the bloody mud, he tried to think good thoughts about the Young Boar, hoping and Praying that it had found some Happiness on its life Adventure.

6

The boy was energized by spikes in adrenaline after witnessing the assassins' bloody assault and could not sleep. He wiped the sticky tree sap from his hands and legs. Along with the pungent smell of the tree bark combined with the Wild Boar midnight mauling the boy was suddenly brought back. Back to the dilapidated laborer's Shack, a shabby construction made of old cut pine weathered and worn from the salty sea air in the rolling hills of Mataró high above the Mediterranean. The boy had spent many an afternoon and evening there with the Old Man and the memory, once conjured, held most of the details intact.

It had been a long day in the Spice fields, the boy remembered. His hands smelled like Tarragon the only spice the boy could identify. The Old Man was seated across from him in the dark space slumping diagonally to his side in room's only chair, his engorged septuagenarian legs patterned with a network of raised varicose veins and crossing haphazardly at the thick swollen ankles. The boy sat cross-legged on the floor in the dark corner.

'The harvest looks fine this year.'

'Yes.'

'We did well today. You worked hard.'

The Old Man reached forward and laid down some Pesetas on the table. 'For you. You deserve it. But don't tell anyone you have money.'

'Yes,' the boy said.

The Old Man's eyes dragged around the shack's interior. 'Place needs repairs. The roof is rotten. Termites too.'

The Old Man coughed thunderously then and his failing chest erupted into a series of short volcanic blasts. When his lungs had calmed he leaned over and released what was in his mouth to the spittoon by the chair. His spit contained the Red Waters of his body and the boy identified it as the same fluid he had within himself.

'Yes, that's blood,' the Old Man told him perceptive of the boy's possible thought. 'You know blood when you see it, don't you?'

The boy remained silent and his mouth curved pleasantly across his face. He did not understand really.

'I am old, Gonzalo. The Stomach Devil has its grip on me.'

Santoro groaned then less a release of pain and more of regret, but the boy could not know that. They were surrounded in the dingy cramped interior by rusted tools and shovels and the stench of damp enriched soil and fertilizer, a spare kerosene lamp hanging from the crooked wooden ceiling and burning with a faint hiss. The real inhabitants of the shack, the Spiders, climbed and swung on a secret network of trapezes and danced joyously in the corners unafraid. Nor did they need to fear. The Old Man considered them friends.

Santoro let out another sigh that was peaceful but no less troubled.

'I am not angry. It is not a dignified way to go. Done in by parasites. But what can I do?'

'Yes.'

'But I am ready,' the Old Man said. 'There is whiteness in death it is said.'

They sat in silence for a while and the silence was fat and good.

'The Great One,' the boy said finally.

'Again?' and it made the Old Man react somewhat proudly and the creases and crags of his face found themselves and folded sideways at his eyes and vertically at the bottom of his face forming a flat grin as warm as a founder's hearth.

'Yes.'

'Padre Miguel has taught you things. You know words. You can finish thoughts. And express them. That is good. Does he treat you well?'

'He tells me to look out and see the world.'

'Traveling is the poetry of men short of words. But adventure is the opera ...'

'Yes.'

'Padre Miguel has made you excited to see the world?'

With that the boy tried to explain to the Old Man and it was difficult to decipher what he was saying and the boy continued with his limited specialized vocabulary full of his Journal Words and after several minutes with many long pauses as the boy could not speak in full paragraphs, Santoro stopped smiling all of a sudden and he became very serious.

'I see,' the Old Man said measuredly and let whatever it was be, if in fact it was anything at all.

'Pass the blanket to an Old Man, will you?'

The boy got up and retrieved the blanket hanging on a hook and handed it to his Best Friend.

'Are you hungry?'

The boy did not answer nor did he ever answer that question. The Old Man knew anyway; he was aware the boy was not eating well at the abandoned house. Nor had he ever been fed consistently in the household of Tuko before he disappeared, who was constantly leaving him at the Church in order to not provide for him.

'Ok. I will tell you once more about the Great One. But please dim the light. It's making me sleepy.'

The boy rose up again and twisted down the lamp and the room glowed faintly with an amber hue. The sun was going down outside and it's final colors of dusk added an array of pinks and mauves to the musty brown-orange interior. The special lighting was fading but gave the room an ambience of hope.

'But first we must feast. The black hoof, the pata negra, is hanging above in the corner to the table. Cut it down and bring it here, por favor.'

The boy took the carving knife and sliced the string from which the carved leg of black swine was suspended. It was jamon iberico, Iberian ham, an exquisite Spanish delicacy steeped in tradition and history. More than a meal, it had been stated within the special marbleized meat was the soul of the country.

'I have no jamonera clamp. We must use the vice.'

The boy propped the leg upon the workbench and placed it upright in the rusty vice with the carved flank face up. The long, thin furry leg of ham with its black hoof still intact had a deep golden hue to its fat, the meat dark red and marbled with veins of grissel. Gonzalo knew how to position the leg for carving as Sama had showed him several times. But she did not trust him with a sharp knife and it was the Old Man who taught him how to slice meat.

'You can carve today, Gonzalo. I am tired.'

The Old Man's mind danced off into a dream of Carmen then. He had been missing his wife for thirty-seven years. But he missed her even more now. He was happy he would be seeing her soon. He remembered them as sweethearts and her walking La Rambla on Sundays in her dresses with the bright floral patterns. He coughed deathly then and it snapped him out of his reverie.

'I know you want to hear of the Bengal. But first I must tell you about pigs.'

The Old Man took a small mug from the table beside his chair. He leaned over and moaned from exertion as he drew the plastic tube protruding from the wide jug of homemade orujo, pomace brandy, resting on the dirt floor. The orujo was made from the grape skins, seeds, and stalks fermented in a vat and then distilled in a copper kettle and heated over an open fire. The Old Man distilled his own home brew every summer.

Santoro poured himself a drink and took a short sip and looked over again at his young friend who was now slicing the ham into long thinly sliced strips and laying them on the table.

'As a Spanish boy you must know. Our most noble creature. The black Iberico. The original Catalan swine. Tamed over centuries. Big. With a long snout. Thin legs. And the black hoof is kept for the aging. Not like Serrano. The Iberico is plump. The fat runs through the muscle. It can cure longer. That's the magic. Of the Iberico flavor. Intense. And sweet.'

The Old Man was breathing hard, speaking in shorter bursts. His wind was failing. His talk was chopped.

'Tonight's Ibérico is special. The ham is bellota. In the pastures of the dehesas the oak trees produce acorns. Called bellotas. In fall and winter. Prized pigs chosen from the rest feed on acorns. Herbs and grasses too. A bellota pig eats ten kilo of acorns. A day. Acorn transforms the fat. In the meat. To a marble pattern. When the pig is 200 kilo it is ready. For the 'sacrifice'.'

The boy extended a freshly carved strip to the Old Man who took it, raised it high, and eased it down his throat. The meat was sweet, nutty, and not too salty to the taste.

'Wait,' the Old Man determined. 'It's cold.'

'Yes.'

'The fat must melt. To release the full orchestra of flavors.'

The Old Man sipped from his mug again and thought about world. He knew his time was short and it was evident in his speech. He was summing things up at every opportunity. To show himself what he had learned on his journey. And inform the boy too.

'Minnows,' the Old Man said. 'We are minnows in a fish bowl. We think we are masters. Because we can think. And go to college. And have the power of reason. What is reason if it is unreasonable? What is thinking if we do the unthinkable? What is mankind if man is not kind? I know, I am getting nasty as the sun sets on me ...'

'Yes.'

'I learned things. The best words came from the Great Nietzsche. Who said, *There are no truths. Only interpretations.* Do you know of interpretations, my son?'

The boy shook of course as the Old Man knew he would. 'Interpretations, Gonzalo, are how we see things. How we understand things. With no interference from others. And how they see things ... their interpretations. Interpretation is a Big Thing—you follow?'

'Yes.'

And the Old Man told him to repeat it. And he did. 'And what does it mean my son?'

The boy hesitated a while. The Old Man was patient.

'How we see things.'

'Bravo. As I was saying, we minnows ... interpret everything like we own it. Like we are entitled. That the world is our due. And that guilts can save us. That the Man with the Brown Beard saves us. And why do we need to be saved? Because of our stupidity. And carelessness. We make excuses. For everything. The truth is—we are a cancer. Cancer on this earth. We consume all we see. Worst of all we consume nature. Nature is dying. Before our eyes. And we tell our little lies. To others. And ourselves. While smiling our little smiles. Like it's all okay. Like it's a May morning. Because we interpret our stupidity as we want. To manipulate. And rationalize. All we've destroyed. To make us feel better.

'We are animals, Gonzalo. We pretend we are not. We pretend we have been created in the image of God. But we are the worst animal. Because we lie. The antelope does not lie. The black Iberico does not lie. Nor the eagle. Or the bengal. We lie to them. They don't lie to us. I am sorry. I am of short-temper now. This fine black pig spends his day feeding on bellota—to provide for us. Noble creature of the highest order. We are not noble. Manipulators. Deceivers. Savages, yes. I apologize, best friend. I am old. I am dying. Perhaps bitter. Cynical, I grant you ... But I see better now. We are no better than the Stomach Devil who inhabits my intestines. Consuming all it touches. Eating my last days. We are parasites, Gonzalo. Minnows. I never hoped to be king of the minnows. Is a life of dignity out there? If not how to have death with dignity? Or integrity?'

The boy was listening as he carved the ham in paper-thin slices as the Old Man had taught him. He listened intently to everything Santoro was saying, as he always did, but he did not comprehend, just a few words here and there. He laid the *jamón* strips lengthwise on the table. They had no plates.

'The fat is melting. *Gracias,* little brother,' he addressed the *pata negra.* 'You have brought honor to our earth. And honor to my table.'

The Old Man explained to the boy the meaning of Honor and told him it was a Big Thing. They ate then and had a marvelous feast. They could not know but it would be their last.

'Minnows,' he repeated as it had become his bitter mantra. 'Minnows who tell lies. To all we encounter. But mostly ourselves.'

He poured himself another orujo from the homemade mash and drank. He was tipsy.

'Forgive me, blessed boy. You are better. Born perfectly. Truly blessed by the Man in the Brown Beard. Born without disabilities. Without our handicaps. You are the model we should strive for. A great human being. You are perfect. I toast you, Gonzalo.'

The man tried to raise his mug but was forced to pause from the roiling within his rib cage. He coughed thunderously and it occurred to him then his time on earth would be shorter than anticipated.

'If I had a son I hope he would be like you. Perfect. If there is such a thing. But there is. As you stand here. You are proof. I am honored. Humbled our journeys crossed. A gift. I am grateful God presented this gift to me. Before my passing. You are my best friend. You are my son.'

The boy could not know what the Old Man meant but he heard him and remembered his words. He knew he was the son of Tuko and that did not change. But the Old Man's words would be delivered to him again in his grab-bag mind.

'The Great One,' the boy said and it made the Old Man stop in the middle of another morose meditation. He noted the boy's new capacity for concentration and thereby progress and it made him smile. Aravella may have been right all along, he thought. He raised his mug then.

'¡Salud, to your sister. The angel ...'

'Yes ...'

'It is in Rajasthan—' the Old Man began as he had done many times for the boy. 'Deep in the forest. There is a ravine. A water hole for the animals. When the spring rains and the monsoon season hits. So that all the creatures of the jungle can drink from it. And feed their babies. This is the home of the Great One. He is a Bengal named Zephyrles. He measures 13 feet. He and his brothers are likely the reason God created this earth. His paw is velvet. His coat tawny. His fury has no remorse. Nor should it. His heart beats with the universe. Within his soul is all of recorded time. And the Life Force of a Krakatoa volcano. Do you know what a Life Force is?'

The boy shook.

'The energy. The power. The will. Of any living being. The will to survive. The determination to live. Explore. Learn. Study. And seek answers. To go on adventures. Striving, searching, evolving ... to do our duty. And better this planet. With honor ... if it can be found ...'

He took another sip.

'We are Life Forces. You. Me. Aravella,' the Old Man added and he coughed and took a breath. The very concept was riling him, exciting him in the last excitements of his life.

The detour inspired by the *orujo* pushed the Old Man from his train of thought even though he'd just begun. So he continued with the derailment.

'It's what got me to India ... to see the Great One—my Life Force ... as pathetic as it is ... Most Life Forces are wasted. By the young, especially. When they have the will ... the enthusiasm ... to harness the energy ... the power that lies within ... the curiosity ... and follow it wherever it leads ... the strength of youth ... don't waste a Life Force, Gonzalo ... a crime to the planet ... most wait until its too late ... I am drunk ... where was I? ... You see? I'm not too bright. But that's always been part of my charm ... Oh ... that damned story ... but it is a good one ...'

The Old Man returned to the tale he knew the boy loved.

'... So ... with the power of dumb youth I made it to Sariska,' he began. '... I am ashamed to admit—I was seeking him. A beggar with no eyeballs told me in Jaipur. A bengal has his own territory. The ravine was his. ... *Pánichéda* it is called ... Reserved for him. By him. With the gift of the monsoon, God filled his cup every year—at the water hole. That was the playground of Zephyrles. El Gran.

'It started as a chorus. Of alarm calls. The most chilling voice to an animal ... A note hit beyond fear. It is blind terror. The horned antelope spoke. Caracal spoke. Wild boar squealed. Golden jackal whined. Striped hyena shrilled. The hare hopped in flight. The gray partridges, bush quails, the Great Indian horned owls gave versions. Warning brothers the Great One was near. And with it death ...

'Then came panic. Two score of Rhesus and Langur shot past me, fighting in the chaos ... thrashing monkey fangs, drawing blood. The brand of terror incited. As the Rhesus scaled trees I knew of his presence. My heart leapt forth ... like a salmon. Not knowing what to expect, I dared myself to stay put. Then I heard it. The voice released from the larynx. Part lightning. Part thunder. A crack! In the language of cat. Thrown like a tempest. It did not endure. It was replaced by chuffing ... snorts forced through the nose. And the chuffs getting louder. I spotted him near the water hole, I knew to take cover. I debated succumbing. But I wanted more, the minnow that I am. I had to observe his magnificence. His majesty. His perfection.

'Yes, Gonzalo, he is as perfect as you. The Father of the Man on the Cross with the Brown Beard had His best day when he created the Great One. And Zephyrles was his prize. Must have been. There was no explanation. Is no explanation. Even for God. A happy accident, maybe ... Unintended. Stumbled upon. But deliberate. God was sculpting something—a masterpiece. Bengal is His masterpiece. Living art. Living sculpture. The perfect creation. The Emperor of all living things. The ultimate proof ... that all Animals are not created equally. And my thought—the thought of a petty narcissist, a pathetic minnow—was, at best, I was shamefully honored. And humbled. To be in his presence. The slashing stripes. Fiery orange pelt. Paws the size of automobile tires. And that gaze.

'The Great One stepped over the muddy bank and drank from his cup. Water must have tasted sweet. He deserved water however it pleased him. I gave thought to sacrifice once again. Nothing could ever top that. I was his. If he would want me. If he would look at me. To give him nourishment. An only gift worthy of him. But I was a fool— young and dumb to believe I could live a noble life. Still. The minnow that I am.

'I directed senses to take in what I could. Water seeped into my eyes until flooded. I wiped them so I could see. He raised his crown, all sensory. He was being watched. He spotted me high on the branch. As if I was nothing, which I was, just another helpless pitiful minnow. And he continued to drink. He spun around on a quick hop and disappeared into the brush. I never saw him again, of course. I cried. Like a newborn. And several times later that afternoon.

The Old Man took a final swig of *orujo* and finished the mug.

'But who was I? So arrogant to think he would want me. A minnow like me … The Jungle Ranger inquired if I had made a sighting. I could only shrug. Not discuss it. I would not. I could not betray him. Like a newspaper reporter. That was my gift. My petty gift. To him. For giving me that moment. I wanted him to go—anonymously—from where he came. Wherever. And make passage. With pride. Mystery. And luster intact. With greatness. Not to be gossip of minnows.'

The mug held in the Old Man's hands fell from his grip. The boy got up and retrieved it for him. He then poured him another. He had never done that before. Santoro was well aware of it.

'The world never saw such a Life Force. And may never again. Energy of the bengal snatched me. By the throat. And took my wind. Suffocated me. Rid me of pretension. Pettiness. Resignation—to mediocrity. Changed the chemicals in my gut. Altered my flickering soul. Forever. Forced me to face—the world—as it really was. But within too. Who was I? I trespassed on the jungle a dumb kid … and I came out … well, a drunk … '

The Old Man laughed then, a spontaneous outburst and it made the boy Happy to see it.

'Then I got married!' the Old Mane laughed harder.

'Yes—when I returned to Spain I married my Carmen,' he trailed off with, adding a wry smile for her. 'She has Zephyrles to blame. For that—'

'The Great One,' the boy said.

The boy handed the filled mug to the Old Man. He could only oblige and take a sip. Santoro would take only little sips now. He did not want to lose his balance when he got up. His eyes were flooded, but the boy did not notice.

'If the Stomach Devil did not grip me I would go to him now—that beautiful beast. Likely he's long gone. But he may have a son. Or grandson. Or granddaughter. I would give myself to his family. How I wish. But I could never. Not to El Gran. Give him old meat. Diseased meat. Full of parasites. Full of the Stomach Devil. All my life I wished a noble death. Dying of the Devil is not noble. It is nothing. To die from parasites. A coward's death. It is the death of a minnow.'

Santoro took one last brief sip and he shivered then and the hair stood straight on his arms.

'Finish the *jamon*, boy, *por favor.*'

Gonzalo then ate the last pieces. He chewed slowly even though he was hungry still. He was too focused on the Old Man at that moment.

'My Sister the Angel,' the boy said.

'You will see her again, blessed boy. I promise.'

The boy thought that the Old Man might say it again as he had many times before and he wanted to hear it.

'Grab the winter coat. We sleep here tonight.'

The boy twisted off the lamp. The two lay down on the dirt floor of the shack beside each other. The boy could see the stars through the holes in the roof. Spiders frolicked nearby undeterred; they had a busy evening ahead.

The boy could hear the storm in the Old Man's chest as his breaths were labored. And loud.

'Do not go to Padre Miguel. This is a Big Thing. Do not return to the Church. Ever. Do you understand?'

'Sí.'

'Repeat it, boy.'

He did. And he finished it with, 'It is a *Gran Cosa*.'

The boy remained awake awhile and he could smell the alcohol coming from the Old Man's breath though he did not know what it was. Santoro coughed some more too and then the boy heard him release a mouthful into the spittoon. Eventually the Old Man fell asleep and began to snore loudly and it kept Gonzalo up even longer. The boy watched the stars with a pleasant curve to his face. When he was awoken hours later by shards of dawn sunlight streaming through the holes in the roof, the table had been cleared except for his wages and the Old Man was gone. And the boy never saw him again.

The Old Man died several days later. There was no funeral or burial. His body was cremated, as was his wish. But it was reported the urn was lost and thereby his ashes too were never to be found. For this reason there was no memorial service or ceremony to celebrate the life of an honorable man of considerable Life Force and generosity of spirit who had fastidiously spiced the foods of the community for decades.

As it was, Gonzalo never went to the local Church again. He never set foot in any Church again. Ever.

It was a Big Thing.

(What the boy could not know is the reminiscence he'd just conjured in his compromised mind had been a stunning occurrence. The boy never entertained memories suggested by smells before, a positive development in itself; but it was more than that. The boy could have recalled many arboreal experiences from the scent of tree sap; in this case he was reminded of the fragrance of the damp wood in the Old Man's field shack. Combined with the olfactory deliverance, what really jarred the boy's memory was the death struggle between the Young Wild Boar and the Hyenas. The felled Boar at the Water Hole and the *pata negra* feasted on by him and the Old Man, swines of different habitats at different times—was the more elaborate connection the boy reconciled in his mind. The triggered recollections from two sources reflected an active subconscious. With respect to the boy's condition, it was a showing of considerable progress; in medical terms, a breakthrough.)

7

The boy tried to stay up as long as possible to the hours before first light when the Great One was likely to appear. The Old Man had informed him more than once that the Bengal preferred that hour to drink water and hunt. But the boy was so exhausted from the tragic excitement of the late night massacre that once his adrenaline stopped surging, he had unintentionally dozed off.

The orange and fuchsia beams of sunrise blessed the clearing with their magic and on this morning of the Third Sleep, the boy woke up in a panic as if he'd missed something. He immediately thought he had heard the sound of savage clawing and scratching and had been awoken by it. But he did not know if that really happened or if it occurred hours before; or if it had been placed in his mental Box during sleep like a Dream the way Aravella said it could. In the end he thought the hazy recollection was a result of his Mental Problems.

[What the boy could not know was that he had attempted to analyze this recollection, a brief contemplation as to the derivation of the clawing sounds, and how and why they might have been placed in his mental Box.]

The boy was redirected to the present and he noticed at his mid-section Waste Pipe One was firm and long again and it stuck out uncomfortably like a tree branch. He swatted it several times which was his method to make it go away and eventually it shrunk back to normal. The fact is this bodily reaction had been happening to him for a while now during early morning sleep and he did not understand it and he was sure it was because of his Mental Problems that it was taking place. He had not taken notice nor could he remember that this seemingly strange development had been initiated after the night in Tarifa when he did not return to his maid's quarters on the Summerwind and he stayed with Sofía Carrion on the sand Dunes instead because she had asked him to.

But it was not this biological nuisance or the early morning splash of watercolors that had stirred him from sleep. Rather it had been a faint rhythmic din coming from far off—and by now the din was getting louder. As the noise increased, the sound of rattles being shaken and bells clanging accompanied by a voice chanting could be heard and it seemed the commotion was getting near and approaching. For some reason the noise was irritating the boy, an emotion he was not familiar with, and he did not know why. He clambered down the tree to investigate.

Gonzalo ran through the Jungle in the direction of the bells and rattles and took position by the main path. Crouching beneath a wide stump of a fallen Bengal Fig, he observed a man dressed in a bright orange sequined robe with a horned hat, bells on his fingers, a rattle in each hand, and a small drum suspended from his neck. The man had dark skin like an Indian and he seemed to be chanting a language the boy had never heard. The boy quickly retreated back to the Ravine and climbed his borrowed tree that had become his home now for Two Sleeps.

The Man in the Orange Robe made his way into the clearing and paused in his chant to take in the lush ravine. He resumed his song and shakes as he rounded the muddy bank of the Water Hole and came upon the bare rib cage of the fallen young beast soaking in a pool of fresh blood, its meat stripped from the bone. The man knelt low and swirled a finger in the scarlet pool. He drew a blood-red line down the length of his nose and angled a look to the sky. He began to tap first then pound on the small drum while performing a dance to his drumming. His ritual lasted several minutes. When he was finished he reached his arms high as to touch the heavens and said a poetic prayer in ancient verse to the open sky.

The boy had a concern. He did not want interference or anyone to disturb what he had set out to do. He did not want to be interrupted. He had never entertained such an emotion—worry—but he felt it now. He did not want anyone to scare off the Great One or keep him away and that plagued him. This preponderance was the source of a freshly felt stress, an unfamiliar negative emotional grid never encountered prior; first the irritation, then the worry.

The man seemed gentle even peaceful enough and the boy who didn't see the darkness in other beings climbed back down the Dhok. Yet he remained there at the base of the tree and stood motionless while behind him, a clan of black and snow Rhesus monkeys watched intently but silently from within the line of Khair bush—a straggling shrub devoid of leaves but sprouting red coral blooms—at the edge of the clearing. The green tendu berries and bárwa blossoms of the Khair served as a staple food to impoverished villagers in times of scarcity and famine. (The blossoms were boiled then seasoned with salt and pepper; the mash was spread on course bread as relish.) Several Rhesus picked at the tendu berries and munched them as they watched the spectacle of The Man in the Orange Robe as if eating popcorn at the movies.

On the bank of the Water Hole the man had relaxed to his haunches and was preparing a bowl of dried bright green buds in a small pipe. He then lit it and puffed. The sweet smelling aroma wafted past the boy and he remembered the smell from his days on the Hashish Farm in Morocco though he did not reconcile the memory at the time.

Eventually the man looked over and saw the boy observing him. His head with horned hat wobbled curiously from side to side and he smiled warmly.

'Namaste,' the Man in the Orange Robe greeted him in Hindi.

The boy stayed where he was so the man took another puff. He rose up and called out to him again.

'Mera naam Nani hai.'

The man interpreted the boy's shyness as fear.

'Nani,' he said repeating his name for the boy. And his head wobbled sideways again while offering the same amicable smile. When Gonzalo did not react the man drew again from the pipe. Then he extended it in the boy's direction.

The boy shook his head. 'No. Gracias.'

'You are Spanish?' he said switching languages, his proficiency near perfect. The man spoke slowly, softly, in near whisper and the boy found his voice to be soothing to the ear though he could not express it. Gonzalo had never heard such a voice as he was used to aggressive voice patterns like that of his Father.

'Sí.'

'I took Spanish in school,' he continued. 'My name in Nani. And who are you, my son?'

His head wobbled again as was the Indian way.

'Gonzalo.'

'You are by yourself?'

The boy did not answer him now but he was drawn to the pleasant man and he did not know why. He strode slowly toward him.

'Don't worry. I do not mean you harm. I am a shaman. Do you know what a shaman is?'

'No.'

'I am a guide of souls. There is a religious festival in the village. But I am meant to be here. I felt the energy. A calling. When I found the hunted beast I knew why. The Sky Spirits had summoned me. It is my purpose.'

The boy did not feel fear; he had concern again but this time about the Great One. That it had been two days and he had not even seen a trace of him. It was the second time the emotion had crept into his psyche in his entire life. But now the feeling was more intense.

'This is cannabis. It is medicine. It helps me contact the Sky Spirits. And direct souls of the departed to them. Would you like some?'

The boy shook as the he approached closer. He walked a path not directly toward the shaman, but at an angle to the side albeit bringing him in closer proximity to the man.

Unbeknownst to Gonzalo, the sneakiest Rhesus of the clan had been waiting for him to vacate the Dhok and the monkey immediately vaulted up the tree and sought out the origin of the sugary smell. He came upon the boy's satchel and tore it open and snatched all the spears of dried mangos and quickly darted back down the tall tree. He disappeared into the brush where he was ambushed by his brethren and amid the calamity, pushing, and shoving they devoured every last piece.

It was the boy's last bit of food.

'The rib frame is small. A young boar, yes?' the Man in the Orange Robe asked him.

'Yes.'

'His soul has been released. So that he may live in peace. And communicate with his brothers. And tell them not to grieve. That he lived a good life and it was noble to be hunted in the jungle. That it was his path on earth. And it was an honor to die this death. And let them know it is okay for them to be hunted and killed too. That it will be their greatest achievement. That they will have done their duty and served the planet well.'

The boy hesitated as something was being delivered to him seemingly haphazardly in his Kaleidoscope mind.

'Spiritual,' the boy said conjuring the word Aravella had taught him that night on the beach.

'Yes, my son. Spiritual. A matter for the Sky Spirits. Because always remember this: In life there is death, and in death there if life.'

The boy immediately repeated the saying hoping to put it to memory. He enjoyed the feeling of being taught things again.

'And if that was not the case,' the shaman added with a wry smile, 'I would be out of a job.'

The boy was reminded, for no particular reason, of the conversation he'd had with Zosimus the Fisherman after the Old Man died.

'Listen, Gonzalo. A funeral is the celebration of someone who has died. It is usually held in the Church.'

The boy understood Celebration and he knew he could not attend this Celebration as the Old Man told him never to go to the Church.

'But Santoro will have no Church funeral. He did not want it. So they burned his body as was his wish. And they have given the urn to me. And I will give the urn to you. That was the Old Man's wish. That you put a pinch of his ashes in your Satchel and bring them on your travels away from here. Wherever you go. For his final adventure.'

'It is an Honor. And a Big Thing,' he added.

'Repeat 'Honor'.'

And the boy did.

Zosimus did not bother to tell the boy he had stolen the urn from the Town Administrator's office as it was going to be dumped in the city's communal tomb in Barcelona reserved for remains that went unclaimed by proper family. The prudent and loyal man of the sea knew the only family the Old Man recognized was the boy. He had called him his son on many occasions.

'Zosimus?'

'Sí?'

'Satchel——?'

'The one Santoro took on all his adventures. It's in the shack. His gift to you.'

The boy ran over to the tree and quickly scaled it. He was surprised to see the Satchel hanging precariously from a small limb. It must have fallen there. When he opened the bag he saw the Mangos were missing, but the Knife and the sack of dried Dung were there still. But there was no Urn. It was gone.

'What are you searching for, my son?' the shaman called out to him.

'My best friend.'

'In the bag?'

'No. The Stomach Devil.' And he said more but his phrases wandered and swayed and were unintelligible as he jumbled words including Honor, Urn, Celebration, and Parasites in and out of sentences.

The shaman did not understand entirely and advanced on the tall tree, but noticed the pewter relic lying on the ground nearby.

'Here is your urn,' the shaman said.

The panicked boy looked down and the shaman was holding it aloft. It had fallen to the ground when the Rhesus absconded with the boy's food.

'These are his remains—?''

The boy eyeballed him intently. 'Celebration.'

Then the wise man thought he understood the boy for the first time. 'You wish for a celebration of your friend—'

'Sky Spirits,' he blurted. 'Gracias.'

With that he gave the Urn back to the boy.

'Come, my son. We will free your friend. But first we must gather flowers—'

The boy followed the Man with the Orange Robe as he passed from tree to shrub, picking ravine blooms and placing them in a small sack; the bright fiery orange petals of the Flame of the Forests, the pink Gugal blossoms, the yellow blooms of the Kadaya and Gol, and white flowers from the Khair and Ber. The two made their way back to the Water Hole as pinkish golden beams of the rising sun speared through the tree line. The boy expressed sudden concern again, receptive to the emotion an impossible fourth time including the recent panic.

The shaman released from beneath his robes a canvas bag. From it he withdrew a hanging incense burner, a small pot made of brass suspended from four foot-long chains and adorned with intricate and ornate designs. He knelt to the ground then at the bank of the water hole and placed a small slab of incense in the tray.

The boy was not free from worry still and it came from him in a rush and he blurted, 'Stomach Devil!'

The shaman looked up at him and smiled.

'There is no Stomach Devil here, my son. These are the ashes of your friend—the purest form of his body. And the earthly world needs him. To replenish the soil with his nutrients. The parasites are gone. The Stomach Devil has been destroyed. Forever. It cannot hurt your friend ever again. There is only goodness and honor here in our celebration. Do you understand?'

The boy did not answer. Whether he was concerned that the ashes containing the Stomach Devil would poison the water and thereby harm the descendants of the family of Zephyrles is not known. It is possible the boy had taken in the Old Man's words and processed them in his fractured subconscious and now they had been delivered back to him in some form of theory at long last as to what Santoro had been saying: that he would never offer his old, infested, or contaminated body to the Great One as a sacrifice, that he'd had his opportunity when he was a young adventurer and let it pass. And he'd regretted his choice. But whether that contemplation was the source of the boy's unrest will never be known.

'And as the earth needs what is left of his body, my son, the sky needs his soul.'

The man's head then wobbled again.

The shaman lit the incense and let it burn for a minute. Once the end glowed orange and the pungent wisps rose from it, he stood up and let the smoky trails laden with spice envelop them. He inhaled it through his nose, his eyes coming to a close. Then holding the dangling pot the man walked a path around the entire rim of the water hole allowing the aromatic smoke to spread so that it could hover over the ravine. At the same time he sprinkled the bright petals and blossoms atop the water.

The boy remained by the bank and identified an advanced analytical connection; the aroma of the incense was a fitting tribute for the Old Man who had been a cultivator of spices.

Eventually the mystical man who had appeared out of nowhere finished his procession and returned to him.

The shaman then began to tap the drum, shake his rattles, and clang the bells as he did for the young wild boar. He then quoted a prayer from ancient Sanskrit texts. After the incantation he looked to the heavens and chanted and sang a song composed of raw sounds, onomatopoeia, and the calls of animals. He began tapping the drum again in cadence to the song. Then he performed a dance that concluded in an extended shake of bells and rattles. Then nothing.

'It is time, my son. The Sky Spirits are ready.'

The shaman gestured too indicating the Urn.

'Let him go.'

The boy seemed to understand, giving a cautious look back at the shaman who nodded assuredly. The boy then bent low, raised the Urn, and poured the contents from above the surface of the water. All of it. Both the boy and the shaman watched the ashes being swept through the air, floating beyond, and then landing silently, haphazardly, everywhere atop the water, spreading further out and away with wind blown ripples.

'Your friend has been guided to the heavens. From there he will talk to you. If you will let him. Will you let him?'

The shaman looked over at the boy and noticed a single tear had made its way down his cheek. The boy remained there transfixed on the water and the floating ashes for many minutes. As if on delay the boy responded to the shaman's final question.

'Yes.'

When Gonzalo snapped out of his reverie he looked up. The Man in the Orange Robes was gone.

But the boy did not feel alone or abandoned. He was feeling Happiness. And thought the Old Man would have been pleased with the Celebration. And he was already looking forward to the time when the Old Man would talk to him. He missed their conversations.

'¡Hola! Santoro!,' he called out and waited for a response.

Gonzalo spun around and walked toward the Dhok but something caught his eye. The small brass pot was curiously placed at a distance now on the muddy bank at the other side of the Water Hole. The shaman must have forgotten it, the boy thought.

Gonzalo maneuvered around the rim and past the violent ruts and slashes of upturned soil from the Boar mauling. When he approached the pot he noticed the fragrant wisps still rising up, the coal still aglow. As he squatted low to gather the chains and raise it, his eyes were drawn to something on the ground beside the burner. At first he did not know what he was observing, a wide flattish stamp in the mud in the midst of all the haphazardly strewn soil. When he realized what it could be he was filled with excitement. Amongst all the tracks of Animals that had been stomping the damp earth during their morning treks, there appeared to be a footprint all unto its own and it was enormous—the footprint of a Bengal!

8

The boy was hungry. At the same time he was too enlivened from his hopeful discovery to notice. He'd studied the area around the giant paw print. He had also rounded the Ravine four times but saw no other mold of its kind, but that did not temper his enthusiasm. It had been a Sleep like no other. It was a Footprint and that was a Big Thing! It would seem a giant Bengal, perhaps from the family of Zephyrles, had visited the Ravine and recently. Perhaps after he'd dozed off after the mauling.

It was high noon and the boy waited in the Dhok with paciencia. He'd witnessed many things in the hours since the shaman had disappeared as mysteriously as he'd come. The source of life that was the Water Hole had been the nexus of Animal activity like a spontaneous stage of survival throughout the morning. From the pilgrimage of the large Sambar deer with enormous antlers, joined by the spotted Chitals, to processions of families of Wild Boar, the stalking Golden Jackals, and the jungle assassins, the Striped Hyenas who had provided a harrowing execution the night before. From the air Bush Quail, Golden-Backed Woodpeckers, Gray Partridges, Peafowl, Tree Pies, and Sand grouses, to the Great Indian Owl, even a Serpent-Crested Eagle, all convened to settle their thirsts. And the boy had witnessed each assemblage from his preferred vantage point in the lofty perch.

'Ho! Niño!' was called out just like it had been Two Sleeps before.

Gonzalo peered down from the Dhok and saw the Man in the Olive Uniform With Stripes once again.

'I told you—*vamos!*' the jungle operative shouted in half-Hindi, half-Spanish, clearly perturbed.

The boy said nothing.

'Come down!' Static and inaudible voices blasted from the Walkie-Talkie at his hip.

The boy quickly left the convergence of tree limbs and hoisted himself down from the tree.

'You sleep here?' The Man posed stomping his boot on the ground.

The boy shook his head thinking the Man was indicating sleeping on the ground exactly where he stomped his foot.

'You sleep in tree last night?' the Man qualified still jumbling Hindi and Spanish.

'Sí.'

He gave the boy an annoyed look. *'Nombre?'*

The boy told him.

The Man with the Olive Uniform was about to write his name on his Clipboard but he paused. He studied the boy smeared with Dung from head to toe with bloodied cuts on his hands. He could tell by the boy's expressions, gestures, and the way he spoke that Gonzalo was 'different.' More important, the Man could see he was not a threat. He was obviously poor too. From the Man's growing furtive expression as he contemplated this, it was clear something strategic was on his mind.

'You want Bengal, Gonzal?'

'Sí.'

'Mi nombre es Yamir.'

'Yamir,' the boy repeated his name.

'Sí, bravo. This'—he pointed to the uniform and stripes—
'my trabajo. Guardia Sariska.' Then he swept his arm across
indicating the entire jungle area. 'My section. Todo. Mine.
Comprendes?'

The boy nodded thinking he understood.

He pointed at the Gonzalo putting his index in the middle
of the boy's chest.

'You work for me,' he said in his unique Hindi-Spanish
mix. *Trabajo. Guardia los animales.* All cats, *todos los gatos—
leopardo, bengal, caracal, jungle cat, gato de la jungla*—' He raised
two fingers pointing to his own eyes. 'Me *guardia,* you *guardia.
Bueno?*'

The boy understood and nodded, but let loose a smile he
had never known; one that seemed freshly sensitized,
reflecting a capacity to feel a new high in emotion he had
never felt before. This would make his Fourth Job and the
boy knew a Job was a Big Thing. He was more than Happy;
he was Joyous but to an enhanced degree—it was the best
job he ever had, he could ever think of; to look for the Great
One and tell the Man in the Olive Uniform with Stripes if he
saw it. Gonzalo was radiating.

'Guardia. Explorador. Mi amigo—'

The Man stepped forward and draped an arm around the
boy's shoulders and smiled, to show they were in fact friends
now. The boy gazed up at him, still glowing, and nodded
enthusiastically.

Yamir stepped away quickly and said, 'Our secreto,
bueno?' Then he put an index to his lips while producing a
'Sssshhhh!'

The boy remained silent then and the Joy was neutralized.
The word 'Secret' made him pause and if asked about his
hesitation he could not tell his reasoning. He did not know.

'And *atención amigo!*'

The boy nodded and smiled, his divergent thought wiped away.

'Hasta la vista, Gonzal.' The Man winked at the boy too.

Yamir continued onward past the Water Hole, giving a quick glance at the stripped rib cage and violently disturbed mud from the overnight death struggle—but he soon spun right back around.

'Leopardo?' he posed.

The boy shook.

'Bengal?' And the Man followed it with a strange smile and chuckle as if he was making a joke. But the boy could not know that.

A memory popped suddenly and Gonzalo was about to speak up, to mention what he had already seen—the possible existence of a Bengal footprint. But he recalled what the Old Man said, that he would not speak of his sighting of Zephyrles once he had observed him in the wild—to anyone. The boy stayed silent and watched the jungle operator, Yamir, his new friend, disappear into the brush at the far end of the clearing.

As the boy climbed back up the Dhok he was confused. He wondered, in an uncharacteristic spontaneous reflex analysis—how he could do his new Job if he couldn't speak of the Great One?

Though the boy had rightfully uncovered a conflict, it was a positive sign. The boy's mind appeared to be receptive to more stimulation, but more than that, his brain was showing signs of being able to process incoming data—reflective of an opening up—even if just a crack. This perceptual awareness of course represented another breakthrough for the boy. In addition to the boost to the emotional registry, he was utilizing elevated logic and deductive reasoning for the very first time.

The boy looked out over the Ravine from his hideaway in the tree and pondered his new Job. He entertained another cause for concern—how could he do his new Job and carry out his Plan? Gonzalo was baffled again until he came up with another solution to the second conflict. He could work at his Job for Yamir until he carried out his Plan!

The boy sat there is a state of marvel. He remembered how Worried the Old Man and Zosimus the Fisherman had been when they learned he would be traveling on an Adventure. And his Sister the Angel had always shown her concern for him. Not only had he made it all the way to India with some Money in his pocket, but now he had a Job! How proud of him they would be! It was the Happiest thought the boy had had since the Joy he saw on Aravella's face the night of her Sixteenth Birthday Party.

9

The boy could not know the Sariska jungle operative who had just given him a job as scout—*explorador*—had a considerable reputation and not a good one. On the job he was known to be disinterested and lazy. He skipped work, days at a time, meaning he did not adequately patrol his section of the jungle with the vigilance required of his position. The man was not terribly concerned with the business of Project Tiger either, the protection and conservation of the populations of the Bengal. He was known to be shrewd and opportunistic. He was also a rake. It was reputed he had received the position because he dated the daughter of a well-known politician in the Government of Rajasthan. There was talk as well he had a wife and family in New Delhi—and a mistress in the holy village of Dehmi with whom he spent most evenings as well as the days he did not go to work. (For this reason the boy saw him on his First and Third Sleeps. On the day of his Second Sleep Yamir had not shown up to work.) There were reports of other liaisons too, with a Project Tiger secretary, as well as others too many to count.

It was for this uncommitted posture and inconsistent work ethic that the sketchy jungle operative hired the boy (for no Rupees)—to cover for him in his absence. The boy could be his eyes and ears, to let him know what transpired in his section—the most active area being the ravine—while he attended to more pleasurable personal pursuits. The operative could then fill in the logbook, the paperwork to his position. And it seemed the Spanish boy who spoke no

Hindi and had disabilities was perfect for the appointment and an assignment that needed secrecy.

As for the expansive territory Yamir was responsible for, not only had the mighty thirteen-foot male bengal not been spotted for several years, it hadn't been seen in all of Sariska. Villagers in Alwar, many of whom did not like the man, passed rumors he had either sold the prized cat to a private zoo or for its body parts on the black market; or that the celebrated bengal had been stolen or killed by poachers under his watch because he was a frequent absentee.

As a person the jungle operative was not likeable. He was arrogant with is colleagues at the Project and dismissive with the poor villagers. Off work he wore fancy clothes and watches and often frequented the bars and nightclubs in New Delhi and brought prostitutes to the Lake Palace Hotel in Jaipur. He drove a black Mercedes convertible too. And of course the villagers in Alwar all speculated where the money was coming from. Needless to say the rumored extra-marital affair with the devout woman in the holy village had been the height of scandal.

Beyond the rumor mill, in actuality, the conduct of Yamir the jungle operative was far worse. The reports were mostly true—all of them, as loyalty for such a self-serving, unscrupulous type was hard to come by and people talked. Eventually. But the scandalous behavior only told part of the story. Unbeknownst to anyone, the corrupt jungle operative had secretly sold at least two bengals from Sariska to an underground Chinese black market consortium.

As it happened, Yamir had negotiated the purchase of the grandson of Zephyrles for a handsome sum. The underworld criminals from Beijing searched the territory day and night. But the mighty animal was too elusive and then disappeared from sight altogether never to be spotted in the jungle again. Using a helicopter in the black of night, the Chinese hoodlums seized a female bengal from an adjacent-patrolled section to the jungle instead. Prior to this abduction, however, the same Chinese crew had been responsible for a disaster of terrific magnitude during their first secret raid. While attempting to airlift another Sariska female, a male bengal attacked from the jungle out of nowhere and killed two of the Chinese thugs. The female bengal was shot and killed in the process.

It was a tragedy, the deal also arranged and coordinated by Yamir for a hefty price. To this day the tragedy remained a secret and Yamir's official report to the jungle Warden for all the missing bengals read, 'Whereabouts Unknown.'

For his corrupt practices and dirty dealings, Yamir the jungle operative stashed away hundreds of thousands of dollars as his compensation. And the Chinese had not gone away. The latest requests and thereby targets on the black market consortium's list had been and were—leopards.

Once again for all the wrong reasons, Gonzalo was the right candidate to be Yamir's explorador, but the boy could not know any of this. Nor could anyone. And no one did.

10

That afternoon Gonzalo lay back against the thick rising branch of the limbs' convergence high in the Dhok tree. He was waiting again. *'Paciencia,'* he reminded himself. But this time he had a Job while he waited. Though the jungle operative did not know or even care, the boy was trained for it. He was sensitized to that feeling again, pride, and a bolstering of confidence followed too.

Gonzalo thought of all the hours he waited in the van for Tuko, and how he had sat in the chair in the wash closet room for endless periods waiting for Aravella to return home to teach him; he waited in his maid's quarters on the Summerwind for the Carrions to be in need of his services; he sat patiently in the daily car commute into the Rif Mountains with Aziz; he waited on the long train ride from Barcelona to Paris with the Dutch Girl, then the longer ride alone from Paris to New Delhi, as well as all the other trains and ferries he'd endured. Compared to all that, waiting in the tree was no arduous undertaking. He did not feel the passage of time like a normal boy as it was, and was immune to boredom. Besides, he was waiting for the Great One. It was anything but boring; rather, a rapturous thrill!

The boy felt increasing Happiness with his thoughts for the most part too. There was a clarity that seemed to be coming over him. It would appear, and he could not know this, but, Aravella's hopes that the boy's mind would come to a point of righting itself over time seemed to be well founded and cast. She had studied the brain (the 'cerebral cortex') and learned of its miraculous capabilities; that it had the capacity to produce more neurons, in essence, heal itself (the 'hippocampus') augmented by proper stimulation, programming, and rehabilitation. And with time. That the brain could reroute its nerve traffic to avoid the deadwood patches, non-working paths, and injured zones and find new ways to send and deliver messages. Her research had given rise to optimism about her young brother's condition. How happy she would be if she only knew it appeared to be happening as she hoped and prayed for!

At the same time, the boy was beginning to experience more complicated emotions. In addition to the positive feelings of joy, excited anticipation, and love, he was entertaining increasing spikes of annoyance, fretting, and worry, even panic, all progressions that led to fear.

A thought came to the boy just then, a thought he had just embraced minutes before. He wondered when the Old Man would talk to him like the Man in the Orange Robe said he would (this type of quick recall never happened before; in days previous, the boy's meditations would pass through his spiraling mind like gusts of wind and be gone). But he had a feeling the Old Man must be very busy with the Sky Spirits as his soul had just been released and welcomed to the Sky. The boy initiated a momentous proposal. He decided to make the Sky Spirits a Big Thing. All on his own! With no help from his Sister the Angel or the Old Man or Zosimus the Fisherman. Hallelula! they would all cheer. He had experienced another episode of advanced cognitive thought utilizing deductive reason as the professionals would attest.

It was golden hour now on the day of the boy's Third Sleep. The sunlight had transformed from the bright white of high noon to the color of brilliant gold ore. Gonzalo was hungry still but there was so much to contemplate as thoughts and ideas seemed to be attacking him at once. But the thoughts did not lay idle and pass as before. He had the capacity to do something with them now. And it took much more time. The boy was bombarded and overwhelmed; then the most poignant proposition of all was delivered back to him: what was he going to say to the Great One?

The boy knew he must speak, that it was part of his own Celebration. Worry crept in again. What would he say to this marvelous creature, a grandchild from the family of Zephyrles? So many Big Things came to mind flooding his cerebral circuitry, a network that seemed to have bypassed the blockades of scarred nerve tissues, rerouted and expanded.

It came to mind then the one who had taught him to speak properly, the one who helped him expand his sentences, and try to talk in organized paragraphs—Padre Miguel. And he recalled the Bible study classes identifying his classmates by name and conjuring the teachings of the pious man. He wondered, What would Padre Miguel say? and better yet, How would he phrase it? And he wished the learned priest had been there to guide him with a choice of words.

Then the curtain fell.

The boy began to feel light-headed and woozy. His thoughts became sticky again. And his mind clouded up and closed down. In no time he was reverting back to his former self until he was trapped in the merry-go-round mindscape again, unable to recall, unable to experience heightened emotions positive or negative (perhaps a good thing), and unable to control his thoughts, much less make any inferences, identifications, deductions, or process causal relationships. Cognitive thought, situational and perceptual awareness had been suffocated again. He was back to Gonzalo from the Special Class even though he'd showed incredible resolve, albeit unknowingly, and was 'lucky' to have made it this far—as it could be said he made his own luck perhaps because of his disabilities. He had taken action at the right moment and seized his opportunity (having embraced 'kairos' as Fisherman Zosimus had suggested; that there was no such thing as luck). He had always been fearless because fear never registered on his flawed instrument. A boy of normal intelligence and emotional standing likely would have never made it to or certainly out of Morocco, let alone reach India. That be as it may, the boy was his old self again—for better or worse.

Though the boy's mind had closed shop, a trace of the day's recent meditations during which he'd experienced a raised level of awareness remained. He knew he had to speak to the Great One; Padre Miguel was somehow coupled to that thought, but he could not remember how. And it made him reminisce about a special day when Padre Miguel had taught him a crucial lesson that he would remember forever, designated a Big Thing by the priest. It was perceived as important, so much so that he mentioned it to the Old Man when the question was posed to him during their final black *bellota Iberico* swine feast in the laborer's shack on the Spice Farm.

But the boy was alone in the jungle, waiting, and merely remembered what happened that day at the Church and nothing more and he did not attach to it any further significance. Yet it did pass through his mind like another sudden but aimless breeze of wind.

After Tuko made his plea to Padre Miguel for assistance and his request granted, he began dropping off the boy at the Church daily after lunch; but when he realized how accommodating the man of the cloth was, he started to leave him there even sooner, after breakfast. His own breakfast, that is. The boy had never been fed well even though Sama tried her best. But Tuko was greedy of course, and cheap, even with the grocery bill. He did, however, contribute to the boy's lunches at the Church though he claimed the money was for the collection plate and thereby was indirectly, but directly, awarding himself with another discount, a two-for-one deal as it were.

At this earlier hour Padre Miguel directed the boy's Father to bring him by the rectory, his own private residence located on the Church grounds. There they talked, Padre Miguel even gave him bread and juice. After breakfast the boy would do chores around the cathedral, pulling weeds from the garden, sweeping the aisles, taking out the trash, and dusting the impressive reredos. The boy performed these duties on and off through the day, at the rectory too and Padre Miguel taught him to do many household tasks.

As a teacher the priest was committed to informing Gonzalo about the Lord and the basics of the Christian religion in Bible Study classes. He even discussed more mythical and ethereal subjects like Angels. He described an Angel to the boy as a winged Spirit of Goodness possessing the powers of protection for those who followed the Christian precepts. He covered the anti-Christ too, the Diablo, and the doctrines of Evil which the boy could not comprehend as he saw the good in everyone.

Padre Miguel taught Gonzalo also about the Ten Commandments and tried to explain them in the sparest of terms so that perhaps the boy could, if not understand now, some time in the future. Aravella, who attended the priest's

Church sermons regularly on Sundays, consulted Padre Miguel as he was spending long hours with her Brother and she shared with him her theories on the boy's condition— she was hopeful even confident the boy might 'wake up' one day and if he did, he would perhaps have all this knowledge waiting for him in the storage of his mind, the very knowledge she was imparting to him as well as the teachings of the priest.

It was around this time that, at the prodding of Padre Miguel and at his suggestion, the boy began to see his Sister Aravella as an Angel on earth as it was clear she possessed similar angelic traits. 'My Sister the Angel,' the boy eventually said and Padre Miguel who had the utmost respect for Aravella and her unwavering and fierce dedication to her brother responded, '*Sí*, she is. Bravo, my son.'

As the two, boy and priest, spent many hours together, sharing breakfast and lunches, his teachings were not all religion-based. He taught him about life too, in the same way the Old Man did. And this brings us to the memory the boy conjured while waiting in the Dhok on that late afternoon of the Third Sleep after the Man with the Orange Robe had suddenly appeared, conducted the Celebration for the Old Man, and then vanished just as suddenly and mysteriously.

After the boy had learned to speak in expanded sentences, although his delivery was still disjointed with jumbled words, boy and priest were able to have more lively conversations and detailed discussions. Speaking in the gardens one afternoon, Padre Miguel asked him about his home life at the house by the railroad tracks and his travels with his father in the van. The boy recounted fractured stories of the 'guests' who would visit, the errands his Father ran at the Port, and the trips to Barcelona, to the Train Stations and public Schools. Though the boy's accounts were delivered in what could only be considered scattered narratives, of course Padre Miguel, without leaping to conclusions, picked up on the fact that at the heart of each story there always seemed to be girls, immature girls, girls of all colors involved in the boy's albeit mixed-up renditions. And then came several references to the town's infamous if not feared Don Pepe.

The priest continued to guide and reposition the boy's thoughts, inquiring constantly with repeated questions, until he could ascertain the whole story. He would not let the boy drift off to silence or other meditations due to his spiraling mind as was the boy's habit. He always brought him back to the subject at hand.

After much prodding, the boy attempted to describe to him the day he chased the cat into the backyard of Don Pepe's ostentatious but luxurious villa, and though Gonzalo did not know what he was saying, as he did not understand or recognize what he had been witnessing, he offered the most modest details of what anyone of sound mind would identify as a free-for-all orgy by the pool.

'Without Clothes,' was one of the boy's phrases employed from his inconsistent recall.

Over time, as in a matter of days, Padre Miguel had heard nearly everything there was to know about the activities that afternoon at the *finca* of Don Pepe. And yet, he did not inform Tuko or Aravella about anything the boy had told him. When the story had been disclosed to his satisfaction, as in fully, the priest told him that everything the boy had recounted to him was their 'Secret.' And that a Secret was a Big Thing, having been apprised of Aravella's ingenious and effective shorthand for helping the boy remember important concepts.

'Secret,' the boy repeated as requested.

From then on, the daily activities of the boy and Padre Miguel took a dubious turn. On certain days, the boy performed errands around the Church and the rectory. The boy still attended catechism classes and Bible study. On other days Padre Miguel had a new set of educational plans for him. He sent the boy on 'Field Trips', as he called them, but in actuality they could be better described as missions.

The priest initiated this phase of the boy's schooling by showing the boy a route to walk that bypassed town leading to a path through the woods and up the hillside to the estate section, and all the way to Carrer Eucaliptus and the grand villa of Don Pepe. The boy's assignment was to slip under the hole he had dug in the fence and hide behind the hedge and simply wait and watch what transpired, whatever it may be—and report back to Padre Miguel exactly what he saw. He explained to the boy in simple terms that these exercises, his required verbal accounts, were part of his learning process and that it would help him speak better with extended phrases and sentences as well as expand his vocabulary, the priest assisting him frequently in his word choice. Padre Miguel added, however, that this part of his instruction was also a Secret and he insisted on the fact that the boy must not let anyone know of their Secrets.

As it was, on those mission days the boy was sent up the hill, and a considerable time later once he'd returned to the Church, he would express as best he could exactly what he saw, if anything. The boy complied of course with the new curriculum and never mentioned a word of it to anyone, not even Aravella or the Old Man. His fractured, scattered accounts when properly pieced together depicted stories of complete and utter debauchery and ill repute and the details were often harrowing even disgusting (of course). It wasn't long before the priest had the boy recount these tales more formally in the Church's confession booth as one would a confession—also part of the boy's religious training. The priest listened patiently and questioned the boy methodically, like an attorney would on cross examination, a process which could take days, until he had heard all of the details, sordid and the like, in the boy's available language and level of competency.

Unquestionably the boy began to express himself better with enhanced word choice during this process and Aravella was thrilled with the boy's development and was incredibly grateful. She showed her appreciation by bringing pastries and desserts, baking cakes, and even cooking for her brother and Padre Miguel. In wintertime, she knitted black socks and gloves and a fashionable silken white scarf for the priest as well which matched his clerical attire, the black and white tab collar. And of course she contributed what she could to the Church with any money she made from selling her stylish clothes at the Saturday market in the Town Square.

Unbeknownst to the boy or anyone obviously were Padre Miguel's own private intentions with his schooling methods devised for the boy. During Gonzalo's forced but completely innocent 'confessions,' on the other side of the confession booth the man of the cloth was discreetly and perversely satisfying his latent and suppressed biological urges in the most physical manner. And these confessions were all kept quiet under the cloak of secrecy. As it was, Padre Miguel had enjoyed an immaculate reputation; universally considered a figure of high morals, integrity, faith, and piousness. The priest had been a pillar of strength for the community with an exceptional following.

Parishioners came from many miles away to hear his sermons. If the parishioners only knew! Such were the goings on at the popular Church in Llavaneres, the *Iglesia de la Inmaculada Concepción*, with all of the ironies of life unfortunately in play.

Yet the disturbed and deviant priest made a mistake. And this is where we return to the boy in the Dhok tree as he was trying to somehow figure out what he could say to the Great One, the mighty Bengal two generations removed from the magnificent Zephyrles. And that thought was oddly coupled in his Kaleidoscope mind to that special day at the Church and rectory with Padre Miguel. He remembered that day he did not go on his Field Trip to Don Pepe's villa high on the hill; instead, after he was finished with his chores around the grounds, he was asked to meet the priest in the upstairs drawing room of the rectory.

There Padre Miguel positioned the boy before the window facing east which offered a sweeping view of the azure Mediterranean at left and the Catalan hills—an expanse of forests and lush foliage, a picturesque mix of palm trees, junipers, and ponderosa pines—at the right, with the run of beautiful *fincas* aligned and perched majestically on the hillcrest. There the boy was asked to place his elbows on the windowsill, close his eyes, dream of far away places he'd heard about and imagine himself traveling the globe.

'To go out and see the world,' was the priest's educational message that day, a pastel lesson in philosophy as well, and what became his oft-repeated phrase. As has been stated, it was a lesson the boy would never forget. In fact, Padre Miguel truly wanted the boy to learn that traveling was good for the soul; that it 'nourished' and 'fueled' it. And he underscored his lesson by saying that the entire phrase was a Big Thing.

The boy put to memory the entire phrase of course, but he also fervently took it to heart as he became intent on venturing beyond Llavaneres and actually—seeing the world; and having learned of the Great One as well as being given the Old Man's remains in an Urn, the boy had a purpose and a destination—a Plan—which resulted in him being in the very place where he was at that moment. At the Water Hole waiting with paciencia. And his Plan had all been sparked and inspired by Padre Miguel's teachings that day as he faced out that second story window of the rectory.

The mistake the priest made was having never told the boy that on the days he was summoned to the drawing room, that whatever happened there was to be once again, a 'Secret.' The lesson to be put to memory was about traveling the globe and not anything else and since it had been processed by the boy as a Concept of equal importance, it overrode their previously unbreakable pact of Secrets on which they had colluded for nearly a year.

As the boy sat in the Dhok tree feeling hungry and passing the time, he recalled all those days in that rectory room upstairs dreaming of the far away places. He remembered closing his eyes. He remembered raising his Arms high as Padre Miguel removed his Shirt (as it was customary to do so). He remembered his drawstring Pants being untied. He remembered standing there Without Clothes and feeling the cool Air against his Body. He remembered the priest entering his frame from behind him, pressuring his Waste Pipe Two. He remembered feeling Pain the first Sleeps, but that over time the discomfort became less until it didn't hurt. (And if it did hurt, as his Red Waters would stream down his legs on occasion, Father Miguel would treat him to cookies and chocolates.) And as these activities would take place, the boy remembered dreaming of France and India and Morocco and Italy and England and the Canary Islands and all the places in the world he had heard about and he would visit them all. Those afternoons in the rectory were like travel for him, he remembered.

And finally he remembered telling the Old Man in the rundown shack in the Spice Fields about all this 'traveling' he did; all those afternoons upstairs he'd spent with Padre Miguel at the rectory. It was the last night Gonzalo and the Old Man were together and the boy recollected he had delivered his account to his best friend in vivid detail, not only because the priest had taught him that 'seeing the world' was a Big Thing, but also because he thought the Old Man would feel Happiness for him, that he had listened to all the Old Man's Adventures and that maybe it showed he could be perhaps an Adventurer too—and that would make the Old Man Happy.

As it was, the day after the boy and the Old Man had their final feast of pata negra and homemade orujo, Padre Miguel left Llavaneres for good and was never seen again. Rumors swirled that he had been transferred to another parish, others said that he had become a monk and was living in a monastery in the north, others claimed he had been promoted and went to Rome, still other stories had him retiring from the clergy altogether. The only person who really knew what happened to Padre Miguel was the Old Man. And the Old Man died two days later.

Morocco

11

The boy awoke from a nap and his neurons were firing again, allowing him to come out of what appeared to have been a temporary regression. The incense had long since burned out in the brass pot, but he could still smell the spicy aroma ever since he'd placed both the pot and the empty Urn in his Satchel. He was filled with Joy, however, and to conjure the triumph of the Celebration for the Old Man he decided to take another look at the ornate brass hardware.

A freshly curious Gonzalo opened the lid to the pot exposing the incense tray. He pulled on the metal pinch tab and lifted the tray. In the bowl beneath he spotted several bright golden-green dried plant buds. The Man in the Orange Robe had left the brass pot seemingly as a gift, but he had forgotten his 'medicine'. But the boy did not process that fact as he had not understood a word he recognized—Medicine—used in the shaman's special vocabulary and context. 'Medicine,' to the boy, meant the disciplinary actions Tuko would administer to him with his leather belt because things he had done wrong as a result of his Mental Problems. Aravella always tried to intervene and Sama too, to prevent Tuko from giving the boy his Medicine but the cruel man would overpower them and locked them out of the room.

The boy inspected a golden-green bud and gave it a quick sniff. The odor was strong and it prodded his spiraling mind immediately once again, as it had already hours before, to recall the Hashish Farm and Aziz and the desperate young Dutch Girl (though he did not remember her as anything but as beautiful as Aravella and generous as she had given him Pesetas) and her bold and daring escape.

The Carrions had thrown a good-bye party for Gonzalo onboard the Summerwind the night before he left after their weeklong cruise in southern Spain. The next day they bought Gonzalo a Ferry ticket and saw him off at the Port in Tarifa. Before the boy boarded the Ferry, he shook the hand of Sr. Carrion who had been good to him and had paid him fairly. Then Marie José pecked him on both cheeks.

Their daughter Sofía approached him and began to lean toward him for a kiss good-bye but then shied away. Under the scrutiny of the others she was intimidated from showing him any affection. In addition, Gonzalo could not know this, but Sofía was overcome with memories they shared of the night before on the sand dunes, unbeknownst to her parents and boyfriend, and was suitably embarrassed. She had written the boy a letter though and had secretly wedged it in his passport in his satchel. She offered a warm smile and embraced him briefly as her good-bye not knowing how much the boy would remember, if anything.

Before the boy boarded the vessel, Sr. Carrion asked him one last time if he had his Passport as he would need it in the foreign country. The boy said he did. The Carrions were concerned for the boy of course but they had fully investigated his plan to work on an orange grove and date palm farm in a beautiful town boasting cliffs on the sea, El Hoceima. They had even spoken in person to Aziz the proprietor of the farm and they had made an accord that the boy would be met and picked up by Aziz in the port at Tangiers.

The way the boy's sojourn to Morocco came about and the web of personalities involved was somewhat spontaneous and convoluted. Aziz had been a friend of Tuko, Gonzalo's father, and after Tuko disappeared from Llavaneres under mysterious circumstances, through the intervention of Sama, Aziz offered the boy an open invitation to come to El Hoceima and work for him. As it happened, Sama (who had returned to her hometown in La Ronda to live with her parents) had heard about the disappearance of Tuko and the death of Aravella, but when she was alerted of the Old Man's passing she tried to locate the boy whom she knew now had been abandoned. She contacted Aziz though she had never met him but had spoken to him many times on the telephone as he contacted the house often looking for Tuko. Aziz was also seductively charming. He would make her laugh and they would carry on conversations in the most amicable of terms. Sama was not aware Aziz was Tuko's marijuana and hashish supplier and dealer who enabled the profiteering Tuko to engage in his other illicit industry, selling drugs to wealthy Spanish clientele for whom he provided other services noted.

Had the Carrions contacted Zosimus about the boy instead, this plan never would have taken place as the fisherman did not trust Tuko or anyone friendly with him. As it was, the Carrions had never met Gonzalo's father and knew little of him and no suspicions had arisen. At the same time they had heard Tuko had been raised a Muslim as had been Sama, and thereby the boy had been raised in a Muslim household (even though he was introduced to Christianity by Padre Miguel). In the end, the conscientious Sr. Carrion perceived the boy's venture to Muslim Morocco as appropriate if not thematically correct and that the boy's absent father would have likely approved.

As for Gonzalo, he was Happy his voyage was taking shape and he was on his way. He had told Zosimus of his Plan to go to India, the only person he had confessed his intentions to, and the wise fisherman had secretly helped him coordinate the trip with a map. 'The Plan' he devised for the boy was to hide his Money always and save it and never give it to anyone—but in the event he ran out—he would need to take Jobs along the way to pay for and continue his travels. He underscored the strategy by teaching him that The Plan was a 'Big Thing'. He also gave him enough Money for food and transportation though he feared the boy would spend it or lose it to opportunistic strangers. But Zosimus had his ailing parents to care for and he could not manage any further responsibility or vigilance. Once the boy took the voyage with the Carrions, Zosimus remained hopeful things would work out.

But there was a major discrepancy. Zosimus had set a route for him to go north, to Paris, to catch the overland Train to India from there—not go south. He was supposed to start his Journey by taking the Train from Cadaques after his initial trip north with the Carrions. Yet that schedule was forgotten as the Carrions treated the boy well, like family even, and gave him his Second Job with fair pay and Gonzalo was attracted to this inviting and peaceful household having never experienced this brand of calm before in his family Casa by the Railroad Tracks. And he was attracted by it. The more time he spent with the family, the more he enjoyed it, cruising the Mediterranean with them too, all the way south to Tarifa. In his discordant mind, by joining Aziz in Morocco the boy processed he was satisfying The Plan devised as he had been given a Third Job, which he knew was a Big Thing and something Zosimus advised him he should do in order to get to India.

For this reason The Plan was not followed exactly and Zosimus lost touch and was left out of the chain of communication. In the end it was Sama's intervention out of her genuine concern for the orphaned boy that resulted in Gonzalo's detour to North Africa. As it was, Gonzalo had learned of Morocco from the Old Man's adventures in Marrakesh and the boy's Ferry to Tangiers was also part of Padre Miguel's traveling the world teachings. Thereby, in the boy's confused state, a product of his pin-wheeling mind, he thought he was still following The Plan and was on the right path to meet the Great One.

This brings us to the golden-green marijuana buds the boy sniffed in the brass pot which were so pungent and aromatic, he received another olfactory-driven recollection of those days in Morocco when he labored at the Hashish Farm in the Rif Mountains.

Each morning at 6 AM Aziz would wake up the boy in his bedroom of the apartment Aziz kept for guests. The apartment was upstairs in the building from Aziz's home residence where he lived with his wife Nuna, a traditional Moroccan and Muslim woman, and their three children. For breakfast he gave the boy a piece of bread and water and then the two drove in Aziz's car, a run down jalopy with no muffler or window handles. Aziz had more money and could afford a more comfortable car but he dressed down his possessions to the level of an impoverished so as to not arouse suspicions of the Moroccan Police Nacional (SGCN).

On their daily journey Aziz and the boy first picked up several other young teens around town who also worked on the Farm. Together they traveled up through the hills of El

Hoceima and onward to the Rif Mountains, down long and winding dirt roads eventually arriving at the well-concealed Farm and warehouse where the cannabis plants were harvested and the resin extracted in the making of the 'kif' as it was called or Moroccan hash.

For his Third Job the boy was stationed in the warehouse where it was his daily task and the task of the other kids to pound on the harvested cannabis plants with rubber mallets to release the resin. The plants were brought to the warehouse from the fields strategically hidden behind acres of date palm trees. The plants would be laid down over porous cloth fabrics and covered with plastic. The plants were then pounded so that the resins would fall to a bucket beneath in the form of a fine golden powder. This potent-smelling powder was the hash product. It took many pounds of plants to yield the smallest quantities of kif extract.

'You must Conserve your Energy, Gonzalo,' Aziz would say. 'And your Strength. So that you can work long hours without getting tired. That's what I pay you for.'

These were the only Big Things the boy learned from Aziz and though they were not identified as such, the boy understood what the man was articulating as they were akin to Job commands from an employer.

Gonzalo performed his job admirably for several months. For his efforts he received meager wages paid in Dirhams after the sums of his daily room and board were subtracted. Like Tuko, Aziz was also a profiteering capitalist in the most selfish and miserly of ways.

It was when the young Dutch couple visited the guest apartment that things changed. Gonzalo could not know this but the couple, Gerrit and the gorgeous Danique, had come to engage in hashish commerce. Gerrit sought a top-notch supplier of Moroccan hash to sell to the numerous hash cafes back home in Amsterdam where the drug was legal. He was just starting out and had learned from friends as well as his online research and a chain of contacts that the Rif Mountain region was the place to find a reliable source. The young Dutch sweethearts were both 'stoners' as well which was often the case for those engaging in such activity.

Gerrit had been unaccomplished most of his life. He had been in rehab for a heroin addiction and had settled on hash as his remaining vice. His sojourn to Morocco was a plan to make money and get his life in order. Danique had pretty much followed Gerrit since high school where they had become a romantic couple. Danique was very attractive as she had honey-blonde hair, an abundant chest, and perfectly carved figure like a knife in a sheath. She had posed for a corporate clothing campaign as a model, but hadn't enjoyed the experience and all the attention it brought her as well as the constant harassment from agencies to get her to move to Paris and New York annoyed her. She was happy to follow Gerrit, smoke a little hash, and hang out. She was a modern hippie, but dedicated to her man.

Aziz met Gerrit through the underground handler system. One Moroccan Gerrit met in Amsterdam through a friend from rehab led to another contact in Marrakesh, which led to another in Ketama, which led to Aziz in El Hoceima. Once Gerrit and Aziz spoke on the phone, the couple was invited to come to offer their proposed business. They were shown to the guest apartment to be shared with Gonzalo. The layout consisted of two rooms separated by an adjoining wall with a wide arch in the middle from which colorful beads hung. There was little privacy. For a bathroom there was a little closet with a hole and a rusty shower of low water pressure and fleeting temperatures.

As soon as the couple arrived, Aziz played the consummate host. He had Nuna prepare a terrific feast of lamb and couscous. The evening started, however, in the couple's quarters where Aziz turned them onto his hash product using a Sebsis, an improvised pipe made from a cannabis stalk. They smoked and laughed and the foreigners were astounded by the potency of the product. They found Aziz to be most agreeable with an excellent sense of humor. He spoke of the hash trade and how the effects of a George Bush presidency on the government had forced a crackdown but that had been eased since many poor Moroccans survived on the hash trade as there was little industry and few opportunities for gainful employment in the country.

Even through the effects of the hash, Gerrit and Aziz came to a quick agreement on numbers and quantities and Aziz sold him several full Zip-loc bags. While he was there Gerrit wanted to make the most of the trip so he spent all the couple's money on product. To ensure his safety out of Morocco and back to Holland he decided on boat and train for transport, foregoing the scheduled flight. The sudden change was actually a recommendation from Aziz who'd recounted disturbing tales of reckless ill-advised travelers trying to fly out of Morocco with contraband and how they ended up in the country's tough prisons for years.

Danique wanted to join her boyfriend on the ferry from El Hoceima to Barcelona, but Gerrit thought it was too risky, and that if he got caught she would be an accomplice. Gerrit was well apprised Danique drew a lot of attention wherever she went—always—from all comers whether in line at the grocery store or at a café; he did not want any unnecessary attention placed upon him. His girlfriend had been detained many times at customs at the whim of inspectors just so they could spend more time with her. Danique understood the risks posed and agreed it was better to keep her scheduled flight. It was decided then that Gerrit would leave on the midday ferry and Danique would keep her plane ticket and fly later that afternoon on the pre-booked flight. And the couple would then meet back in Holland.

Aziz offered to give Gerrit a ride alerting him to the fact that some cabbies worked undercover and were spies for the government—an offer that he accepted. Aziz also offered a ride to Danique but remaining understandably cautious, she thought a taxi was the safer option for her.

That night the group enjoyed a fabulous dinner with Nuna's home cooking, the flavors accentuated magnificently by the effects of the hash they had smoked. Their taste buds were enlivened terrifically. Traditional Moroccan music was playing and they drank wine as well though Nuna did not approve of that aspect. She understood however it was a 'business dinner' with Christian clients.

Of course Gonzalo was invited to the table also, but he did not understand much of anything since the group was speaking English like they had been during their business and departure transportation discussions. The boy found himself transfixed by Danique, however. He had not seen a woman this beautiful since his Sister the Angel. No one could ever be as beautiful as her in his mind, but Danique was close. So very close.

Dinner conversation was lively and animated especially after more wine was consumed. Born into poverty, Aziz spoke of his days as a street urchin in Marrakesh and how he became involved in the hash trade. Gonzalo listened but he could not understand. He did notice that when Aziz spoke he was constantly addressing Danique. And looked at her often. This interaction did not go unnoticed by Aziz's wife, Nuna, either. Gerrit was relaxed and stoned and was less conversational. After a lull Aziz asked Danique how she got her 'beautiful name.'

'It's a combination,' she said in Dutch-accented English.

'A combination?' Aziz posed with a wide charming grin. 'To a lock?'

They all laughed uproariously, all except Nuna and Gonzalo.

'Of what combination do you speak? Can you give us all the numbers of this combination so that we may open your lock?' he posed in a playfully flirtatious if not seductive tone. The fresh comment caught Danique by surprise, until she realized he was teasing her and she broke up.

'No,' she said giggling freely. 'It's a secret combination. No one knows but my mother.'

They all laughed some more to the stoned banter and then the table went silent.

'Your mother,' Aziz repeated soberly. 'I never knew my mother ...'

The Moroccan seemed to get lost in a downcast reverie a beat. Then he raised up and glaring directly right at Danique, lasering into her beautiful cobalt blue eyes and said somewhat intimidatingly, 'I grew up on the streets. I'm all street—'

He smiled after as if he was hinting at something, perhaps a show of menace in some way. That he was a man of the streets and all that was implied in that. Yet it was more than raw intimidation or warning, it was sexual—and she felt it.

His comment pierced the Dutch girl and she reached for her glass to break up the moment.

Gerrit meanwhile was circling in his own hashish-induced orbit, oblivious to their interaction.

'And you Dutch boy—?' the Moroccan redirected. 'You two are together how many years—?'

'Ten.'

'—and you know nothing of this mystery?'

'I know of this mystery,' he said. 'It's—' and he paused for effect.

'It's what—?'

'It's mysterious!' he said bursting out and Aziz threw his napkin at him and they all laughed hysterically.

'Okay, so you're not going to tell me! I've had enough! Out of my house! Give me my hash back! Go home! I will take you to the row boat at noon and you, mysterious one, you take the donkey cart!'

Their sides were splitting again.

Later in the guest apartment, Gerrit spoke of how he liked Aziz and felt they'd been very fortunate; that with all the potential risks involved in coming to a place like Morocco, known for its conning and thievery, it would seem he had found a suitable supplier and potentially someone they could trust. But that also, he did not want to get ahead of himself either. They would play it day by day. One thing of which Gerrit was completely confident, however, was the fact that his clients in Holland's hash cafes were going to love the product and would certainly be seeking out more.

Danique agreed that they should still be cautious. She did not mention her charged if not unsettling repartee with Aziz though silently she was wary of him.

The couple then turned out the bedside lamp and Gerrit climbed in the spare double floor mattress. Once the light was off Danique changed out of her clothes. The boy watched her between the spaces in the hanging beads and took in her beautiful body alit from the window by the streetlights below. He observed her neutrally and without eroticism as she spread lotion on her legs, and arms and breasts—just as Aravella used to do in front of him. Her wonderful breasts hung with heaviness due to their size but perfectly, naturally, as can happen only on the young. Her rear was as exceptional and curvaceous, her feminine convergence trimmed to a small bar. When she spun slowly around and bent over to withdraw a change of underclothing from her bag, he noticed her private flower then and the tiny folds as he had seen when his Sister bathed and dressed in front of him.

This vision made him Happy and not because of any biological reasons or incitements of a sexual nature because he was not configured that way. His Happiness was attributed to the Joyous memory of his sister and he thought of her constantly as he watched the Dutch Girl. Danique then stepped into a pair of black thong panties and joined Gerrit on the floor mattress.

The following day, Gonzalo was retrieved early by another driver who took him and his young coworkers to the warehouse in the mountains. Aziz drove Gerrit to the port where he made the noon ferry. Danique went along for the ride to say good-bye. The couple had decided to allow Aziz to take her to the airport right after. As the two drove in silence Aziz lit up a joint and took several puffs. He offered some to Danique who declined. At the airport she got out, thanked him and bid him farewell. Aziz offered to escort her inside anyway as there was an unruly group of ogling Arabic men aligned at the curb.

Inside, the young Dutch girl tried to check in. She produced her ticket but when they requested her passport, she could not find it. She searched her bag through and through but it was missing. She became very upset. They went outside to check in the car, but the passport was nowhere to be found. Danique immediately phoned Gerrit but she could not get him on the line. Aziz suggested he take her immediately to the Dutch consulate in Rabat a five hour drive, but she resisted, still in a state of shock and unable to fathom the reality of her predicament. Rabat was after all 500 kilometers away, a drive of five hours, and she still wasn't going to surrender to the misfortune so easily.

Aziz quickly telephoned his wife and asked her to scour the guest apartment. They spoke in Darija, the Moroccan Arabic. Nuna called back ten minutes later and claimed the apartment door was locked and the key was missing. Aziz contended Gerrit must have taken it with him by mistake. Danique continued to try to phone Gerrit and finally her boyfriend answered. Gerrit claimed he gave the key back to Aziz.

Aziz asked Gerrit to check all his pockets. Sure enough he was holding the key in his small jeans pocket. Aziz informed them he had another key stashed in his apartment and he could take her back so they could try and retrieve her passport. Gerrit thought that was the wisest approach as it would likely take a week to get documents replaced in Rabat.

Danique was beside herself but tried her best to hold back her tears the entire way back to the apartment house. Aziz let her in and she searched and searched, but her passport was not there. She spoke to Gerrit again and he advised her to make the trip to Rabat in the morning as there was not enough time that day. She could get a hotel there and wait for a new issue. Danique thought the best plan was to take a taxi there immediately, but Gerrit discouraged her as he didn't trust any Moroccan cab drivers on a five-hour drive.

Aziz brought her a glass of wine to calm her down, but she declined it. It was late afternoon already by now and she was exhausted. She asked to be left alone and Aziz complied. Danique locked the door from within and took a long nap. She was awoken when Gonzalo returned home and knocked on the door. She cautiously opened it for the boy.

Later that evening Nuna brought over some chicken and rice and the boy and Danique shared a meal together. The boy told her that he was on his way to India to see the Great One, and though she understood Spanish she was too nerve-racked to listen. After dinner Aziz knocked on the door and the boy answered. Danique was taking a wall shower that consisted of the faint trickle of lukewarm water. Aziz then rudely entered the bathroom frightening her. He extended a glass of wine to her over the opaque plastic partition as he took in fully her naked body behind it. The startled girl asked him to 'please leave.' And he did leave after hanging around too long—the bathroom.

When Danique emerged from the bathroom wrapped conservatively in a towel, he was sitting in the guest bedroom smoking a bowl of hash from the Sebsi pipe. He offered it to her with his charming smile and without answering, she gathered her clothes to change in the bathroom still perturbed he had barged in while she was showering and likely saw her naked. As she got dressed she called Gerrit, but she could not get him on the phone.

A fully clothed Danique sat on her bed across the room from the Moroccan man. He began to discuss the logistics for the following day; he would drive her to Rabat first thing in the morning and help her find a suitable hotel. She did not answer him, but silently she decided she would accept neither. He lit up another bowl and was as pleasant and positive as can be, assuring her that everything was going to work out. He even made her laugh. Aziz switched off the glaring overhead light and lit candles claiming the effects of hash were best appreciated in candlelight. After some more prodding by him, the young Dutch girl decided to have a smoke, to calm her nerves after such a harrowing day. Then they talked about many things for a couple hours.

When Danique indicated she would like to retire to bed the man's eyes narrowed eerily to a neutral expression. He did not move. She then asked him to leave and again he said nothing and didn't move. She was very stoned and not thinking properly. In a paranoid rush she tried to grab her bags and he immediately rose up and stopped her. Freaked out and fearing worse, she began to whimper. She begged him to let her go.

'Tomorrow,' he said.

'I want to go now. Please!'

The man shook and sat down omnipotently. 'Your boyfriend is greedy—'

'No, he's not …'

'How could he leave you here, a beautiful girl like you?'

'Please—'

'He cared more about the drugs than you—'

'No—'

'He's a two-bit hash smuggler. And the creep owes me—'

'He paid you, I saw it! Let me go!'

'He paid for the hash. He didn't pay for the room.'

'No, don't say that! You can't say that now!'

'You have any money?'

'I can get it for you! My father—' she pleaded.

'—too late—'

In the candlelit room Aziz rose up and moved toward her. She extended her hands to fend him off but she was too stoned to really fight. He embraced her and began smooching her neck. She shoved him away hard and that's when he tossed her on the mattress and began to tear away at all her clothes. She fought as best she could but he ripped off her blouse popping the buttons, then yanked off her bra with a snap releasing her ample bare breasts. She kicked as he tore down her pants. When he got to her thong he shredded it in two leaving her totally naked. She spun over to cover herself and he smacked her hard on her bare posterior and flipped her back over and when she screamed he walloped her across the face drawing blood from her lip and stunning her.

The monster pushed her back and she stopped fighting. She wailed as his mouth devoured every inch of her spread legs and breasts and he placed his fingers everywhere. Then he turned her over on her stomach. She cried out several times again and each time he did, he smacked her until she fell totally silent and was without will. He traced his tongue in and out of every part of her body. She was stoned too, trapped in a horrific nightmare of which she could not escape. She cried and her ribs heaved into the mattress.

He propped her up on all fours and braced her shoulders in place so she couldn't move.

'No!—please no!'

The man penetrated her deeply and she shrieked in horror and collapsed down and he smacked her again. He began to bounce in and out of her frame as she bawled into the pillows. He spread her arms wide and held them there and with his mouth pressed next to her ear he asked her again, 'See the *puta* you are? Your boyfriend is gone a few hours and already you're *follado* a guy you just met! See?'

'No, no, no!' she wailed.

The evil man's illicit businesses were often spoken in Spanish and he knew the slang better for nefarious activities—even sex, forced or otherwise.

'And the mystery of your name, *perra?* What is the combination?'

When she didn't answer he penetrated her harder and deeper and harder again until she screamed from the pain. Then he smacked her in the head.

'*Respondéme!*'

She stuttered it through the wails as he rammed her. 'It's Danielle,' she said finally. 'And Monique ...'

'Who gave you that name—?'

'My mother ...'

'If your *madre* could see you now—the filthy *puta* you are!'

Just then he gave her a final crack to the head that almost knocked her out. She was dazed. Then he reversed from her and using his finger he teased her in that most taboo, feared, untouched, her most private place. After circling the target he injected his thumb within with the looming threat of sodomizing her. She wailed and reached a weak hand back.

'Please,' she pleaded. 'I'll do anything, but not that—'

'No, eh—?'

With the incentive he'd sought, he rose up and surged forward, crashing through her, violating her there with his deepest thrust yet and she yelped in pain and got hysterical again. But he smacked her each time she burst out until she was silent again.

'Bueno?' he posed. 'You like?'

She knew to answer him now and nodded weakly.

'... This is what happens when you don't pay the rent ... how is your vacation now, tourista? ... welcome to Morocco ... and get used to it... there's mucho more to come—'

After what seemed an interminable time he turned her over and forced her in his lap to feed on him. She was in shock and too disoriented to cry anymore.

'Mamalo, puta!—'

And she did. He forced her to. Until he didn't have to anymore.

'That's right ... bueeeeno ... You like?'

As she performed fellatio on him he pulled her hair for a response. She nodded. He grabbed her hair harder ripping strands—he wanted to hear it. 'Respóndeme, concha!'

'Yes, I ... like it—'

'You like what?'

'I like ... doing ... it—'

He demanded she use the more descriptive verb and identify his anatomy too. She complied of course.

'When you wake up! You're going to mamalo! Sí?'

'... Sí ...'

Repeating for him in the foreign language was the worst reminder of the nightmarish and dire predicament, that it was not just a bad dream; it pulled her from the protective state of merciful shock, and tears streamed down her face all over again as she obliged him.

'Whenever I want, right? Say it!'

She did.

The monster held her to it. He took fortification pills and alternated their positions for hours, continuing to penetrate her both ways, invading her, as if she were a dog, then having her perform acts on him, whatever he wanted. Then he shaved her vagina and smoked hash off her breasts and made her smoke too, to alternate between the pipe and his organ.

And the boy listened and watched the bodies thrash through the night beneath the fractured glow of the streetlights streaming in through the windows. When Aziz got up early to drive Gonzalo to the mountains, the Dutch Girl was passed out. He told the boy to meet him in the car. He then grabbed her by the ear and forced her head in his lap and he held it in place for many minutes until he received his pleasure, making sure she imbibed him.

'Gooooood ... You like the way I taste?'

She nodded.

'From now on—like that!—you hear me?'

(Every morning for three weeks, as soon as she woke, without being prompted and trained like an animal in fear of being whipped, it was the first thing she did until the act came to its full completion. Some mornings he shoved her head away preferring to sleep still.)

But she still had to survive the first night ...

'If you try to leave I'll kill you,' he whispered to her. 'And take a shower.' Then he kissed her harshly and bit her lip and told her he was not going into the mountains that day; that he would remain close by which was a lie.

When Danique woke up at one in the afternoon she could barely walk. She was bruised, aching all over, and had no strength. And of course the apartment door was locked from the outside. He had taken her phone too. She was trapped.

When he came home that evening he went directly to the guest room. She was in panties and a T-shirt smoking a cigarette sitting on the floor in the corner of the room. She was sipping on a glass of wine too from the bottle he had left.

'I see you found the wine.'

'Sí. Gracias.' The compromised girl thought using Spanish would please him.

'Did you shower like I said?'

She said she had, again in Spanish.

The monster then lit up the Sebsis and extended it to her. Danique smoked without protest. After she'd taken a few hits, the last ones pushed upon her by him, he stood above her and extended his hand. She clasped it and stood up and he guided her by the hand to the bed. He eyeballed her fiercely. She took off her T-shirt and panties in response and he ravaged her again. She did not complain or resist. He poured coconut oil all over her body and had her from every angle. With the slightest nudge she sensed what he wanted and she performed each and every task. And she told him everything he wanted to hear when asked.

The boy who had seen everything from his bedroom the last Two Sleeps, until he could stave off sleep no longer, was awoken in the middle of the night. He needed to pee and he crept into the adjoining room where Aziz and the Dutch girl were asleep in bed. Inside the bathroom consisting of the hole in the floor for relieving Waste Pipe One and Two as well as the wall shower and opaque plastic, he released the tie in his drawstring pants and urinated. As he did this he noticed the yellow Towel the Dutch Girl used to dry herself hanging from a wall hook. The towel was spotted with traces of Red Waters.

The ravaging of the Dutch girl went on for nearly a month. The monster forced itself upon her repeatedly each afternoon and through the night then left for the warehouse in the morning. One night he had another girl come and had them perform for him. Then he had them both. Another time a man came. Aziz engaged himself physically with the other man and then he watched the 'guest' have Danique too every which way. And all along the way Aziz continued to feed her bowls of hash from the Sebsi and glasses of wine.

He had effectively turned her into a slave.

'What's your name?'

'Dani.'

'Whose property are you?'

'I belong to Aziz … I'm all his,' she said. 'Forever …'

12

The days passed and Gonzalo continued to be the silent witness to the series of aggressive spectacles unaware that he was really witnessing true horror. And evil.

'Your boyfriend never loved you. Say it—'

'Never loved me, never …' she parroted dreamily.

'I couldn't hear you, what?'

' *I love you, Aziz,* I said.'

Danique was so gone in her faculties she actually meant it. Her distorted mind plied the day long with hash and drugged wine made her fall in love with him, deeply, to the point where he brought other girls to enjoy in front of her which at this point made her jealous.

One time Aziz was atop the Dutch girl, her head banging against the wall. Her eyes caught the stare of Gonzalo as he was watching through the hanging beads. A lone tear made its way down her cheek and the boy could see it reflect off the light from the window. But the Dutch girl's eyes rolled back in her head in some form of ecstasy. She couldn't know why she'd shed a tear, she didn't know which way was up. The animalistic episodes were so indulgent and the Dutch girl was so compliant the monster began to get bored of her, treating her badly, smacking her at will even when she was making her best efforts to please him.

Aziz had more men come to have pleasure with her, however they wanted it, and he was paid for it. Drug dealers took her as partial payment, snorting cocaine off her intimate parts. Aziz's friends negotiated her price in front of her and had her do acts in front of a crowd and had her satisfy a line-up. They laughed as they spray-painted her posterior and privates.

One morning when the boy was waiting outside by the car, Nuna appeared from the front door and approached him.

'You must help, boy.'

Gonzalo did not respond as he did not know why he was being told this.

'The Dutch one,' she said. 'He will kill her.'

The boy had never heard of such a thing and of course he remained silent with nothing to say.

'You must save her, Gonzalo.' She reiterated the murder threat. 'Speak, boy!'

'Save?' he posed finally.

'Because ...'

The boy again was speechless, unable to process what was happening.

'He watches futbol this night. Tonight you go. Far away. I put passports under bed. Give to her, the Dutch one. And tell her no wine! This is our secret!—'

When the boy heard the word he knew it was important. He had learned that and would never forget it. This coming from a woman he did not know, yet it held the same significance for him. Her command was an order sealed with a Secret—it was a Big Thing.

Nuna heard Aziz coming down the stairs and she became panicked and dashed off.

'Under your bed. Tonight,' she reiterated while scurrying away. 'I go. He will kill her ...' Nuna said again as she fled in a panic, then spun back hurriedly servicing a need to explain. 'Because she's beautiful—'

Then Nuna quickly disappeared behind the back of the apartment house as Aziz emerged from the front door entrance.

'What's the matter?' Aziz posed taking in the boy's serious expression.

The boy said nothing and got in the beat up car.

That night when the boy went home, Aziz let him in the door and followed him inside. He had another animalistic session with Danique. (He no longer had conventional intercourse with her; it was only her posterior.) Then he took off locking the door behind him. He left another opened bottle of wine for her.

The boy looked out the window and saw Aziz get into a car with a group of men. Gonzalo went to his room and lifted the thin mattress. As communicated, both passports were there. The boy had not been aware his Passport was missing.

Having showered, Danique stepped from the bathroom in her yellow Towel washed clean of the blood. She was holding a fresh glass of red wine about to sip. Gonzalo was standing there clutching his Satchel and her Passport.

'Here—'

'Wow …' she remarked as if it was a relic from some far away memory of a distant life. 'Where did you get it?'

'He will kill you. We go now—'

'What?'

Just then the door was unlocked and flung open and Nuna rushed in. She snatched the wine glass from her hand. 'Don't drink! Come!' she said panicked.

The wife of Aziz knew from experience the wine for female 'guests' was laced with Rohypnol, a powerful drug that incited delirium and disorientation, and thereby a loss of will and rational thought. The Dutch girl's eyes teared up until they were flooded.

'But—'

'No time!'

'He'll do things to me if I go—'

'He will kill you if you stay! I have seen it!'

Nuna grabbed her and a dazed Danique did not move as she was still under the effects of all the drugs consumed. Nuna then smacked her across the face.

'Wake up!'

The Dutch girl stood there delirious so Nuna packed her bag for her in a rush and they hustled out the door.

'I sorry. But you in danger!' Nuna said in apology.

Outside, Nuna, whose face was covered in a traditional black veil, handed the key to Danique.

'Drive quickly!' she said.

They all piled into Aziz's car and took off.

Danique drove confused and unevenly trying to pull out of the consumption fog as Nuna guided her to the Port and commanded her to park the car behind the hauling trucks. She advised the two to conceal themselves in a storage hut reserved for giant rolls of fishing nets.

'Take first boat. Any boat. You have money?'

The boy wondered if he should speak up about the money he had saved. Zosimus told him not to. When he checked his special Pocket sewn into the drawstring Pants he drew the contents and saw there was no money, just a stuff of papers written in Arabic. The Pesetas from Zosimus and the petty Dirhams he'd received for his Job at the Hash Farm were gone.

Danique though unstable she checked her purse not knowing she'd already done so. 'I have a money card.'

'Go!' Nuna blasted. 'Stay hidden! He will come! He will kill you!' she warned again.

She cursed then in Moroccan Arabic. Nuna did not know how to drive. She knew she would be beaten either way. But Aziz would not kill the mother of his children. She walked all the way home taking a circuitous route. It took several hours. She would be beaten that night within an inch of her life. Nuna would never see in one eye again.

The two huddled together deep in the storage hut behind piles of nets. It was pitch black outside still and dark inside the hut.

Not long after, Aziz arrived at the Port with several men. They located the car first then combed the docks at the ferry launch, checking inside the nearby buildings. One mustached man entered the storage hut but couldn't see. As soon as he left, Danique grabbed the boy's hand and they climbed through the back window and ran down the docks away from the ferry launch where the fishing boats were lined up. They boarded a rusted out trawler and climbed down into the cabin and found the bathroom. She locked them inside. Though she was terrified, adrenaline aroused her wits. She hadn't sipped the wine and she was coming out of the fog of forced consumption.

Danique Prayed then and had Gonzalo repeat her Prayer. She squeezed his hand hard.

'Thank you,' the Dutch Girl whispered and she erupted into tears then while covering her mouth, a full release from the clearer realization of the horror of her captivity. There would be more spontaneous tears for her the rest of her young days.

An hour later, they heard the voices of men boarding the boat. It was 4AM. Soon after the engines rumbled.

Suddenly, the bathroom handle was tugged then twisted aggressively. A man's voice shouted in Spanish. There was commotion and then banging on the door from multiple men all speaking Spanish.

A key was heard inserted and the door swung open. At the same time Aziz and his band of henchman were scouting all the fishing boats and came upon the Spanish vessel. Aziz spoke Spanish to the fishermen and as he did he could hear voices in the cabin below.

'What's going on in there?' he posed in perfect Spanish.

'I'm looking for my wife. She's Dutch. We had a fight.'

At the same time, Rodrigo, the boat's Capitán who opened the bathroom door, informed the pair, 'I'm sorry. We can't take stowaways—'

'Por favor—' Danique pleaded in a whisper, sapped of her strength, and the man could see the fear in her eyes, a terror deeply layered in her expression.

'We could be thrown in jail. It's Morocco.'

Rodrigo moved through the cabin and up and out to the deck. He spied Aziz as he was articulating his plight while employing his affable qualities, the others already laughing at his psychopathic charm, his gift. He had already handed the men some hash too and Rodrigo witnessed it.

The Capitán faded back inside to address the fugitives.

He spread the door. 'You'll have to go—'

The strung out and shell-shocked victim pleaded with him and spoke in quiet hysterics of being raped repeatedly by the monster as soon as her Dutch fiancé had left the country.

'He will kill her,' the boy who was not quite right said suddenly.

Rodrigo could not explain it but the boy's comment resonated with him in some far off and inexplicable way.

'Are you transporting drugs?' he posed fearfully.

She shook. 'No, I swear!'

The Capitán told them to be silent and sealed the door shut locking them inside. Danique grabbed both the boy's hands and Prayed again. Rodrigo returned to the deck and gave orders to his crew to untie and ready the boat for immediate departure.

Aziz and his henchmen tried to rush the trawler and a scuffle broke out. The Spanish fishermen held them off; several of the Moroccans were hurled overboard, physically tossed into the water.

Then the slow moving fishing trawler motored off. Not long after, a Moroccan police boat was in heated pursuit. But Rodrigo made a wise and bold move as only a savvy man of the sea could. He commandeered the boat to the next Moroccan port west and stationed it there blending his vessel in with a row of similarly docked trawlers. They waited a couple hours. The Spanish boat's registered destination was Marbella, the direction the Moroccan police boat took. When the time was right Rodrigo guided the trawler on a detour to Gibraltar instead.

After an hour back on the sea, the Capitán invited the boy and terrorized Dutch girl to join everyone on deck as it was a beautiful sunny morning. Danique was in a state of horror-induced shock and could not move. Rodrigo returned with a cold Estrella beer for her.

She took it, her face and chin rippling uncontrollably as she fought back more tears. She produced a sad smile and said, *'Muchas gracias.'*

'De nada,' said the honorable Captain.

Danique burst into tears again and Rodrigo tried to console her, but she was unable to be receptive to the touch of a man or anyone—except the boy. And yet her latest release was a welcomed one, one of profound relief; her and the boy's prayers had been answered. The Dutch girl's desperate ordeal in Morocco was over.

From Gibraltar the two boarded a train to Malaga and continued onward all the way to Madrid. Danique purchased the tickets. Most of the time the Dutch girl gazed out the window at the passing vista, but really she was staring off into oblivion still in shock and gripped with fear. Each hour she was increasingly free of the effects and aftereffects of weeks of drugging, more horror crept into her mind. The boy saw singular Tears streaming down her cheeks every several minutes. Then he dozed off. Eventually, she did too but it took a while. Her head collapsed on his shoulder; she was still clutching both his hands.

When they arrived in Madrid's Puerta de Atocha station three hours later, they were forced to wait for the evening's overnight train to Paris. The Dutch girl was still terrified and panicked. Now that she had sobered, she was so deeply ashamed and together they found refuge in the deep recesses of a café a good walk from the station. While the boy ate a sandwich Danique ordered draft beers in an attempt to calm her nerves. She was so fraught with misery and shock (while consumed with nightmarish flashes of memory, images she could not prevent), she hadn't asked the boy his travel plans even though he'd mentioned it in El Hoceima.

'India,' he said. 'To see the Great One.'

'*Quién es?*' she asked in her broken Spanish and she broke down again as she said it. It killed her to speak Spanish because it was the language employed perversely by the Moroccan monster Aziz, she was reminded.

He tried to explain but the words were jumbled. 'But I must get a Job first,' he added.

Danique purchased a prepaid telephone card. She phoned her parents and through her sobbing, without revealing any details, she begged her father to deposit money immediately into her account. He obliged. She did not call Gerrit. And she would not contact him ever again. After living at home a while and undergoing extensive therapy she would move to New York to start a new life.

With the influx of cash and her orientation temporarily restored, Danique brought the boy to a travel agent outpost near the Puerte de Atocha station. There she purchased for him a train ticket, not only to Paris, but for the overland train to New Delhi. She handed him a wad of Pesetas too.

'Job?' he asked of her.

'*Perdóname*, I have *no trabajo*. It is my gift to you. *Regalo*.'

After a while her timid hand looped inside the arm of her traveling companion as they ventured around the neighborhood in proximity to the station. They were brother and sister.

'You saved me, Gonzalo. You're my angel.'

Her comment made the boy consider Aravella then.

'My Sister the Angel,' he said.

Danique did not know what he meant. His comment possibly signified it was Aravella who had liberated them from the mess in Morocco as she was a real Angel. They did not speak much the rest of the day nor on the overnight train. But she held on to him even as she slept and they stayed close through the entire journey. They arrived at Gare d'Austerlitz in Paris the next morning and Danique brought the boy in a taxi to Gare de Lyon. There she bought him food, water, and chocolate for the long journey and waited with him for his transcontinental train that afternoon and put him on board to make sure he was safe.

The Dutch girl kissed him good-bye on the cheek. Her time with him had given her the faintest trace of hope, in humanity even. She could live on that for now and for the challenging days that lay ahead.

'I will never forget you, Gonzalo,' she said in English.

He did not know what she had said; it was because of his Mental Problems he was sure.

13

It was late afternoon when the boy snapped from his lengthy and detailed reminiscence of the days in Morocco. He was now touring a circle around the Ravine. He had witnessed more treks of Animals from his high perch in the Dhok as they visited the Water Hole to hydrate; a small herd of Nilgai the blue bull Antelope, several Hares, numerous Birds, a team of Gray Langurs, Chinkaras the Indian Gazelle, and the Rhesus of course. A family of Wild Boar rumbled up too and spent time investigating and sniffing the stripped rib cage of their perished brother.

The boy had observed these processions while politely awaiting his turn to drink, albeit in a detached way, too consumed with the harrowing recollections that now made him sad. (He was so invested in his meditation he even saw a feral Dog sniff the Footprint of the Bengal. Though he was looking right at it, the observation did not register.)

It was the boy's turn now to drink. As he squatted low, Gonzalo splashed water on his face. He had been crying. The plight of Danique was affecting him dramatically now. The pinwheel in his mind had stopped spinning if for only a short while and he had the capacity to focus more exactly on what had really transpired. He remembered the Dutch girl eyeballing him over Aziz's shoulder and the single tear on her cheek as her head slammed repeatedly against the wall. He now knew she had not been Happy when she glanced at him.

The boy was entertaining more complicated sentiments and complex emotions. Sorrow was gripping him unlike it ever had in his life. He was feeling the Pain of the Dutch girl and he now understood increasingly more of her situation as the details came to him. It produced Anger in him toward Aziz. And then he became Angry when he thought of the Boys at School. Then he became Angry with Tuko too, his Father. Most of all, of course, he became Angry with Don Pepe. This man made him so Angry he had to stop thinking about him. What was surprising, in a good way, was the fact that he could drive unpleasant thoughts away. He had the capacity to control thoughts and emotions and drive them from his mind.

The clarity of thought he'd experienced in the morning of the day of his Third Sleep had returned. As he sipped from cups of water in his hands, eventually he was reminded of his mission and Plan and wondered once more what he would say to the Great One. He repositioned himself on the Bank next to the Footprint and drank from there and pretended he was sharing a drink with Zephyrles.

The boy looked older now. He was hungry. He decided to inspect the rib cage of the young Boar felled by the assassins. He tried to peel off tiny scraps of flesh and any soft residue remaining on the bone. He used the Knife Zosimus had given him but he was largely shaving off chips of bone. He ate them anyway.

Not satisfied, he took a stroll to see what he could find in the Jungle. After an hour, he had the great fortune of finding an accessible lower branch to a towering Bengal Fig tree. Most of the figs had been pilfered by the Rhesus and Langur, but there was one hidden high up. He climbed to snare it and flicked the worm away and ate it immediately. Another fig he found on the ground hidden beneath the leaves. He ate fig leaves too.

Gonzalo ventured onward and across the service road. He marched in between the rows of thick Ardusta bush. He spotted a bloody object in the soil, a fragment of a Chital jaw bone from a fresh kill likely perpetrated by one of the jungle's feline predators, a Caracal, Jungle Cat, or Leopard. The boy immediately chewed on the bloody gums until only teeth and bone remained. He was too famished to fear an ambush.

The boy's quest for food was cut short. He experienced concern again, sensing he must return to the Ravine and not miss anything. His goal was now sticking to the moment, holding on to present time while keeping the Plan in the forefront of his mind and what he must do. His enhanced mental capacities served to keep him on track, and as important, did not allow him to get sidetracked. A deliberate thought process with intent—prioritizing—had never happened before. For this reason the boy knew his appetite was not a priority and his Hunger could wait.

* * * * *

At the same time the boy was being carefully studied from a vantage point unseen—the expansive canopy of that very Bengal Fig tree from which he had just extracted a fig— from a medium-sized predator known to be the best disguise artist in the jungle. The predator had stalked the boy three days now and two nights, his every movement watched. It had clawed the trunk of a nearby Gugal tree to mark its territory the night before which the boy had heard in his sleep, but could not be sure. Yet Gonzalo could not know of this presence, nor could any human of sounder mind. This was a stealth master and the toughest foe to any creature in the jungle.

* * * * *

When Gonzalo returned to the Ravine he sidled up to the bank of the Water Hole and rubbed more Dung on his body, using the water to help spread it over his skin. He was ready again though he was mindful the Great One usually appeared in early morning. Still he was ready.

That evening, as the boy waited high up in the Dhok, he heard a radio sound below. He peered down the trodden Animal path, the widest one, and the figure of Yamir appeared in the distance and he was approaching. In one hand he was holding his Clipboard and the other held a handset. He was talking into it in Hindi.

More static noise erupted from the oncoming Yamir's handset. Then he switched it off as he arrived in the clearing and reattached the Walkie-Talkie to his belt.

'Gonzal!' he shouted still dropping the 'o' in the boy's name.

The boy tapped the tree trunk with his brass pot.

'Hoa!' the uniformed man greeted him. The boy returned the greeting citing Yamir's name.

The jungle operative asked the boy then if he had seen a small girl. The boy looked at him blankly.

'Girl,' Yamir repeated, having forgotten the boy spoke only Spanish. When he said 'Niña,' the boy, whose mind was in the moment and not pixilated or fogged, understood.

In more Hindi-Spanish, a mix of language the boy could not understand, Yamir launched into a brief story, that a small girl had been missing from the nearby village of Burrad and he wondered if the boy had seen anything.

'No,' the boy responded. 'No niña …'

Just then the man drew from his shirt pocket a granola bar and unwrapped it. He broke the choco-almond bar in two and stuffed the first piece in his face and munched. The ravenous boy watched him intently, his eyes locked on the food and the operative caught it.

'You hungry? *Hambre?*'

'*Sí.*'

'You are living in a salad bowl, amigo! Ensalada everywhere.' He pointed out trees and shrubs in the vicinity. 'The dhák leaves over there. The khair blossoms. The adusta fruit. *Ensalada e fruta.* What more do you want?'

The selfish man then gobbled up the second piece of his granola bar and burped while he chewed.

'*¡Buen apetito,* Gonzal!—'

The man pointed two fingers at his own eyes again conveying keep an eye out! He kept walking past the Water Hole toward the other end of the clearing. He was on a search for the young girl though he did not seem panicked. Then Yamir stopped suddenly and seemed to be examining a twelve-foot high Gugal tree. He traced a hand over its papery bark and eyed the thorny branches. It seemed to give him pause.

The jungle operative then swiveled back. 'Have you seen the Leopardo?' he reiterated once more.

The boy shook his head. And Yamir again disappeared into the thick brush. From the thicket he yelled back.

'*Guardia,* Gonzal! My *Explorador!*'

Having watched the operative the boy immediately treaded over to the stunted Gugal tree even though he was famished. He got a close look of the pink and red flowers each comprised of four petals. Upon closer inspection of the tree, he noticed a dense series of scratch marks slashing down the trunk shredding the thin bark. He was not sure what the marks were. For a brief second his sleep the night before came to mind but he could not decipher why.

The hunger got the best of him and the boy scurried over to the nearest Dhák tree and grabbed a fistful of its leaves; he picked the green tendu berries from the Khair shrubs Yamir had pointed out and followed that with a raid of yellow-red fruits from the Adusta. He made a pouch of his shirt and placed all the foodstuffs within and settled at the based of his borrowed tree and feasted.

'I need Energy for El Gran. And Strength,' he thought aloud in a rational and causal analysis of nourishment that was different for him. Before he'd responded to the hunger reflex without thought. 'Bueno—'

The boy immediately pondered the lost Girl and he was confused from what would have to be considered another logic-based standpoint. Yamir had enlisted him as his *explorador* or scout, but he never asked to help him search for the Girl.

* * * * *

On the night of his Third Sleep, the boy made a Fire with a final Match. He had prepared the Fire ahead of time before retiring to the Dhok for a nap so that it would be ready when he awoke. He had been napping again through dusk as the day had been a long one and he had been up late and arose very early. The moon was bright still though it had passed the point of total fullness. It looked as if it had been sanded down on the right side. The boy was surrounded by the darkness of the middle of night but the moon's silver blanket illuminated the Ravine brilliantly.

As the flames to the fresh Fire rose as a tall beacon to catch the eye of the Bengal, the boy's cerebral improvements were further enhanced and he was perceptive and alert. He brought to mind immediately his most recent recollection, that of the lost Indian Girl from the Village. He hoped she would be found. He even gave thought to helping to Search, yet he recognized also he must follow his quest. Though he could not identify the thought as 'selfish' as he was not familiar with negative emotions, he had never tasted a feeling quite like it before. He did not like its taste either. He anticipated the Girl must be very frightened if she was still lost in the Jungle. He considered scanning the nearby area in case the Girl had come to the clearing.

At the same time, Yamir had not commanded him to Search; he wanted him to perform his Job and watch for—guardia—the Animals. The boy was still perplexed by this. The Animals lived in the Jungle; this was their home and they knew to protect themselves to the best of their abilities. The Girl could not. She had no protection. It was then through his rational weighing of the situation using logic as his tool, Gonzalo decided to Search for the Girl.

The boy did not know how to make a Torch but he thought perhaps his Satchel poised on the end of his Stick could burn brightly. He did not want to burn the gift from the Old Man but he thought Santoro would understand that he was following a Good Thought. That's just what he did. First he stuffed the Satchel with small twigs and Branches. He stuck the pointed walking Stick with the canvas Bag attached to the end in the Fire. He was pleased to see the Bag light up. His idea had been rewarded and he felt more confident. He raised his Torch high and felt orgulla as in proud of his creation though he did not know the word— just the feeling. Then he walked to the rim of the clearing and crept along and chose the widest of the Animal access Paths to the Water Hole, and stepped softly past the enormous granite boulder rising beside which marked the trail.

* * * * *

At the entrance to the access trail from the eight-foot tall chunk of granite, the florescent yellow eyes glowed brilliantly, reflecting the moonlight; the consummate predator lay nestled in the recess to the massive rock boulder, stealth-like and crouched. This beast, a veritable engine of destruction quite equal to its far larger cousins due to lesser size, could conceal itself in places impossible to the lion or bengal; its need for water was far less, and in diabolical cunning coupled with an uncanny sense of self-preservation and surreptitiousness when danger appeared, it had no equal.

As the bright flame to the improvised Torch passed below, the fire was mirrored in the dauntless feline's eyes, pupils dilated to eternity. The beast had an aversion to fire having faced it in village raids and it recognized any injury sustained could be life threatening. Fire had that capability and it was the element the daring predator feared most. There would be no offensive, not now; it could wait. Its clock was set on jungle time and with the waterhole as bait there was all the time in the world.

* * * * *

Gonzalo continued into the thick of Jungle, pausing at every bend of the Path to listen. Perhaps he could hear the Girl if she was laughing, he thought. Or crying. It would be crying he decided then—because the girl must be very frightened by now. As the boy went deeper still through the lowlands of dense scrub forest he could barely see the Fire at the Ravine. He had concern that the Bengal would come while he was gone, but the thought of a lonely little Girl, likely terrified like Danique the Dutch Girl had been, was his immediate priority. He still was not used to the taste of selfishness and did not care for it. It made him almost Happy again to discard it. For others more experienced the 'almost Happy' sensation he now assumed was relief.

As he traversed through the tree line, he recalled a story Aravella had told him one day. It had happened when they were in the Orphanage, how she had run away once when she was nine years old. She explained that she escaped from the house and hid for Two Sleeps in a portable toilet. She was very frightened. She had told him she fled because she didn't like the way Prado, the man who ran the Orphanage 'touched' her. And that she told Prado's wife Isadora, but the inappropriate behavior did not stop. Then she informed the Doctor, the one who conducted the outfit's medical examinations. Soon after, both Aravella and Gonzalo were adopted legally by Tuko, their Father. To leave the Orphanage brought much Happiness to Aravella. She confided that she was no longer scared—of anything. That the experience had made her 'Strong,' a state that was a Big Thing. The boy processed the story afresh and he intuited how scared the lost little Girl from the Village must feel now.

'Gonzalo—' the boy suddenly heard whispered aloud. He looked around and no one was there.

He stopped moving and listened more intently. Then he heard it again. The voice was louder. He could decipher the voice; it belonged to Aravella, his Sister the Angel.

Aravella was calling out to him, trying to communicate with him like the shaman, the Man in the Orange Robes said could happen. Only it was the Old Man whose voice the shaman said could be heard—if he let it. The boy knew the Old Man's Soul had been guided to the sky to be with the Sky Spirits. In the boy's lucid state of mind he deduced that Aravella, whose voice he had just heard plainly and clearly, must be with the Sky Spirits too. Finally he identified where she was and by the sound of her soothing voice she must be Happy and in a good place, perhaps the very best place. The Old Man had called it Heaven. She probably was spending time with the Old Man if Heaven and the Sky were close by each other. She may have greeted him and thrown a Celebration. The meditation filled the boy with immediate Joy, so much so his eyes began to fill with water.

The boy's Torch went out then as all the canvas had burned through. The sky was still very dark and tall trees were blocking the moonlight and Gonzalo was so deep in the jungle he could not see the Fire at the Ravine. Rather than venture out further the boy decided to wait until the darkness of night faded a bit. Then he would return to the Ravine and resume his wait for the Great One.

As the boy sat there he could not stop it, not now. It started with the voice whispering to him again, the voice of Aravella his Sister the Angel communicating with him from the Sky. It was his final memory of her, the last days he saw her, the One Sleep comprising her sixteenth Birthday Celebration and the One Sleep after. And he had his wits about him, enough to recall the Two Sleeps in their entirety.

14

The 16th Birthday Party for Aravella on the beach by the Port was stupendous. It took place at the Cantina de Playa. The wife of Zosimus the Fisherman had helped Aravella prepare the fiesta. Tables were festively arranged on the beach with candles and colorful tablecloths. There were multi-colored Christmas-type lights rimming the roof of the cantina and balloons suspended of pink and white.

The seamstress also helped Aravella design the most beautiful dress for which the birthday girl had saved up her hard-earned money. The flamenco-style dress was white with a stretchy bodice and side zip, tight to the torso. The circular skirt was enormous with gorgeous flowing panels, accentuated by a bright scarlet band frilled at the hemline. The hand-sewn creation was made of silk and it swished and swayed when Aravella walked in her red high heels. Her raven locks were tacked in a Spanish chignon bun, with red flowers—Poinsettias—attached; she had small ruby red drop down earrings and matching thin necklace. She was tanned and glowing like the sun for her big night and she could not have looked more beautiful, so much so, that when Gonzalo saw her he was filled with Happiness.

The birthday girl had invited all her friends from previous schools, even one girl from the Orphanage, Violeta, who had recently gotten in touch with her. Violeta was older, 21, and after considerable therapy, she had survived the challenging days with the proprietor of the Orphanage and was now going to college in Barcelona. She was happy again and prideful. Aravella designed a dress for her too—Spanish-styled with panels of ruffles cascading down in a unique sunset shade of violet to playfully coincide with her name.

(The celebration was contributed to by an anonymous donor who had mailed Pesetas to Aravella in a sealed letter with no note. No one knew for sure, but it was believed the unknown benefactor was the Old Man whose health was rapidly failing. There had been a determining factor. The envelope itself was enlivened with the bouquet of spice.)

The party began before dusk and this was intentional so the young group could enjoy refreshments and witness a gorgeous Mediterranean summer sunset. A DJ had been hired and he was playing an assortment of music, starting with some Spanish guitar followed by soothing Café del Mar-style ambient music to initiate the evening. In addition to girlfriends, Aravella invited a select group of well-mannered attractive boys—to dance with of course! But there was one boy to be seated next to Aravella, and one boy only—Gonzalo.

Once the sun faded below the horizon with the sky streaming with brilliant hues—fuchsia, pink, violet, purple, red, and orange—the group settled at the beach tables. They feasted on mixed paella: a Valencian rice dish combining seafood, prawns and mussels in their shells, and meat, chunks of beef and chorizo sausage, enhanced with numerous seasonings, saffron, onions, and garlic. For this occasion there were two paella dishes prepared, one spicy, which the birthday girl preferred.

Several of the girls took sips of sangria too. Arturo the barman at the cantina would not serve minors, but as he had known Aravella most of her life, somehow, some way, a docile mix of the fruit-filled wine beverage was magically left in a pitcher on a table behind the cantina along with a stack of plastic cups. Violeta of course was of drinking age and she was able to enjoy champagne directly from the bar.

Once night fell, a birthday cake was presented (with sixteen flaming candles spiritedly extinguished with the help of Aravella's young lungs) and the DJ shifted his playlist to electronic dance music, known to the clubs of Barcelona and Ibiza— popular and familiar selections that only boosted the enthusiasm of the youths. The group danced on the beach to the upbeat sounds. Aravella danced and danced, experiencing the time of her life. She even had Gonzalo join her, each time to rousing applause. There was one boy on whom she had a crush—Eduardo Sanchez—and he was the recipient of a good deal of her charismatic charm and warm attention.

'Birthday,' the boy said to his Sister the Angel several times and she hugged him introducing him to all her friends, most of whom he'd met already but didn't remember their names. The third time he wished her a happy birthday she excused herself from the small cluster with whom she was speaking and clasped Gonzalo's hand, removed her heels, and steered the boy to the water's edge, a private union between the two of them.

'Are you having a nice time?'

'Happy.'

'I could not have asked for a better night. Know why I chose this location to have my party? On the Sea?'

The boy shook.

'Well, the water and the beach are beautiful of course any time. But I wanted the serenity. And peace. You know? And I don't want to give you another science lesson, not now— but—all Living Beings originally, millions of years ago, came from the Sea. Are you aware of that?'

He shook again. 'The Sea.'

'Yes. And for this reason when we're at the sea, or the ocean, or on a lake, or on a boat, we as living organisms, feel a sense of calm. It's because the mind and body are at peace when close to the water. Because we are made of water. And we grown in water before we are born. And our waters are in harmony with the sea and they compliment each other when we are in each other's presence. This reduces stress and tension.

'Here's the science. Water is composed of tiny molecules and negatively and positively charged ions. It's those charged ions in the water that produce the calming effect.' She paused. 'From whence we came—' she added as an afterthought, more for herself than anything.

She laughed a marvelous release, that of a girl who was beyond her years; she had become a woman early, even before this night. But now her 16th birthday was the peak of her life experience to date and she was radiating the goodness of life and this special aura glittered to all and highlighted the perceptions of all the rewards her goodness would bring her. The future for this talented, selfless, loving young woman could not have been brighter; the sky was the limit.

'Here I was not trying to teach you a lesson—and what am I doing? Teaching you a lesson!' she guffawed. 'Don't worry, it's not a Big Thing—'

She hugged her brother and kissed him. 'We have always had our best times by the water, haven't we?'

The boy nodded with a smile and she looped her arm in his and they strode back up the beach to rejoin the festivities.

Tuko drifted in to the party smelling like hashish and immediately sidled up to the bar. He came without Sama that was his habit but this time his 'fiance' had returned home for a week to confer with her family, to discuss the 'future' with this man. Eventually Tuko congratulated Aravella, planting a kiss on her cheek that she accepted neutrally. He tried to embrace her too, but she stiffened in reverse so he could not. Then he shuffled back to the bar and remained there drinking shots of tequila. When he spied Violeta approaching and then wait patiently for an order, he moseyed up and introduced himself.

The moment of unrest came when Aravella was seated at a candlelit table furthest from the cantina and closest to shore having a private chat with Eduardo. She was flirting and laughing. She was a little tipsy too from the cups of sangria secretly fetched for her. As it happened, when she looked up she was stunned if not startled and not in a positive way. Her heart leapt, only held in place by her rib cage. She had sighted the silky predator eyes of an uninvited, unwanted guest, Don Pepe. Two of his swarthy henchmen Gonzalo had witnessed at the finca were advancing behind. And the unwanted presence was carving a direct path her way.

'I came to wish you a happy birthday,' he said in his raspy, throaty voice, overdone by tobacco products, alcohol, and most narcotics under the sun. 'Congratulations.'

Eduardo eyed her uncertainly, but the gay atmosphere forced Aravella to be gracious. 'Gracias—' she said measuredly.

'You've grown up to be a beautiful young woman.'

She nodded anemically while her pulse fired. The man of ill repute lit up a cigarette then, taking his time.

'Your father and I are old friends—'

She said nothing.

'I would like to give you a present.' His henchman at the ready reached forward and handed him the sapphire velvet box and Don Pepe extended it to her.

'Perdon. I cannot accept.'

'Please. It's your birthday. I never attend a birthday party empty-handed.'

'No, I'm sorry.'

Before he could finish his next sentence, Aravella excused herself to Eduardo and got up from the table and marched a deliberate path to the bar, her heels clacking loudly, an intoned gait of disturbance. She was burning from within.

Tuko was chatting with a smiley Violeta who'd had several champagnes already. Aravella's long lost friend was beginning to sway and slur some words. Tuko ordered her another glass.

'How could you bring them here?' Aravella fired at him.

'Aravella. Be polite,' he said sternly. 'It's a party—'

'Yes—my party,' she whispered harshly. 'That I saved up for and planned on my own—'

Zosimus the Fisherman who was standing nearby observed the disagreement. It was of little surprise to him that Tuko had not contributed anything, even his time, to the fiesta.

'They were not invited. Please ask them to leave—'

'Keep your voice down,' Tuko warned.

'Now!—'

'They're my friends. I invited them to your 16th birthday party—'

'You ask them or I will tell them—'

'Don't be rude, Aravella. I'm your father and—'

'I'm your pay check!'

Violeta was coherent enough to see this exchange was headed in an unsightly, perhaps regrettable direction. She clasped Aravella by the arm and quickly maneuvered her onward through the crowd to quell the tension.

'Gracias! Father!' she added sarcastic as she was pulled away.

'Don't ruin your night, amor ...' Violeta consoled her.

'Can you believe him? ... He brought those pigs!'

'It's not worth it ...'

'You shouldn't talk to him either—he's one of them!'

The boy observed as Violeta guided an infuriated Aravella for a walk down the shore in an attempt to calm her. They both removed shoes so the heels would not dig into the sand. Amid the party swirl, Gonzalo settled in a chair and gazed out at the two of them. Aravella took in several deep breaths to calm herself. After several minutes, the two returned to the Celebration. Aravella instructed her brother to head home with Tuko. She hugged him for an extended period and kissed him too, a fierce smack on the cheek of enduring love and adoration.

Her composure restored, Aravella swished past the tables, found Eduardo dancing with a cluster of revelers, grabbed his hand, and pulled him from the throng and they carved a direct line down toward the water.

From the cantina, Gonzalo watched the handsome Young Man and the Birthday girl as they walked along the Shoreline, her Shoes in hand. As they shrunk in the distance, Eduardo clasped Aravella's free hand and they continued onward along the shore disappearing beyond the jetty. To this day there is speculation as to what happened. But it is safe to say Aravella was very happy to be in the young man's company.

The boy got in to the van along with Violeta as Tuko had promised her transport to the rail station to catch her train back to Barcelona. Tuko had a brief chat with Don Pepe and his henchmen before getting behind the wheel. Then he started up the vehicle.

'Let's stop by the after party—'

'There's an after party?'

'In a beautiful villa. Everyone's coming now.'

'But my train leaves shortly—'

'Aravella would be disappointed if you left early. I can drive you to Barca too—'

Having remembered what Aravella said about her Father, Violeta declined the offer but made him promise he would take her to the platform an hour later for the next departure. She was tipsy of course and unsuspecting. She reached back and held the boy's hand affectionately.

At the entrance to Don Pepe's finca, the guard opened the retractable gate and let the van pass through. Violeta got out and was greeted by Juno the Portuguese man servant who summoned her in and immediately proposed a house tour. She was too consumed and distracted by the villa's opulence during her tour of the house to wonder what happened to Tuko and the boy. Beyond the candlelit patio, there were several African girls in evening dresses sipping champagne by the glowing pool. Violeta was then served a flute from a tray and absorbed the elegant surroundings and atmosphere.

The boy was fast asleep when Aravella tiptoed in with her red shoes in hand and spread the baby door to his closet-sized room. Her hair was no longer tightly tacked in the chignon; it was mussed and cascading to her shoulders. As the boy sat up she put her finger to her mouth gesturing to keep quiet. Like a cat she stepped noiselessly into her bedroom.

Moments later, the boy heard a loud discussion. Tuko had been waiting up for her. An argument ensued.

Aravella who could no longer hold her tongue resented now any authority the man who called himself her father tried to impose upon her. Tuko was scolding her for coming in late and was rifling questions at her. 'Who were you with? What's his name? What did he do to you?'

The boy could hear every word.

'It's none of your business!' she sent back defiantly, her voice raised.

'It is my business! I'm your Father!'

'You are not my father. You're a fake!'

'You're drunk!'

'Everything about you is a fake—'

'And you've been kissing boys! And what else—?'

'You have a fake family! All for money!!!' she shouted.

'Watch your mouth, little concha!'

Then the young, but fiercely independent and spirited girl who was increasingly feeling the strength of modern womanhood could hold back no more. And she unleashed the load that was roiling within her interior, the poisonous lava boiling inside and paining her for years with regard to her false Father and his corrupt ways. The chemicals in her gut had changed. There was no going back now.

'You are selfish! And cheap! You buy terrible food and keep him in a closet! You don't care about us!—me or Gonzalo! You never have!!! But it's worse—.'

The boy could not see them but if he had he would have witnessed Tuko cowering in a corner enduring the barrage, like a cornered animal, witnessing the strength of a smarter, superior species. He knew Aravella had his number and he hesitated purposefully, allowing sufficient time to plan a strategy—and he needed it.

'Those girls. You bring them here and call them *guests* and pretend you're getting them jobs as nannies! You get them jobs all right—as prostitutas!!!'

'The only one acting like a prostituta is you!' he sent back in a futile attempt to douse her fury. But he could not.

'How many girls have you turned into putas? Young girls with dreams! And hopes! How many lives have you ruined???'

'You know nothing of my business!'

'I know what you do! You feed them as meat! To that despicable animal! Underage girls of every color! And you do it all for Pesatas! And his sick pleasure! That puerco sucio drugs them and violates them and rapes them! Everyone knows it! And you call him your friend! And you have the nerve to bring that pig to my party! And his pig friends! You're nothing but a pimp! You're disgusting!'

The boy heard a scuffle then and he got up and positioned himself at the door so he could see.

'Get away from me!' his Sister the Angel admonished him, her eyes aflame.

Tuko slapped her across the face and Aravella screamed at the top of her lungs.

'I'm telling the Policía Nacional! About your filthy business!'

'Be my guest—'

He charged her again and shoved her to the couch and she fell back. 'About that puerco too! You sell young girls, you sell drugs, I'll tell the Guardia Civil and the Agente de Aduanas too!

He pounced on top of her then.

'Go ahead—he's my best customer!' he volleyed referring to the customs agent.

Tuko then undid his pants and tried to tear away at her dress, forcing his hand beneath to rip away her underwear. To his shock she was not wearing undergarments.

'Putita de mierda!' he fired as a response. And he resumed with his assault.

'Don't touch me, *puerco!!!*'

Aravella, who had the sharpened claws of a lioness swiped wildly scratching him through his eyes and across his face; she then coiled a gam back leading with the bone of her heel and with the leg thrust of a ballet dancer, she slammed him in the testicles, sending him careening back. Tuko yelped and cried out in agony and was temporarily stymied. Enraged now, he cocked a fist and punched her as hard as he could in the crown, knocking her into semi-consciousness.

Tuko scrambled into the kitchen and grabbed the serrated steak knife. He splashed a pan of water on her face to rouse her. When she came to, coughing, the cold blade was already pressed to her neck. Once she was fully conscious he forced her to rise up from the couch, the wielded knife still pressuring her jugular.

'Want to be a putita on your birthday? I'll make you one. And get paid for it. If you resist—in any way—I will kill the *retardado*. You hear me?'

She let out a gasp to breathe.

'Did you hear me?' he shouted.

She nodded still breathless.

'Yes, what?'

'I will … do … what you say,' she said in between gasps. 'But please … let me get my things—'

'What things—?'

'… clothes …'

Tuko immediately perceived her request as a stratagem; but then thought the better of it. He realized she needed to have underclothing—he could not give her away without. He viewed the situation now as a business deal—a very profitable one. He had contemplated this day many times before and always wondered how it would play out. Now it was upon him and it was easier than he'd anticipated as she'd forced the action, basically delivering herself to him. He was well aware, he had always been aware of what a prize he had with her—the most coveted—and what she would command on the local market. But he also recognized if he didn't act now he would lose her and a most generous windfall.

More important, with her mention of the Cuerpo Nacional de Policía (CNP) and the Guardia Civil things could get problematic for him—and Don Pepe too. And if things went bad for Don Pepe, Tuko would be in the most perilous situation of all. He knew of the fates of men who had crossed him. Aravella was too smart. Unchecked she was a liability of the greatest proportions. He had to criminalize her, to get her engaged in illegal acts with evidentiary proof. And he had to move now.

Things had changed for him too. There was no going back.

'You're a virgin, you hear me?'

She nodded without hesitation. 'Clothes … *por favor*—'

Tuko instructed Gonzalo to go to his sister's room and get her a change of clothes—jeans, a top, and some undergarments, choosing alluring colors out loud. He ordered the boy to place the garments in the van directing him to go to the Church to see Padre Miguel first thing in the morning.

Tuko escorted Aravella outside and to the parked vehicle still under the threat of the knife. With tears in her eyes Aravella looked at the boy a final time.

'Don't worry, amor. I will see you again. No one ever dies—'

'Let's go!' Tuko said.

'No one ever dies!' she exclaimed louder. 'And that's a Big Thing!'

She told him to repeat it. And he did. Aravella told Gonzalo she loved him then as Tuko shoved her in the front seat, snapping shut the door locks. The corrupt man who had assembled an artificial family for money was confident Aravella would consider his threat to kill the boy a real one—and that it would merit her compliancy. He was right.

Tuko settled in the driver's seat tucking the steak knife beneath it. He turned over the motor and steered the van across the train tracks and through the town's outskirts and up the hillside without further incident. While he drove Aravella asked permission to change her clothes. He ordered her to put on undergarments—'rosa'—but 'leave the dress on.' As told, she squirmed into the silky pink pair.

'*Por favor*, Tuko,' she called him now, pleading. 'Tomorrow. I will do whatever he wishes. For as long as he wishes. I will make you lots of money. But not tonight. Permit me my last hours. Of youth. And happiness—'

The greedy procurer comforted by visions of newfound profits said nothing in response and for the duration of the ride. Aravella sobbed, her tears rivering down her face and falling to her birthday dress. She cried silently though. She would not exhibit frailty or let him perceive any weakness. Ever. She would die first.

Tuko, always mindful of raising the stakes of business, spoke up finally to address her pledge. 'As long as your friend behaves too—'

The news was horrifying to Aravella, a second kick in the stomach. Violeta had already fallen prey to Don Pepe. She wept for her friend as well.

As it turned out, Violeta had not been harmed—yet. Don Pepe was busy with the hired girls. He did not want witnesses to see his treatment of the newcomer, in addition to the fact he could not resist hedonistic services already commissioned as in the prostitutas from Barcelona. The man's hypersexual licentiousness was in step with Tuko's proposed arrangement and the two came to an accord: that neither newcomer would be touched that night—as long as they were as Tuko promised, 'cheerful and agreeable—to everything.'

For this reason, Don Pepe made a most handsome offer to Tuko. But the procurer had a request; he wanted a first turn at Violeta. After mulling it, Don Pepe approved the final clause in the negotiation, but only after lowering his initial bid.

Don Pepe was secretly thrilled with the transaction, but also with the fortuitous turn of events. He was getting the town's if not the city's starlet, beautiful Aravella, after all these years; and as much of her as he wanted—without protest. As determined, he could wait one more night. And he would receive Violeta as a bonus. Lascivious if not pornographic visions danced in his head; an uncontestable triumph for the miscreant man.

15

The boy was still crouched in the jungle blanketed in the black soup of a deep jungle night. As the wide canopies of lofty Kadaya and Bengal Fig trees blocked the moonbeams, the boy could not make a move and needed to wait for darkness to pass. He remained vigilant in the hopes of hearing any sound that might indicate the whereabouts of the lost little Indian Girl.

Yet, with his injured mind temporarily healed, uncluttered and freshly enlivened, he was able to draw from memory nearly on impulse. He continued to rehash a recollection of those Two Sleeps. After all, the fleeting clarity he was entertaining allowed him to not only recall in more detail, but also understand better what had actually transpired. And with a boosted and burning curiosity, he wanted to.

As his recollection served him, after Tuko drove off with his Sister the Angel he could not fall back to sleep. When the sun rose he made his way to the Church as his Father had commanded. The boy stepped through the big doors to the cathedral and saw the grand structure was completely empty. He recognized then from experience to go to the rectory where Padre Miguel lived.

Padre Miguel heard him come in through the door below and he dressed himself. He met Gonzalo downstairs surprised to see the boy so early. He fed him toast and juice before sending him back to the Church to dust the woodwork of the pews and sweep the aisles. The boy returned to the rectory and vacuumed floors on both levels.

In the garden he did some light weeding and watering of the flowers.

Padre Miguel inquired about his sister's birthday party and the boy spoke but only briefly and in jumbled sentences. The priest moved them on to the confession booth thinking his memory would be stirred by the formal setting to which they had become accustomed. Yet the boy was unusually quiet. He didn't have much to say to the priest's disappointment.

After lunch, Padre Miguel sent the boy on another Field Trip up the hill. The boy took the usual route that bypassed town and led to the Path in the woods. It was a very hot summer day and the boy was sweating. He arrived at the villa of Don Pepe and squirmed beneath the Fence as he was trained to do. Then he waited behind the high Hedges for anything to observe so he could recount it later in Long Sentences.

The boy heard the soothing sounds of ambient music coming from the main house. He noticed two men—Don Pepe's bodyguards—playing cards at a table near the outdoor lounge beds near the pool. One henchman, the rotund one, had removed his jacket and the boy could see the shoulder holster and the butt of a Gun sticking out of it.

A half hour later, the boy was enthralled to see his Sister the Angel and Violeta emerge from the main house and cross the patio as they approached the pool. His energy and excitement was boosted the way a golden retriever responds to the sight of his master. His pulse quickened too. Both girls were both wearing white terry-clothed robes. Don Pepe was trailing them from several steps behind. The three settled at an outdoor dining table set for lunch beside the pool.

'Did you two sleep well?'

'Very,' Violeta said pointedly.

The group was served lunch, a selection of sliced beef, sea bass, salad, and fruit. Don Pepe's manservant Juno poured mimosas from a pitcher. The girls declined the offering for the moment preferring to finish their coffees.

At one point, Don Pepe leaned over and kissed Aravella on the forehead that evoked from her a shy smile. Moments later, she returned a peck to his cheek. It was enough of a showing to incite the infamous man to lean in and kiss her lightly on the lips. Aravella laughed. That led to an embrace across their chairs until they were locked at the lips for a long, enduring kiss. All the while Violeta watched as would a disinterested but discarded third wheel.

Not long after, the boy saw Tuko appear from the house and he joined the group at the pool. He poured himself a mimosa and then extended his hand to Violeta. She rose up and he guided her past the pool to an outdoor lounge bed covered by a tent-like structure from which white draperies hung and fluttered with the wind.

'Can we hear something upbeat?' Aravella posed referring to the music.

'Juno!' Don Pepe called out. 'Change the music. So we can dance!'

Don Pepe smiled at Gonzalo's Sister the Angel and they shared a laugh together.

The boy could not hear their voices well and he knew Padre Miguel would ask him to repeat what he had heard as was the nature of his academic exercise on the Field Trip. He crept closer kneeling behind the large shrub in the expansive back lawn. The conversation was then rendered perfectly.

'It's nice getting to know you …'

'And you,' he produced suavely.

'You have quite a reputation.'

'I wish I had as good a time as my reputation.'

'I hear you have better.'

'Oh?' he mused with a laugh. He was privately exulted Aravella was flirting with him. Her noted compliancy if not sensual willfulness and charm were bringing out his best behavior. Their interaction could not be unfolding any smoother in his estimation. Especially since the pulsations from her toward him had never been positive; he thought she detested him. His natural inclination with a *resistente* was wholly perverse and those were the types of thoughts he had been harboring for Aravella—for years.

But the young girl of exceptional character was showing herself to be anything but resistant and Don Pepe was no longer charged in a sexually vengeful way. Her coy but accessible and down to earth way had neutralized his lasciviousness if not dismantled his perversions. And he was enthralled with the turnabout, even his own. The man had been living on the fuel of short-term lewd and libertine unions with women he could care less about. This liaison perhaps was showing itself to be different and Don Pepe could not have been more thrilled.

As a testament to Aravella, she had the capacity to bring out the positive qualities if not goodness in anyone, even him. She made people better.

'A German philosopher once said,' she proffered, '*There are no facts. Only interpretations.*'

The dedicated academic she was, Aravella had heard the Old Man recite this quotation once and she wrote it in her journal and never forgot it.

'Precisely,' Don Pepe avowed. He was suitably impressed. She was becoming more important to him by the moment.

'Now. Will you accept my gift?'

'Of course,' she sent right back.

He slid the velvet box across the table. She spread the top from the bottom of the casing revealing a thin gold chain with a diamond suspended from it.

'It's beautiful,' she said warmly.

'May I ask you to put it on?'

'Why don't you put it on for me?' she posed with an inviting smile.

Don Pepe got up and moved behind her. He fastened the clasp at the back of her neck and planted a kiss on her nape too. Then he poured her a mimosa and she took it.

'Let's toast. To your interpretation—'

'And yours,' she countered raising her glass though she did not drink.

'Don't you like champagne?'

'Yes. But I had sangria last night. I'm a little—'

'Hungover?' he posed with another indulgent laugh.

'I'll bring it to the pool. A swim will wake me …'

'At your leisure,' he said.

She hesitated. 'But not with an audience—' she said cautiously, indicating his bodyguards.

'You mean Kiko and Raoul? They work for me. They've seen everything.'

'Not me,' she noted suggestively, as if a naked swim was on her mind—already.

The loaded remark excited the man, prompting him to revert to his lewdness and envision the gift he was about to receive. Implied though was once again something he wasn't used to; there was an attractive bashfulness in her character too and an integrity which enhanced the gift's immediate value; it made him feel special in a way. That what she possessed beneath the robe was too good for an audience. Yet he was welcomed to it, as in, the chosen one. He was decidedly honored. And completely aroused. When it came right down to it now, he didn't want his thugs eyeballing her either.

Don Pepe smiled warmly. So did she.

'You haven't forgotten my age, have you?' she feathered with a sparkle in her eye.

'No,' he said politely, though silently he was basking in his landslide victory and luck once again.

The man let out a whistle communicating with his men like they were trained dogs. They both stood up to attention and Don Pepe gave a short wave of the hand and the men moved off and into the main house—to ogle the security camera monitors of course.

'And turn everything off!' he commanded almost on response cue to the bodyguards' most certain kinky meditations and intentions. On this point however they would silently not comply; not with this young girl as a showcase. They would let the cameras roll, a decided perk of their employment in the profligate household.

'Gracias,' she said. 'Sorry, I'm still shy.'

'You're sixteen. You should be,' he said. Don Pepe was indulgent enough in his own psychosis still that he wanted to hear the words aloud. It was an aberrant way to pinch himself, that this twisted miracle was really taking place.

'What do those men do for you?'

'They're friends really. But they protect me.'

'Do you need protection?'

'Everyone needs protection. Even you.'

'Are you going to protect me?'

'With my life,' he said.

Aravella smiled wryly, a showing she was pleased with the answer in some way. 'You care for me, don't you?'

'No. *Te amo.*'

'Why? You don't really know me—'

'I know more than you think. I've watched you, I've seen you grow up. And become a woman. Before my own eyes. There is no mystery to you. Which is important to a man like me. Though you are mysterious.'

Don Pepe caught himself just then. His words were flowing from his mouth spontaneously, words that seemed to reflect his true desires without the usual artifice. He was envisioning the two of them as if they could be a couple. And he was campaigning for it.

'But there are so many girls out there.'

'Not like you.'

'And you've had most of them.'

'I've made mistakes.'

'What's so special about me?'

'You're strong-willed. Independent. And very smart. Mature beyond your years. Because you're an old soul. And you love like no other—I mean your compassion. I can tell these things. I am an old soul too. But I got sidetracked. And have had difficulty finding my way back.'

It was the most honest declaration of himself he'd made in a decade.

'What happened to you?'

'That, amor, is for another day.'

'Have you found your way back now?'

Don Pepe removed his sunglasses so that she could see his eyes, the ones normally aglow like Caribbean waters with pirate ships. But there were no pirate ships now. There were sailboats, elegant ones, on calm, turquoise seas. He leveled his naked eyes on her and said it directly and with conviction.

'I believe I have. You could help me make sure of it.'

She reacted with the vaguest of smiles a moment, but then ended it on a collusive wink. The wink told Don Pepe his words had flattered her more and that they were floating in close proximity, in some way already linked. He had not felt this contented in years. Or hopeful.

Aravella could inspire those euphoric feelings in people. If she wanted to. It was her gift.

'You know, I've never had a man …'

The man would not speak nor could he. He only hoped she could not hear his pounding but trembling heart. It could safely be said Don Pepe was in love.

The exceptional one rose up from her chair, stepping from the table. She moved to the edge of the pool, her back to him. She dipped a toe in then eased herself down a step. The waist tie to the robe was undone. She let the garment fall from her shoulders and flung it on a chaise lounge chair. As the gift was being unwrapped, Aravella's naked backside was left before him held barely in check by the pink thong panties. Don Pepe took in her gorgeous posterior, producing a spare but famished grin of which he wasn't even aware.

Aravella descended the last steps into the water until she was in to her waist in the shallow end. She turned back then and smiled at him. He got a glimpse of her deeply sunned upturned breast produced tantalizingly in profile.

'Join me,' she tethered.

'I don't like pools.'

'… For me?'

As a response Don Pepe stood up from his chair and released his white linen pants. He was wearing black tight underwear, his form and contour perfectly exposed. The man was tanned and hairy.

'You make me do things I wouldn't normally do.'

'Normal isn't everything it's cracked up to be,' she said somewhat seductively out of the corner of her eye. Don Pepe was in heaven. She had that going too, he thought, an adventurous spirit if not a wild side.

'I think we're mates ...'

'Oh?'

'Soul mates ...'

Aravella cast an eye toward the backyard. Tuko and Violeta were lying beside each other beneath the tent on the lounge bed. They were laughing and chatting like lovers. Violeta suddenly returned a carved, penetrating look Arevalla's way at the same time as if she'd been waiting on it.

Gonzalo, still peering out from a squat, was taking in them both looking back and forth as if he were attending a tennis match. He wanted to call out to his Sister the Angel, but Padre Miguel forbade him from interacting. It was their Secret that he was even there.

Don Pepe made a running dive into the deep end of the pool and swam toward his prize awaiting him in the shallow waters. As he did she submerged a hand below and hooked her thong at the hip with her thumb and drew them down the length of her legs. She stepped out of the panties. Then she raised the prescribed pink pair hanging from her finger so he could see them. As he was lured if not magnetized to her she extended them to him and he clutched them with a laugh. He moved in close to her until he was a foot away, his eyes dancing between hers and her gorgeous green eyes and perfectly formed breasts, her nipples erect like hard candy.

As he made his move forward to finally take hold of her and consume her, suddenly, Aravella's gaze was seized by something above his shoulder in the distance beyond.

'Look at them,' she said indicating the pair entwined on the lounge bed as her hand landed softly on his shoulder. Don Pepe swiveled around, his guard relaxed with nothing to fear; it had been the best day of his life in years, if not ever. As he did, Aravella raised the serrated blade she'd removed from beneath the driver's seat of the van—the steak knife wielded to threaten her—and from behind the despicable man with all her might she slashed the blade across the animal's throat, slicing his neck apart, effectively slitting his throat in two. Had she had more leverage than just a hand on his shoulder, the thrust with which she exerted on the pull of the blade would have decapitated him.

The evil one clutched his neck and felt the warm Red Waters pouring out. He spun half way around to look at her, his face contorted with shock, and terror, his eyes popping, as the blood squirted and flowed down his hairy chest. He collapsed softly to his side in the water and what remained of maniacal dreams flowed quickly from his body. The pool turned bright red as if there'd been a shark attack. And there had been.

At that very same moment, as the assault had been well coordinated, Violeta drew a knife she'd spirited from the lunch tray, raised it high and with both hands plunged it deep into Tuko's chest. Then she did it again. And again. The greedy procurer tried to fight her off but she was drawing upon years of abuse and suffering at the hands of men like Tuko. Aravella had apprised her the night before of her 'father' the pimp and his lifetime's worth of nefarious conduct while they devised their collusive scheme. As a result an impassioned Violeta kept stabbing and cutting still, even when the profiteering polluter of women and destroyer of lives was no longer taking breaths.

'Violeta! Vamos!' Aravella yelled.

The boy did not know what to think. He was so startled he was unaware he'd stood up and Aravella spotted him.

'Gonzalo! Get out of here! Run!'

The boy quickly pivoted around and away to flee.

'No! Come with us!'

But the boy could not hear her and he continued running toward the only place he knew, the Fence. At the same time the bodyguards were tearing down the back of the house and across the patio. The girls naturally reversed and fled directly to where the boy had disappeared.

In the break in the high hedge, Violeta who'd had a head start, saw the puff of soil dust and located the hole beneath the fence.

'Here Aravella! Run!'

The boy heard the shots ring out as Violeta squeezed herself beneath the barrier. But Aravella, his Sister the Angel did not come. They waited and waited until finally they heard the urgent voices of Don Pepe's henchmen.

'Gonzalo—we must go!'

Violeta clutched the boy's hand and they ran through the tree line and out to the road; they stopped the first car that passed and got in and were motored to safety. The girl was bikini-clad, wise to have left the bloodied robe on the lawn of the finca.

Aravella never made it to the barrier. She never made it past the back lawn. She had been shot in the back of the neck while fleeing. The courageous girl of exceptional character died instantly. Gonzalo did not witness the tragedy of course but Zosimus the Fishermen at the request of the Old Man who'd become very ill, revealed to him the truth the following day.

Nearly the entire town showed for Aravella's funeral in the Church and Padre Miguel delivered the eulogy. It was a Celebration even though many people cried, the boy remembered. Even the Old Man whose health was deteriorating fast attended the ceremony using a crutch.

The Old Man told the boy outside the Church, 'Your Sister the Angel is Resting in Peace and she has gone to Heaven. And that my son is a Big Thing.'

The boy did not understand this or what had happened at the time. But sitting in the jungle while trying to locate a lost little Indian girl he processed the tragic days as accurately as to his enhanced capacities.

The two girls had taken the lives of his Father Tuko and Don Pepe and caused an End of Sleeps. He was sure of that. But he did not know why they had done what they did. Most importantly, he recalled his Sister's final words to him.

No one ever dies.

For this reason, he knew now it was Aravella's voice he had heard an hour before as he was passing through the Jungle brush. She must have seen his Torch, he thought; she was letting him know she did not die. It was the final confirmation his Sister the Angel had joined what the shaman referred to as the Sky Spirits.

Very few knew exactly what happened at the house of Don Pepe that fateful day. Except Violeta and Don Pepe's bodyguards. And Padre Miguel. The Guardia Civil never launched an investigation. The official story provided by the

Policía Local was an armed robber had broken in to the finca and murdered Don Pepe and the adopted daughter of Tuko. In what appeared to be a separate development, and was deemed as such, Tuko had disappeared and was considered a missing person.

The fact is, Kiko the bodyguard had shot and killed Aravella though he had not intended to. Yet neither man who worked for Don Pepe reported any crimes. Later that afternoon they burned all the security tapes and removed the surveillance equipment and thereby any evidentiary trace of the indulgent activities that took place at Don Pepe's. They raided the house of course and stole whatever they could and the raid was purposeful. When night fell they hauled Tuko's body in a car and rowed it in a skiff out to sea and tying two cement blocks to it, they dumped it overboard. When they first saw the man's body they were shocked to see he had been relieved of his manhood. They were concerned the castration would sensationalize the case and discredit the legitimacy of their staged robbery. Don Pepe was left floating face down in his scarlet pool. Aravella was found on the back lawn. The bodyguards had the decency to put the robe back on her though they pilfered the diamond necklace; an act she would have been happy they had performed.

The only 'credible' person not involved directly who knew what happened was Padre Miguel. The boy had provided him with a detailed account. But the priest did not come forward. He did not want to be thrust into any inquest of any kind. The boy would be involved too and the scandal would require further scrutiny, potentially placing their incriminating Secrets in jeopardy. Like Tuko, Padre Miguel disappeared soon after never to be heard from again.

The Policía Local and the Customs Agent searched the premises for any incriminating clues; as in clues that could incriminate them. They were stunned to learn the security tapes were missing and remained forever fearful damaging evidence may surface. Behind closed doors they found no compelling reasons to investigate the two murders further as it was not in their best interests. The case was determined an armed robbery double homicide and was officially closed. The Policía Local could live with that—for obvious reasons.

16

Batta-tat-tat!

The Golden-backed Woodpecker hammered away at a nearby tree trunk inspiring the Great Indian Owl to hoot in a series, twice each time between pauses. As darkness receded to a deep purple overhang, the boy could almost see enough of the Jungle surroundings to attempt a retracing of his steps back to the Ravine. He had *Paciencia* still and hoped the Fire was still burning and if not, that the Orange coals were still aglow.

The boy was settled at the base of a high and wide tangle of deep thorny Khair brush. He had chosen the spot so that he could not be snuck up upon from behind; the deep thicket of thorns would keep any predator away from the rear, forcing it to approach from the front which would enable the boy to at least see what was coming.

Just then Gonzalo shifted to stretch his legs and he felt an immediate jolt of sharp pain. Twisting over on a hip he saw he was sitting atop a prickly branch studded with needle like-spires. He carefully removed a two-inch thorn from his backside producing a smear of Red Water. As he flicked the thorn to the ground, the boy saw it out of the corner of his eye—like a bolt of Lightning. His head swiveled toward the movement and saw the predator recoil and spring and fly toward him, eyes flared, jaws cocked, a flash of ferocious incisors protruding, with paws outstretched, retractile razor claws sprung. The incredible leap seemed to last forever, suspending time, a ferocity in flight, a force of nature unleashed and at its finest.

The boy reacted, ducking and rolling quickly to get out of the way of the clawed and muscled missile and the Animal went soaring over him having misjudged its prey if only temporarily. Had Gonzalo not moved the mighty Jaws would have hit its target in a perfect bulls eye and administered the death bite. But the vault represented such a violent surge that the beast overshot and flew head first, feet flying after into the middle of the deep thicket of thorny brush behind the boy. The sheer velocity had flipped it over to its back, and it yelped and snarled in combined cries of pain and fury.

The Animal spun fiercely with the strength of seven men in the bed of baby knives roaring with a rage to rival the Monsoon. But the more it twisted and spiraled aggressively to wrestle free of the overwhelming tangle the more it became ensnared, pierced by dozens of thorns and spindles—a veritable quicksand of deadly brush. The predator, now trapped like a netted marlin, snarled, hissed, and cried like the caged beast it was. It would summon all its strength to ferociously fight the thorny death web and it would continue the exhaustive struggle for hours. Out of its element, having forfeited its element of surprise, time was no longer its ally. The light of Sariska dawn was coming too fast and so were the breakfast crews.

Gonzalo sprinted as fast as he could but the dark blanket still enveloping him made a maze of the Jungle. He charged to any void that seemed an opening, zigzagging past clusters of Trees, his pulse firing, the hair to his body standing on end; he was sweating profusely. He'd never experienced a fright like this—few have—at a time when he had just begun to be receptive to fear. Meandering at a swift clip through thick brush, heart pounding, he came upon the semblance of a Path padded by single-file treks and migrations of the Hare, the Wild Boar, Chital, Nilgai, and others—though he could not know that. As he crosscut the Jungle, traversing through the tallest Trees and thickets, and locating the gaps by trial and error, he Prayed silently that his Plan would not be interrupted or thwarted.

'Not now. I am not ready—'

Somehow the boy successfully navigated past the densest part of the forest and as the trees became shorter, the sky opened and streaks of moonlight broke through to the jungle floor aiding him like a spotlight. The first clue to previous passage revealed itself as he located the walking Stick he'd carved at the spot the improvised Torch had gone out. The boy reoriented himself, confident now he was on the way back. The widening Path also indicated the Ravine was near.

Proceeding quickly and to his sudden amazement he heard high-pitched spikes of what seemed laughter, human laughter; that to a baby or small Child. The boy redoubled his pace and charged down the home stretch, the final Animal access Path to the Water Hole, forearming away brush and dangling branches.

As the boy reached the clearing he came upon the most startling sight. The small figure illuminated in silver by the receding Moon and the glow of embers still smoldering on the Fire, appeared to be the young Indian Girl, maybe four years old, sitting near the Bank of the Water Hole. Miraculously she seemed unharmed. Her face was covered with mud and he could see the trails down her plump Cheeks demarcating tears that had run down. Her Knee had been scraped and she had scratches but she seemed fine. The boy's impression was enhanced by the fact that she was laughing seemingly spontaneously for no reason.

It was then the boy witnessed the second miracle. Out of the brush and prancing before her was—a Bengal Cub! It was so very small though it seemed to be infectiously curious about the little Girl twice its size. It would run toward her on the hop cautiously then dance away. The playful movements had caught the Imagination of the Girl who thought it a big kitten, like the feral cat adopted and domesticated in her impoverished local village home. The boy scanned the area in every direction; there did not appear to be a parent Bengal to the Cub in the midst. Thereby he put the sighting in its proper context; he'd come upon two lost Children in the Jungle!

When the Indian Girl heard the boy approaching she looked at him breathlessly in a frozen stare. Sensing the potential Danger, the boy rushed up and immediately took her in his arms and hoisted her on his back; with all his might he scaled the Dhok a foot at a time. The Girl began to cry of course, the fun with a furry friend cut short. When they reached the convergence of limbs, the platform to his makeshift hideaway, the boy drew from his special Pocket the last pieces of Bengal Dung. He applied Saliva and once moistened, spread the Dung over the Face and Body of the little Girl until she was covered in the brown smears; she cried throughout the process. He then held her close to keep her Warm, the way Aravella often handled him, he recalled.

The boy was attuned to the fact the Great One must be somewhere close. He also concluded from Aravella's lessons in Biology, with proper social inference—that—since there was a Cub, the Great One from the family line of Zephyrles must likely be a Female, a Mother. This caught him by surprise as he envisioned the Great One to be Male, reminded also Yamir had called him a 'son of a son.'

Then he heard it. The piercing Roar was unleashed with the force of a sixteen-inch gun, exactly as the Old Man had described it. Though the thunderous cry was muted and seemed far off, it was no less menacing. In actuality, in the language of the Bengal the calling out was fearful if not frantic. The Bengal knew if the missing Cub was alive it was in grave danger, lost and alone in a jungle fraught with night and day predators, from sky and land.

But the boy did not recognize Bengal speech intonations and thereby could not decipher or assimilate what he'd heard. To him the outpouring was merely an announcement of power and dominance, perhaps even a warning. A big one, no less. After tending to the needs of the Girl and making sure she was comfortable in the perch, he looked below and focused on the clearing once again only to discover the Bengal Cub was gone.

The boy hoped he hadn't missed his chance. At the same time it appeared he was closer to his realizing his Plan than ever. First the Footprint, then the Cub, and now a signature Roar. His highly anticipated meeting with the Great One seemed so very close.

The boy was enduring a flood of emotions he could never have been prepared for at a time when he'd just become receptive to them. First the terrifying, near-death confrontation with another savage feline predator and now the pronouncement by the long sought-after Great One, that he had arrived and was in the vicinity. He had gone from heart-stopping fright to exhilaration, having never experienced either.

The boy was thunderstruck. But this did not adversely affect him for long. He listened to the hammer of his heart, he could sense his Red Waters surging, and his hands and legs tingled to their tips. Never had he felt this excited or vital, so very alive—his adrenaline still boosting. Yet he recognized he had to calm himself for what lay ahead. This was perhaps the hour, this was perhaps the day. To gain a semblance of control of his raging interior, an enhanced situational awareness signaled him to revert back to what the Old Man (experienced in many Adventures as well as this very Ravine) had imparted to him, which had become his overriding mantra since he left Llavaneres and was rediscovered the moment he set foot in the jungle.

'Paciencia,' he reminded himself, his heart still stammering.

He looked down upon the peaceful, innocent face of the little Girl who was so exhausted she had fallen asleep in his arms. Gonzalo clutched her closely still the way his Sister the Angel held him all those years. This brought him serenity once again. His poise reclaimed, he thanked the Man on the Cross With the Brown Beard for answering his Prayers and getting him through the series of considerable challenges.

17

The maroon late night sky was fading to a deep shade of violet, iris, and periwinkle and first light was nearly upon them. He considered his predicament now and the Plan of action he must take in a logical analysis and well-deliberated cause and effect way.

He could accompany the Girl to the village. But that Plan was Dangerous as the Bengal may be nearby as well as the other night assassins. He could search for food for her; any predator scraps, fruit rinds, even tree leaves could provide her with at least some sustenance. He could wait for daybreak and hope that Yamir, The Man in the Olive Uniform with Stripes, might pass through again to rescue her.

He could also get the Girl some water from the Water Hole. Surely, she was thirsty. At the same time, she was now asleep and comfortable. He could not risk leaving her at present asleep in the tree—to do anything—as she may roll and fall out.

The boy decided to wait for first light, perhaps an hour away. When the Girl awoke he could then get her some Water then look for Food. While gathering these items, he considered her old enough to fear falling (rather than relinquish safety and try to suddenly Escape), the way a frightened kitten might behave. Maybe then he could bring her to the Village himself.

But more unsettling thoughts bombarded the boy. What if the Great One showed up now at the Ravine? What if this was his only opportunity? Here he was sidetracked with a situation that was getting in the way of his Plan, his Celebration and hopes for Double Happiness. This type of feeling had racked him the day before. And he had not enjoyed it. And still did not. He had come all this way, traveling so very far—to Cadaques, Ibiza, Sitges, Barcelona, Formentera, Tarifa, Tangiers, El Hoceima, the Rif Mountains, Gibraltar, Malaga, Madrid, Paris; the overland train stops to Vienna, Budapest, the Bosphorus Ferry, Istanbul, Tehran, Karachi, New Delhi, and finally the Bus to Sariska. (He remembered too the chaos on the Train—in southeast Iran near the Pakistan border though he did not know the location—when Men with Guns took Money from passengers, but the Pakistani Woman with Four Children who spoke Spanish called them 'bandits' and made him hide with her Kids in the Bathroom, the way he hid with the Dutch Girl on the Spanish fishing trawler).

All the places of his Journey came to him with his memory defogged and his Kaleidoscope mind no longer twirling, but restructured. He had exhibited much patience; he wanted to fulfill his Plan and now. The boy was confused again but in a different way. He was enduring more sentiments from the negative emotional complex for the first time—frustration and anxiety—though he did not know the terms. It was not a Happy feeling and thereby he did not find Joy in his present state of mind.

As he continued to hold on to the sleeping Girl he realized he cared for the Child though he had never met her. He already had felt closeness to this little person, along with a desire to reunite her with her Mother. And suddenly as if an epiphany was at play, the feeling became stronger and he began to untie another tangle of thoughts. He understood how a Mother and Child could be so attached. And this feeling must be the Love of which everyone spoke; the Love that his Sister the Angel spoke about that night on the Beach when they built a Fire and went swimming and she told him the Double Happiness tale hoping he would 'experience Love one day.' He wondered what the Indian family from the Village was thinking; that the Mother of the young Girl must be so very Unhappy and Worried about their missing child. They must have so much Love for this little person and now she was gone, he thought. Or missing. Or Dead and gone to the Sky Spirits. And thereby he felt Worry for the Mother too.

The Bengal Cub came to mind then and he pondered what the Great One, the Cub's Mother must have been thinking, her young one missing too. And that as a Mother, like the Indian Mother, though an Animal, it must feel similarly, as in deeply Worried and concerned. It was then he reconsidered the Great One's Roar. Perhaps it was not an Announcement to him as he first thought; rather the Cry of a desperate Mother trying to locate her Child. Just like that an emotional awareness had crept into the boy's psyche and a rush of sentiments flooded his cerebral circuits.

A newfound emotional understanding combined with enhanced memory inspired him to go back in time and contemplate the history with People he had known. Of course the warm feelings he had always felt for certain people he now suspected had been a form of Love all the time. He felt Love for the Old Man. And Zosimus the Fisherman. And of course he felt Love for his Sister the Angel who had told him she Loved him on a daily basis. He perceived it now clearly. Everything she had done showed her Love for him. He reflected on all the Hours she spent with him, talking to him, teaching him Words, and Numbers, and Big Things, protecting him from Strangers and Mean Boys, and making sure he was fed and was Happy. These were demonstrations of her Love. And he had never been able to respond to her Goodness because of his Mental Problems. That saddened him just then. He had never told his Sister the Angel he Loved her and how he wanted to now.

So he did. 'I love you, Aravella.' He was confident she heard him.

(He was reminded again then how Aravella had hoped he would find Love someday, the kind exhibited in the Double Happiness story. And yet that seemed different, like another type of Love, though he could not understand why. But he would not consider it now. He was contemplating the People he knew to determine who Loved and perhaps those who did not and he had already decided for himself it was a Big Thing and he did not want to be sidetracked.)

The boy did not have similar warm sentiments for Padre Miguel. The priest had done things to him that made him feel physical Pain in the rectory upstairs. He did not feel Love for Aziz either as he could see now the Pain he had caused the Dutch Girl. In fact, Aziz seemed to fit the Concept of Evil (he'd learned in his Bible Study Classes) unlike no other he had ever encountered. For the first time he could see why someone would want to force another into an End of Sleeps—that is, murder them.

In the same way the boy did not have positive feelings for Don Pepe so he knew it must not have been Love. And he trusted Aravella's opinion too because of how much she Loved. She did not Love Don Pepe, just the opposite. Therefore he must not have been a Loving person. If he had been his Sister the Angel would have Loved him too. But not only did she not have Love for him she caused his End of Sleeps, that he must have been Evil like Aziz. He concluded then that Don Pepe and Aziz were similar Evil types and if Aravella had met Aziz and he had done to her what he did to the Dutch Girl she would have caused his End of Sleeps too.

He remembered the Boys at School who had caused him Pain when they hit him constantly and hoisted him in the air by his Underwear. He remembered them laughing at these Painful stunts at the time—and he himself laughed along with them—but now he knew better. They were not his Friends and they did not show him Love.

Sama cooked Food for him, but she made him sit in his Room for hours and then she moved him out of the house and into the Backyard, still seated on a Chair. Waiting he learned was not fun. It required Paciencia. He did not feel Love for her nor did he feel it from her.

Then there was his Father Tuko; he had caused him much Pain, hitting him, 'disciplining' him, giving him 'medicine', making him wait, and not sharing his Food when he was Hungry which was often. If he had been a good Father he would have made sure to give him Food. (Like Aravella did. Like the Great One must have been doing for her Cub.) He would have given him a Good place to sleep too, instead of a little Closet as Aravella pointed out during their argument. It was stated that he was a 'fake' and did things for Money and not Love. That must have been true. And then of course Tuko hurt his Sister the Angel enough to strike her. He punched her so very hard; it looked like he was going to cut her in the neck with a Knife too. And he brought her to Don Pepe who did not Love. Why would Tuko cause her Pain and force her to go to a place where there was not

Love? It must be that Tuko did not Love either, he processed.

From these memories now clarified in his unencumbered mind he deduced that these had to be the reasons his Sister the Angel and Violeta turned on Don Pepe and Tuko and ended their lives. The Men had not shown them Love. They must have been trying to cause the Girls Pain instead, to treat them with Evil, he decided.

Otherwise—why would they do such things?

The behavior of these Men seemed different than the pack of Hyenas who killed the young Boar, he thought. The Man in the Orange Robes had explained that it was an Honor to be killed by another in the Jungle. The Hyenas were not trying to hurt the Boar and make it feel Pain. They were doing it for Food, to keep themselves and their Families alive, and at the same time, allow the Boar to be given Honor. As it was the Death of the Boar helped the Hyenas; that there was Honor in this type of Death. And that sacrifice allowed its Soul to go to the Sky Spirits.

The boy now finally had a clearer understanding of the Big Thing Aravella had been speaking of Nineteen Sleeps before her Birthday Celebration: Love. And that it was Love— like Good Thoughts and Faith—that helped the World, he recalled.

The World seemed Smaller to the boy then. His thoughts were making it Small, making it shrink, as he began to decipher its ways and figure things out if even in the slightest ways.

Sr. Carrion and his wife Maria José seemed to Love. They treated him like a member of their Family. That was Love. It had to be. He felt the Kindness in their actions. Especially Sofía's. Her Friend Massimo did not Love him. He smacked him in the face Three Times and it caused him Pain. The boy did not have Positive feelings for him.

For some reason Sofía Carrion continued to command his attention as he tried to consider all the People, preventing him from continuing. He had never processed the warm sentiments of Sofía as anything beyond that when in her company, but all of a sudden he received them now in a surge like a huge wave crashing to shore. And recollections of her on the Tarifa Dunes came back to him and made him digress from his run of character profiles and analyses.

On an August evening the Summerwind was anchored off Tarifa opposite the famous high Dunes close to shore. The Flames of several Beach Fires could be seen dotted along the beach. Hot Summer Winds—the same name as the boat, he thought!—were still blowing and it had been a good day for the windsurfers. The boy had watched them flying past the Boat all afternoon. But all was quiet and still now.

The Carrion Family was assembled on the deck at the dining table. The boy was serving the Pink Wine, pouring a glass for each of the family members. Calm melodic Music was playing and the parents and their daughter were chatting and laughing. There was much Love at that table, he remembered. He was able to identify it now. This Positive and Warm atmosphere was not like his home by the Railroad Tracks where there was always yelling and fighting; it was not Positive or Warm. Except when Aravella was at home.

The boy traveled in his mind then and thought how Fun it was to think of all these things—People, Places, and events in his life—in a new way, from a new perspective though he did not know the word. It was a completely different World to him now, with his eyes open to it and with a fresh understanding—of everything. It was if he had been in the dark Closet of his former wash closet room unable to understand things. Now he could understand things. Now he could see things. And remember. He felt Free.

18

And he could think whatever he wanted whenever he wanted. And what was relentlessly occupying his mind now was the time he'd spent with Sofía, a memory that had been buried. But the early morning bombardment of meditations had brought it to the surface.

After Dinner on board was concluded the boy cleared all the Dishes and helped in the Kitchen then he went back to his maid's quarters Bedroom and lay down. He heard a knock and so he got up and opened the door. Sofía was standing there with a beach Bag over her shoulder.

'Ola, Gonzalo—'

He did not say anything, he recalled. Her blonde hair was falling off her shoulders and she looked very pretty in her Turquoise Dress. She was summer tanned but seemed to have an even deeper reddish glow from sunning herself all day once again on the Deck Chairs. The boy knew that because he brought her things throughout the afternoon—Sunblock, plates of Fruit, occasional Pink Wines, and her Secret supply of Cigarettes she hid in her room.

'It's a lovely night,' she said.

'Yes.'

'I want to go to shore. To see the stars. But I don't want to go alone. Will you come see the stars with me?'

The boy said he would.

The two scaled down the ladder to the back platform of the big boat. The ship's skipper Armando, was waiting for them in the outboard tender holding the line, the engine humming. Armando extended his hand and helped them both hop on the inflatable outboard. The skipper then spun the small craft around and motored to shore.

When the tender hit the sand they both eased themselves over the side, Sofía tacking her dress high so as to not get it wet, holding her flip-flops aloft as well. Sofía informed the skipper she would call when they needed to be picked up.

The girl, saddened by the state of affairs with her wayward boyfriend Massimo, had not had a fun summer. Yet on this night she was excited and enthusiastic; she ran up the beach as if she had not a care in the world. The boy could not know that, but he did see her smiling a lot at him without saying anything.

'Vamos,' she said and she extended her hand. 'I want to climb the dunes.'

Clouds were covering the half-moon and robbing the beachside setting of any glow. The Bonfires spiked with occasional Laughter and the faint din of Music were far off and didn't offer any additional light. The boy could barely make out where they were going and yet it was not far, only the width of the beach.

Where the Clouds were not muting the Sky, the Stars were brilliant.

Sofía clasped the boy's hand and they walked together. She had the softest hand he remembered, much like his Sister the Angel's. She seemed to glide across the Beach too while he labored with Smaller Steps and every few paces he had to half-run to catch up. He looked down and captured the faint image of her Long Legs, how her Feet twisted at each step in the deep Sand to get traction. And when he shifted his gaze up again he saw it. It appeared through the darkness as an immense White Wall rising before them and running in both directions as far as he could see. He had never witnessed anything like it. He hadn't put together he'd been seeing these Dunes from the Boat for days, but up close it was different. These were the famous high Dunes of Tarifa.

'Magnifica, no?' she posed. 'Let's climb to the top.'

And the two started up releasing their hands as the incline was steep and challenging. The boy soon became winded. It was like climbing steep stairs made more difficult by the thick sand.

About a third of the way up, the boy paused to catch his breath and as he did, he saw his own Shadow emblazoned on the glowing White Sand. He swiveled and saw the Clouds had cleared giving them the splash of silver Moonshine, albeit at half power. Yet it still reflected off the granules of white sand highlighting their whiteness.

Gonzalo looked ahead and Sofía was nearly at the crest. Moments later, she called out to him adding a spontaneous laugh. He was huffing but eventually he reached the top and spun around and took in the expanse. He could see the Bow and Stern Lights of the Summerwind and the lights of other boats positioned offshore and anchored nearby. The warm wind was rippling through his spare clothes and it felt soothing. It truly was a magnificent sight.

'Gracias,' came from his mouth through the panting.

'You like it? See?' she posed with another chuckle, while trying to catch her breath too as her own lungs had been tested. 'I'm not so crazy after all—'

'The Stars,' he said.

'Aren't they beautiful?'

The black sky now looked like a special holiday blanket. There were thousands of yellow, white, and silver stars twinkling and glowing as far as the eye could see.

'Come have some rosado with me—'

Sofía had spread a thin fleece duvet on the ground and was sitting cross-legged. She pulled out the chilled Bottle from her beach Bag and he moved to open it, as it was his Job, but she had already removed the Cork on board.

'Do you know what rosado is?'

The boy shook his head. He was still standing as she poured the Wine into two plastic Cups.

'You call it pink wine and that's a little true. It's pink because it's a light-colored red wine. Let me tell you how it's made, if I can remember—' She smiled self-deprecatingly too knowing she had to concentrate now to recall what she'd read on the Internet.

'How do I say this? Ok—' She laughed some more at herself as she tried to organize her thoughts.

Under normal circumstances it would not have been challenging for Sofía to articulate what she'd learned. The fact is, she'd been recently deconstructed. The lovely Sofía was reprogrammed by an overbearing Italian macho presence that kept her off-balance with her confidence and insecure about her diction. She had been negatively conditioned by Massimo and though unaware, she was still accessing him and their relationship as she spoke with the boy. The Lupo had gotten under her skin; she had opened herself and given herself completely (especially physically) to this undeserving man, her first love. She still projected his daunting, narcissistic presence even when he was not there in person. He had been in to her too deep for her not to be affected.

Massimo made fun of her when she spoke or said things that seemed silly or dim and the gaffes would make him laugh. And since humor was derived for him from her seemingly ditzy comments and actions, she was fragile enough to let herself become negatively programmed to play the role to replicate those moments of joy for him. She compromised and undercut herself and her gifts in the process for the sole purpose of pleasing him. So she played up the 'intellectually-challenged girl,' because that was what he liked, that was what placed him in his comfort zone as it was all about him, another superiority junkie, selling herself short in the process. The regressively conditioned version of her was what he wanted. Yet what was positive for him was negative for her. For this reason alone they could never last as a couple since, as the degradation formula goes, she would become boring and useless to him. She had lost herself in him and it would take time to become deprogrammed; to rid herself of the negative conditioning and rediscover her thoughtful, kind and confident self again. So she could get back to being the lovely spirit she was born to be with the very unique gifts she possessed.

'I'm not good at explaining, but, there are the dark grapes, bueno? They're stomped and crushed and they have the dark skins, right? And the seeds, and all the grape gunk, stems, everything—are in these big tubs with all the grape juice. But only for a short time. That's the key. Then the skins are taken out quickly. That's why it's pink. For red wine the skins are left in for the entire—what's it?—fermentation? And so the color gets really dark …'

She paused then. 'Actually, you know how I know this?'

The boy shook. He liked Sofía a lot. The way she spoke, her voice was Soft and Gentle and she was not an aggressive, threatening, or demanding presence like others. He liked being in the same room with her and he liked the way she talked, as in the Music of her delivery. Though these were the reasons he liked her, he could not express them or even think in those terms. He just knew he liked being around her.

At that moment, it was the boy's great fortune to recall she had Kissed him on the Cheeks that one night and association memories never happened for him. (This occurrence must have been coincidence; that the roulette wheel that was his mind would have to land on an association memory eventually, like a broken clock can tell time once a day). The boy liked her even more now that he remembered that.

'It was a bet. With Massimo. I said rosado was a type of white wine. We checked Google. I lost. I always lose bets with him. He's very smart. I shouldn't bet him. Because he wouldn't bet if he didn't know, you know?'

She laughed again. 'Don't say I never taught you anything—.'

The boy smiled.

'In France they call it rosé ...' she added as an afterthought. 'But they do it differently. It's called saignée. Or bleeding ... Lose a bet and you become an expert—'

Sofía snapped her lighter and lit up a cigarette then. A silence hung over them a moment as she mourned her depreciated romance though the boy could not know that. The hurt was ripe and the sour meditations came and went.

'Come sit down!' she blurted, not registering he'd been standing all the while, too consumed with her psychological detour into relationship gloom.

The boy settled down on the spread blanket at the other end of the duvet. She handed him his Cup. He had never tasted alcohol. The thoughtful girl had waited politely for him though.

'¡Salud—!' she toasted and she had to lean forward to touch his cup. She sipped hers then.

'What are you doing over there?'

'Watching … Stars,' he said.

'Try it—'

'Pink Wine?'

'Yes, that's what I've been telling you. Aren't you listening?'

The boy smiled then and took a sip, his first sip of alcohol.

'Do you like it?'

He winced slightly as though he had sucked on a lemon. He was not expecting such a taste; it was bitter to him. He nodded however even though he was not sure.

Sofía laughed heartily and moved over to sit closer to him. She felt comfortable in his presence. Though he was considered to be 'off,' she didn't perceive it entirely that way. Though compromised at present, Sofía was developed in ways beyond her intelligence quotient; in ways people considered 'smart' were not. She had instinct. And intuition. But it was something more, something indefinable. She could see things from a different angle—the unconventional angle. And that angle when expressed came off as lack of intelligence. She could see the future somewhat too. These were her gifts.

Macho marauders like Massimo (though he was no galactic thinker) who ran on the fuel of egomaniacal and hollow charm would undermine her, tease her, overwhelm her, and in effect, bulldoze her and her gifts to the ditch. When in fact it was he who, like most, didn't understand. He was only concerned with her abundant physical gifts.

Sr. Carrion, her father, was well apprised of this imbalance in their union. But he allowed his daughter to follow what he considered to be the healthy impulses of a young teenage girl. And she had been selective—Massimo was her first and she was already nineteen. He was fully aware they would not last as a couple, that the relationship had a time fuse that was burning.

And that was what held the kind and considerate Sofía in her present morose state. She had given herself to this albeit unappreciative man, but once she had done so, the chemicals in her gut and her orientation to her life had changed. He became a priority. She enjoyed their physical relations. But it made her disoriented like would a drug. And she needed to withdraw from the drug in order to be cured. She recognized that.

But the Lupo wasn't the first to take advantage of her. Jealous schoolmates had done the same. And when it came to other girls no one could incite the envy more than Sofía. She could rob the boyfriend of any girlfriend in seconds and the girls knew it. So the female complex was always a slippery slope for her too. She had trouble having normal girlfriends. They were cruel to her. They shunned her. And it hurt her and set her back.

Over time Sofía became less confident about her gifts. And she shied away from exposing them. Or herself. And so she kept to herself. The slick Massimo had found the key to her lock. A grand seducer, the Lupo, like all seducers have a highly developed social awareness; the capacity to open locks by trying and testing different things—if one approach does not work then another might and with a full repertoire of possible approaches they keep throwing them in a barrage until one sticks or until the right button is pushed—the key to make them liked and appreciated inspiring a desire in the target or victim to have closer relations. (The proper infusion of humor is perhaps number one on the list of techniques for seduction.)

Massimo, like many Italian men, had the talent to open up the repressed Sofía with humor enough so she could enjoy herself, and laugh, and he could pretend to like her and what he heard. (The cliché clincher was to say 'I love you,' which Massimo articulated seven times, on the occasions when a tryst did not seem to be forthcoming.) By way of these age-old deceptions, she fell for him. Meanwhile he didn't care for her emotionally nor had he ever. Only the conquest was important to him. Meanwhile the chemicals in her gut had changed. To be free of him, Sofía needed to alter the chemicals again.

Sofía had always liked the boy. She felt some commonality with him. They were both underappreciated. And undervalued. And misunderstood. She was not fearful of divulging her unconventional thoughts to him either. She felt completely at ease with him unlike anyone she had ever met. It was not the fact that he was uncomplicated, spoke little, or was fractured in his thinking that was of course due to his condition. But at the same time he seemed to have an integrity; a quiet nobility seemed to exist beneath the surface of his compromised casing. It was a feeling she possessed deeply within her core, born of another dimension—her gift. Sofía could sense this boy had more going on. She could see it in his eye. And that it would be revealed in the future. Aravella maintained that perception too, but Aravella's prognosis was more hopeful in nature. Sofía knew it would be as if it were fact. To her it was fact.

Sofía moved over again this time sitting right beside him. She reached for his hand again and held it, spreading her fingers to interlock with his.

'See the rosa one there? That's Mars. The Red Planet … The rosado goes with the planet nicely, no?' she posed with a warm smile.

19

The Peafowl and the Grey Partridge were starting to chatter through the brush. The Bush Quail and the Tree Pie were conversing higher up. The Serpent Eagle had already claimed a lost baby Hare as it scampered across the clearing. The boy looked out to the clearing and the forms of the trees, the Water Hole, and the rest of the Ravine were starting to take their shapes and become distinguishable. First light had finally descended upon the jungle. The pitched sounds of the early birds caused the sleeping Indian Girl to stir. The boy pet her head affectionately. She was peacefully out once again.

While holding on to her, with his other arm Gonzalo extended up and snapped off the small branches that were in his reach. The Dhok had many branches and he broke off as many as he could gather. Then one by one, he assembled them in such a way as to create a fence in the convergence of the grand limbs he had inhabited for Three Sleeps. Once the makeshift barriers were in place he clambered down the Dhok and began to snap off Bamboo stalks at the edge of the clearing. He hoisted the pile up the tree and then returned to the jungle floor to gather Sapling Strips that resembled string. The Old Man had taught him this process in the Spice Field when they tied fallen spice Plants to Sticks to keep them upright.

The boy piled in his shirt as many Sapling Strips as he could find. On his march back to the Dhok he passed the Gugal tree he'd inspected earlier. He saw the slashing scratches again but then spotted three feet above a new series of violent scratches, these marks much deeper and wider than the original series below. He realized these were more than scratches. They were claw marks. But they were different. The ones below were nearly vertical. The new series were coming at a diagonal. The boy pondered the sighting and realized an Animal must have been responsible, if not two, perhaps one of the cats. But the marks were high up enough on the trunk—seven and ten feet, respectively— to indicate these marks were not belonging to the smaller cousins, the Jungle Cat or the Caracal. There were only two possibilities that came to his enhanced mind. The Bengal or the Leopard. Or both.

Could the Great One have done this? he wondered. If so it would be a third if not a fourth indicator (counting the Cub and the Roar) El Gran might have visited the Ravine and recently. Perhaps it had been visiting the Water Hole with its Cub and the Cub got left behind. Or maybe this was the work of the Leopard instead. He remembered Yamir asking him if he had seen the Leopard after viewing the Gugal tree. He must have been reacting to the Claw Marks. This incited a fresh fear in the boy. At the same time Yamir hadn't seen the Paw Print or the Cub or heard the Roar of the Bengal. He couldn't be sure but he was hoping the markings were not those of the Leopardo. He did not want his Plan interrupted much less ended. He hoped for the Great One more than ever. He Prayed again then.

The boy climbed back up and resumed with his project. He tied all the branches together and reinforced them with the Bamboo stalks. He then fastened the improvised fence to the bigger limbs. It took time but when he finished he would have the Indian Girl safely enclosed in his small makeshift structure, almost like a baby's crib. This would prevent her from falling out while sleeping.

With dawn steadily approaching the Water Hole began to reappear from its muted shadowy shapes and gray hue to pop with color and offer life again. A clan of Rhesus flew through the Bargad trees at the far edge of the clearing, cackling and snarling, playing an early morning game of tag in the treetops. While tying tight the last Sapling Strips to secure the improvised barrier crib in the Dhok, Gonzalo continued to entertain his meditations on that freshly memorable night in Tarifa, and what took place in the aftermath.

While Gonzalo was sitting there with Sofía atop the high Dunes, he was reminded of thinking about Massimo and how now, with a clearer mind and better understanding of human emotions, he did not have Love for him. The Man had mistreated him and said things to him, using Words he'd heard often enough, words that Sofía told him not to say, as if protecting him. The boy identified 'dumb,' 'stupid,' and 'imbécil,' but there was one Word he remembered more than most. He had heard the word before when the School Boys used it. He heard it from Sama too. And finally Massimo. He had always wanted to know what it meant and tried to remind himself to ask Aravella many times, but he never did remember. But he recalled bringing it up that Warm-Winded Starry Night.

Sofía was clutching the boy's hand still and with the other she refilled her cup. She sipped briefly and after enjoying another feast of the stars she kissed him on the cheek and placed her head softly on his shoulder.

'What is retardado?' he posed suddenly and seemingly out of nowhere.

Her head sprung up from his shoulder. The question had caught her off guard and she needed to give a proper answer some thought. She was not conscious of the fact that, out of nervousness, her hand had reversed itself from their interlock. Their warm connection had been interrupted and she unknowingly called back her appendage in response to the change in atmosphere.

'Retardado,' she said, 'is a word that means doesn't understand—'

'Doesn't understand,' he repeated.

'Sí. But it's not the person being called retardado who doesn't understand. It's the name-caller who doesn't understand.'

The boy said nothing and took a longer draw from his Cup, finishing it. Another swift but warm summer breeze flew past and through them. And they sat side by side again. Holding Sofía's Hand had made him feel Happiness, he remembered then. He had wanted to feel it again. So he reached over for her Hand and held it.

She looked to him, so very touched by the gesture and gladly surprised at the same time. He had never done anything of his own volition like that in front of her. Their warm connection was flourishing again.

Sofía moved into him and her head approached his and she gave him the faintest peck directly on the Lips. He smelled her Breath and Perfume that were pleasant and it filled him with more Happiness. She retreated momentarily and then kissed him again but this time—longer. He learned to kiss from Aravella who had taught him the polite greeting Custom with Females. But he knew only to kiss Both Cheeks, not the Lips.

Then Sofía drew back again and spun around showing her back to him.

'Will you unzip me?'

The boy had performed this ritual several times before for her, but usually the reverse—zipping up—and he always left the room right after. He reached and slid down the Zipper of her Turquoise Dress to just above her posterior.

'Gracias.'

Sofía rose up then to a stand and released each shoulder strap, guiding them down the length of her arms. The dress fell and she stepped from it. Spare red panties with frontal lace form-fit her hips and swollen rear. There was no brassiere to hold in the gorgeous breasts. She revolved around slowly, facing him.

'Look at me, Gonzalo—'

He did and his eyes did not remain in one place. Her sizable breasts hung high while cascading down, beautifully-rounded and shaped. Her slender figure was elongated as she was tall and curved to perfection. In the boy's mind, she resembled the Statue of the Goddess in the Town Square Fountain, much the same way Aravella did.

He remembered feeling warm then, warm all over his body as he gazed upon her. She knelt down directly before him and kissed him again as she untied his drawstring Pants. She released him and held him. He felt the Heat of her Lips and the Coolness of her Hands. The sensation was unlike any he had ever felt before. Her Lips retreated from his then and she bent low and into his lap. The Feeling got even better.

She rose back up eventually and slipped out of her rosa tonga and removed his lightweight pants. They collapsed back to the soft duvet and laid side by side kissing for a while occasionally feathered by brief warm gusts.

'Do you know about love, Gonzalo?'

The boy hesitated at first. He then tried to explain what his Sister the Angel had told him about Love, but he jumbled his phrases. She caressed his forehead and face, her way of reassuring him that everything was okay.

'Love is,' she continued, 'the greatest thing this planet has to offer.'

He felt very Happy. 'Greatest …'

'I believe that …'

Sofía made love to the boy of indeterminate age on the top of the Tarifa dunes overlooking the Mediterranean, the hot winds blowing over them beneath the sparkling blanket of yellow, white, and red stars, with the lights of North Africa glowing in the distance.

As their bodies were pressed together she whispered in his ear, connecting her previous thought.

'… And making love is the most beautiful moment two people can share—'

'… Moment …'

'We are making love now, amor—'

The boy was unknowing and unprepared of course, but Sofía guided him, assisted him, while imparting more soft and gentle thoughts, even complimenting him sweetly in most imaginable ways.

And then they stopped. And then they started again. Until they could no longer. Until it was no longer possible. They dozed off curled in a roll of the duvet wrapped in each other's arms—until Sofía's eyes snapped open in a panic a few hours later.

The tender came to pick them up around six in the morning. Sofía asked skipper Armando to not speak of the extended evening, but the loyal man knew already to look the other way unless his loyalty needed to be prioritized; unless confronted by the one who paid his salary.

On the short ride back to the main boat, the two sat in the back of the tender exchanging occasional glances. Sofía clasped his hand again gently and smiled warmly. She knew he was leaving that afternoon for North Africa. She would miss him. She missed him and his silent dignity already. She also suspected she would never see him again.

'We did bad things,' she whispered to him naughtily.
'Bad things?' He was startled and confused, interpreting her comment as if as if he had made a mistake in his Job.

Just then she realized what she'd said was too subtle for the inexperienced one to pick up. She had meant it, collusively, intimately, because she had enjoyed herself and the taboo nature of what they'd done together. But the boy couldn't know that and rather than explain off the complex subtlety she dropped it after assuring him she was joking and that they and certainly not he had done anything wrong.

'I'm going to write you a letter,' she said louder over the growl of the outboard motor. 'Try not to lose it, amor.'
'Yes.'

The parents were still asleep. But not really. Sr. Carrion had done the best a father can do. He had taught his daughter to make the right decisions. So the early morning hum of the tender was not disturbing to him. Rather, he found comfort in it. He was confident his lovely Sofía had washed the portrait of the Lupo from her canvas. Forever. And had been responding to and enjoying the healthy impulses.

20

The boy reflected then on the last time he had seen Sofía. It was at the Port in Tarifa when the Carrions were seeing him off as he was boarding a Ferry to Tangiers. The expressions on her face that day, all of them, he recalled. And how she had stayed away from him somewhat. He attached her distant behavior to the reminiscence of the night they spent together on the Sand Dunes. He understood better why she did not give him a kiss good-bye, not even the kiss on Both Cheeks. Because they had 'shared' that 'moment,' the 'greatest moment between two people,' as she had put it. That, it would seem, was more important than kisses on cheeks for politeness; but he was not sure. But in some way he recognized their night together had made things different.

There it was. The pressure at his mid-section. Waste Pipe One was thickened and rising high again in his pants. It came to him suddenly now as past events were quickly clarifying in his mind. This extension from his waist—the Male Organ as Aravella taught him in Biology lessons—was not happening because of his Mental Problems as he'd assumed only the day before; rather it was conjured by thoughts of Sofía and what they'd done in Tarifa. He remembered how it felt and how it caused this changed state to his body and what she had done to connect it to her physically. Because the Organ was more than a Waste Pipe he figured. It had a Second Job.

Again his Sister the Angel's Biology and Human Reproduction lessons (which she initiated that night of the Beach Fire and swimming, followed by home study) came to mind. That, what he and Sofía had done in Tarifa, 'the most beautiful moment two people can share' was how children were made. So 'making Love' was making infants. Perhaps it was 'beautiful' because a Couple could Reproduce which is how Aravella instructed, 'life happens.'

The boy was amazed. Pondering the surging new thoughts he noticed the Organ had shrunk—again. He had not needed to swat it away this time, like every morning since around the time he'd 'made Love' with Sofía, he determined.

The Concept hit him harder now causing new Feelings for her, for Sofía, with whom he'd experienced the 'beautiful moment.' He felt warmth toward her, now very strong. He missed her. He had Love for her. He wanted to see her right then. And share his thoughts, his new thoughts, and inform her of his Plan and hear what she might say about it.

Maybe this warmth he felt toward her was the Love Aravella hoped he would find 'one day.' And perhaps he had! He and Sofía seemed to be that 'Couple' Aravella spoke of, which his sister had noted in his Schoolbooks, 'who share a Connection, a Bond of the Mind, and a Bond of the Body too.' But that also, 'they come together like lines of poetry. And that is Double Happiness.'

Had the pieces fallen into place in his mind? Just like that?

The boy was not sure about everything it was so unbelievable, but these new thoughts circulating in his head were helping him envision things he'd never understood before. An overall picture of the World, Biology, and Love that was appearing, changing, transforming right before him, each Concept becoming tuned in clearer by the moment in his freshly fortified mind.

Had he found Double Happiness with Sofía? But how could there be without Two Lines of Poetry matched together? he wondered. There was no Couplet to signify the Love.

The boy was reminded of the Letter Sofía mentioned. He had never seen it. Ever. Yet he knew she Loved and he reasoned she would not say it if it was not True. And yet he knew there were 'no Truths, only Interpretations' from the Old Man's favorite quotation. He was getting confused now.

But perhaps Sofía wrote him a Line of Poetry in her letter. So he could combine it with a Line of his own. And both poetries juxtaposed would form the Couplet for Double Happiness; which implied they were a Couple themselves who had found Double Happiness. But how could that be if she was not with him? Without her, there was no couple to enjoy Double Happiness. It was difficult to understand.

Then he recalled the Overland Train ride from Paris to India. He had had to hand over his Passport in each and every new country. And when he eyed the Passport there was always a loose piece of Paper sticking out that he figured was part of it.

Perhaps that piece of Paper was the letter? his mind leaped to. But where was his Passport? He hadn't seen it in Two Sleeps. He had the Urn still, the Knife, and the Brass Pot with the shaman's Medicine and one dried Dung inside. Did he drop the Passport in the Jungle? Did he leave it in the Satchel? But his Satchel was burned as a Torch. Did he burn his Passport? And the Letter too???

Dawn was breaking colored in pastels on the Sariska sky and peach and fuschia streaks slashed through the trees painting everything hit with a pink glow—the beginnings of another perfect jungle sunrise. The Ravine was blazing with color again. The boy watched the Indian Girl sleeping soundly on her back. He scaled down the Dhok and began his Search. There was nothing at the base of the tall Tree he had been living in for Three Sleeps. He circled the Water Hole and surveyed the mud and the drier soil beyond. He searched the paths in the Jungle leading to the Ravine. Still nothing. He fumbled through the Bushes and Shrubs. Stuck in a pile of leaves was his book of Matches now empty and damp from the dew. It gave him Hope.

Gonzalo searched everywhere and then high up on the branch of a Kadaya tree he saw the little red booklet spread across the limb folded in half. (The boy could not know this but when the Rhesus were playing tag in the treetops it was actually a game of keep-away, the Passport the coveted object of pursuit. The document had traveled from monkey to monkey following the initial raid on the boy's Satchel and resulting theft of the dried mango spears, his remaining food.)

The boy shimmied up the first branch of the Kadaya, climbing further to snare it. But the piece of Paper he had seen inside on the overland Train was not there. He scanned the ground and kicked around piles of Leaves. All the while he thought about Sofía and their night together in vivid detail. He saw her smile clearly and remembered the soft words whispered in his ear. Where was the letter? He had never wanted to find something so badly in his entire life. (Of course with his fresh orientation to everything, most things were 'firsts' for the boy now.) He was entertaining anxiety again and it was not a good feeling. But he was getting more comfortable with it. He had learned it came and went, that it would pass.

After a long search, the boy climbed back up the Dhok and reminded himself to have Paciencia. The young Girl just then uttered deep sleep gibberish. He peered in over the barrier of the makeshift Bamboo shelter. As if she knew he was watching her—on cue—she rolled over. And when she did, there was a white piece of Paper laying there! Stuck to the Bark of the Tree. The Girl had been sleeping on it. Gonzalo reached in and held it up, a damp wad thicker than Paper. It was an Envelope and written across it— 'Gonzalo'—and he recognized the curves of the 'G'.

The boy was thrilled and excited. He tore open the flap and drew out a lone thin sheet. The problem was, he could not read. He assumed since he was now understanding the ways of the World, he would be able to read too.

But he could not. If he could he would have understood her words had been intentionally written in the simplest terms for him.

Caro Gonzalo,
Gracias, dear one. I am writing you to apologize. I fear what we did you were not ready for. Perhaps I took advantage. Because of sadness in my life. Yet it seemed right. If things were different I know you would be the right one. For me. I feel it deeply in my soul. But you have shown me what to look for. Remember always, love is life's greatest gift. And making love is life's greatest sharing. You are the most beautiful and gentle spirit I have ever met. I can never forget you. You will always be in my heart.
Love,
Sofía

The boy was anxious to hear what Sofía had written. How could he find out? Perhaps Yamir, the Man in the Olive

Uniform with Stripes, could read the Letter as he knew a little Spanish. He placed all his available focus on this.

The fact was, he reasoned, she was not there with him. That would mean perhaps she did not have Love for him in a Double Happiness way. If she did she would have told him so. And asked to join him on his Journey to see The Great One. But he had never mentioned his Journey or his Plan. He never even brought up the Great One and perhaps he should have! He was upset with himself then and it made him have resentment for his Mental Problems which he was sure were the reasons he had not divulged this to her.

And yet, he reflected on the fable. The Chinese student went on his Journey. To get a Job. That was his Plan. And he had left his new Love for a long time. Once he won the Job, he returned for her. They enjoyed their Celebration and Married and they found their Double Happiness.

Perhaps he could see Sofía again and they would Marry! And she did write him a Letter too which may contain her Line of Poetry—that he could Match with his own.

But was he mixing up the Story? He had always mixed things up because of his Mental Problems. Perhaps he was doing it again. And what of his own Plan? Didn't Marrying Sofía go against what he had come to India for? He was perplexed once more.

He was reminded of their last goodbye at the Port in Tarifa before his Ferry to Tangiers; Sofía had not said much to him, even kiss him on Both Cheeks. Before he thought that was because they had already had their 'moment' that was so much more than polite habits or behavior. They had already 'shared' the 'greatest' that two people can share. But in pondering it now, it did not seem right. That if she had Love for him she would have told him or done something to show it. He could not recall if the Chinese girl had told the Student she had Love for him before he left to see the Emperor. But she did want him to return. This request showed him she had Love for him.

Sofía did not do that. And yet maybe that was what she was saying in the Letter: to come back for her! Though he could not read he did recognize the word 'Love' in her Letter as one would remember a picture made up of short lines circling and straightening. And she did call him 'amor.' He knew what that meant.

Gonzalo realized then how challenging was Love; and hard to reason. Or maybe it was just he who didn't understand Love and everyone else did; that he still had Mental Problems and everything he had been thinking in the last days was another big mix up, a jumbling of Big Things, Stories, and School Lessons. Perhaps he was producing Crazy Ideas and unrealistic Theories and ill-conceived Concepts and things he thought were True were not; and that his Mental Problems were still at play—or getting worse.

* * * * *

[The boy could not know this or think in these terms yet, but he was confronting the challenges of being a human being invited into existence on Planet Earth; and as such, like all others, placed in the bottom of the deep and dark well of the human condition. And like people considered 'normal,' there in the Sariska jungle, he was scratching and clawing to try to see and find the light high above, to do his best to climb out of the well, using knowledge and spirituality as his ladder in order to attain a life of love, integrity, goodness, and enlightenment. His mind was no longer spiraling out of control, his memory no longer a Kaleidoscope sieve, his brain no longer a pinwheel that randomly spouted colored confettis of information he'd absorbed; he was able to listen, remember, analyze, infer, deduce, and reach conclusions. His entire Box and its contents, stored in the recesses for all those years were now available to him. He'd been blessed with above average mental capacities, but the gift had been blocked and thwarted due to a lack of oxygen at birth from a frightened teen mother who home-delivered him in secrecy and shame in an abandoned building basement unbeknownst to her parents, and left him in a trash receptacle—a cubo de basura—only to be found by the Barcelona sanitation department, a garbage can infant as it were; but his rescue had given him a chance.

Now, these years later, beyond the mistreatments of life and through the magic of love of those who cared, his mind had successfully re-righted itself after toiling, laboring, reworking daily at the molecular level; his brain was able to rewire itself, reorient itself to a point by way of the wonder of biology that the circuitry was repaired and reconstructed and able to fire and snap properly. It took more than a decade and a half but at the synapse level, it had found the proper detours and bypasses to outsmart the stunting blockades and derailments, aided by consistent rehabilitation techniques and teachings of good souls with whom he had come in contact. Aravella's methods had made the difference, her unconditional love rewarded, and her prayers had been answered. Had she not been there for the compromised boy he would have remained in darkness, his mind in the cerebral shadows, and his earthly experience relegated to the ditches and landfills of life where most evil mistreatments thrived. But she, and others, had given him a second chance, to have the opportunity to (climb out of the well) and find the path to enlightenment.

The boy had been right all along: Aravella was an Angel. And if exposed to the concept earlier he'd have called her a Saint.

It could be safely said, at this point, he was no longer 'retardado', far from it.

But it had happened so fast. What the boy lacked was the sagacity of experience to help him make the proper choices to get out of the well. But he was seeking, searching, like most human beings, poised there in the jungle, in a Dhok tree, and grappling now minute by minute, second by second with the intense life issues of the human condition that most take decades to undertake if ever confront. The fact is, he was better than most. His mind spiraled still, but it was a spiraling of speed and efficiency. A Kaleidoscope of brilliancy. A pinwheel of instantaneous recall. An uncommon matrix of home design. It could operate quicker, fire faster, recall clearer, and reach appropriate conclusions with enhanced analysis. His microprocessor was superior, his intellect undeniable and everything he had ever absorbed was available to him. He had not reached the level of normalcy once hoped and prayed-for. He was better than normal. And he was just a boy of undetermined age.

Though the boy had assumed control of his gifts in calculation and analysis, the area in which he still lacked was an emotional intelligence quotient. And understandably so. The wide range of feelings to which he was previously unreceptive was overwhelming him now. The influx of emotions never experienced had crept into his awakened state and he did not possess the maturity to handle them. Most significant and apparent, the concept of love befuddled him and it would take time for him to process—and only time could tell when that moment would arrive.

But the boy could not know any of that.

21

In the dilapidated shack on the Spice Farm days before Santoro passed away, Gonzalo recalled the Old Man repeating something he'd heard, memorized, and believed. And the Old Man was not mixed up in his mind. That there were 'no facts, only interpretations.' It was determined a Big Thing too. The Old Man told him that.

This recollection was important to the boy. It gave him the confidence to know he was not mixed up. The boy was seeing things, interpreting things, his own way without interference or relying on or adopting the perspectives of others. He perceived and deduced this was the right way; it was his own understanding of things that mattered.

But he still did not understand Love.

How he wished he could talk to his Sister the Angel. Or the Old Man. Or Zosimus. Or the Man in the Olive Uniform. Or the Man in the Orange Robes. Because they had Experience. And Maturity. Surely they would know if Sofía had Love for him. Surely they could read her Letter and find the Line of Poetry if there was one. Surely someone could tell him the contents of the Letter. And then again what could they tell him? They would be imparting their own Interpretations, not necessarily what was accurate or true for him. Or Sofía.

The boy concluded then Love itself was a Mystery.

Maybe the Sky Spirits could solve for him the Mystery of Love. But from what he had learned he needed to Die With Honor in order to speak with them. Or get the shaman the Guider of Souls to help. How he wished the shaman would return to the Jungle if only to try to find the Brass Pot he'd forgotten. Then he could ask him.

Then an idea was delivered to him mercifully as he had his entire mind with a full Box of History and Memories from which to choose. He had not thought of him in a while. But he knew he could talk directly to the Man in the Brown Beard. The priest had told him so and though the boy had become skeptical of the man, Aravella believed in speaking to the Man. So he asked the Man out loud in a Prayer and he hoped his Prayer would be answered. (And soon!) Because he had Faith. And Faith saved the World according to the priest.

At the same time he questioned this. Because Padre Miguel hurt him. And therefore the man must not have Loved. And perhaps what the priest told him, what he always told him had not been true. It was just his Interpretation and perhaps he should not accept it. The boy had identified the Sky Spirits and the Man in the Brown Beard as Spiritual Concepts. What was the difference? From his own Interpretation they both seemed to speak of and perhaps do the same things. They said Prayers, sang choruses, and they did Celebrations when earthly Animals died. So how could he talk directly to the Man in the Brown Beard when he could not talk to the Sky Spirits?

He gave thought to the young Wild Boar who had been killed by the Hyenas. The shaman claimed the beast needed him to guide his Soul and could not do it by itself. But maybe that was because the Wild Boar had already Died with Honor and therefore could not speak to the Sky Spirits and do it for itself. So it needed the Man in the Orange Robes to speak for it. The same way Padre Miguel spoke at his Sister the Angel's Celebration and helped send her to Heaven.

It was the boy's Interpretation then he could talk to the Man with the Brown Beard and have Faith that he would answer his Prayer. And he hoped it would happen quickly. And maybe the Sky Spirits would respect his Faith and hear him too.

The boy was fatigued as he'd been through quite an ordeal through the night and had not really slept. He was exhausted mentally too and he tried to release his mind from all the difficult analytical thinking and wait with Paciencia for answers to his steady stream of questions. And yet he could not sleep. His enlivened brain was firing away to new paths of thought, offering an array of logic-based responses and potential answers, proposing idea after idea to satisfy valid queries. And thereby the boy was buzzing, more sensitized than ever. And that vital feeling was most pleasing to him. In the end the boy did not want to sleep. He could not sleep. He would not sleep.

22

The assassin scout scurried through the thicket of dense forest and brush with savage intent. The overnight hunt had been unsuccessful and yielded little and the scout decided to scour the paths to the ravine. Its ears perked suddenly to the rustling of twigs and faint sounds of a struggle. The assassin moved swiftly in the direction of the sound, alerted further by the sharp snapping of branches. Moving in on the source, it stopped short suddenly, cautiously, its olfactory senses struck by a notorious signature scent. The assassin peered out from a thick Arjun tree to witness the uncommon spectacle, keeping its panting to a minimum.

The excited assassin let out a howl but not an alarm call of warning. A different high-pitched snippet, the special octave communicated a message that a potential kill had been located. Howls, cries, and whines from different points far and near erupted through the deep jungle as the predator missive was responded to and passed onward. Each and every assassin was a scout in its own right and the entire pack had been combing the environs of the ravine for prey, the water source its most effective trap in the beasts' arsenal.

The spotter scout unleashed another cry to confirm location and within minutes the pack convened from all directions and assembled. Together as nasty brothers they would begin to mount an offensive. The pack converged on the desperate animal trapped in the thorny bed, its body suspended and spiraled, wrapped in a near cocoon of vines and thorns. All attempts at spinning free from its overwhelming tangle had backfired. Its frenzied maneuvers had been performed with such a fury and awesome brute force that the more fiercely it tried to liberate itself, the more shackled it became. The two-inch thorns had dug in deeper to its golden rosette coat with its densely arranged black spots all streaked in scarlet, as it had wrestled the deadly web through the night and was nearing the point of exhaustion. The enraged feline had lost a lot of blood, its superhuman strength waning.

The trapped cat caught sight of the oncoming pack and snarled viciously exposing its incisors to intimidate and inspire maximum fear, as always. This was after all the fiercest, most dangerous predator pound for pound in the jungle. But in this case its angry growl and flash of fangs were hollow pretenses before experienced assassins that, like the ensnared feline, were soldiers trained daily in the art of death. They recognized easy meat and the enchained beast, though dangerous still with powerful jaws that cut through bone, was the preferred prize of all. It was the assassins' most feared enemy in the forest and they would exact their revenge—mercilessly.

The team of pitiless, unforgiving Hyenas unleashed their war cries and charged the immobilized feline and attacked. Whines and hisses countered the thunder and lightning screams, roars, growls, and gnashing of fangs. The noise alone could be heard for great distances. Langurs were already stationed high above nearby and the Golden Jackal had picked up the scent and lay low and concealed behind a fallen Kadaya, biding its time.

Though the feline was a thick seven-foot slab of pure muscle, the heads and snouts of the Hyena were nearly as robust and the snap to their jaws almost as powerful. And they had numbers. Snouts mounted to thick necks cabled with taught tendons began spearing, chewing, and digging through the prickly brush. When they reached the raging cat, they thrashed and tugged and nipped and bit its arms, legs, and coat. Caught in the suspended tangle the feline could not swipe or lunge or provide leg thrust to vault. The only part of the feline freed from entrapment was its fearsome broad and massive head, but it could not bend or launch its deadly points or even fend off. Its prized attributes—speed, agility, ability to climb, stealth, even its uncanny sense of self-preservation and escapability—had been neutralized, an unintended consequence of what had amounted to an overzealous leap, a regrettable misfire on curious prey the cat had been stalking for days—and underestimated. But of course the feline could not have known the total transformation in sensory awareness the elusive prey had undergone in those very same days.

The entwined one spit and hissed and roared courageously, invoking all cunning from its savage arsenal; it tried with all its remaining might to fight back, to bite back, but was reduced to the fate of a helpless fly in a spider's web—confronted by a pack of hungry spiders. Ten minutes and a thousand nips and rips later, in addition to the massive loss of blood, the trapped feline had been weakened unfairly and diminished fatally. This had never been a just fight but the ultimate jungle predator had made its living on taking unfair advantage. And now that dial had swung back around.

Its screams of defiance became cries of pain and the diabolical squad could hear the strained, desperate octaves, the pack fluent in life and death languages of prey and fellow predators. They knew it was over. Numerous muscular jaws sawed through the chains of thorny brush still inhibiting the pack from making the final kill. When the coils of studded vines had been snapped away, the assassins were able to get at the feline's body and administer the deathblow, tearing away the softest part to any male beast, the cojones. From there the Hyenas proceeded to feast from inside out on their most menacing and feared rival with relish.

Minutes later the awesome feline that had been menacing and bullying the Pánichéda for a decade, that had terrorized the Striped Hyenas for years, invading their dens and mutilating their pups, was dead. There would be no more clawing of Dhok trunks or three AM nocturnal stalks and raids. The adept, agile, mysterious, cunning, and stealth force of nature that was the Leopard, having never had a chance, succumbed and died with honor like the wild boar the day before.

23

The boy looked in on his Guest then and was Happy she was deep asleep still and getting much needed rest. He studied her pretty face and small everything and he felt Love for her. Her face and body disguise of Dung had dried somewhat, flaking in places. He had concern for her still and wondered how to handle the situation if the Great One appeared. He thought then to retrieve Water and Food for her so when she woke up she could have nourishment. But first he would refresh the Dung on his own body in the event he was confronted by one of the Jungle's many predators that could stifle his mission.

The boy clambered down the tree clutching the Urn. He advanced unsteadily his legs still asleep from hours seated prone in the Dhok. He fought through the prickling sensation in his limbs and their numbness. He collected as many edible berries, leaves, fruits, and blossoms he could and pouched them in his shirt. Then he made his way to the Water Hole and kneeling in the mud he blew into the Urn to ensure the last ashes of the Old Man were released. Then he washed out the Urn and scooped it full of Water.

The calls started from far off and blended in with the savagely natural setting. A team of nervous Langurs flew past the edge of the clearing with much commotion. The boy observed the group shooting up the nearest trees available, one by one, choosing perches high up as if to spectate. These were not the sounds of monkeys at play. Frightened suddenly, they were shrilling high-pitched cackles of fear. A trumpeting of critter chaos sounded off, desperate alarm calls betraying the anxiety; the Sand grouses, the Sambar Deer, the Nilgai, Chital, Chinkara, and the high-pitched squeals of Wild Boar, one call more urgent than the next, blasting from all directions, creating an atonal jungle chorus of abject terror—respectful lesser beasts drawn to attention and now poised on fearful watch.

The visitor appeared as silent as a ghost at the far other side of the Ravine. Though thirteen feet-long and enormous with paws as big as saucers it was made invisible even to the periphery of perfect vision. The transversal of black coal stripes and the dappled tawny coat dissolved any silhouette to jungle relief, breaking it up completely as if it just melted into the shadows—a phantom entrance.

As Animal alarms abounded the boy froze on his haunches and scanned around the Ravine. Cautiously he hesitated, rising up slowly to reclaim still-numb legs starved of blood and awaiting more. The boy twisted left suddenly at an awesome presence felt but not seen. Skipping a breath, he was shocked once he located the source of the silent energy and power, another fresh emotion he'd never experienced.

The boy's pulse pounded rapidly, a reflection of his racing heart, though he stood mesmerized as he took in the Great One standing stoically in all its majesty. Not only had the phantom crept up on him without a sound, it was poised there gazing directly at him, its ember-orange and black slashes once again blending harmoniously with trees and brush behind. The huge convex head hung heavily and smoldering golden eyes with black vertical slits glowed like Spanish doubloons as they pierced the boy's stare. The boy lowered his head and bowed slightly, a gesture of deference as one would to a God.

The boy paused briefly to take in the marvelous form of El Gran recalling the Old Man's description—Living Sculpture—the long body, firm head, and short muzzle; bulky, broad in the shoulders, back, and loins, with stout legs ending in the wide paws. Upon further scrutiny Gonzalo noticed a feature that caught him again by surprise. The Bengal possessed the Male Organ and thereby the Roar the boy had heard the previous Sleep was not likely that of a Mother. The Roar belonged to this Bengal, most certainly the Cub's Father. At long last, the boy had located the Grandson to Zephyrles; he had found the Great One, Emperor of all Earth's Animals.

A single lonely tear made its way down the boy's face; not an expression of sadness or fear. He had never witnessed such a creation. It was all the Old Man had said. And more.

The Bengal raised his head jousting his nose higher to better sniff the air and identify everything around including the boy. He gave a short Roar and a sharp twist of the head that did not seem angry; rather it was announcing an arrival, its power, and its intentions. This was Pánichéda, its territory, and no other creature could dare lay claim to it. The enormous cat calmly approached the Water Hole, its head hung low, its shoulders bunched, its muscles rippling as it padded closer, chuffing sharp exhales through its nose as it advanced.

The boy stayed in place and remained absolutely still. He was excited of course, elated even, but his heart was hammering against his rib cage as he watched the Great One creep down the muddy Bank while carefully examining the immobilized curiosity across on the other side. He offered the boy another Roar with a head twist as a warning.

Without further ado, the gigantic beast knelt low and lapped up mouthfuls to satisfy an overnight thirst. The squadron of Langurs watched nervously from above, a theater they had attended many times, a play of which they had understandably never tired.

The boy, thinking of the Indian Girl and her eventual but certain need for sustenance, faded back measuredly in retreat from the Bank, step by step, his eyes not leaving the Great One. He moved steadily and picked up his pace across the clearing back to the Dhok, clutching the Urn and gathering numerous Stones along the way. He climbed the tree to his hideout swiftly; he did not want to keep the Great One waiting or allow it to get bored and vanish as phantom-like as it had appeared.

Within the makeshift safety enclosure that penned in the Girl, he placed the Urn filled with Water in the corner supporting it upright with the Rocks. That way the Girl could not topple it and when she woke she could see it awaiting her and have a long satisfying drink. He then lay down the plant foodstuffs hoping she might try them. (The boy could not know this but these items picked from the surrounding shrubs were well known and considered valuable resources in times of famine. The girl would recognize them easily.) As a parting gesture Gonzalo gently rubbed more from the last chunk of Dung to her exposed Skin using Saliva again to dampen it. He placed what remained of the Dung in the Brass Pot and left the relic behind in the tree.

The Bengal was on its way to drinking its second gallon as the boy scaled back down the tree. He retraced his steps to the Bank of the Water Hole on the opposite flank from where the Bengal sipped. Yet, suddenly it hit him—he hadn't prepared the Couplet as he'd been busy caring for the Girl while navigating through the deluge of memories, emotions, and fresh perceptions of past experiences. He had played with his revamped brain like an infant would a new Christmas toy, albeit to make sense of a past life immersed in the shadows of ignorance, but also to understand the World better. The meditations had completely seized his attention through the night, a cerebral onslaught unlike he'd ever known. And now he was caught unprepared for the biggest day of his life, rendered speechless with not an idea of what to say.

Having satiated its thirst, the Bengal reversed itself from the bank and spun and appeared as if it would take off. But several meters beyond it found a patch of dry grass and soil the dawn sun was baking with warm light. Then it collapsed with a lazy groan and began to lick its outsized paws, unconcerned with anything else for the moment including the boy.

'Ho—!' the boy blurted helplessly from across the Water Hole, at a loss to think of anything else to communicate.

The Great One, golden eyes aglitter and made more brilliantly amber while reflecting the peach and pink sunrise, angled up and offered a brief glance for the boy and then went about his cleansing, disinterested.

'Ola, El Gran … I call you Great One … because you are … the Great One …' he fumbled reverting to speech patterns of the past, though this was different. His mind was misfiring but it was not because of any disability. The boy was simply awestruck.

Gonzalo was flummoxed. Here he had attained a private meeting in a private setting with the great beast—something for which he'd waited years—and he was jumbling words again and twisting things in his mind. The fact is, as his injured Brain had been reconfigured and cleared he had become increasingly sensitized which made his psyche and nervous system more receptive to the full range of life's emotions. Where he had been fearless and unflappable, now he felt tentative, unsure, and lacking in confidence. He was intimidated by the Bengal. So the thoughts that surged through his head were of a doubting nature. He began to question his mission. What was he was doing there? Who was he to be addressing such a marvel of nature, the Emperor? How could he even be worthy of such an encounter?

To add to the boy's uncertainty the Bengal didn't seem to care about his presence at the Water Hole one way or the other. As if he was not even worth the Bengal's bother or the wasting of its time. Feeling all emotions and with heightened sensitivities, mostly negative, he was humbled to the point of despair. What was it he had to say to the Great One anyway? And how could he not have anything to say if it really was that significant?

The boy reasoned that he needed to convey at least something. He contemplated the vast array of issues he'd been deliberating in the wee hours of his Third Sleep. He decided to just launch into a spontaneous dialogue to keep the Great One mindful of his presence. Before he lost him to the Jungle.

'I am Gonzalo … a minnow … the smallest person … Do you know about Love, Great One?' he asked in another awkward rush, too unsure of himself still to organize thoughts properly.

The boy recognized he had erred too. A discussion of Love was ill-conceived as he himself did not understand it.

He did not want to pretend to know more than he did. It would be a Sin to deceive the Great One. He was racked again with insecurity. But why would a Creature so magnificent want to engage with someone so unknowing? But he looks asleep, he is not engaging! But maybe he is resting and listening to every word!

Gonzalo was rattled. To prolong their meeting and keep the dialogue alive he began to spout off things he was confident he did know, but wasn't sure entirely as his fresh Deductions and Interpretations had never been spoken much less tested. He had processed these thoughts only recently, within the hours, in his own refabricated, uncluttered mind.

'I realize Great One that it is important to go out and see the World. And keep Faith and have Good Thoughts because they help the World. Along the way. And though I do not understand Love—it's a Mystery—I can feel it. And I know there are people, Animals, who Love and those who don't Love. And each Animal must be careful of those that don't Love, to beware of Secrets that can be Dangerous and can hurt. There are Animals who will give Pain and they must be watched out for. Though there may not be Truths and only Interpretations, it is important for an Animal to decide what Interpretations to adopt for itself. Interpretations are made up of Big Things and the more Big Things—Knowledge—an Animal learns the better chance it has to arrive at proper Interpretations. Once Interpretations are discovered they must be remembered, followed, and lived by ...'

As the boy spoke, the Great One was lying on its side dozing now, enjoying a morning nap, having tongued all four Paws, Limbs, and the Organ. At one point it raised his head and speared its nose forward and up, its head twisting to and fro, as if to recognize a particular if not special fragrance from the full and rich bouquet of a thousand jungle smells. The heavy Head remained held high until its desire to relax took over once again; until it reclaimed its sleeping posture and its Eyes drifted to a close.

'From the gathering of proper Interpretations a Plan can be made to follow. But the Plan needs a Life Force driven by Faith. That Life Force comes at birth no matter what Animal, Man or Minnow—or not—as all Animals are not created equally. Angels can help as they respond to Life Forces—but only if there is Love and the Life Force has embraced Faith too. Angels will look out for those Life Forces who show Love and Faith, to Protect them and guide them to carry out their Plan—'

As the boy continued to deliver his speech designed to grab the attention of the Great One, he could see that it was landing upon deaf ears. The mighty Bengal it would seem was not bothering to hear him out, ignoring him, likely considering his thoughts gibberish. Or boring. Because surely the Great One knew everything he was saying and had it within him already in a highly developed Soul reflective of his almighty Life Force. And perhaps he, the boy, was an annoying newcomer to the land of Interpretations. Or perhaps he had made it all confusing; or that his message itself was confused. That was the boy's immediate perception as he spoke while a full range of emotions, positive and negative, was firing in him instantaneously now like shooting stars.

What was significant was rather than give up, the boy continued on to try to communicate, and that he had the will to do so, indicative of his own Life Force that had always been there, beneath the layers of disconnected wires and preventive disabilities, a Life Force that had gotten him all the way to the jungles of India, and the more he articulated his personal Interpretations and heard his words aloud, the more valid he recognized they were and the more comfortable and confident he became. That he was in control of his thoughts and—himself.

And perhaps also, his Interpretations were valid for him, but not the Bengal.

What the boy could not have known was, the great Bengal, master of the Pánichéda dominion, had never remained at the Water Hole for any length of time. Ever. Nor did it lie down in the Ravine or any other Jungle clearing and make itself vulnerable to the Striped Hyena or Leopard or any other albeit foolish would-be attackers. Yet the Great One had changed his habits on this Sleep because of the special smell of the boy and the sleeping Indian girl in the Dhok. It was wafting off the Dung rubbed to their Skins, the Dung of a Female Bengal; a special Biological blend of urine and excrement, and thereby an unmistakable scent, and the Great One was comforted and did not feel threatened. In fact the fragrance was appealing and the Bengal remained there drawn if not magnetized to the scent. But it was respectful too at what it perceived to be its female counterpart and thereby it maintained its distance—for now.

'All Life Forces need a Plan,' the boy continued, 'and by taking action and seizing the right moment—Kairos—with the guidance of Angels and those who Love, and by winning Jobs and Working Hard at them the Plan can be carried out. Animals show their Love by treating other Animals with Respect and being Honorable. The Animal that Loves can be an Angel too. And maybe help another Animal, or Life

Force, with a Plan. And Protect it from the Life Forces that don't Love. And when it comes time for a Life Force to part from this Earth, an End of all Sleeps, after many Sleeps, an Animal who Loves can Die with Honor because it has done its part to make the World better. Then that Life Force will Rest in Peace. And its Soul can be delivered to the Sky Spirits or Heaven whatever the Life Force's Interpretation, to join all others who Loved and Died with Honor, because No One Ever Dies. In Life There is Death and In Death There is Life. And there is Love in between ...'

'These are the thoughts of a small person. A Man. A Minnow. A tiny Life Force. And that is my Interpretation. Of a Life lived so far on this Earth. And I offer it to you, Great One, the great Warrior you are, the Emperor of all Animals, on this day of our meeting, a meeting of two Life Forces who Love.'

The boy was prideful he had communicated his message. He had spoken eloquently in summing up his philosophy of the World, an Interpretation—formulated by and composed of Big Things—he had originated and concluded just hours before in the sleep-deprived overnight. (Aravella, his Sister the Angel would have been proud. So would have the Old Man.)

Yet the boy still had one challenge left. Though he was able to more than adequately express himself and his Interpretations now, he had not dreamed up a Couplet to provide to the Emperor, El Gran. He was confused and drained and he pondered it there on the bank of the Water Hole while the sleeping Great One lay prostrate in the clearing taking up thirteen long feet of the Jungle floor not counting its tail.

The boy decided to call on the one Life Force he had always relied on most who taught him the Big Things, protected him, looked out for him, and who had shown him more Love than anyone. His Sister the Angel. At first he spoke to her his head angled to the Sky. But she did not address him in return as she had in the Forest the Sleep before. Then he Prayed to her. But nothing happened and no Couplet came to mind.

So he settled down on the Bank and began to target memories of their interaction in his now highly developed Pin-Wheeling, Spiraling, Kaleidoscope mind. And he flashed through all the events, the quotations and sayings, all the Big Things learned, until the wheel of his mind stopped suddenly. He recalled a science lesson one Sleep by the shoreline—the night of Aravella's 16th Birthday Celebration—when his Sister the Angel had taught him that 'all Living Beings had come from the Sea' and were made of water and it was the reason the 'Mind and Body felt at Peace when close to the Water.' That the 'ions were charged' in such a way that it produced a 'calming effect.' She'd laughed at herself for instructing him on the night of her party and said it was 'not a Big Thing'—and yet he remembered it now.

It was an instinct based upon learned science that he should plunge into the water. He was aware if he went in all the Bengal Dung would wash off. But so what? he countered in thought. What did he need the Dung for anymore? It had been administered to his Skin to protect him from other Predators, not the Great One. With the Great One he could be himself.

That Interpretation however caught the boy by surprise. It indicated all this time he had not been himself before the

Great One. He'd been tricking the mighty cat, albeit unintentionally. His real Body had been covered in a Mask. The Dung of the Bengal spread over him had disguised him. In this way he must have been deceiving the Great One. He did not want to do that. It was a cheat; the work of an impostor, a Life Force that perhaps did not Love. It was likely the reason the Bengal slept before him, disinterested and bored; and why it did not seem to care about any of his Words or his Interpretations of Life. The highly developed Bengal knew to stay away from Life Forces that did not exhibit Love. Perhaps that was how the Great One perceived him; as a Life Force that did not Love.

The boy made up his mind. He wanted the Great One to see the real him, the authentic Life Force he was, a Life Force that Loved like the Bengal himself. So without giving it another thought the boy jumped in the Water Hole creating a terrific splash. He stayed underwater while he washed his face and body off, freeing himself of the disguise. As he did he thanked his Sister the Angel once again for providing him with the Knowledge, helping him pinpoint where he'd strayed from his Plan while resolving the dilemma and guiding his Life Force on the right track yet again.

Above the surface however, at that sudden spike of commotion, the sound of the boy's plunge and the splashing of water, way across on the opposing bank of the Ravine, the Great One vaulted high from his slumber and spun around with a swiftness rarely seen in nature, savage senses alerted to a possible threat, ready to defend or attack. Though the boy was no longer visible the all-instinctual and sensory cat noted the trail of bubbles and aggressive swirling to the water's surface and was lured to investigate.

The Great One, the grandson of Zephyrles, padded noiselessly down to the muddy bank of the water, its muscles convulsing, its shoulders flexed, and it paused at the water's edge not far from the rib cage of the fallen wild boar. Rather than get wet, it waited, and settled back on its haunches in an upright sitting position. It had a playful look as it studied the turbulent water, the expressions of a curious kitten, like those of his cub that had pranced before the Indian girl. The Great One had never looked younger.

At the same time, while submerged, the boy felt liberated. He'd washed away the foreign matter and was feeling peaceful and relaxed. He was mindful of what Aravella had taught him; how all Life originated from water and thereby it had a calming effect and he noted it. He could almost feel the charge in the particles surrounding him. It served to not only deliver him back to a state of equilibrium, but invigorate as well, like he was refreshed and renewed. In this moment he let go of his overtaxed, overworked mind and let the cerebral processor rest and he just floated there. His mind downshifted and became placid and serene, open and receptive. With no attempt to focus his mind was left to wander and roam and his synapses to fire at will. Or not. This cerebral surrender placed him in an imaginative, almost dreamy state during which he was gifted two new Interpretations that just presented themselves to him from seemingly nowhere.

As the boy did not force anything, it was the original fable of the Chinese student that came to mind likely because it was playing in his subconscious. The story revolved around the love of the Chinese Student and the Mountain Girl who nursed him back to health and how they achieved Double

Happiness by each combining Two poetic Lines and forming a Couplet—a testament to their Love.

But in contemplating the story the boy found an area of confusion if not disconnect, something that did not seem appropriate. Though admittedly Gonzalo found Love to be Mysterious and he did not understand it, he recognized there were different forms of it. Thereby he wondered, Why did the Love in the fable that resulted in Double Happiness have to be the romantic type as in the Love of two sweethearts? Why could not a Life Force achieve Double Happiness with another type of Love, like the Love he had for his Sister the Angel or the Old Man? He knew enough about Love that it did not have to be romantic Love or making physical Love to be Love. In the boy's freshly processed Interpretation, Love was Love no matter what form.

Secondly, the idea of Double Happiness had been somewhat corrupted; the Student never provided a Line of poetry for the Mountain Girl which she had requested from him. He had lifted the Line authored by the Emperor and matched it to hers to form the Couplet. The Emperor had nothing to do with their Love and yet he had supplied half the Couplet with his Line of poetry resulting in their Marriage union in Double Happiness. The boy felt the Student should have written something of his own reflective of his Love for her of from his heart—his personal expression—to be Matched with hers if the Double Happiness were to be properly achieved; and not borrowing from someone else. This made it awkward to Gonzalo—a lacking in respect of the couple's Bond or union. In addition words authored by someone else and lifted, borrowed, or even stolen, were simply a mild deception if not a cheat.

The boy exercised forethought as well. He recognized it could be stated about his critique of the fable—'but that is not the story'—as it had been passed down for centuries in Chinese history and there was no altering it. To that end the boy concluded he was not satisfied with the Story; that it was inappropriate and tainted, and he decided it was within his right to change it and make his own rules to the Double Happiness Couplet. His new rendition may not have satisfied the Chinese Life Forces, but it would serve his own vision of what the Love Couplet should be, in the same way there was a Heaven and there were Sky Spirits and both were viable and valid and a Life Force that Loved could choose either. And that his modified Double Happiness Couplet would have the spirit of the Chinese one, it was just an alternative version—his Interpretation—and he felt free to author it and embrace it.

But the boy wasn't done as his relaxed mind had an influx of more imaginative meditations, in the form of last questions. Why did the Chinese couple that expressed their Love in a Double Happiness Couplet need to reside in the Earthly World? Why couldn't their Souls have been released to Heaven or to the Sky Spirits and still enjoy the magic of Double Happiness? Because In Life There is Death and In Death There is Life and No One Ever Dies. Again the boy generously-Interpreted the Concept of Double Happiness and felt welcomed to modify it. Instead of a famous Chinese fable's version, he'd made the Concept his own and infused it with his own Big Things which were reflected in his own Interpretation.

While the boy still hovered with liberation beneath the water's surface in the Water's Hole's deepest point, his final analysis combined with a freely-associating imagination had produced a new and fresh Interpretation. And he hadn't even been trying to think about anything, it had just been delivered to him. But it all happened in water, perhaps inspired by Aravella's 'from whence we came.'

The boy's head broke the surface with a surge and he swam closer to the Bank until he found footing. He checked his chest and arms and confirmed they'd been cleansed of all the Dung. As he waded in the shallower water he spun slightly and angled up; it was then he noticed to his amazement, the Great One sitting with Paciencia at the far bank of the Water Hole no less than twenty-five meters from him.

The boy smiled and stepped forward until he was neck-deep, only his head protruding. He looked directly at the Great One and while peering into its glittering golden eyes that held the light of all of eternity within, he delivered:

The howling wind of the Angel's laugh, a beauty clothed the air in red and white and love without limit for a mystery beyond celebration...

And he continued with the second Line:

Fields of green and gold run beyond a blue winter's swine, spiced by Heaven's fleeting minnow and a sun splashed adventure forever more...

A Couplet had been adequately rendered, but the boy was not done. He added a third Line:

The darkness that may be felt, carries the stars' shared joy, a fresh awakening to behold beneath the glory of jungle's bite.

The Three Lines composed and offered to the Great One were complete. The boy had chosen a Triplet to signify his brand of Love split amongst three; for the two people who had shown him Love itself, taught him most of what he knew which enabled him to embark upon a Journey and carry out a Plan for a Celebration as proof of an Enlightenment. Aravella and the Old Man were unquestionably joined with the boy in a Bond of what he now termed Triple Happiness—for all of eternity. That was the boy's Interpretation and there were no second opinions.

And there they were, Bengal and boy, in the early hours of morning, the Great One's beloved hour, the departed Leopard's too, two Life Forces who Loved poised opposite on the banks of the Water Hole in the jungle wilds of Sariska. Having delivered his Triplet, with hopeful eyes locked on those of the Bengal, the boy faded back several steps to shallower water exposing his shoulders, then his chest, and waist, until he was standing in the mud on the Bank across, completely free of disguise.

The Great One chuffed and took in the morning air thick with jungle scents, though its curiosity was exclusive to the unknown beast at hand; the scent of a Female Bengal was no longer in the air. The Animal making all the noise was odorless now due to a film of water covering it.

'Take me away, Great One,' the boy beseeched, 'and share me with your Cub. I only suggest you carry me deep to the Jungle, so that an Innocent Life Force does not see our Celebration. We as those who Love don't want to disturb her Peace or disrupt her Journey on this Earthly setting with something she does not understand.'

The boy's skin exposed to the hot sun was drying and his movements emitted more of a fragrance and the Bengal could smell now the hide of the different Animal. The Great One lifted from its haunches, the large brilliant goldens narrowed, zeroing in, which resulted in a quick flick and swish of its tail, an indicator of a readiness to commence assault. But in the presence of an Animal it did not recognize, firing a set of unique pulsations with which it was not familiar nor had it ever encountered, the Bengal hesitated tentatively and retreated a step, uncertain whether to leap into the water and swim a direct route or dash the perimeter. Vaulting forward then back then starting left then pivoting right, the Great One began to howl and whine, and then let out a snarling roar, bothered by its unwelcomed predicament.

At that moment the boy—embracing Kairos once again to take action at the right moment and conjure his own luck—made the decision for the Great One. He swiveled around suddenly and sprinted heading toward the nearest Animal access Path used for hydration treks to the Water Hole. The boy ran as fast as he could, but he did not run out of fear; he'd perceived the Great One's uncertainty and he guided it from indecision by proffering its most comforting posture: pursuit from behind. The boy's instantaneous modification to his Plan also provided no opportunity for the sleeping Indian Girl to witness an End of Sleeps—his Celebration—an Interpretation she could not understand and would not for many years.

The Mighty Great One galvanized its massive body with a power twist and vaulted off in a flash, tearing around the water's rim with an eye on the unusual Animal's passage, leaping over shrubs to shortcut distance. There would be no hide and pounce today; it had lost the element of surprise to this uncommon beast that now offered a stunning challenge. But the Bengal, grandson to Zephyrles, possessed lightning bolt swiftness and the jungle agility to compensate. This was its finest hour, the early morning of the predator, and its favored contest, a hunter's charge from the rear as the boy intuited, the Great One's tried and true method in the art of death with honor and nobility.

The boy continued to pump his legs and felt so gloriously vital as he did. His heart gonged, his pulse popped, and he ran the blissful clip of an Olympic sprinter, boosted by adrenaline and Hope—but Love most of all—so he could extend his Celebration as far away from the Water Hole as possible until he was enveloped in a thick wood with trees and brush comforting and blanketing him all around.

The team of Gray Langurs swung like acrobats along treetops, leaping from Dhok to Kadaya to Bengal Fig in order to spectate from lofty branches, a scene they'd witnessed dozens of times. But they had never seen anything like this. They witnessed the uncommon Animal stop suddenly and spin around and hold its ground with the steely courage of a Mongolian Warrior. As soon as the boy did, The Great One, having sprung on the run from a power coil, was airborne in mid-vault already and it landed upon the boy, its fangs dug deep into his neck just as quickly, cutting off his air.

The boy was stunned at first but did not feel Pain, only Peace. He was numbed, his head prickling, and he was dizzy. His windpipe had been smashed and blocked and he felt the Red Waters retreating warmly down his neck. Death would come quick, a fine End of Sleeps with Honor.

The boy was seeing dreamy White as the Great One took his air from him with a vise of jaw, held him locked in place, immobilized. And then Gonzalo gasped and the gentle calm of Death set in. He was spinning, disoriented, in the unyielding grip of the Great One, permitted now to fly far away to the outer pavilions of consciousness where he was delivered a final free-association gift from his freshly enhanced mind: a last Interpretation.

He saw through the canvas of White all the Faces of those he had Loved and who had Loved him and he felt the Warmth and Generosity and the Goodness all at once. Love was all around him. His Sister the Angel. The Old Man. Zosimus. And Sofía. And his Schoolmates. And the Langur and the Rhesus. The Wild Boar. And the Jungle of Sariska. And of course he felt the Love of the Great One. The boy Loved them all. He Loved everyone. And that's when it came to him—mercifully—the answer to what had been perplexing him on the overnight to his last Sleep. As he lay there dying a Good Death with Honor in the Jungle he'd discovered the answer—his answer—to the Mystery of Love.

A Life Force was not defined by being Loved. What was important was that it Loved without hope for anything in return. The contents of Sofía's Letter did not matter nor the fact they had made love, life's greatest sharing. What mattered was he had Loved—regardless. That offering Love, being of giver of Love, was what defined one as an Animal of Integrity. To give Love—that was Life's greatest thing. And in his final thoughts the boy designated the epiphany a Big Thing—and this was his final Interpretation.

Having resolved the Mystery for himself, with Love all around him, Gonzalo died with Happiness in Triple. The boy had lived a Life of Love, he had carried out his Plan, he'd done his Duty, he had become Angel to two Life Forces and guided them on their Paths, he had done his part on the Planet, he had scaled the walls of the dark well of ignorance and understood the Universe as best he could and achieved his Interpretation of Enlightenment; he had lived a beautiful Earthly life filled with Joy, Integrity, and Nobility— and Love.

Fittingly, this uncommon Animal Died with Honor, his Life Force poised to sail on to the Sky Spirits to join his Sister the Angel and the Old Man and all the Animals throughout History that had Loved. The boy had achieved Triple Happiness, a glorious Earthly Celebration in a World it took him Two Sleeps to figure, One Sleep to fathom.

'Gracias, El Gran,' were the boy's last words and he was hopeful his celebrator would understand.

24

The young Indian Girl they called Kayisha awoke to the sound of the sand grouses flying overhead, hundreds of them, landing one by one on the bank of the water hole. The stubby birds had been waiting for the bengal to leave and now the coast was clear. Her pretty bright eyes buzzed around realizing she was hemmed in by the makeshift enclosure. She stood up and looked out over the edge and saw the sand grouses filling their beaks.

She gazed high and low and looked all around. She wondered where she was. She had an itch and noticed the dried brown film flakes on her arm and scratched until the flakes were all gone. She didn't bother with her legs. She held on to the edge of the enclosure and shook it. Then kicked it. She tried to climb over the barrier and fell back. It was too high. And sturdy. Then fear crept in. That she was all alone. And thirsty. And hungry. Kayisha began to cry.

When she could cry no more she sat down resigned to her predicament. Looking down eventually she saw a handsome rock formation, in the form of a person. It looked like a toy or a doll made simply from several rocks. Feet, stomach, head, and two twigs for arms. She smiled sparely and took off the head. She located the Urn behind surrounded by more stones. She freed the Urn from the protective pile and inspected it. The Indian Girl drank the water without hesitation, every last drop. She spotted the pile of blossoms and berries and she knew them from the relish her mother made to spread on bread and she ate each one. Then she put the head back on and almost smiled.

Yamir, The Man in the Olive Uniform with Stripes, the Sariska jungle operative for Project Tiger passed through the area two hours later. He'd been calling out intermittently but Kayisha had not heard him. Only when she heard the static of his Walkie-Talkie did she begin to cry out.

The Man with the Olive Green Uniform with Stripes scaled the Dhok and brought the girl to safety. They spoke in Hindi and she told him about the boy. That he had taken her up the tree, fed her something that tasted 'yucky' and then she fell asleep. Yamir radioed for an ambulance and he carried the girl out of the Pánichéda ravine and through the clearing onward to the jungle path to the road. The ambulance retrieved them a short while later.

On the ambulance ride to the Village Medical Clinic in Alwar the jungle operative had another question for the girl.

'Did you see the bengal?' he asked in Hindi.

'No.'

'No bengal?'

'Baby bengal ...'

'You saw a bengal cub?'

She said 'sí,' but Yamir did not believe her and chalked it up to the excited imagination of a child. Unknowingly, her innocence perceived had just saved the cub from being apprehended and sold.

Yamir then asked her if she'd seen the Leopard to which she shook her head. Of the boy, he remarked wistfully, 'He was a good scout. We could have used him.'

'Maybe he'll turn up,' the driver said.

The jungle operative was not so sure. He'd observed the series of bengal tracks around the water hole (hence the questioning of the Indian girl), some indicative of a full sprint; and bengals did not sprint without intent. Yamir would never mention the existence of the tracks in his report, however; nor would he offer up the name of the boy.

In Alwar the villagers called Kayisha's rescue a miracle. Her parents had cried day and night thinking the worst. No one had given her a chance, at her age, her size, in a jungle full of the fiercest predators. Everyone of course spoke of Gonzalo and they called him 'the Spanish boy' because no one knew his name. The parents wanted to locate him to reward him with all they had which were the blouses from their backs. Yamir claimed he wanted to give the boy a job with the Project. But he had his suspicions that Gonzal as he called him had not survived; that the tracks indicated the Bengal had chased him and if attacked, the outcome was certain.

But the opportunistic Project operative did not say a word about his suspicions or his observations from the ravine; the existence of numerous paw prints. It was good for the outfit to have boasted a successful rescue and he did not want to take away from that. A story with a happy ending was good for the Project, but most importantly for Yamir as he was also heralded as a hero for his 'exhaustive vigilance'. It was better for the public to not know about the plight of the Spanish boy. The story incited wonder and a bengal killing a human had never been good for business. The corrupt man presumed correctly. As the open-ended story passed around, more and more people began to visit Sariska and give money to the Project.

The story of the girl's harrowing ordeal became an instant legend in the village and the legend passed to other villages. And there were many embellishments. The most popular version had the boy fighting off the mighty bengal to save the child and was eaten in the process; that he had given his

life for the girl. Most of the stories did involve the boy
sacrificing himself in some way. Or why would he have
disappeared? The boy was considered a hero and the story
excited the imagination of many. The devout villagers often
gave prayers for the boy and those who loved had love for
him even though they'd never met him.

Kayisha of course could never forget what happened and
what the boy had done for her. As she got older she was able
to appreciate what he'd accomplished and was marveled all
the more. The experience and the memories of it had
changed her life forever. When the girl was older a Spanish
name came across in conversation.

'That's it!' she cried. 'That's his name!'

From then on the legend had a name and books were
written. The first was entitled, 'Gonzalo and the Tiger.'
Others included 'The Boy and the Jungle,' 'Sariska Scout',
'Kayisha's Story', and 'The Rock Doll'. The attention the tale
garnered was good for Project Tiger funding and the scaly
jungle operative was promoted to Chief Executive.

As for Kayisha, not a day would pass when she did not
think of Gonzalo. She loved him from afar and her nightly
prayers included him. She turned into a stunning, comely
girl, but one of excellent character too. She was given offers
to be in the movies and endorse products. But that did not
interest her.

In her own life she avowed to save herself for one man, a
man who exhibited the qualities of her hero Gonzalo, the
Spanish boy. She would live a life of Love and Integrity and
Honor. She would work for the government in social
services helping the poor people of her country. But Kayisha
she would never marry.

Once in a while Kayisha would visit the water hole after the Monsoon season. She didn't care to see the ravine when it was experiencing drought. She preferred to see the water hole at its fullest. When it gave life. As she remembered it. These trips were emotional for her and they provided much happiness; sitting in the jungle setting and dreaming of the day when the miracle happened. And envisioning the Spanish boy who saved her life, smiling at her all over again.

25

Beyond legend, and as it really happened, several curiosities occurred at the Water Hole the morning the boy met his End of Sleeps and found Triple Happiness. While the Indian Girl lay sleeping and before the Man in the Olive Uniform with Stripes arrived, the possessions the boy left behind experienced their own individual sagas and Journeys.

Once the boy died and the Great One dragged his body deeper into the Jungle (and shared him with his awaiting Cub), the sneaky Rhesus that had profited from the boy's habitation in the Jungle already, investigated from afar the vacant Dhok looking for more food or booty. Upon closer look it spotted the makeshift enclosure penning in the Girl and was lured by it. The Rhesus charged up the trunk of the tree and clambered high to the convergence where it examined the bamboo barriers. It boosted up and peered in careful not to disturb the sleeping Girl smeared in brown. The savvy Rhesus smelled the scent of Bengal but was not fooled as it resembled too much a monkey.

Two other Rhesus of the clan curiously pursued their brother, but were hissed and shrieked off. Sufficiently rebuffed, the younger smaller Rhesus spotted Gonzalo's Passport and snatched it immediately as the youth had been the object of the game of keep-away, as usual. Satisfied with a prize under normal circumstances it could never attain, the snowy monkey took off proudly and disappeared into the brush. The second follower received a swiping clawed paw to the face and it fell back and out of the tree entirely, knocking the Brass Pot to the ground in the process. Once it shook off the fall, the dazed Rhesus located the relic and attempted but could not negotiate the latch. Trying every which way, eventually the frustrated monkey left the item worthless to it at the edge of the clearing.

This left the sneaky Rhesus alone again to resume with his raid, to see if the small sleeping Animal was easy food. As it hoisted up the enclosure barrier about to leap in, a thrashing snarl erupted from beneath. The Rhesus knew the sound all too well—a dangerous rival—and the monkey sprung to a branch higher and then another until it found one from which it could launch itself to the safety of another tree.

The usually nocturnal but fearful Caracal had received enduring whiffs of the happenings at the Water Hole and decided to forego its tree hideout by day and descend upon the Ravine. Normally it stayed away as the Pánichéda was the Leopard's territory, but the scent of its larger more ferocious cousin was absent. It had stayed hidden in a Kadaya tree and witnessed the boy and the Bengal running off. That's when the Caracal left its vantage point and silently treaded up to the water source. By now it had hydrated itself and was moving in on the enclosure, creeping slowly. That was when the sneaky Rhesus fled to avoid a confrontation. As the Caracal advanced the pungent smell got worse and not knowing what was inside the barriers it decided not to engage any surprises that could be threatening; especially when the scent of a female bengal was wafting. The Caracal thought the better of it and took off to wait for nightfall and unsuspecting ground critters to satisfy its appetite.

As for Sofía's Letter, it had been wedged beneath a slab of bark and went unseen during the rescue of the Girl by the Project Tiger operative. It remained there until a late afternoon crosswind swept it away carrying it to the Water Hole, the envelope fluttering and landing atop the surface of the water.

As the news that day passed around the neighborhoods of Alwar and nearby villages that the missing Girl had been found, the shaman took particular notice. He learned of the rescue and the Spanish boy's involvement. Though he asked questions of the villagers he never mentioned he'd seen the boy the day before. Late that afternoon he made his own pilgrimage back to the Water Hole where he had met the boy and released the boy's friend to the Sky Spirits.

The Man in the Orange Robes came upon the clearing and noticed the enclosure still intact in the convergence of the Dhok where the boy had set up his camp. Then he took a stroll around the perimeter of the Water Hole and was amazed to spot the many Bengal prints, the flat stamps as well as the upturned earth that implied swift, attack-style movements. The shaman did not need to see more. He knew what had happened. It was a just a feeling, but feelings and visions were his specialty. He was certain the boy had sacrificed himself in one way or another. What he could not know was how, or that the sacrifice was purposeful, especially since the boy he'd met seemed to suffer from disabilities. Gonzalo's mind had not fully reawakened.

The boy had gotten in over his head, the shaman thought.

But when he circled back around to the other side of the Water Hole he saw the boy's tracks. They showed mostly normal footprints indicating walking speed. Then he found one trail and one trail only showing the boy had been running. And both tiger and boy sprinting tracks headed off in the same direction. And yet there were so many tracks of both. Walking tracks, peaceful tracks. As if they had spent time together, communicating, if not talking. One on one side, one on the other, as if exchanging ideas.

And why would the boy put himself in harm's way? He'd already protected the girl in the tree. Why hadn't he just stayed with her? The Bengal could not climb a tree like that. And if he'd found her why hadn't he just escorted her back to the village midday, the less threatening jungle hours? It was clear to him the boy knew he was not coming back. That was why he made the enclosure. So she would be safe when he was gone.

The shaman understood now. The boy had sacrificed himself with intent; to join his friend from the Urn perhaps, in the sky with the Sky Spirits. He had been waiting for the Bengal. And when he had his chance he did not want to waste it. Otherwise he would have brought the girl to safety himself. The boy had rescued the girl and then gave himself to the Bengal after perhaps much interaction or discussion.

It was then the shaman saw the object floating on the surface of the water. He tossed off his orange robes and swam to it bringing it to shore. The envelope that had been opened, the boy's name written across it. The shaman drew out the letter, unfolded it, and read.

At the conclusion of the letter, the shaman refolded it and inserted it back in the envelope. He said it solemnly.

'The boy had been loved. And he died with honor.'

With that, the shaman tossed the envelope back into the water hole, the only article handy belonging to Gonzalo. Then he donned his orange robes again, gathered flowers and blossoms from the nearby trees and shrubs, and performed a celebration for the boy. He smoked cannabis, burned the incense, walked the big circle of the water, tossed the blooms atop and spread the smoke over it; he clanged the bells and shook the rattles, he danced and he sang songs and he said prayers and he called upon the Sky Spirits to let them know a boy of integrity who died with honor was coming to join them. And he guided and released the soul of Gonzalo to the sky.

In the middle of the celebration when the shaman was dancing with the bells and rattles, his eyes closed, a chorus of desperate animal alarm calls erupted nearby. Though the man heard the urgent commotion he was too entranced in his private ceremony to be lifted from it. He was communicating with the Sky Spirits in music and prayer, a benediction type ritual never to be interrupted so as to not lose the connection with the sky.

When he had completed the ceremony the shaman, the boy's Man in the Orange Robes was exhausted, more so than usual. He collapsed down and sat by the bank of the water hole just where the boy had delivered his Triplet to the Great One. He gazed out over the water and took in the stillness. His head wobbled a final time and—he cried—something the holy man never did.

'He was a good boy,' the shaman addressed himself. 'His equal will not soon walk this way. If it were not to be the bengal himself.'

As he sat there the shaman soon heard more alarm calls and twisted around, looking in every direction. Immediately he scampered to the Dhok and scaled it. He remained in the convergence beside the enclosure for an hour until he saw a small heard of Chitals, the spotted Indian deer, stride up fearlessly and take drinks. Then he knew the water hole and the area nearby was safe again and he was clear to make a passage back to town.

The shaman never spoke of Sariska or the boy or the letter or the tracks he witnessed by the water hole—to anyone. He was too familiar with the opportunistic if not greedy qualities of earthly beings to utter a word. All that mattered to him was the boy had died with honor and he had guided his soul to the sky.

26

Not long after the Rhesus gave up on the Brass Pot, a curious Gray Langur hurdled past and scooped it by the chains and took off. The family of five followed their patriarch into the thick brush where the Langur tried to break open the Pot. Again it would not give. The sons and daughters tried too. Then a snarling fight erupted. Not done, the patriarch was instinctual enough to transport the Pot onward through the forest, all the way to the service road. There it smashed the brass relic against the asphalt. The Langur father spiked it down again and again, denting it in the process. But the lid would not budge. Again the others tried. They smelled it, smacked it, smashed it—but to no avail. They too abandoned it, leaving it on the side of the road, mangled as could be.

At approximately the same time the shaman was delivering his ceremony for the boy, a Bangladeshi drifter hitchhiking across India came upon the Brass Pot lying on the side of the road. He picked it up and popped the latch. The lid sprung open and the drifter was delighted to find the pungent chunks of cannabis. Immediately he drew out his pipe as he was an experienced marijuana enthusiast and lit up several bowls. The cannabis was so strong the scent had permeated that of the dung and the man thought they were one and the same and he smoked a potent mix of both.

The drifter became very stoned and experienced a different sort of high; it made him dreamy and introspective and he even hallucinated somewhat. He wandered into the woods and took in the dazzling nature and propped himself against a Kadaya tree. He ruminated about his life and how he had fallen short; he'd left behind a trail of failed family relationships, friendships, and romances. Yet those failings had never been his intention. Somehow he had gotten derailed; how it had been his dream in life to make some kind of a difference but resentments had taken over and poisoned him.

The significant high the man was experiencing kept coming, getting stronger, and he marveled at the cannabis' potency. His perceptions were getting more expansive; but not entirely. He philosophized; how 'we as living beings are composed of the same star stuff, that we're all in this together—this magical mess and swirl of totally inexplicable chaos we call life. And so, we might as well embrace it, have fun with it, and be a little extraordinary while doing it. And it is our purpose.'

The drifter continued to smoke the cannabis laced with dung throughout the rest of the day until it was all gone. Little did the Bangladeshi man know the Chinese Emperors as far back as Tang Dynasty had been smoking bengal dung for over a thousand years to enhance mind expansion, as they used every part of the bengal for healing benefits and numerous medicinal uses and practices.

When the contents of the Brass Pot were empty, the man lay back in repose against the tree and eventually fell asleep. He awoke in the middle of the night in a panic filled with anxiety. He had sobered but his mindset had been revamped if not altered. He pondered the meditations of hours before and came to some startling realizations; he could not be so carefree and idealistic in his life. He could also not be so irresponsible. The drifter was penniless, living hand to mouth, and he had fathered a daughter he would not recognize. And now he felt ashamed. He decided then to return to Bangladesh and visit his daughter and formally recognize her. Then he would get a legitimate job. And it was a start.

27

What the Man in the Orange Robes could not know was while he was dancing and praying for the boy, and invoking the Sky Spirits, dissolved seamlessly and without silhouette in the jungle brush was a ghost. The ghost had padded silently, feet at a time, to the last line of Dhok trees, positioned low behind shrubs while melting into the shadows, as if waiting for unsuspecting prey to pass and pounce. Though the animal alarm calls fired, the ghost had not returned for sustenance. Noiselessly and without as much as a chuff, it sat there upright and gazed out curiously through golden doubloon eyes and watched peacefully if not piously the spectacle of the Man with the Orange Robes as he performed a shakes and rattles Celebration for the boy. The ghost, the Great One, grandson to Zephyrles, the mighty Bengal, had returned to pay his respects to the different human being, the exceptional boy.

And the boy would have been proud to know it.

28

The Golden Jackal lurked through the forest stalking the satiated Striped Hyenas in parallel, shielded by dense thickets while keeping a safe distance and treading decidedly upwind. Downwind the carnage profiteer could smell the scent of bloody muzzles to the assassin pack and was hopeful to find a trail of meaty scraps. An hour later what the scavenger was left with was a flattened, densely-spotted rosette coat of soft fur streaked with Red Waters of which it was content to lick until there were no more and the Jackal lapped it long after the scarlet traces were gone.

What the boy would never know was, the engine of destruction that met an End of Sleeps in a thorny brush spiral, had been stalking the boy day and night. For Three Sleeps each time it crept close—by the Water Hole, the access Paths, even several noiseless prowls up the Dhok while the boy slept—the pitiless feline was neutralized and turned away repeatedly by the stench of Bengal. The boy did not appear or move like the cat's more formidable relative and the normally fearless Leopard was confused if not confounded. Even when Gonzalo passed beneath the beast's boulder perch wielding a Torch, though there was no scent of Bengal, the masking smoke and intimidating Flame kept the concealed predator at bay.

The frustrated feline was further stymied by the return of the Great One, the grandson to Zephyrles whose family line had ruled the Ravine for decades. But in the Bengal's absence, the Leopardo had taken over the Pánichéda and terrorized the tropical forest freely and dauntlessly for years.

But the Bengal reemerged with its Cub, the product of a union with a Mother murdered by Chinese poachers. The Great One sent the Leopard a message written in Bengal claw on the trunk of a stunted Gugal and the Leopardo's short-lived reign of the Ravine was over—it was getting pushed out.

On that fateful night, while the boy was waiting in the dense dark Jungle for first light to carry out a Plan, and the anxious and threatened feline charged suddenly—stout legs recoiling with sinewy strength to launch and lift off the retractile-clawed meteor of muscle that it was—the consummate predator once more caught a savage waft of the female Bengal; for this reason the usually indomitable cat elected to soar beyond intended prey and in doing so plummeted into a thicket of brush to avoid a deadly confrontation with what it assumed to be the better beast. The jungle master had been duped—again.

As it had happened, the Bengal scent of the boy had been temporarily disguised by the stench of smoke in his clothes and the lack of any signature predator scent goaded the anxiety-ridden and zealous Leopardo into making its move. But at the last second, the doomed feline received the sparest whiff of its superior cousin on the boy's skin as the smoky smell had dissipated, causing the cat to second-guess an assault in mid-vault and meet a fate in the most unlucky and—uncharacteristic—of ways. In the end, the young Life Force that was the boy had been the triumphant one having outsmarted on successive occasions the most cunning and stealth Animal creations the Planet has ever known, and by a show of superior daring he was able to preserve a glorious Celebration and the very Triple Happiness he now enjoyed.

29

Eight years later, the young woman boarded the train in València and arrived at Barcelona Sants in less than three hours. She had not been to Barcelona in quite a while and she harbored little hope, but she recognized the need to try one last time and hear the results first hand. She stepped into the agency now located on the Diagonal and the chief administrator was at lunch. Her assistant who was of course apprised of the situation spoke to her. There was no news. They'd had an investigation conducted, but the records of the boy had been lost or destroyed long ago and there were no fresh leads. The proprietor of the foster home where he had lived had been incarcerated and died in jail and that she knew already.

The young woman was now convinced she would never learn the fate of her baby boy whom she had anguished over nearly every day of her life since it had happened. He would be twenty-five years old now. The young woman took a taxi to the Sagreda Familia cathedral a final time (Aravella's favorite church designed by Antonio Gaudí).

Wherever her boy was she prayed he was enjoying a beautiful life—a life of love and happiness—a better life than she could have ever provided for him at the time. Her last hope was to be reunited with him in Heaven and she asked the God Almighty to grant her that wish. She carried that wish with her not as a burden but as a jubilation to be for the rest of her days.

Propaganda

ALLURE OCTOBER 1995

Original publicity stills and cover art tries with Ingrid Seynhaeve, photography by Peter Beard

Model Citizen

*The story of a man who never met a
stunningly beautiful woman he didn't like.*

THE SHALLOW MAN

*By Coerte V. W. Felske.
243 pp. New York:
Crown Publishers.
$21.*

By David Kelly

LOVE, H. L. Mencken said, is the delusion that one woman differs from another. Nick Laws, a marginally more enlightened fellow, claims that one woman in every 50,000 is quite different from the other 49,999: she's drop-dead gorgeous, and he's determined to sleep with her.

Nick, who narrates Coerte V. W. Felske's amusing first novel, "The Shallow Man," is 30 years old, lives in SoHo and works by day as a hand model, by night as a party promoter for clubs with names like Cafe D&A. He knows how to ask "Would you like to take a bubble bath with me?" in 10 languages, and he has committed to memory the Victoria's Secret 24-hour toll-free number. With the exception of his Harley, all he cares about is what he calls, collectively, "Thing": "fashion models, beautiful women and general hotness." He happily acknowledges his obsession right at the start:

"I never met a model I didn't like. The revelation came to me early one morning when I was in that dreamy state, beyond the point of sleep but too comfortable . . . to get up. I thought about the previous night's interludes, the hair, the sweet smells, the lips and the curves rarely seen by most mortals. It made me smile serenely. Since I don't have a great attention span, I thought about this for a short while, then went on to other thoughts."

It's too bad about those "other thoughts." When Nick contemplates "the sweetest joining of limbs known to man," his company is agreeable. But during the couple of weeks described in the novel, he tangles with his brother, his confidante and, of course, models' boyfriends, all of whom demand that he re-evaluate his life. Unfortunately, he does. By his own account, he is neither very bright nor very witty, and a dullard's earnest ruminations can only be dull — or, as Nick would put it, as exciting as York Avenue.

Before long, though, he is back to his old unreflective self, proving that the unexamined life is well worth living. To Nick, everything resembles conjugating the verb, and if your mind works in similar fashion ("mind" may be the wrong word), you'll probably understand his ruling passion:

"Anyone who claims there is nothing sexual about playing the game of pool doesn't like sex. The long, slender cues ramming forth, the shiny balls dropping into the pockets, the rack is even the shape of a triangle. Everything about it suggests sex. And when Thing plays, there's nothing better on the planet. When she's good, forget about it. From any angle, it's art. My kind of art. You see her grip that stick in one hand and slide it through elegant, feminine fingers on the other. If you're watching from behind, let's not forget her posture: she's bent over at the waist, her posterior in perfect view, her breasts lightly skimming the felt, her shirt hangs lower than normal and you get a good peek. Then *smack!* She drives the stick through the ball."

In Nick's opinion, competition isn't healthy. He hates actors, "rock apes," Wall Streeters and anyone else who might horn in on his territory. Besides, men just aren't "life-enhancing." Women, however, are sublimely spiritual as well as sublimely physical:

"There's nothing in the world as magical as Thing's bathroom. It smells exquisite, has wonderful feminine adornments and is usually very clean. I've been known to stay in a bathroom of this sort for quite some time. Especially if we haven't slept together yet. You go in there and really get a feel for her. . . . You see the soaps, the shampoos, the creams, the lotions, the pink razors on the rim of the tub. You see the droplets of water on the bathtub basin and you know she was shaving her slender gams hours before. . . . Short of actual penetration, it's the only place you really get a sense of her deeper roots of sensuality. Stepping into Thing's bathroom is a voyage into Thing's soul."

ONE feminist writer has used the term "penised humans" to refer to men. Mentally, at least, Nick Laws is as penised as a human can get. When he awards Audrey Hepburn the crown for "pinnacle hotness," it is only because Mr. Felske has nodded; surely his hero, who craves tall, leggy, curvaceous women, would choose someone like, say, Julie Newmar, or RuPaul.

Nick detests the beach, but this novel is perfect for it. (It's too slight for the subway ride to the beach, so wait till you get there.) "The Shallow Man" is also perfect for shallow men. On the other hand, women may think the title is redundant. □

David Kelly is an editor at the Book Review.

The New York Times Book Review

July 9, 1995

Hope you have many more !!!

*Love,
Dad*

P A G E S

for detail and a poet's soul, beautifully captures the ebb and flow of life at this edge of marsh, sand and sea.

Stealing to the beach, she describes primitive horseshoe crabs mating under the night's full moon—and the morning-after carnage when shore birds arrive to pick at the carcasses of crabs overturned by waves. Patiently watching telephone poles and channel markers, she describes the monogamous osprey and its peculiar nest-building habits (she has seen males bring in cornstalks, cow dung and a toy shovel). Ackerman even manages to evoke sympathy for the mother mosquito's astonishing egg-laying powers —fueled, of course, by blood meals— during the single, brief summer of her existence.

A former staff writer for *National Geographic*, Ackerman offers much more than a chronicle of a seaside community. Interweaving reflections and a bit of personal history, *Notes* is a celebration of finding a home, wherever that may be, and savoring the "rich broth of life." By book's end she has

▲ **COERTE V.W. FELSKE** Sure, his hero dates models, but don't call him *The Shallow Man*.

readers all too happy to wake up and smell the sweet stink of the mud flats. (Viking, $21.95) ■ **PAULA CHIN**

▥ THE SHALLOW MAN
by Coerte V.W. Felske

I may not have been the king of Generation Face," proclaims hipster Nick Laws, invoking his superficial peers in screenwriter Felske's first novel, "but I was definitely one of its princes." A hand model and party promoter at Manhattan's coolest clubs, this ne'er-do-well signs his checks with an X and an O, knows how to ask "Would you like to take a bubble bath with me?" in several languages and carries a tattered copy of *The Letters of Vincent van Gogh* to impress "Thing," his catchphrase for models and other impossibly stunning women. Nick can't get enough of Thing; his every waking moment is devoted to bedding them and their friends—as long as they're not Civilians (regular-looking women).

It would be easy, but inaccurate, to dismiss Nick as a misogynist. For one thing, his acidic classification system

extends to men too. "Guys can be Dialtones [bimbos]," he concedes. Besides, Nick's trash-talking and sex fiestas are transparent escapes from pain, which underscores a disastrous jaunt to Miami (a Thing-ridden place) and his unrequited love for the Catsuit Feminist (his pal Alexis, a student of women's studies who hussles drinks clad in Spandex).

Spiked with original Nickspeak and hilarious dialogue, Felske's depiction of the physical elite is so clever in its anthropological detail that we can forgive his piggy protagonist just about anything. Besides, *The Shallow Man* harbors a few glimmers of Nick's humanity. You just have to dig—deeply—to find them. (Crown, $21) ■ **JENNIFER KORNREICH**

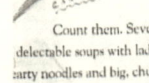

Count them. Seve delectable soups with ladl arty noodles and big, chu very bowlful. What more

See? You're 1

You can bite into a juicy h

People Magazine

Speaking of the Devil

OR children growing up in a churchly way, the devil is no joke. Any creature that goes by such incantatory names as Beelzebub or the Prince of Darkness and can consign you to eternal torment is worthy of, at the very least, a morbid respect. Princeton professor Elaine Pagels's brilliant new book, *The Origin of Satan* (Random House), comes as a release from all that. Her Satan is more of a political stratagem than something Billy Graham could work up a sweat saving us from.

Pagels traces the origin of Satan to a certain Judeo-Christian tendency to define oneself by demonizing those most nearly like you. She locates the roots of this I'm-right-so-you-must-be-the-devil theology in pre-Christian Jewish splinter groups like the cave-dwelling Essenes, who placed a higher value on their own ascetic brand of Judaism than on the "chosen" status of the entire tribe. The authors of the New Testament Gospels took that exceptionalism and ran with it, bolstering the case for Jesus' unique godliness by portraying their own people, the Jews, as more devilishly culpable in the Crucifixion than the Romans.

Reading Pagels, you can't help but wonder whether the squabble over Jesus among the Jews of Palestine—just the latest prophet or the Messiah?—might be one dispute that should have stayed in the family. Once Jesus becomes the property of the gentiles, Satan, heretofore a minor meddlesome figure in the Old Testament, comes into his fearsome own as the personification of heretics and certain nonbelievers—like, for instance, the Jews. (For an update, check out Pat Robertson's *The New World Order*.)

It might be argued that Pagels isn't giving the devil his due. She doesn't seek out satanic evil in the murky depths of the human psyche or in the cruel indifference of the universe. That's another story and one she knows all too well, having lost a child to illness and a husband to a climbing accident. In *Origin*, her subject is what she calls "the social history of Satan," an examination of the group interests that are served by playing the devil card. When we hear religious and political leaders talking about the "Evil Empire" or the "Great Satan," Pagels reminds us, it's time to duck.

Family feud: The devil was a tool (Hans Memling, circa 1470).

Shallow Waters Run Deep

THE STUNNING but unreflective man, playfully dismissed as a "himbo," knows a lot more than you think. Behind those big blank eyes and that deep tan is ... well, there's not much. But it's something that women find hopelessly tempting: a healthy disdain for thinking too much.

In a slender holiday from anything remotely resembling a meditation, Coerte V. W. Felske's *The Shallow Man* (Crown) makes a case for the unexamined life. Since he can't be bothered connecting the dots, he maps out the sexual politics of the jejune and Gitanes with an easy straight line. Reading the quick-witted prose, one begins to think less about things and more about Thing, the Shallow Man's tag for the women he dates: gorgeous, seemingly unattainable models.

The Shallow Man is hardly stupid. He's more like Hamlet without the mental baggage, tumbling Ophelia by Act II. So what if behind all that cigarette smoke and charm lies a lean mentality? Oscar Wilde had his number: Only the shallow know themselves.

Esquire Magazine

BOOKS

By DIGBY DIEHL

IN HIS first novel, *The Shallow Man* (Crown), Coerte V.W. Felske spins a clever tale of the narcissistic world of fashion modeling. In this comic send-up, Nick Laws is the shallow man whose every thought and word reflect his sole interest in life: boffing models. From the late-night clubs of Manhattan to the art deco bars of Miami, Nick searches for beautiful women to take to bed. That's all he does. He's so perfect, he's hilarious.

Is there a man with a soul so noble that he has not entertained this fantasy? In real life, no one could stand around all day in his motorcycle jacket and sunglasses, purring platitudes to curvaceous dimwits. But Nick's relentless, self-conscious pursuit is very funny.

True to the cliché, there is one knockout woman who won't give in to Nick's charms, and she's the one he loves. With her he discusses erotic philosophy and reads passages from *The Letters of Vincent Van Gogh*. The skeletal plot of this elongated joke hinges on the resolution of their unconsummated love affair, but as Nick reminds us, "Never judge a book by its contents." Certainly not this book. *The Shallow Man* is fun, flash and filigree—a sexy, witty spoof of the Nineties.

Lawrence Thornton, on the other hand, is one of our most challenging novelists. His sequel to *Imagining Argentina* is *Naming the Spirits* (Doubleday), a deeply moving tribute to the "disappeared" who died in Argentina's Dirty War. Thornton evokes the Latin American tradition of magic realism to animate the spirits of 11 people who were executed on the pampas. They come to life again through a survivor, a girl named Teresa who suffers from aphasia as the result of a bullet wound. The spirits offer eloquent testimony to the bravery of ordinary people murdered by a brutal regime. They haunt the living. It's a novel you will not forget.

Following his engaging series of Cold War thrillers that feature the dashing Blackford Oakes, William F. Buckley has written a fictional saga that tracks a friendship from World War Two through the Vietnam war. *Brothers No More* (Doubleday) opens with Danny O'Hara and Henry Chafee in Italy in 1944. Danny is the grandson of Franklin Delano Roosevelt and has the charismatic confidence of a man born to privilege. Henry, of modest family background, is reserved and scholarly. He is also Danny's roommate at Yale and his lifelong friend. Danny marries Henry's sister Caroline and becomes a successful hotelier. Henry rises through the *Time* magazine hierarchy to become chief correspondent in Saigon in 1963. True to a

Coerte V.W. Felske's *Shallow Man*.

The pursuit of beautiful women, a William F. Buckley saga and Anne Rice's theology.

Buckley novel, the grandson of FDR is a scoundrel. But his friend Henry is principled. That basic tension in their relationship—the secrets they share and the intertwined lives they lead—keeps the plot rattling along, with some creative coincidences. What makes this novel so irresistible, however, is Buckley's wit and erudition. He revels in re-creating scenes at his alma mater, pens an exciting scene of sailing in a storm off Nantucket, provides Caroline with a strict Catholic conscience, makes Danny's mistress a scholar of Spanish literature, brings to life a portrait of Henry Luce and comments through the characters on the politics and great events of the post–World War Two era.

White Bucks and Black-Eyed Peas (Scribner) is an eloquent and insightful autobiography by Marcus Mabry, who is now a foreign correspondent for *Newsweek*. Born into a poor family near Trenton, New Jersey, Mabry used help from Aid to Families With Dependent Children, food stamps, Medicaid, Head Start, college grants and affirmative action to graduate from Stanford and become a professional. His observations about welfare, racism (his own included), family, France and education are eye-openers. As the "exception" who made it, Mabry meditates on what it means to live in the different worlds of impoverished blacks and well-to-do whites.

Finally, Anne Rice has published the fifth volume in her Vampire Chronicles

series. We have long admired Rice's artistic bravery in dealing with vast historical canvases, philosophical issues and wild leaps of imagination, but in *Memnoch the Devil* (Knopf), she goes too far. Her familiar protagonist, the vampire Lestat, is offered a Faustian pact. Being a good businessman, he considers all the angles. He visits both heaven and hell, meets God and the devil and generally rewrites Christian theology. As if this weren't enough, Lestat also time-travels back to witness the creation, reconciles it with evolution and then zooms through human history. Along the way, he meets Jesus Christ on the road to Golgotha and sinks his vampire fangs into the son of God.

Memnoch the Devil offers passages of poetic brilliance, but with so much else going on in this epic, a reader can't stop to appreciate the fine points.

BOOK BAG

Literary Las Vegas: The Best Writing About America's Most Fabulous City (Henry Holt), edited by Mike Tronnes: Hunter Thompson, Tom Wolfe and Noël Coward are among the writers celebrating the essence of the American Monte Carlo.

The Night (Alone) (Little, Brown), by Richard Meltzer: A raucous coming-of-age novel from the man known as "the Thomas Paine of rock writing."

Total Health for Men (Rodale Press), edited by Neil Wertheimer: The first encyclopedia written solely for men covers every significant male health issue, including your sex life.

If You Leave Me, Can I Come Too? (Atlantic Monthly), by Cynthia Heimel: In this fifth collection, our *Women* columnist continues to help us laugh our way through life without Prozac.

Zhirinovsky: Russian Fascism and the Making of a Dictator (Addison-Wesley), by Vladimir Solovyov and Elena Klepikova: Further evidence that this bigot ought to be locked up before he becomes president of Russia.

Burning Angel (Hyperion), by James Lee Burke: In this ninth Dave Robicheaux mystery, Burke continues to mine the bayou and again comes up with hard-boiled literary gold.

What's Love Got to Do With It? (Anchor), by Meredith Small: An anthropologist's thorough, lucid, nontechnical descriptions of why we mate the way we do and how human sex has evolved.

Back Fire: The CIA's Secret War in Laos and Its Link to the War in Vietnam (Simon & Schuster), by Roger Warner: A grim, well-documented and important addition to the shadowy history of Southeast Asia between 1960 and 1973.

![Playboy rabbit logo]

PLAYMATE DATA SHEET

NAME: Priscilla Lee Taylor

BUST: 36   WAIST: 25   HIPS: 34

HEIGHT: 5'8"   WEIGHT: 118

BIRTH DATE: 8.15.71   BIRTHPLACE: Miami, Florida

AMBITIONS: To run my own modeling agency. To be very famous, very successful and very in love.

TURN-ONS: Secure, confident men with dark hair, strong bodies and even stronger personalities.

TURNOFFS: Laziness and rude comments.

NOTHING COMES BETWEEN: Me and my Mexican food — authentic Mexican is by far the best.

I DON'T LOOK GOOD IN: Turtlenecks — they look horrible! I dread New York winters.

I'D LIKE TO: Shake the hand of the person behind the Absolut vodka ads. I've framed every one.

FAVORITE BOOK: "The Shallow Man" by Coerte V.W. Felske. It's about a very shallow man and his involvements with models.

MY APARTMENT: It's like a giant game room on the ocean.

In the beginning...   Ken meets Barbie   Sssmokin'!

Sagas to enjoy from now to Labor Day

Les Misérables sparks a sequel

Laura Kalpakian's *Cosette* (HarperCollins) seems like a sequel to Victor Hugo's nineteenth-century novel but is more like a kissing cousin to the popular stage musical. As every child in France knows, in Hugo's story little Cosette is the abused waif eventually adopted by the bread thief Jean Valjean, who symbolizes the downtrodden Parisian masses. Kalpakian extends Cosette's life by 35 years and two children, giving her a glorious second career as Mea Culpa—a sassy political pundit who's sort of a French Republican precursor to Molly Ivins (except that Cosette must guard her safety with a pseudonym). The saga also tracks fresh denizens of the Paris underworld. Prime among these are the Starling, an up-and-coming bread thief, and Nicolette, a frond carrier at the Paris Opéra who has too much fun as the mistress of Parisian swells to settle for a conventional marriage with Cosette's bourgeois son, Jean-Luc. If Kalpakian's sequel behaves like a miniseries, it's no surprise: A couple of movie developers hired her to *Scarlett*-ize the saga. As a frankly commercial proposition, *Cosette* may be loved most by those who always *meant* to conquer Hugo's magnum opus but somehow kept slipping into not-so-*misérables* sagas like *Mistral's Daughter* instead.

Hurricane Pat

Pat Conroy's new novel, *Beach Music* (Nan A. Talese/Doubleday), is not a sequel to his last, *The Prince of Tides*, a long-running best-seller. But the plot promises similar swells of psychodrama. Considerably suaver than the hero of *Tides*—who emerged from a dirt-poor family of shrimp-boat operators—*Beach Music*'s narrator, Jack McCall, is the son of a judge and a Charleston, South Carolina, belle. A southern exile in recovery from post-Dixie traumatic stress disorder, Conroy's hero may despise the South he's left, but he can't stop talking about it. He's severed his roots to live as an expatriate food-and-travel writer in Rome. What holds him there, besides great eats, is a custody feud with his in-laws back in Charleston. The dispute dates to the suicide leap of his seven-year-old daughter's mother, Shylo—the eldest daughter of Holocaust survivors. Against their wishes, Jack spirited the child out of the United States in hopes of shielding her from her tragic family past. There's also a Vietnam-anniversary subplot in which filmmaker friends of Jack's are searching for a missing high school pal, a general's son who vanished 20 years ago while allegedly building bombs for the antiwar underground. And that's just the plot's outer casing. You never leave a scene in *Beach Music* without feeling that a whole lot of living has gone on, historically and in the present. Maybe Conroy is our Victor Hugo. He's got the big heart, the big memory and the big mouth.

110

Where cosmic meets cosmetic

Watching a good man get befuddled over a femme fatale always makes for a diverting read. To that end, Liz Rigbey's sophisticated mystery debut, *Total Eclipse* (Pocket), showcases a hero blinded by love who ought to have spent his summer reading *The Beauty Myth*. Call him Lomax: a disarmingly unkempt astronomer who finds himself romantically involved with Julia Fox, a lab colleague who's a prime suspect in a domestic murder case. The unsolved double slaying of Julia's husband and stepdaughter prove no impediment to Lomax's obsession with her; meantime, Lomax's friendly ex-wife, a spa manager, is stunned by the transformation in her former spouse, who shaves off his beard at Julia's urging. During a forced sabbatical from the observatory—where, coincidentally, he's party to an ethics investigation—Lomax becomes an extra telescope for Julia's defense team. As a suspense writer, Rigbey is more of a stockpiler of intriguing data than a thrill artist. The payoff comes with a revelation of plot duplicity that would make Alfred Hitchcock shake his jowls. Hint: Don't look too far into the cosmos for clues. The murder motive lies not in the stars but in the killer's cosmetic compulsions.

Did his lover commit murder? Liz Rigbey's hero investigates.

Deep thoughts from a male model

The Shallow Man (Crown), by Coerte V.W. Felske, humorously portrays Nick Laws, a model and club promoter who's happy to let "Thing" (the allure of beautiful women) dictate his conversation if not his life—to the point where he's mastered how to say, "Would you join me for a bubble bath?" in every language spoken by supermodels. Aware that his lifestyle annoys "dromes" (average-looking people who resent the beautiful), Nick argues that it's not his fault that "4-B girls" (beauty, breeding, brains and bank account) were created, or that men are compelled to pursue them. He frequently hauls out his tattered copy of Van Gogh's letters to prove that history's purest artist was also a model muncher. Set up by a "catsuit feminist" (one with beauty *and* brains), wary of "donuts" (male models who are stuck on themselves), a too-frequent partaker of "the Dracula nap" (sleep all day, come out at night), Nick is a lot of laughs even as his promiscuity takes on the aspect of an addiction passed from father to son. The plot's not exactly *Hamlet*, but fans of Jay McInerney and P.J. O'Rourke should be amused.

Who's afraid of a "catsuit feminist"? Not Coerte Felske's smart-aleck hero.

Glamour magazine

moment.) "After a few months," he says, "you can't help it—your girlfriend will start to say, 'Hey you're a nice guy, and really smart.' And that's not exactly what you want to hear. It's the beginning of the end. Like once on a party cruise, I was talking to these two women. We were getting along great, I thought. And one of them said just that: 'You know, you're a great guy, smart, from a good family'—and then she splits. I mean, what was the point? She split."

Diane Shader Smith, who is now married to a lawyer, offers a possible explanation. "A guy who's intelligent and high-powered carries the weight of the world on his shoulders. Male bimbos know how to have a good time. Another thing they're better for is sex. They're not worrying about waking up early for that important meeting."

Sometimes, however, even women who knowingly get involved with male bimbos are amazed at their vapidity and self-absorption. "All I wanted was to have sex with the guy," says an exasperated young Ph.D. candidate. She was talking about her latest himbo, an aspiring screenwriter cum security guard who later kept her on the phone for an hour talking about...himself. "He didn't ask one question about me," she complains. "I even tried bringing myself into the

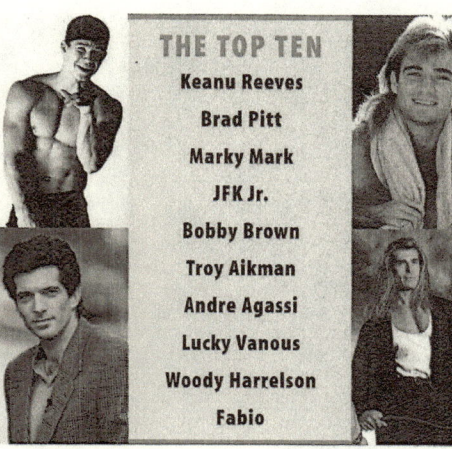

THE TOP TEN

Keanu Reeves

Brad Pitt

Marky Mark

JFK Jr.

Bobby Brown

Troy Aikman

Andre Agassi

Lucky Vanous

Woody Harrelson

Fabio

MOVE OVER, JAY MCINERNEY

Author Coerte Felske

Coerte V. W. Felske, the 33-year-old author of *The Shallow Man*, wants you to know: *he* is not his title character. The narrator of his forthcoming novel, he says, is a composite of a number of men whose antics he witnessed on the model circuit. "I used to live with a fashion photographer," he explains, "and these characters would show up at all the fashion shows. They'd fly around the world. They could be lawyers, restaurant owners, party promoters."

Felske says he himself doesn't even date models. "OK," he admits, "I have gone out with a few, but only very briefly. All my girlfriends, though, have been Cat-suit Feminists." This is Felske's term for women who are both intelligent and gorgeous. He introduces a number of such swell terms for young women in his book, which he says he wrote in five weeks. For example, Civilian Girls (anyone not fortunate enough to

be a model) and Dial Tones (women so stupid they might as well emit one each time they open their mouths).

"One of the challenges of the book was keeping Shallow Man from being too smart," says the Ivy League–educated Felske, who until recently lived in Hollywood writing screenplays, including one for Mickey Rourke he'd rather not discuss. "Shallow Man doesn't want to be deep. He's introspective but tries to avoid it." *The Shallow Man*, Felske insists, is a book for the nineties. "It's different from the eighties," he says, "when money and power were the big things. Now glamour is eclipsing intelligence in a lot of ways, rightly or wrongly."

In any case, Felske asks, "What's wrong with caring about beauty? Shallow Man thinks it's life-enhancing." As Forrest Gump might have put it, shallow is as shallow does. —*D.M.*

EXCERPT: HITTING THE WALL WITH THING

It was typical banter but we had come to the point in the conversation where you either take it higher or you hit *The Wall*. The Wall is a God-awful, excruciating mental state. It is that helpless feeling you get when you've exhausted all normal conversation with Thing and you find yourself unable to produce anything else witty or amusing to keep her interest. It's the point where nine out of ten guys fuck up and though it's painful to experience, it can be rather funny to watch.

Guy looks at Thing, she looks at him. She expects him to say something. But, with the pressure of her eyeballing him, he chokes, and looks away. He looks back at her but now she has turned away. His lips then part to utter something, but only air shoots out (or something stupid that he kills himself for saying later). He then notices Thing getting fidgety. She shuffles a step. The more uncomfortable she gets, the more he can think of nothing to save himself. He'll try anything. He looks over her shoulder, smiles falsely, as if to greet some imaginary acquaintance and POOF! She's gone....

I used to hit The Wall with regularity in my twenties but it doesn't happen very often now...

—*From* The Shallow Man, *by Coerte V. W. Felske*

Buzz Magazine

Ocean Drive Magazine

IT'S BEEN QUITE A YEAR for novelist Coerte V.W. Felske. He was greeted last summer with phenomenal reviews for his first novel, *The Shallow Man*, a satirical send-up of the modeling industry. From the *New York Times Book Review*, *Esquire*, *People*, *Glamour* and *Playboy* came comparisons that placed Felske in the same league as literary icons Tom Wolfe and Jay McInerney. The book-launching party held last summer at film producer Ted Field's estate in Southampton turned out to be a blowout for a thousand people, while Felske's book party in Los Angeles drew the likes of Jack Nicholson, Harvey Keitel, Ed Begley, Penny Marshall and Kiefer Sutherland.

Though his long, blond hair lends him the air of a hippie artist, Felske has traditional roots. He hails from a town in the fashionable Hamptons and attended the country's most prestigous schools; he was graduated from Dartmouth College, where he was a Romance Language scholar, in 1982. In 1986 he received a Master's in Fine Arts from Columbia University's film school.

Before joining the literary lions in New York, Felske worked as a screenwriter in Los Angeles. He has a dozen screenplays to his credit, most notably Mickey Rourke's *Homeboy*, which he co-penned with the actor. And in addition to writing well, Felske writes fast – he completed *The Shallow Man* in six weeks, and his latest project took only

As the hot new author of the moment, novelist Coerte Felske makes his mark with *The Shallow Man* and continues on an uphill swing

order

By W. Douglas Dechert

three months. He has his next six books outlined and will begin writing the screenplay to *The Shallow Man* after he finishes the Miami leg of his five-city book tour. It is to be produced by English producer Michael White (*Rocky Horror Picture Show*, *My Dinner with André*), who was given the book by Jack Nicholson. Nicholson wants to direct. Johnny Depp and Nicolas Cage are being touted to star.

DD: What is *The Shallow Man*?
CF: *The Shallow Man* is a satirical take on the modeling and fashion businesses. It deals with the beauty drive and glamour obsessions that our modern culture is entrenched in. *The Shallow Man* called it "Generation Face." There are many drives that are similar. The greed drive, the money drive, the power drive, they all involve superficiality and shallow pursuits. Men throughout time have been attracted to beauty. The story itself involves a hand model by day and party promoter by night who in essence carves through Manhattan nightlife in search of the ultimate beauties. He goes wherever he can to find them. That's how he gets through the day. It's a drug for him. And this guy is [faced] with the decision at the end of the story whether to continue living that way, after a series of setbacks, from family, from friends, who call him on his shallow ways and make him re-examine and reevaluate his existence, or turn it around. The main tension is whether he will revert or be redeemed.

DD: *The Shallow Man* seems to address contemporary issues of male-female interaction. Are there any trends in that arena that are at the top of your mind?
CF: Therein lies the significance of the character of the Catsuit Feminist. She's the walking contradiction. She's a woman who espouses the feminist platform yet at the same time enjoys being admired for her beauty and will stuff herself into a catsuit. I found it was important to have the Catsuit Feminist having problems finding a connection with a male. I see that every day. The modern woman, no matter what anyone says, is much more empowered. She has alternatives professionally and sexually. The Catsuit Feminist opts for a woman in the end. There's a feeling of "I just don't need a man." And I'm all for women and men expressing themselves however they wish. But let's not ignore the consequences – certainly separation of the sexes.

DD: Have you gotten any negative feedback from feminists?
CF: The book was received incredibly well. They were all incredibly supportive, even the most hard-line, so-called feminist reviewers. It's important that they got it. I wasn't sure if they would. It's a satire. Satire can fall flat. Or be taken in the wrong way. But readers of the *The Shallow Man* understood that the book was not an objectifying of the women but rather a disrobing of the men. It was stupid, shallow, male behavior being examined. It was putting you in the mindset of a guy

that does think this way. About women. About numbers. About variety. About sex. About commitment. About marriage. There are many men out there like that. For women, the book can be a warning. I was worried about the men feeling ratted out more than I was worried about the female readership. *The Shallow Man* is a composite of characters I have absolutely known. The book is a literary documentary. Of quotes I've heard, scenes I've seen, things I've experienced. The protagonist's generic pronoun name for beautiful women is Thing. It immediately brings to mind some kind of objectification. When really, he places women on a pedestal. He adores them. He doesn't get involved with any women that he knows are either vulnerable, emotionally crippled, too young, or someone who he senses may fall in love with him and therefore will get hurt when he goes on to the next one, which is his pattern. He stays away from that. He gets involved only with

"Writer's block has never been an

option for me. The Shallow

women who know the deal going in. It's all planned and thought out. Nick Laws is not in the business of lying to and hurting women. The Jersey girl rips him apart. *The Shallow Man* is not scorching the lives of women. The humor aspects soften the book, too. I was happy the groups who read this book got it. And wrote about it.

DD: You've sold the screen rights to *The Shallow Man*. It appears Jack Nicholson may direct the film. Any comments on that process?
CF: I was flattered to know he was a fan of the book. He attended the book launching party in Los Angeles. He read it and sent it to English producer Michael White, who is now producing the project. With respect to Jack, the only thing is when you get involved with stars of this magnitude, your worry is when they can free up and do your project. They say Jack's schedule is locked for a specific period of time. I hope he retains his enthusiasm for the project. If not, we'll go forth. Jack gave me a great producer in Michael White in any case and for that I am grateful.

DD: While we're on the subject of Hollywood, you spent ten years out there screenwriting. How did that affect your approach as a novelist?
CF: Fortunately, the first six years of that were in New York. I wrote screenplays out of New York. That helped. It gave me that edge I desperately needed from New York. And I lost it in Los Angeles when I was there. First of all, a publisher a long time ago told me it may well be easier to get a novel published than it is to get a screenplay made. I don't know what the numbers are but he may have been right. That's what happened. I was always told by my agents in Hollywood that I wrote screenplays like novels, that I really wanted to be a novelist. Three of them urged me to write books and, as soon as I did, the book sold.

Screenwriting for me was like training camp. It gave me discipline. I wrote fourteen screenplays in five years. Writer's block has never been an option for me. *The Shallow Man* was written in six weeks. My newest novel was written in three months. The writing is the easy part. It's the preparation of the story prior to the writing that takes time. Even though my work appears to be closer to stream of consciousness than anything so structured, it's organized from the beginning. I know my ending before I start. Many novelists just write and thereby make the entire process a discovery. I make the discovery within the framework of the skeleton I have laid down. I attempt to give it that fluidity and spontaneity and discovery that makes material biting and powerful.

DD: What's your socioeconomic background?
CF: We had some money, but not always. I'm no inheritance boy. Or trust-funder. I've had to make it on my own. My father was a successful real estate investor in the Hamptons. We lived in Quogue, Long Island, then Bronxville, New York. Both

Man was written in six weeks."

towns are upper middle-class communities. My mother is a brilliant and very articulate woman. It gave me an understanding of the privileged classes or those in a higher socioeconomic bracket. My dad is a salt-of-the-earth type, which was a grounding influence. I never went too far in either direction. I never fully adopted either world. But I understood both. As a writer, I never wanted my creative product to be steeped in anything so myopic, so one-sided that it reeked of artificiality, so it didn't ring of truth and reality, that it was bullshit and I didn't know my subject matter. Pretentiousness is what I'm talking about I guess.

DD: One thing I've found that's useful in growing up with a reasonably privileged background, is that you're able to delineate pretension very quickly.
CF: For me I think, the grounding force is that understanding of the different socioeconomic groups. It's the gauge which enables you to see through the bullshit. I've never been too far removed. I played three sports year round. And that gave me a sort of brotherhood with everyone else. We lived out in a summer resort town in Long Island, but all year round. So I hung out with the locals in the winter and the privileged types, the inheritance boys, in the summer. And my dad was an in-house check system against the phonics, the pretension. His senses are very keen that way. I purposely stayed away from all that country-club, cocktail party stuff. I didn't like it. Too boring. Not enough originality. And it was going to take me nowhere. Right into the land of social climbing, pretension, golf muscles, artificiality and certainly no career I felt worth pursuing. It was like the reverse of the ghetto but with the same results. Nowhere. I'm glad I got out of there. And I did it on my own. ❖

IS THERE A WAR BETWEEN THE SEXES?

Author Susan Faludi on what men are so mad about.

*B*acklash (Crown), Susan Faludi's 1991 bestseller, struck a nerve with readers as she chronicled the ways our male-dominated culture has sabotaged women and the gains we've made. "I marshaled enough evidence to convince myself and a lot of other people that there was a lot of anger out there toward women's equality," says the journalist who is now a contributing editor for *Newsweek.* With her second book, *Stiffed: The Betrayal of the American Man* (William Morrow), Faludi set out to find the roots of that anger. Beginning in what she thought was the obvious place—at a therapy group for men who'd battered the women in their lives—Faludi soon discovered that physical abuse was but one "leaf of the artichoke" of male anger. At the heart, she says, is male rage at a culture that has robbed them of their definition of masculinity. In *Stiffed,* she observes and talks to many different men—from porn stars to laid-off aeronautics engineers to born-again Promise Keepers to Citadel cadets—and comes to some interesting conclusions about the current state of manhood in America. SELF's editor-at-large, Sara Nelson, spoke with Faludi about her findings.

SELF: The subtitle of your book includes the word *betrayal.* Who do you think men have been so betrayed by?

SUSAN FALUDI: So much about being a man in this society is winner-take-all, be number one, have the biggest SUV. And if you can't be number one, you're nothing. I would argue that the root of the problem for men is in the cultural shift from a society in which men have a role to a consumer culture that is ruled by retail values.

SELF: But we have always lived in a competitive society. I bet cavemen competed over who brought home more skins. Isn't score-keeping a normal human tendency?

SF: Maybe, but I think what has happened is that those impulses used to be balanced by other values—like

A man's view of sex, love and romance in the new millennium.

*O*n the surface, Coerte V. W. Felske's *The Millennium Girl* (St. Martin's Press) couldn't be more different from Susan Faludi's *Stiffed.* Felske's book is a novel, its protagonist is a woman and it's written by a man. But like *Stiffed, The Millennium Girl* deals with what Susan Faludi calls "the ornament culture" in which what you look like, drive and have are the most important things.

The heroine of *The Millennium Girl* is Bodicea Lashley, a twentysomething "Digger"—a veritable prostitute; think Holly Golightly meets *Sex and the City*—who travels the world hooking up with rich, powerful older men who'll keep her in Prada. Convinced that she only has a 10-year window (from 20 to 30) to snare herself a rich "Walletman" and that how she looks, where she goes and who she knows are her most valuable attributes, Bodicea has what her creator cheerfully agrees are "self-image problems. She thinks men are the answer."

The explicit sex, shopping and globe-trotting in *The Millennium Girl* is exactly the sort of shallow consumerism Faludi targets in *Stiffed.* ("[This is a culture in which] there's nothing to do between the time you wake up and the time you go to bed besides eat and go to the movies and jog," Faludi says.) And at first, Felske's book seems as superficial as the world it depicts. Women are routinely called "girls," when, that is, they're not given faux Native American names that describe their behavior: "Three Minute Princess" or "Earning Every Penny." The sex is of the notch-in-the-belt variety and everybody's interested in money. Yet Felske's story—like his previous novels, *The Shallow Man* and *Word,* not to mention Jay McInerney's megahit *Bright Lights, Big City,* to which it will likely be compared—aims to be uplifting and hopeful. Bodicea really does evolve over the course of the book from a piece of professional arm
Continued on page 130

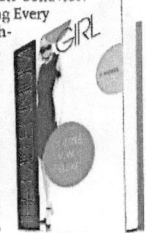

Self Magazine

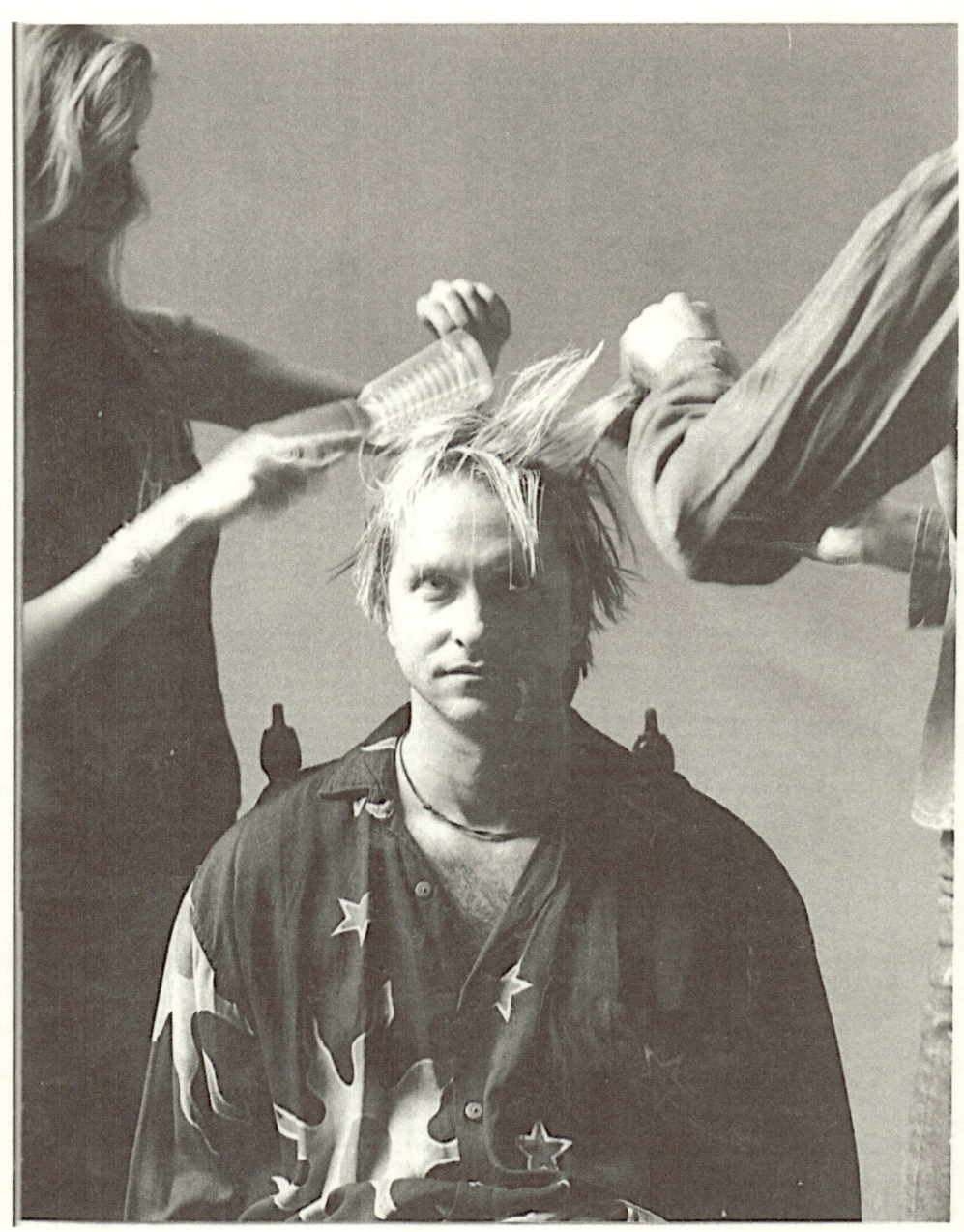

New York Magazine

His latest tale, *Word*, is a jazzy, ironic appreciation of writing, filmmaking, and chasing skirt. In two of those arts, at least, downtown novelist Coerte v. w. Felske seems more than passingly adept.

I

T'S AN UNEXPECTEDLY HOT, STICKY NIGHT IN LATE NOvember, and though the police are trying to persuade the hundreds of revelers gathered around the iron gates of Joe's Pub to move along, inside the three-week-old Lafayette Street club a wild party is in full swing. Pink and red spotlights swirl over the sunken dance floor as models in backless dresses dance to Abba with the men who love them—arch-rivals Donald Trump and Roffredo Gaetano; photographer Sante D'Orazio; tank-topped club impresarios Jeffrey Jah, Mark Baker, and Nur Khan; and a couple of well-known gossip columnists. An open-shirted Kevin Costner takes a breather in a banquette with Chuck Pfeiffer, Bob Shaye, and Peter Brant; from their table nearby, Emma S., Kara Young, and a few more models edging over 30 wriggle their fingers seductively in greeting. A movie premiere? A supermodel's birthday? No, it's a book party.

But one befitting Coerte v. w. Felske, the 38-year-old author of 1995's *The Shallow Man* and the upcoming *Word*, both of which are taut, clever character studies centered on this posse of older roués and slightly over-the-hill models—all of whom the author considers close friends, the kind who come over for late-night glasses of port in the SoHo apartment he shares with gallery director Michiel van der Waal, brother to Frederique, and whichever South African or Dutch or Italian models are passing through town. That is, when he's not in Quogue playing tennis with Taki, or in St. Tropez with his new Czech-Croatian girlfriend who lives in Switzerland, or hanging out in L.A. at Monkey Bar with his old friend Jack Nicholson, who helped arrange for the filming of *The Shallow Man* (for protagonists, Felske's thinking "Pitt, Penn, Downey, DiCaprio, or Cage").

With his surfer's patois, a mellow constitution that he chalks up to being a Libra, and a practiced way of speaking similar to Mister Rogers's, Felske is beloved by all: a guy's guy and a model's guy, whose novels neatly refract their own lives through a highly ironic prism. He does take his shots at ponytailed, Vespa-riding, mannequin-addicted, SoHo-loft-living thirtysomethings who are band models by day and party promoters by night. But Felske sympathizes with the dudes at the end, attributing their flaws to societal shortcomings and a general millennial ill will.

In Felske's world, models are called Thing (young ones are Baby Thing, stupid ones are Dialtones); the rest of womankind are Civilians, His girlfriends are Catsuit Feminists, and we, Generation Face, all live in the notoriety-obsessed Age of A (for Astonishment). His characters often think in these terms; what's more, their feelings are italicized: *"No one wants to be sentenced to life at someone else's table. . . . I want the reservation in my own name. I want my own table and I want to fill it with whomever I fancy."* Less self-consciously writerly than other colleagues who are concerned with this tribe, like Bret Easton Ellis or Jay McInerney, Felske confides that he writes his books in only a few weeks.

"It's all about the voice," he says, often, as if it were a mantra.

Just tonight, Felske comes up with a theory he calls the Ten-Year Window. "Women only have the years from 20 to 30 to really do it up," he says, taking a seat at the bar next to Joaquin Phoenix. "For some, maybe 24 to 34." How to take this comment, delivered, to all appearances, by a guy who's apparently spent a little too much time with Things and not enough with Civilians? Auditing women's-studies classes while a grad student at Columbia's film school, he tells me, qualifies him as a feminist—yet he suggests that women are different from men because they're "ruled by the moon." Oh.

As a samba band tunes up onstage at Joe's, a sunglasses-wearing Ralph Lauren model named Zofia jumps up on a table near the D.J. booth. "God, do I adore Coerte, he is *so* wise," she announces, narrowly avoiding the approaching gang of Felske's high-school buddies, who smother him with bear hugs and painful-looking noogies. "This dude," gurgles the beefiest one, grabbing him by an Armani lapel, "was so popular with chicks in high school that cheerleaders from the *other* team were asking for his number."

Sipping an Amstel Light with three or four undone shirt buttons revealing dark tufts of chest hair, Felske runs a hand through his white-blond, shoulder-length locks before jumping onto a conga line between Mark Bavaro and Daniela Pestova, his five-foot-eleven stature greatly diminished by their hulking figures. He leans in close and confides, in utter mock seriousness, "I'm the Mad Hatter."

O

VER THE DIN AT DA SILVANO A FEW NIGHTS EARLIER, FELSKE takes gulps of San Pellegrino and looks over the crowd—David Duchovny, Helmut Lang, and, to his delight, Robert De Niro eating penne with his family at a corner table: the perfect setting for what he wants to discuss.

"See, the most important businessmen, bankers, film producers, and studio heads don't know squat when it comes to women," says Felske, winking indiscreetly in De Niro's direction. That's what *Word* is about: the Faustian bargain struck between a film writer struggling for credits and a 50-year-old studio head trolling for dates. It's a relationship not unlike Felske's with Ted Field, the fiftyish head of Interscope Records, who is rarely seen without a woman hovering around legal age ("Ted has no problem getting dates," Felske retorts, denying widespread buzz that the character is based on Field). Not to mention Felske's friendship with Mickey Rourke, with whom he lived for five months while rewriting Rourke's boxing movie, *Homeboy*. "I only got respect once he realized that I could get him pretty girls," says Felske.

After dinner, Felske suggests a trip to Lot 61—"I hear it's the hot joint"—but I beg off. He asks if I have a boyfriend, and walks me home. Running his fingers through his mane concernedly, he has one last thing to say before stepping off into the night: "So, what's going on with my hair?"

A Model Wordsmith
BY VANESSA GRIGORIADIS

People are Talking about
books
John Richardson has always been a master raconteur. In *The Sorcerer's Apprentice*, he's at his peak with Picasso, Braque, and the rest of the gang.

a h, the 1950s. Nostalgia for that decade usually brings to mind a nuclear family presided over by a June Cleaver clone, so clean-cut and cheerful it's scary. But here is another, better reason for fifties nostalgia: Back then you could stumble by accident across a neglected French château, nurture it back to health, purchase Cubist masterworks on the cheap in an undervalued market, and amass one of the world's great art collections for what seems today like little more than a song. That's exactly what John Richardson, future author of the definitive Picasso biography, did during a decade-long relationship with the controversial art critic Douglas Cooper. Or, more precisely, as he recalls in his entertaining new memoir, *The Sorcerer's Apprentice* (Knopf), the 25-year-old, impressionable Richardson moved in with Cooper (then the art world's most renowned champion of Cubism), helped him buy and restore the château and amass the art collection, and ended up watching in helpless horror as his reckless and insecure lover self-destructed, bringing their idyllic life together to a disastrous close. The book is a true festival of gossip: Socialites, royalty, and various fifties wunderkinds drop in for cameos, with more substantial appearances by Georges Braque, W. H. Auden, and Francis Bacon. Picasso lived a short drive away and became Cooper's and Richardson's close friend. Needless to say, Richardson's description of Picasso at work is priceless, alive to both his genius and his egomania. The maestro comes off like a noble vampire who even as a deaf old man could suck the life force out of his admirers, sneak off, and "use it to fuel a night of work in his studio." —S.K.

PICASSO WITH HIS WIFE JACQUELINE AND OTHERS, 1957.

Novelist-cum-boulevardier Coerte V.W. Felske explains how to marry a billionaire in 1999.

t he outtakes from the life of Coerte V.W. Felske teem with glamour: The portrait of the novelist as a young man by good friend Peter Beard; a snapshot with model Frederique van der Wal; another with Sandra, his girlfriend-model, in St. Tropez. To Felske, whose previous book parties were held at Joe's Pub and Lot 61, the velvet rope simply does not exist.

For tonight's out-on-the-town interview, Felske suggests we start with drinks uptown at Fifty Seven Fifty Seven ($110). From there, perhaps, we'll move on to dinner at Harry Cipriani ($500) before finishing up with nightcaps at Au Bar ($175). An evening with Felske is enough to make a girl's Prada habit seem positively economical.

By 7:30 P.M., Felske is *books* ▶336

Vogue Magazine

People are Talking about

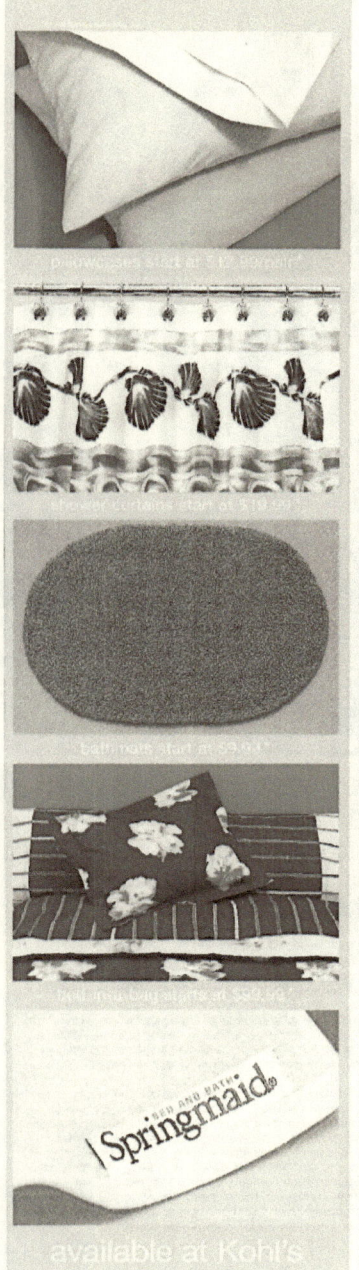

books

THE YOUNG AND THE RESTLESS AND THE VERY RICH ARE AT THE CENTER OF COERTE V.W. FELSKE'S LATEST NOVEL

THE MILLENNIUM GIRL

A NOVEL

COERTE V. W. FELSKE

stretched out at a table in the cavernous bar, ready to talk about his new novel and the events that inspired it. He runs a hand through his shaggy Caesar cut, cocks his head forward, and tries desperately to be heard above the din. "It's a good night." he says, surveying a room of Armani-clad tycoons, endless martini glasses, and the high-pitched laughter of well-dressed women. "Wednesdays are good," he announces emphatically. "The men have finished their business today; maybe there's a meeting tomorrow, but now they have a night or two before they have to go home to their wives. And you get everyone here—Europeans, South Americans, *everyone*. It's prime Digger territory."

A "Digger," mind you, is Felske's term for a woman who targets wealthy men like a heat-seeking missile. And Diggers are at the center of *The Millennium Girl* (St. Martin's Press), Felske's much-buzzed-about new novel. A fictionalized account of his gimlet-eyed social observations, *The Millennium Girl* takes the reader through the marriage market of the nineties. His heroine, Bodicea, is determined to land herself not just a husband but a husband who meets a strict set of financial and social criteria. According to Felske, it's women's lib for the nineties; Bodicea's point of view takes a quick tussle with the fifties (for that perennially chic retro feel), spins through the eighties (for a dose of glamour), and lands firmly in the next century—the goal is still the same (landing the guy), but the white picket fence has morphed into a classic six, several vacation homes, and a Gulfstream V for the commute. The difference is that these women, like Bodicea, approach finding a husband with the steely-eyed acumen of a CEO: Wine and dine at Le Cirque 2000, shop at Gucci and Manolo, summer in the Hamptons, and winter in Aspen. Beyond having the money that allows them to traffic in global finery, these women are looking for men who can spend it with style.

But *The Millennium Girl* is not just another collection of insiders' jargon and "Page Six" gossip. Felske is the real thing: He knows his territory, and he writes about it with wit and style. *Girl* may have taken him only a few weeks to write, but he's been steeped in its culture since childhood. He grew up on the Eastern Shore of Long Island, navigated his way around Manhattan from a very early age, spent his undergraduate years at Dartmouth, and then did graduate work at Columbia University's film school—after which he cowrote *Homeboy* for actor Mickey Rourke. Then came two novels that, like *Girl*, glitter with a diamond-sharp deconstruction of modern life in the fast lane. Both got solid reviews, including *The New York Times*'s; both are being produced for the big screen by New Line Cinema. "It's all about the voice." Felske says, describing what makes his novel different. "It's honest. It's in praise of women who are trying to better themselves in anyway they can. Occasionally you write music and people respond to it, and I think this strikes some universal chords." —DANA WAGNER

*pata ▶338

sugardaddy sinderellas

Author **Coerte V. W. Felske** mines America's goldigger circuit in his new novel *The Millennium Girl.* **Bill Powers** learns why honey makes the world go round.

At a high-profile fete in Manhattan, Coerte V. W. Felske was once introduced to Christy Turlington as "the man who never met a model he didn't like." Just recalling the incident is enough to give him chills. "It's stuff like that that really makes me cringe," says the 39-year-old scribe, taking three steps back as if to punctuate via pantomime, "but I guess it sort of comes with the territory."

When your first novel is called *The Shallow Man* and follows the antics of an urban model hunter leading a barely examined life, there's some inherent baggage an author must learn to accept. Nevertheless, his 1995 debut put Coerte's name on all the right lips, including those attached to Jack Nicholson, New Line Cinema, and *Esquire* magazine.

That winter, the men's glossy assigned Coerte an investigative feature on Aspen's yearly Christmas break influx of goldiggers. The $18,000 exposé was ultimately killed due to changes in *Esquire's* editorial leadership but Coerte's encounters with these 21st century courtesans on the slopes of Colorado's toniest ski town left a lasting impression. Eventually they would serve as foundation for his latest tale of woe and dough entitled *The Millennium Girl.* Coerte recalls his Rocky Mountain excursion over a round of St. Pauli Girls at the Time Hotel in New York:

"I interviewed about 25 or 30 girls. At first no one wanted to talk and, really, what woman in her right mind would want to draw this kind of attention?" he asks with the annunciation of a TV anchorman.

"Then after New Year's Eve it was interesting, the women who hadn't managed to land their guy sort of felt this need to purge. I promised I wouldn't use their names and they gave me the full rundown. That's when I heard about girls studying the names on the *Fortune* and *Forbes* lists. Some girls were going to Brunei the next week. They just disappear for a while – tell their family that they're going to model in Europe or something – and wind up making $25,000 a week. It's a totally viable financial undertaking for a woman. I mean, there's no question what they're doing is prostitution, but they get paid incredibly well."

The assembled anecdotes have been fictionalized into the life of *The Millennium Girl* – a twenty-eight year old Digger named Bodicea – who lives in Trump Tower with her gay best friend Napoleon. Bo is looking to get off Tour permanently, meaning no more St. Moritz in March, June in The Hamptons, July in St. Tropez. She's tired of constantly chumming the bigwig waters hoping to get hooked on the purse strings of unreliable, though often generous, Walletmen. But, she's also wary of settling down. To paraphrase a rhetorical pondering of Bo's: Why have one guy who treats you like shit when you can have 20 who treat you like a Goddess?

"Many of the girls I spoke with think a woman should get what she can," says Coerte. "Let's face it, survival is where it's always been at and some women are more hard-nosed than others. There's a very low success ratio [when it comes to goldigging] and if they play *the game* too long, these women often wind up making compromises they never would have in their youth. In this modern age, as things get more stressful and Darwinian, people start doing things they never would have found acceptable back when life was a little more homespun. My whole thing was to show the warmer side of these women so you know where that money gravitation comes from. Ultimately Bo prevails and gets what she wants on her terms, but it's definitely a low-percentage racket."

"My bedroom is where I dream up things like Writer-Is-Rock-Star or depict a sci-fi world in which writers rule. And then I wake up to find that I'm in my third Writer's Guild arbitration hearing in three years."

coerte felske

author, The Shallow Man *and the upcoming* Word. *He is currently completing a screenplay of* The Shallow Man *for New Line Cinema.*

Also by

Coerte V. W. Felske

for

The DVP

coertefelske.com
thedolcevitapress.com

Cover art, calligraphy, cover photograph of Alessandra Ambrosío and back cover
photograph of Ana Beatriz Barros, Alessandra Ambrosío, and Irina Shayk by
Peter Beard shot on Giant Polaroids in New York City, 2009, produced by CVWF

Cover design by Christian Toms for Red & Jacket or chris@redandjacket.com
and CVWF for The Dolce Vita Press
Cover concept by Jackie Merri Meyer for MeyerNewYork@aol.com
and CVWF for The Dolce Vita Press

"Tom Wolfe rewrites *American Gigolo*."
— *Kirkus Reviews*

"Crass, slangy, egotistical, and reeking of sun bronze, and the turnover of fleshy delights makes the narrator's decision to become an aging roué instead of responsible adult seem like an admirable choice. Felske writes like a gigolo and treats seduction as a dirty sport."
— James Wolcott, *Vanity Fair*

"Model citizen. Nick Laws, who narrates Coerte Felske's amusing first novel, proves that the unexamined life is worth living. Nick detests the beach but this novel is perfect for it."
— *The New York Times Book Review*

"Felske spins a clever tale of the narcissistic world of fashion modeling. Nick is so perfect he's hilarious. *The Shallow Man* is fun, flash, and filigree—a sexy, witty, spoof of the 90s."
— Digby Diehl, *Playboy*

"Tight prose, smooth dialogue, captures characters' gloss with a smart shine of its own."
— *Publishers Weekly*

"Shallow waters run deep. The quick-witted prose makes a case for the unexamined life."
— *Esquire*

"Spiked with original Nickspeak and hilarious dialogue. Very clever."
—*People Magazine*

"Felske's novel *The Shallow Man* turned the fashion world on its head—and introduced the term 'modelizer' into the collective consciousness. Refreshingly moral-free."
— *Detour*

"Deep thoughts from a hand model, fans of McInerney and O'Rourke should be amused."
— *Glamour*

"Make no mistake, Felske's literary Lothario, the Shallow Man, is no ordinary ladies' man. He's an uberstud for the '90s, otherwise known as a model hound, beauty junkie, or, **modelizer**."
— *Details*

"The *Shampoo* of the 1990s."
— *The New York Daily News*

"The *Bright Lights, Big City* of the 90s."
— *Buzz Magazine*

"Generation X's answer to *Less Than Zero*."
— *Sydney Morning Herald (Australia)*

Front and back cover photographs of Adriana Lima by Ellen von Unwerth
Calligraphy by Peter Beard and Chris Toms

Word 2014 cover design Cover design by Christian Toms for Red & Jacket or
chris@redandjacket.com and CVWF for The Dolce Vita Press

Original cover concept by Jackie Merri Meyer for MeyerNewYork@aol.com and
CVWF for The Dolce Vita Press

"**Chandler for the 90s: (*****)** *Word* is pure 40s cool and paragraphs swing with voiceover rhythms that put Harrison Ford's *Blade Runner* monologues to shame. Beautiful babes, New York wasps and sleazy zillionaires flit through *Word*, larger than life and twice as interesting."
— Carrie O'Grady, *The Guardian (England)*

"A torrent of L.A. buzzwords and insider cynicism unmatched since Odets and Lehman's *Sweet Smell of Success* took on Manhattan. The Hell-A hypechat will flick all of your fuses."
— *Kirkus Reviews*

"Flashy and dark, this energetic Nathanael West retake offers a rich Hollywood menu of pandering, ambition, power, and retribution."
— *Publishers Weekly*

"**Magnificent Obsessions:** *Word,* the book Bret Ellis didn't write, is Felske's satire of Hollywood, i.e., 'Star Camp,' and he does a great job with female movie colony characters."
— *Playboy*

"*The Shallow Man* turned fashion on its head bringing the term 'modelizer' into the collective conscious. With tough-talking *Word*, Felske is back, red-eyeing it over Tinseltown's turf."
— *Detour*

"By page 3 of this sharp send-up of all things Hollywood, you'll be patting yourself on the back for having discovered *Word* before *Variety* announces its arrival at a theater near you."
— *Marie Claire*

"**If We Gave Out Book Awards:** Edgiest Boy, *Word.*. Felske's anti-hero hilariously manages to find some beating hearts inside the hippest Hollywood hyphenates."
— *Glamour*

"*Word* belongs to the growing genre of Hollywood novels in which idealistic filmmakers experience disillusionment and con artists and charlatans occupy the positions of power."
— *USA Today*

"*Word* is winningly told, with often ferocious humor, including a fresh, funny argot. Recommended for fiction collections."
— *Library Journal*

"A vicious story of the movie-driven anathema of depth that is L.A, Felske's tale about aching for success and the price of achieving it will remind you why you live in Northern California."
— *San Francisco Metropolitan*

"*Word,* is a jazzy, ironic appreciation of writing, filmmaking, and chasing skirt. In two of those arts, at least, downtown novelist Coerte V.W. Felske seems more than passingly adept."
— *New York Magazine*

"The word on *Word* is all good."
— *"Page Six," The New York Post*

Front and back cover photographs of Alessandra Ambrosío by Raphael Mazzucco
Calligraphy by Peter Beard and Chris Toms

The Millennium Girl 2014 cover design by Christian Toms for Red & Jacket or
chris@redandjacket.com and CVWF for The Dolce Vita Press

Original cover concept by Jackie Merri Meyer for MeyerNewYork@aol.com and
CVWF for The Dolce Vita Press

"How to Catch a Man at the Century's End: A face-to-face with 'diggers,' women who troll resorts in search of millionaires. We know that women like this exist, but until now we didn't have all the gory details. Bo is charming and the book is hilarious and sympathetic."
— *The New York Times Book Review*

"*The Millennium Girl* skillfully takes us through the marriage market of the new millennium. Felske is the real thing: He knows his territory, and he writes about it with wit and style."
— *Vogue*

"The resourceful Felske's latest topic is gold diggers, the sweet lovelies more shark-like than Anita Loos's or Truman Capote's and the author laces every page with a masterful cynicism."
— *Kirkus Reviews*

"Based on a magazine article Felske wrote about young women hustling in Aspen, *The Millennium Girl*, is snappy fun, a box of candy wrapped up with a black latex bow."
— *Booklist*

"A strong follow-up to his previous, *Word*, Felske uses his trademark insight and detail to peer into the lives of sassy, sad women and their encounters with the richest. A complete hoot, sexy, hard to put down, it's 100 percent fun, and recommended for all fiction collections."
— *Library Journal*

"In *The Millennium Girl*, pulse-of-the-Zeitgeist author Coerte Felske sets his sights on 'Diggers,' the globe-trotting hotties on the hunt for 'Walletmen,' the ultra-rich men of their dreams."
— *Detour*

"Who are these lit It Girls?*The Millennium Girl*. 'I'm not a hooker but I do live off men,' says Bodicea. I wanted to hate her, but she was too shameless and too hilariously over-the-top."
— *Mademoiselle*

"Felske's cleverly describes the art of the gold-digger and the folly of their prey. Bo invents cute nicknames for the Diggers and acidic jibes at upper-class hypocrisy, good for chuckles."
— *Publishers Weekly*

"Great fun and more than a racy rehash of *Pretty Woman*, Felske covered the 'digger' scene in an article for *Esquire* and clearly knows the turf. Female empowerment, a having-it-all ending, a pampered husband-hunter, and a flaming gay sidekick perpetuate these pages."
— *Entertainment Weekly*

"*Breakfast at Tiffany's* for the year 2000. A totally titillating read."
— *Woman's Own*

"Bodicea is possessed of a wry sense of humor and eye for detail and she sympathetically picks apart her own insecurities and those of fellow Diggers. Once again, Felske expertly maps the morally dubious interiors of characters who live on a razor's edge of scruples."
— *The Southampton Press*

Cover art, calligraphy, front and back cover photographs of Irina Shayk by
Peter Beard shot on Giant Polaroids in New York City, 2009, produced by CVWF

Cover design by Christian Toms for Red & Jacket or chris@redandjacket.com
and CVWF for The Dolce Vita Press

Original cover concept by Jackie Merri Meyer for MeyerNewYork@aol.com
and CVWF for The Dolce Vita Press

Scandalocity

Author Coerte V.W. Felske's fourth novel, *Scandalocity* (The Dolce Vita Press, 2012) comes on the heels of his highly acclaimed "dolce vita fiction" trilogy: *The Shallow, Man, Word,* and *The Millennium Girl.* Zeitgeist for the Information Age, the book is set against the backdrop of the starry lights and glamorous nights of New York City. Defined as "The speed at which scandal, measured in velocity, can turn you into a star," *Scandalocity* is a sexy, ADHD psychological thriller, and the master of guilty pleasure prose takes on our technology-driven, media-consumed, and celebrity-obsessed culture in a taut, explosive narrative. Protagonist Harry Starslinger is a neurologically disordered online gossip columnist who becomes embroiled in the police investigation of his girlfriend's murder. Like Dostoevsky's *Notes From Underground,* the book takes off in roaring first-person as we ride Harry's spontaneous, insightful thoughts. One of the most connected men in the City, where his high-profile position as a purveyor of celebrity gossip offers him access anywhere, anytime, "Slinger" finds it difficult to founder life-sustaining connections in a rocket-paced world of IMs, iPods and e-mails, social networking sites, and hand-held techie toys. The story unfolds in parallel between the ongoing murder investigation and the burgeoning romance with the victim in the past. There's more murder, a manhunt, and Harry becomes the hunted one. A pulsating page-turner, the novel combines the scalding thematic tones of Odets and Lehman's *The Sweet Smell of Success* with the suspense and dramatic twists of Kasden's erotic cinema thriller *Body Heat.* Felske's fourth installment in his "dolce vita fiction" series, *Scandalocity* crackles with razor sharp vernacular and a lexicon's worth of bleeding edge phraseologies, hallmarks of the author's inimitable life-in-the-fast-lane literature.

the
dolce
vita
press

The Ivory Stretch

Coerte V.W. Felske

Cover calligraphy and back cover photographs by Peter Beard
shot on Giant Polaroids, New York, 2009, produced by CVWF

The Ivory Stretch cover design by Chris Toms for Chris.Toms@live.com
and CVWF for The Dolce Vita Press

Original cover concept by Jackie Merri Meyer for MeyerNewYork@aol.com
and CVWF for The Dolce Vita Press

The Ivory Stretch

Coerte V. W. Felske, noted Zeitgeist chronicler of the skin-deep and shameless age, flits, flaps, flutters, stretches wings, and struts with his latest, *The Ivory Stretch* (The Dolce Vita Press, 2016). Frenetic, idiosyncratic, bedazzling, and uniquely original, this wild ride of a novel showcases protagonist Billy Sixkiller who seizes the reader's imagination and uses him to gaze boldly into the heart of the American psyche in the great literary tradition of Twain, Kerouac, Kesey, Thompson, and McCarthy. Through Billy, the author launches a revenge tale steeped in the Native American ethos to create a vivid snapshot of conflicted America in the 21st century. Aptly named, Sixkiller—a modern-day Odysseus if not Moses himself—is a larger-than-life anti-hero who takes dispirited road companions on an adventure of a lifetime of his own design, a postmodern Vision Quest of spiritual renewal and self-discovery. "Billy Six" slices through the breathtaking settings of the Southwest in a supercharged elongated car made of curves, white beyond white, blasting wide the eyes of his unsuspecting roadies—reluctant accomplice, the Parisian orphaned Frenchy, and his suicidal captive Roland. Billy initially kidnaps the dead-souled novelist for a past crime, but a curious relationship develops between the two men, which is the beating heart of the story. Along the way, the emotionally recessive prisoner develops an amorous bond with sheltered, spiritually-starved Frenchy, Billy's former lover. This ever-shifting three-way and unlikely clashing of personalities and blend of intimate motivations staves off predictability and the narrative not only retains its oxygen, but surprises the reader as it reinvents itself at every turn. When the trio are together taking to the highway in the stretch limo the novel zooms into high gear, comprising one of the great road trips to be found in American literature, rife with unconscious echoes of Least Heat-Moon's *Blue Highways*, Pirsig's *Zen and the Art of Motorcycle Maintenance*, as well as Thompson's *Fear and Loathing*. The dramatic ironies compound as the charismatic, dazzlingly unpredictable Billy, seeking to exact revenge on Roland for the murder of his parents, ends up giving his emotionally voided prisoner a new appreciation for life. Billy hauls him across four state's worth of deserts, forests, and Indian lands for five sleep-deprived days in an effort to peel away a lifetime's layers of anguish, guilt, and disillusionment and blow the winds of life back into Roland's lungs. Because only by having his captive embrace living again can Billy truly have the power to take something of value away from him, that is, the man's life. Why? To give his revenge value and meaning. Which brings us to the grandiose, complex, and magnificent rendering of the Sixkiller character. Perceptive though manipulated, profane yet sacred, gentlemanly but diabolical, and like a bomb going off in a fireworks factory, Billy explodes onto the page spouting his vast artillery of language like shrapnel. His prescient, savvy, irreverent, fuel-injected rants border on the Whitmanesque and his outlaw spirit at once embodies *and* contradicts the journeying aspect of the American character; a contemporary equivalent of the searching characters in Kerouac's *On the Road* and Kesey's *Sometimes a Great Notion*. Almost as uncommonly, the pouty-sexy-feisty Frenchy, Billy's thirsting sidekick, is another full-bodied, unique personage who evolves before our eyes and learns to more than hold her own against him. Simultaneously thrilling, *noir*ish, crackling and detouring, the electric prose masterfully seasoned with philosophies, historical asides, tribal customs, letters, diaries, metaphors, and individual paths to enlightenment gives the tome a hightened reality, while remaining true to the enchanting milieu of L'Amour and sensibilities of McCarthy to forge a new kind of western. Felske, whose previous works lasered in on modern fast lane culture, has gone lyrical, poetic, even classic here, with his boldest and most significant work, shepherding a cast of characters who start out searching for external validation, but find internal truths instead. The author expertly transports his eye for detail and innate curiosities on a different kind of "dolce vita" that is equally sweet, but twice as spicy. Like a gun barrel to the small of the back, *The Ivory Stretch* forces the reader to contemplate the vulgar and divine, entwining sex, lyricism, violence, and spirituality to inspire deeper epiphanies. With its author's mythic vision of a southwestern death trip that transforms into something decidedly more life-affirming, *The Ivory Stretch* claims its place as a vital part of the American literary tradition and Billy Sixkiller joins the pantheon of great fictional character creations, certainly to be one of the most talked about in recent memory. Conjuring hints and evoking whispers of some of literature's finest, *The Ivory Stretch* sets the imagination ablaze with an unforgettable, high-octane, adrenaline rush ride which haunts the psyche well after the story's climactic conclusion.

Chemical / Animal coming Summer, 2019

Completed Works

of

Coerte VW Felske

coming soon from

The Dolce Vita Press

Chemical / Animal

A Touch of Noir

The Dolce Vita Press Presents The Complete Works of...

Coerte V.W. Felske

To purchase Coerte V. W. Felske titles,
request signed or review copies, write to the publisher
or author, or for news, updates, and descriptions
of upcoming releases and an in-depth biography,
please visit the author's Web site at:

coertefelske.com
thedolcevitapress.com

Montauk, 2018

Photo by Peter Beard, Thunderbolt Ranch, Montauk

Coerte V.W. Felske was born in New York City and grew up in Manhattan and Quogue, Long Island. He attended Bronxville High School and received his Bachelor of Arts degree from Dartmouth College. He did his graduate work in film directing and screenwriting at Columbia University. *The Shallow Man*, originally published in 1995, was his first novel. His second novel, *Word*, came out in 1998 followed by *The Millennium Girl* in 2000. In 2010 the independent online literary imprint The Dolce Vita Press was founded in conjunction with Amazon.com to publish and distribute Felske's books. The imprint's inaugural publication was *Scandalocity* published in 2012. Special author's cut anniversary editions of both the acclaimed *Word* and *The Millennium Girl* were released in 2014 followed by *The Shallow Man: 20th Anniversary Edition* in 2015. Felske's southwest psychological drama *The Ivory Stretch* was released in 2016. *Three Sleeps to Double Happiness*, Felske's sixth original novel, is slated for a summer, 2018 release accompanied by a book reading and signing tour in in the U.S. and Canada.

The Dolce Vita Press was established to enhance contact with the readership as well as offer the author the creative freedom to incorporate the talents of top photographers, graphic artists, and book jacket designers. The DVP label derives from the Italian term "dolce vita," which translates to the "sweet life." Felske was influenced by Federico Fellini's cinematic masterwork, *La Dolce Vita*, which tells the tale of a carefree, decadent group of seemingly glamorous bon vivants, nightclubbers, and exotic women as they navigate their way through Rome's high society, all pursued by a dashing playboy paparazzo. The author has often referred to his literature as "dolce vita fiction," stories about nightclub impresarios, serial womanizers, fashionistas, fortune hunting women, entertainment business hopefuls, and scandal sheet writers entrenched in a similar dolce vita circuitry; in essence, characters living modern versions of that illusory 'sweet life' depicted in Fellini's film. In addition to the summer 2018 release of *Three Sleeps to Double Happiness*, the author has two more works completed and coming soon. Felske's *Chemical/Animal*, his second written in first person as a woman, will be released in summer, 2019, followed by the hard-boiled Los Angeles 1940s thriller *A Touch of Noir* in 2020. All Coerte V.W. Felske titles for The Dolce Vita Press are available at the author's Web site coertefelske.com, thedolcevitapress.com, Amazon.com, BN.com, independent bookstores and e-book distributors worldwide. To contact The DVP, request a review or signed copy, or write to the author or publisher please visit the author's Web site at coertefelske.com.

Three Sleeps

to Double Happiness